Demon
Hunting
in a
Dive Bar

Demon Hunting in a Dive Bar

LEXI GEORGE

BRAVA

KENSINGTON PUBLISHING CORP.

www.kensingtonbooks.com

BRAVA BOOKS are published by

Kensington Publishing Corp.
119 West 40th Street
New York, NY 10018

All Kensington titles, imprints, and distributed lines are available at special quantity discounts for bulk purchases for sales promotions, premiums, fund-raising, educational, or institutional use.

Special book excerpts or customized printings can also be created to fit specific needs. For details, write or phone the office of the Kensington special sales manager: Kensington Publishing Corp., 119 West 40th Street, New York, NY 10018, attn: Special Sales Department; phone: 1-800-221-2647.

Brava and the B logo are Reg. U.S. Pat. & TM Off.

ISBN-13: 978-0-7582-6313-1
ISBN-10: 0-7582-6313-9

First Trade Paperback Printing: February 2013

10 9 8 7 6 5 4 3 2 1

Printed in the United States of America

To Katie and Miranda—you hold my heart in your hands.

And to Audrey, my friend, fellow writer, and beta reader. Thanks for giving me that most precious of gifts, your time.

Chapter One

Being a zombie sucks. It's hard to feel sexy when you're bloated and starting to smell. And zombies have little or no job security. Once the zombie master is done with you, you're leftover meat.

Tommy never planned on being a zombie, but then who does? One minute he was standing on the sidewalk outside One Shell Square in New Orleans, thinking about what he wanted for supper, and the next minute he was dead, the victim of a freak window-washing accident. Smacked upside the head by a squeegee dropped from the forty-ninth floor. He had a permanent dent in his scalp to prove it.

At twenty-four, death was the last thing on Tommy's mind. He had a girlfriend and a job managing the Subway Shop on Poydras Street. As jobs went, it paid the bills. There was even a little money left at the end of the month to tuck into his savings account. Tommy had a plan. He was saving up for culinary school at Delgado Community College. After graduation, he and his girlfriend Robyn would open a restaurant of their own. They'd call it The Happy Vegan, and the menu would include things like homemade tortillas served with refried beans and soy cheese, avocado and tomato salad, and sweet fried plantains. It was gonna be kickass.

And then Tommy screwed the pooch by getting himself dead. Sucked didn't begin to describe it.

He was still flitting around his body in disbelief at the morgue, unable to comprehend the wrong turn this bitch of a day had taken, when his new boss showed up. The guy didn't look like a zombie maker. Tall and handsome in a dark-haired, lean, and feral kind of way, he had the loose-limbed grace of a young, fit animal.

He was also way too skinny. Zombie maker dude needed to eat a sandwich.

But it was his eyes that had caught and held Tommy's attention. Purple eyes, the guy had honest-to-God Elizabeth Taylor purple eyes. A man and a woman were with him, a couple of sketchy characters. Dirty and ragged, with the nervous, used-up appearance of meth addicts, they hovered around him, skittish as a pair of stray dogs.

"Fresh," the woman had said, eyeing Tommy's body with ghoulish interest. Her teeth were rotted black stumps in the gaping hole of her mouth. Tommy was *dead,* and this chick gave him the willies.

"He'll do," Grape Eyes said, and waved his hands over Tommy's body on the slab.

Quicker than he could say Jerusalem, Tommy had been sucked back into his body. He sat up and looked around, blinking. The examiner on the night shift had slipped out for a quick smoke. Ironically, his nicotine addiction may have saved his life. No telling what the Maker and his scary companions would have done to the poor sap.

"I have a job for you," the Maker had said to Tommy. Seriously, Grape Eyes was a freak. He acted like talking to a dead guy was the most natural thing in the world, and maybe it was to him.

And just like that, the guy had made Tommy an offer he couldn't refuse. The son of a bitch put a geis on Tommy—a kind of zombie maker curse that gave him total control over Tommy.

That was how, three days later, Tommy found himself *here* on a riverbank at the ass end of nowhere more than a hundred miles from his beloved New Orleans. Hannah, the sign at the outskirts of town had said this bit of backwoods Alabama was called. Tommy had never heard of it. Before now, that is; whoever said "ignorance is bliss" sure as hell knew what they were talking about.

The good news? The Maker had put a spell on Tommy that kept him from decomposing at the regular zombie rate—which, apparently, was roughly the decomp rate of garbage in the hot Louisiana sun. The bad news? He was rotting from the inside out. No one else would probably notice it, but Tommy could smell himself, and it wasn't pretty. He was a fastidious guy who took pride in his personal appearance. He'd rather be dead than stink. Lucky him, he got both.

On the bright side, it could be the inside of his nose he smelled. Who was he kidding? There was no bright side to being a zombie.

He gazed uneasily at the wooden building squatting on the other side of the river. It reminded him of the troll in *Three Billy Goats Gruff,* waiting to pounce on unsuspecting travelers. Beck's Bar, the place was called, and this was where he had to go. Apparently, demons went in Beck's but never came out.

Tommy had gleaned this information by playing dumb and listening to the zombie maker's conversation with his two creeper pals.

"I'm sending him on a recon mission," Grape Eyes had said to the bony female. "There's a place I want him to scope out, see if the rumors are true. I want to know what happened to the missing demons."

"That's good, that's good," the woman mumbled, rocking back and forth on the worn heels of her cheap shoes. She plucked at one thin eyebrow with nervous fingers. "Give the meat his orders and let's get out of here. I need a fix."

So now he was "the meat." Clearly, zombies got no respect in the supernatural world. As an African American, it wasn't Tommy's first encounter with prejudice, but that didn't make it any easier to stomach.

But Tommy was smart. He kept his mouth shut and learned more. More than he wanted to know. He found out the zombie maker's two buddies were demon-possessed humans. That explained their emaciated, worn-out condition. Possession was apparently hard on the human body. Grape Eyes, on the other hand, was something called a demonoid—half human, half demon. The demon half must be the source of Grape Eyes's power. No normal human could do the things he did. And to think, less than a week ago Tommy would have laughed at the idea the boogeyman was real.

He eyed the river with distaste. He didn't have a boat and he wasn't a strong swimmer. Not that it mattered now that he was Deadsville. He couldn't drown. But he didn't relish the thought of going in that brown water. Even less the idea of what might be in it. Suppose a catfish decided to take a bite out of him? A corpse would be a delicacy to one of them big old scavenger fishies. But the onus the Maker had placed on Tommy compelled him to cross the river *now*, boat or no boat, Tommy-eating-fish or no Tommy-eating-fish.

Damn spell.

Damn demons.

He weighted himself down with rocks and started across. It was the weekend before Thanksgiving. The water had to be cold, but Tommy couldn't feel it. The muddy bottom was squelchy and full of silt, and sucked the shoes right off his feet. Too late, he regretted not taking them off but he couldn't go back for them, not with the geis upon him. The compulsion to reach the bar was strong, like the gravitational pull of a large moon. The water was deep and dark. Thankfully, he couldn't see much. Something large bumped past him, and Tommy picked up the pace. Tommy the Zombie, gator bait.

This sucked. This sucked *hard*.

He missed the dock and came up in a slough a short distance downstream from the bar. Dumping the rocks, he floundered clumsily through the water to the ladder at the end of the pier and climbed up the wooden slats. Clothes dripping, he paused half in, half out of the water and looked around. It was late afternoon, maybe an hour before sunset. A couple of boats bobbed at the end of the boardwalk, but otherwise the place seemed quiet. Tommy had a feeling things livened up once the sun went down. Beck's struck him as the kind of place people went under cover of darkness.

Or maybe not. The bar somehow looked better from this side of the river. Cleaner, tidier and less menacing, almost as if it had shed a disguise. No trash or empty bottles littered the porch or the dock. Everything seemed well maintained, loved even, which was an odd thought to have about a dive bar.

Tommy started to lumber onto the dock, but something made him pause on the ladder. The onus was still there, but the urge to reach the bar had been replaced by a sense of expectancy. He and Grape Eyes were connected by an invisible thread, and Tommy could feel him on the other end of the line. The Maker was tense, expectant. Something was about to happen, something the Maker had been waiting for a long time, the real reason he'd sent Tommy here.

Tommy stayed put, nervous, but obedient to the demands of the spell. The screen door on the porch swung open and a young woman stepped out of the bar, a large, scruffy dog at her heels. Judging from the mutt's lean body and rough gray coat, there was Irish wolfhound somewhere in the dog's lineage, and not too far back.

The woman, on the other hand, was pure thoroughbred. Tall and lithe, she moved with the muscular grace of a dancer or an athlete. The black long-sleeve T-shirt she wore clung to her high breasts, and her long, shapely legs were encased in a pair of tight jeans. Suede boots hugged her slender feet. Balancing a bowl and its contents in one hand, she strode across the porch with her head down. Her dark silky hair hung around her face, obscuring her features. She came down the steps and onto the pier.

"I'm worried about her, Toby," she said, talking to the dog. She had a sexy voice, dark chocolate and smoke, the kind of voice that did things to a guy—even if the guy happened to be dead. "She's such a little thing and so thin," she said. "I know she's hungry, but she won't let me near her. Maybe a can of tuna will tempt her."

The dog sat at the bottom of the steps and turned up his long nose in disdain.

"Don't give me that I-hate-catitude. She's just a kitten." The woman knelt on the side of the dock and peered into the thick underbrush that grew along the muddy bank. "Here, kitty," she called softly. "Beck's brought you something to eat."

Nothing stirred in the bushes.

"I know you're there. I'll leave the bowl here, in case you change your mind." The woman settled back on her haunches with a sigh. "Okay, be stubborn. But I'm not giving up on you."

Placing the bowl near the steps, she rose and pushed her silky dark hair out of her face. Tommy stared at her in surprise. She was beautiful with smooth skin and clean, strong features. The word "pretty" would never be used to describe this woman. It was too anemic and sweet. She had a fierce, wild beauty, as perfect as a rose and as sharp and piercing as a thorn.

Tommy's nose twitched as the delicate scent of jasmine drifted past him on the breeze. He squinted, hoping the eye rot hadn't set in. Yep, the chick on the dock looked terrifyingly familiar. He knew her. Or, to be more precise, he knew her male counterpart.

The woman called Beck was the zombie maker's twin. Tommy would bet his afterlife on it.

Chapter Two

Beck left Toby guarding the steps and went inside the bar, waving at Bill, the sound guy for Beelzebubba, the country band she'd booked for the weekend. The music wouldn't start until later tonight after the ballgames. College football was a religion in Alabama, and Saturdays in the fall were holy days reserved for worshipping the boob tube.

Beck didn't mind. Football was good for business. Plenty of folks came to the bar after the game to celebrate or mourn, depending on how their team performed. The food at Beck's was a big draw, thanks to Hank, the new cook. So successful, in fact, that Beck had toyed with the idea of opening the bar to normals.

She'd quickly dismissed the notion. Beck's was a bar for demonoids, the only one of its kind to her knowledge. The norms had a world of places to eat and drink. It was their tough luck that Beck's had one of the best cooks in the state.

Speak of the devil, she thought as Hank stuck his head out of the back.

"Need you to look at tonight's menu," he growled in a voice like a train rumbling over a trestle.

"Sure," Beck said, veering toward the kitchen. The menu at Beck's changed like the weather, depending on Hank's mood. She gave him free rein to keep him happy, "happy" being a relative term. Hank wasn't what you'd call the bubbly type.

He was built like a bulldozer, with hands and feet like concrete blocks. With his shaggy black hair, thick black beard, and surly manner, he reminded her of Beorn, the skin changer from *The Hobbit*. He'd been raised by his mother; that much Beck knew. Nothing unusual in that. Most demonoids were raised by single parents after their demonically charged mother or father disappeared into the sunset, on the prowl for the next high, the next party.

Or the next kill.

Demons were creatures of the spirit world that craved physical sensation. That's why they were attracted to humans. Drugs, sex, and violence were irresistible to them. Mortals taken by a demon never lasted long, a few months, a year at most before their poor, beleaguered bodies wore out and the demons left them to die.

Demons were no damn good; miserable, self-serving parasitic bastards out for themselves and their own pleasure, without a thought for their victims or their unfortunate offspring. A demon was the reason she'd never known her mother, and a demon had killed her best friend. Latrisse Jackson had been a waitress at Beck's back when Daddy still ran the place for norms. She'd been working at the bar a year when she got possessed. Toby and Beck searched for her for months. By the time they'd found her, it was too late. Latrisse was all used up. She'd died in Beck's arms, a broken, wasted thing riddled with disease and aged far beyond her twenty-three years.

Beck had hated demons with a fiery passion since.

And she was half demon.

"Whatcha got?" she asked, plucking the menu from the cook's beefy fingers.

Hank glowered at her but made no response. Mr. Personality he was not. Beck figured him to be around forty years old, but it was hard to tell. Half bloods like her and Hank didn't age, although they sometimes disguised the fact from the norms by adding wrinkles and gray hair to their appearance.

Beck noticed the entry at the top of the page. "Shrimp étouffée? That's something new, isn't it?"

"New for this place, maybe. You think all I'm good for is cooking burgers and dogs?"

Yep, he was Beorn, all right, a bear in human guise—a bear with a sore tail, and just as ornery.

"And wings," Beck reminded him. "Best dang chicken wangs around. That's what everybody says."

Hank harrumphed and stomped back to the kitchen.

"Nice talking to you, too," Beck said.

Shaking her head, she walked behind the bar, a glass block semicircle that dominated the center of the room.

Ora Mae Luker, a pudgy widow with an uncanny knack for growing things, wandered in. Ora Mae was a regular who toodled across the river every afternoon, Monday through Saturday, to have a drink and a little conversation.

Ora Mae's gray hair was freshly washed and styled. She wore polyester slacks with an elastic waist, and a loose, eyelet cotton shirt. Taking a seat at the counter, she blinked at the empty bar from behind her wire rimmed glasses. "Where is everybody? This place is dead."

"Watching the games," Beck said. "We won't get busy until later."

"Oh, yes, of course. I should have realized. How silly of me."

Ora Mae was one of those rare creatures, a Southerner who didn't give a hoot in Hades about football.

"I'll have the usual," Ora Mae said.

"One dirty martini coming up."

Beck sullied the vodka with olive juice, added extra olives, and set the frosted glass in front of the plump matron, listening as Ora Mae rattled on about the bumper crop of squash, pumpkins, and cauliflower in her garden.

Twenty minutes later, Ora Mae finished her drink and got to her feet. "I guess I'd better head home. It's almost time for the news, and I do like the looks of that new weatherman."

Beck smiled. Ora Mae had butt lint older than the new guy on channel 5. "Be careful crossing the river."

Ora Mae waved good-bye and left, and Beck set the empty martini glass in the sink. She was wiping down the bar when she saw *him,* sitting in his usual spot at a table in the corner, surrounded by shadows. Shadows he brought, Beck thought with a surge of annoyance. Conall Dalvahni carried his own black hole of gloom with him wherever he went. With his dark hair and eyes, and his brooding expression, he was the freaking Grim Reaper, if Death were a demon hunter.

Beck couldn't stand the guy, and the feeling was mutual. So, why was he back? The last time she'd seen him, he'd made it clear he thought she was pond scum, an insult to decent, right-thinking creatures everywhere.

He was a demon slayer and she was a demonoid. Polar opposites. Oil and vinegar. TNT and a lit match. I got it, she thought, giving the bar an angry swipe with the cloth. *Loud and clear. So why the hell can't he leave me alone?*

It had been nearly a month since she'd last seen him. Twenty-one days, to be exact. Three whole weeks without Mr. Dark and Gloomy, and good riddance. She should have shrugged off his icy disdain by now, forgotten him, and moved on. But his obvious contempt for her and her kind stuck in her craw. She couldn't stop thinking about him, and that pissed her off.

Everything about him pissed her off. His forbidding, humorless demeanor and his arrogant, holier-than-thou attitude.

And now he was back. Not for long, though. She threw down the bar towel. This was her place. She'd kicked him out once, and she'd do it again.

Hefting a liquor bottle with a metal pour spot in one hand, she stalked over to his table.

"What do you want?" she demanded.

"That depends." His deep, rough voice grated on her nerves and made her stomach knot. "What have you to offer?"

"Nothing you're interested in."

His dark gaze raked her up and down, casual and insolent. Beck's grip tightened on the bottle.

"You are mistaken," he said. "You have information about the demon activity in this area, information that I require."

"Get your information someplace else, mister."

"I am more than willing to recompense you for your trouble."

A flat leather pouch appeared in his hand. Opening it, he tossed a thick wad of hundred-dollar bills on the table between them. Beck stared at the pile of greenbacks. It was a lot of money, several thousand dollars at least.

"There is more where that came from, Rebekah. Much more."

Something hot and hurt flared inside her. On top of being lower than dirt, he thought she was for sale. She pushed the feeling aside. It didn't matter what he thought. She was an idiot for letting the guy get under her skin.

"The name's Beck and I don't need your money."

"Your name is not Beck. It is Rebekah Damian."

"Who told you my—"

"You are thirty-one years old," he continued, as though reciting a series of well-memorized facts. "Although you appear much younger, no doubt due to your demon blood. Your father is Jason Beck Damian, a nice enough fellow, but otherwise a quite unremarkable human. This bar belonged to him—thus the name—until he married and started another family. His wife does not drink and disapproved of her husband running a tavern. At her encouragement, he sold the place."

"Encouragement?" Beck made a rude noise. "Brenda nagged his ass until he caved."

"At eighteen, you were too young to purchase Beck's on your own," Conall said. "So you bought the place with the help of your partner, Tobias James Littleton, and turned it into a bar that caters to your kind. The name you kept."

"My goodness, Daddy's been running his mouth, hasn't he?" Beck drawled, clamping down on her rising temper. "At his age, you'd think he'd know better than to talk to strangers."

"I have supped at his eatery several times in the past few weeks," Conall said with a shrug. "The name of the place eludes me."

"Beck's Burger Doodle," Beck ground out.

"Ah, yes. The Party Burger is a favorite of mine."

"Daddy makes a good hamburger. So what?"

"Your father has told me much about you." Conall reached

across the table and toyed with the salt shaker. The sleeves of his cotton sweater were pushed back, exposing his strong forearms. His shoulders were broad and heavily corded with muscle. He had beautiful hands, strong and bronzed, the hands of a warrior. And not just any old warrior, Beck reminded herself, a demon killer. "He confided, for instance, that he had a three-day dalliance as a young man with a woman named Helené."

Her mother? Daddy had told Conall about her *mother?* Beck stared at him in disbelief.

"She was a dark-haired beauty like you," Conall said, lifting his gaze to her face. "He did not know it at the time, but she was demon possessed. Some months later, Helene returned, changed almost beyond recognition from the excesses of the demon. She had a child with her, an infant girl with a strawberry blotch on one shoulder, a birthmark common in the Damian family. That baby was you. She shoved you into your father's arms and left, never to be seen again."

"Daddy told you all this?"

"Yes."

"Bullshit. My father never talks about his freak of a daughter. He's an upstanding citizen now, a member of the Civitan Club, and a good Baptist. What did you do to get him to spill the beans?"

Conall sat back in his chair. "You think I wrested the information from your parental unit by supernatural force?"

"Figured that out by yourself, did ya? My, you are the bright one."

"You do not like me."

"Ding, ding, ding," Beck said, tapping her forefinger in the air. "Right again, genius."

Conall's black gaze slid from her face to the bottle in her hand. "I see. And what do you mean to do with that flask?"

"I was thinking of bashing you over the head with it if you don't leave."

His black brows rose. "You wish to hit me? Why?"

"Mister, the last time you were here, you all but said you think the kith are nothing but vermin to be exterminated, and now you're back." She jabbed her finger at him. "Seeing as how *I'm* kith and you're a demon hunter, I take your presence as a threat."

"Kith? This is the term for your kind?"

"It's *our* term," Beck said. "For some reason, we like it better than scum-sucking demon spawn."

"Are you always so sarcastic?"

"Only when I'm awake."

He regarded her without expression. Nothing unusual about that; the guy had about as much expression as a two-by-four. "You think I came here to kill you."

"It crossed my mind."

"And yet you confront me with nothing but a bottle in your hand, and I a demon slayer."

"I can take care of myself," Beck said. "I've been doing it a long time."

Conall sprang at her in a blur of movement. The bottle in Beck's hand clattered to the floor as she was swept up and pinned against the nearest wall by more than six feet of hard-muscled male.

"You fascinate me," Conall said. His dark voice was rough. "I cannot decide whether you are brave or foolish. Perhaps both."

Beck went still. The heat from his big body and his crisp, woodsy scent surrounded her. He smelled like a little bit of heaven, she'd give him that.

"Let go of me." She felt the weight of his stare but kept her gaze fastened on his wide chest. She couldn't breathe, not with him so close.

The alpha male jackass ignored her, of course.

"You smell of jasmine and spices. Sweet and exotic," he murmured. His warm breath whispered across her skin. Beck began to tremble. "How . . . interesting. I expected the stench of demon to be upon you."

His last words hit her like a slap in the face. Anger washed over her, bright and hot, followed by an overwhelming urge to escape. Shifting into a column of water, she flowed from his grasp. It was easy, this close to the river. Water strengthened her powers. It was one reason she hadn't wanted to sell the bar and move into town.

The stunned look on Conall's face as she poured out of his arms was priceless, almost worth the aggravation of being around him.

Almost.

She glided across the wooden floor and resumed her former shape, taking care to place the table between them before she re-shifted.

"Out." She pointed to the door. Her chest heaved and angry tears burned the back of her eyes. She would not let him see her cry. She refused. "And this time don't come back."

"We must talk." He stepped around the table. "You remember Ansgar?"

She edged away from him. Distance, she needed distance.

"Yeah, I remember him," she said. "Big, blond guy. Carries a bow and arrows. Here a couple of weeks ago." *With you,* she wanted to add. *The night you found out what I am and acted so disgusted.* "What about him?"

"He was attacked and wounded nigh unto death a few days later. He has recovered, but the wound pains him still and has left a scar."

"He's a demon hunter. I'll bet he has lots of scars."

Conall shook his head. "You are wrong. Death comes seldom to the Dalvahni. We heal quickly and we *never* scar. Do you not see the import of this?"

"Can't say as I do."

"Someone has developed a weapon against the Dalvahni. If this weapon falls into the hands of the djegrali, it could be disastrous. I need your help."

"Guess you should've thought about that before you made the 'You don't stink bad for a demon girl' crack, you narrow-minded ass."

His dark brows rose. "My words were careless and spoken in haste. 'Twas not my intent to anger you."

"Mister, just the fact that we're sucking in air on the same planet pisses me off."

"What can I do to make amends?"

"You can get the hell out of my sight. That would make me feel loads better. Other than that, I can't think of a thing."

Conall moved closer. "That I cannot do, not until I make you see reason."

"You can't *make* me do anything."

To her astonishment, he smiled. "A challenge," he said. "I like that."

A part of her, the female, horny part she generally tried to ignore, sat up and took notice when he smiled, the shameless hussy.

Oh, no. She would not go there. She'd dry-hump a stump before she had anything to do with that stuck-up, sanctimonious, speciesist SOB.

To her relief, Toby interrupted them. Nudging the screen door open with his nose, the dog trotted inside. The silver chain around his neck jangled as he shook himself and resumed his human form. Like his doggie self, Toby was restless and energetic and never still for long. He wore his usual attire on his wiry frame: jeans and a faded T-shirt. His gray hair hung in a long braid down his back.

Toby shot Conall a curious glance. "What's he doing here? Thought we got shed of him weeks ago."

"I thought so, too," Beck said. Something was wrong. Toby looked alert, excited even. "What's up?"

"There's a dead guy on the landing," Toby said. "Thought you'd wanna know."

Chapter Three

"What?" Beck hurried for the door. "I was just out there. I didn't see anything."

Fwppt. Conall was in front of her, barring the way. Beck was used to beings with supernatural speed, but this guy was *fast.*

"I will deal with this," he said. "I am no stranger to death."

"I didn't ask for your help." Beck tried to push past him, but no matter which way she went he blocked her. Frustrated, she shoved her hands against his chest. He was solid muscle and about as pliable as a steam shovel. "Get out of the way."

"No. You could be in danger. It could be the work of the djegrali."

"Djegrali? You think I'm afraid of demons?" Beck laughed. "Get real. *I'm* a demon, remember?"

"You are but half demon."

"Same difference," Beck said. "No good demon but a dead demon. That's the Dalvahni motto, isn't it?"

Conall's expression hardened. And that was saying something, because the guy had a mug like granite. "The Dal were created to hunt down and capture or destroy rogue demons. That is our purpose."

"Peachy," Beck said. "Bully for you. Me, I'm trying to run a bar, not save the universe. So, excuse me while I go see about the dead guy on my pier."

"You are troubled. I offer my sword arm in your defense."

"What are you, dense?" Beck said. "I don't need your help. I don't *want* it. Get out." She turned her back on him. "Toby, you'd better call Sheriff Whitsun. You'll have to meet him at the end of the road and bring him in. Let's just hope he doesn't close us down for the night."

"No need for that." Toby's mismatched eyes—one purple, the other as golden as topaz—shone with mischief. "It ain't that kinda dead guy."

That stopped Beck in her tracks. She stared at him in confusion. " 'Scuse me? What other kind of dead guy is there?"

"That kind," Toby said, pointing to the door.

A man shuffled in off the porch. His clothes were soaked and he was barefoot. He looked young, maybe in his early twenties, although looks could be deceiving, especially among supernaturals. He had a pleasant, open face that Beck liked immediately. There was an unhealthy ashy tinge to his brown skin, but otherwise he looked fine. In the crook of one arm, he held a ragged bit of black fur. A pair of copper eyes gleamed at them from a sharp feline face. It was the feral young cat Beck had been trying to coax out of the bushes for days.

"Hold." Conall drew his sword. As blades went, the sword wasn't pretty or fancy. But Beck had seen Conall in action, and knew that he was wicked good. He pointed the business end of the weapon at the newcomer. "State your name and business."

The stranger's brown eyes widened in alarm. "I'm Tommy Henderson," he said. He had a rich, fluid voice and a distinctive accent. Southern, definitely, but not from around here. "I'm looking for a job. Something temporary."

"Have to be real temporary, 'cause he's *dead*." Toby tapped the end of his nose. "Dog snoot. The nose knows."

"You can smell me?" An expression of genuine horror flitted across Tommy's features. "He said the spell would keep me from stinking. I should've known that lowdown no-good mofo was lying."

"What mofo?" Beck asked.

"The zombie maker. Damn, I hate this." Tommy sniffed his damp sleeve. "You got any air freshener, or maybe one of them Stick-Ups handy?"

Beck stepped back. "You're a *zombie*?"

As part owner of a bar for supernaturals, she'd seen some pretty strange things over the years, but the walking dead was something new and unsettling, even for her.

Toby grunted. "Told ya he was a stiff."

"Don't be rude, Tobias." Beck considered Tommy. He didn't look dangerous. "I never met a zombie before. Gotta say, you're not what I expected. I thought zombies ate people and went around saying *unh uhn*. You talk just fine."

"Brains," Toby said, giving Beck a *duh* look. "Zombies eat brains. Everybody knows that."

"I don't eat brains." Tommy shuddered. "I'm a vegetarian. I hate this. I wish I was dead." His face crumpled. "Shit, I *am* dead. I'm worse than dead. I can't go home like this. I'll give my poor mama a heart attack. And Robyn's gonna be pissed."

"Who's Robyn?" Beck asked.

"My girlfriend," Tommy said. He made a face. "Ex-girl-friend, more like it, seeing as how I'm dead."

"Maybe Beck can help you," Toby said. "Jimmy Earl Flynn's wife caught him messing around and put the whammy on him. The poor sap broke both legs and an arm before Beck removed the curse."

"You are an undoer?" Conall gave Beck a look of appraisal. "That is a most useful talent."

"It was a simple klutz curse," she said. "I've never tried to unzombie somebody before."

"I understand if you don't wanna help me," Tommy said. "I ain't nothing to you. I shoulda stayed at the bottom of the river and let the gators eat me."

Damn, Beck thought. Tommy seemed so lost and miserable. She knew what it was like to be different, to be an outcast in her own family. Tommy the zombie couldn't go home and nei-ther could Beck the demon girl. Daddy had married Brenda, the God-fearing, Bible-thumping Holy Roller, and had a cou-ple of kids, *human* kids, leaving no place for her in his new life.

"It's not that I don't want to help you," she said. "I don't know if I can."

"You are wise not to attempt it," Conall said. "Such a course would be inadvisable and possibly dangerous for someone not well versed in the magical arts."

Translation: he didn't think she could do it. She didn't think she could do it, either, but that was beside the point.

"I'll give it a try," she said, ignoring Conall's growl of protest. "But, I'm not promising anything."

Closing her eyes, she sought the still, quiet place within her, letting her agitation with Conall the Super Jerk and the unsettling happenings of the morning fall away. When she opened her eyes again, she could see the spell surrounding Tommy in a reddish-brown haze. Lines of power, delicate as the shimmering strands of a spider's web, writhed inside the nimbus. If she could find one end of the spell, perhaps she could unravel the whole thing. An impossible task, when the tentacles of the enchantment were constantly moving and changing, crossing and entwining with one another like a writhing bed of snakes.

Maybe if she broke a line of the spell the whole thing would fragment. She gingerly touched one of the humming fibers with the tip of one finger. The spell formed a mouth bristling with teeth and snapped at her.

"Yeow," Beck yelped, jumping back. She stuck her bleeding finger in her mouth. "It bit me."

"Rebekah, perhaps it would be better if you did not—" Conall began.

Furious, Beck reached out and grabbed a handful of lines at once. Power shot up her arm and knocked her to the floor. She stared up at the ceiling, dazed, and tried to catch her breath.

Conall loomed over her. "I warned you, did I not?" he asked, helping her to her feet. "This magic is beyond you."

She opened her mouth to argue with him and shut it again. He was right, dammit.

"I can see the spell, Tommy, but I don't know how to undo it," she said. "But I'm not giving up. In the meantime, you can stay here until we figure something out."

"Inadvisable," Conall said, drawing her aside. "He is the undead. A creature bound to do his master's bidding, a sorcerer of great power as you have already discovered. The zombie cannot be trusted."

"Lower your voice. You'll hurt Tommy's feelings."

"He is dead. He does not have feelings. He is a soulless minion of evil."

"He does, too, have a soul," Beck argued. "You can see it in his eyes, in his expression."

"You are mistaken."

God, he was arrogant.

"Maybe he died suddenly and didn't go to that big Happy Meal in the sky," she said. "Maybe he got stuck, somehow. Ever think of that?"

"Highly unlikely. Necromancers raise the dead after the soul has departed."

"So now you're a zombie expert?"

"I do not have to be versed in the ways of the undead to know that the arrival of such a creature bodes no good. In all likelihood, he is a fiend garbed in human flesh."

"A real glass half full kind of guy, aren't you?" Beck said. She tapped her chest. "If he had a demon in him, I'd know."

He gave her one of his superior I'm-a-demon-hunter-and-you're-so-*not* looks. "How?"

"The same way I can see the zombie maker's spell. Demons are like a dark spot, a cancer inside a person."

To her satisfaction, his condescending expression faded, replaced by curiosity. "Interesting," he said. "Do all the kith have this talent?"

"I have no idea. Take a poll, why don't you?"

He grabbed her by the arm as she started to turn away. "You cannot allow the zombie to stay here. 'Twould be foolishness in the extreme."

She jerked away from him. "Yeah, well lucky for you, it's not your problem. Besides, the cat trusts Tommy. Animals can sense things about people."

"You would make a decision based on the supposed intuition

of a stray animal?" He shook his head. "Such a thing is beyond illogical. It is nonsensical."

There he went again, rubbing her the wrong way, like steel wool on a baby's behind. "I don't have to justify myself to you," she said. "Now, for the last time, go away."

"No."

"No?" Beck's blood pressure rose. All the dive bars in all the world and he walks into mine, she thought. "I've had about enough of this shit and you. This is *my* place. Leave. Now. Before I have Hank and Toby throw you out."

"They are most welcome to try," he said with a lethal smile. "I will endeavor not to hurt them too badly, as they are your friends."

Something like panic welled inside Beck. Ridiculous; she *never* panicked.

"Why are you doing this?" she cried. "There are plenty of demonoids who'd sell their own mothers for the money in that wallet of yours."

"I do not know them."

"You don't know *me*," Beck said. "You don't know anything about me."

From across the room, Toby raised his brows at her as if to ask *You okay?* Beck shook her head at him in warning. Toby was a tough old bird, but he was no match for a demon hunter, particularly this one. Conall might seem all cool and calm on the outside, but Beck had seen the savage current of violence that ran beneath his placid surface.

"You are wrong," Conall said. "I have watched you carefully for weeks and I do know you. More importantly, I think . . ." He hesitated. "I believe I can trust you."

The words sounded forced, like rusted gears grinding back to life.

"Well, I don't trust you," Beck snapped. "Go find somebody else."

Turning on her heel, she walked away.

★   ★   ★

Conall watched her saunter off. The garb she wore hugged her long legs and round bottom in a most indecent fashion. The females of this place and time frequently donned breeches, but few of them looked as delectable in masculine attire as Rebekah. She had a strong, lithe body and moved with a fluid, sensuous grace.

Fluid, indeed, he thought, recalling her sudden and unexpected transformation a few moments before. He'd held a woman in his arms, a supple, jasmine-scented creature of delight, and then she'd slipped from his grasp, as elusive as a *naiad* returning to its elemental form.

She was the most frustrating, annoying, fascinating creature he'd ever encountered. He'd handled things badly, and now he would have to start all over again. Find a way to get back in her good graces.

Back? He had not been in her good graces since they'd met. Their first face-to-face encounter had been less than a month ago; though that was not the first time he'd seen her. He'd frequented Beck's Bar for weeks prior to their "introduction," watching her from his table in the corner. Studying her, but never speaking. She intrigued him from the start, and that had unsettled him. What was it about her that drew him? True, she was comely, but it was more than that. He had known countless beauties through the centuries. None of them had disturbed his equanimity like Rebekah.

After a few nights of sitting alone in his corner, he'd realized with a surge of satisfaction that she returned his notice. She darted furtive glances his way; he made her uneasy. Good. He wanted her on edge, off balance, like him. It gave him an advantage, or so he'd thought.

Until the night she had come to Evie Douglass's defense, a woman she scarcely knew, taking on a demon single handed. He could see Rebekah still, facing the loathsome creature with naught but a bottle in her hand, her violet eyes ablaze. Springing to her aid, he'd slain the fiend with his sword. To his surprise, she had chastised him most roundly for it. Then she'd shocked him further by removing a demon from a possessed human, like a physic lancing a boil.

Rebekah Damian was stubborn, independent, and reckless. She was magnificent.

She was also half demon.

He'd discovered her true nature the night of the demon attack and had been repelled and disgusted . . . and strangely fascinated. She represented a dichotomy, this new creature, this child of the djegrali.

His attraction to a by-blow of his enemy bewildered and disturbed him. She'd been quick to notice his reaction and had angrily ordered him from her bar.

He'd left, returning a few days later, telling himself 'twas his duty to discover what he could about this new race called demonoids. Having parted from Rebekah on bad terms, he'd made himself invisible, studying her, unseen, for weeks, searching for signs of corruption. How could strength, beauty, and goodness spring from evil?

To his frustration, he was unable to detect any wickedness in her, or the taint of the djegrali's influence, in spite of her accursed demon blood.

He had soon grown impatient with his guise. She was too interesting, too intriguing a puzzle. He wanted her gaze upon him, her notice. It was most unsettling, this unseemly attraction. No doubt it was the result of unslaked lust and the lure of forbidden fruit.

He'd told himself to put her from his mind and focus instead on the disturbance in the ranks of the Dalvahni. Three of his finest warriors had fallen in recent months—not to death or djegrali treachery, but to a foe more insidious and subversive.

They had fallen in love. Conall had seen the evidence with his own eyes, though he still found it hard to grasp. Dalvahni warriors did not *love*. Battle rage and lust, these sentiments were known to them and easily remedied by a visit to the House of Thralls and the emptying clasp of a sexual companion. The thralls, in turn, fed on Dalvahni emotion. 'Twas a relationship that had served both races well for eons.

Until now.

Something was afoot here, some kind of strange dark magic. This place, this Han-nah-a-lah was to blame. Deep mischief was at work here, and the djegrali lay at the root of it. He would discover their twisted scheme and foil it.

And Rebekah would help him. What better place to unravel the enemy's latest ploy than a beer hall that serviced nonhumans? Rebekah and her little place on the river suited his purpose exactly. He would linger here and listen. He would learn what he needed to know to defeat the djegrali. It was his duty.

Rebekah's low, sultry drawl teased him from across the room. Her voice was one of the first things he'd noticed about her. Warm and husky, it whispered along his senses and invariably turned his thoughts to sex—with her. He had never been with anyone but a thrall, and then but seldom. He disliked the loss of control.

What would it be like to lose control with Rebekah? he wondered.

He took a steadying breath; best to keep his thoughts away from such things. Rebekah was conversing with the zombie. Perhaps the ghoul would reveal something important. He would join them and find out.

Rebekah was but another weapon to be used in the fight against the djegrali. He must remember that.

Chapter Four

"I can cook," Tommy said in response to Beck's question regarding his skills. He clutched the scrawny young cat to his chest. "I was saving up for culinary school before . . ." He swallowed hard. "You know."

"Already got a cook," Beck said. "There's only one rooster on that dunghill, and his name's Hank."

"A zombie got no business being around food anyways," Toby said. "He's bound to start losing things, sooner or later. I don't care what kinda spell that voodoo dude put on him. Zombie parts in the vittles are gonna be a gross-out."

"Toby," Beck said, giving the bouncer a repressive glare.

Toby shrugged. "I'm just saying. Course, some of the scavenger types might like it. In fact, I know them Skinners would."

The Skinners were white trash, plain and simple. They didn't come into the bar very often, but when they did, they always brought trouble.

Tommy's brow crinkled in distress. "He's right. Shoulda thought of that myself. It's a health code violation to have me in the kitchen."

"Don't worry about it," Beck said. "We'll find something for you to do. Where'd you used to work?"

"I ran a Subway Shop in New Orleans."

"N'awlins," Beck thought with an inward nod. *Knew he wasn't from around here.*

Toby perked up. "You got management experience? Hot damn. He can help out in the office."

Conall waltzed up to them like he owned the place. "Unwise," he said in that haughty tone of his that drove her nuts. "You know nothing about the creature. Before you give him access to your accounts, you should at least query him about his Maker."

God, he was irritating as a pair of burlap drawers, the big Dalvahni know-it-all. Beck longed to tell him off, but her practical streak made her hesitate. Much as she hated to admit it—really, *really* hated to admit it—he was right. They knew nothing about Tommy and less about his Maker. No sense opening the barn door and inviting the wolf in to bed down with the sheep.

"He's got a point," she said to Tommy, ignoring Conall's grunt of surprise. "I need to ask you a few questions. I hope you understand."

"Sure, I understand, Miss—" Tommy looked embarrassed. "Shoot, I just realized I don't know your name."

"I'm Beck, and this is Toby, my partner. We run the joint."

Tommy gave her a shy smile. "Nice to meet you, Beck."

"Enough," Conall said. "Who is your master and why did he send you here?"

Tommy's face went slack and his eyes filmed over. "Uhn," he said, as though his tongue had suddenly grown too big and thick for his mouth.

"Answer me, fiend," Conall said, lunging at Tommy with his sword.

Tommy squawked like a startled chicken and leaped halfway across the room.

Beck grabbed Conall's arm. "Stop it. Don't you get it? He can't tell us about the Maker. It's part of the spell. Right, Tommy?"

Keeping a wary eye on Conall, the zombie tried to move his head up and down without success.

"See? He can't even nod," Beck said. "He can't betray the zombie master's plans."

Conall lowered his blade. "A convenient circumstance, but I will abide by your wishes. For now."

"I'll say one thing for him," Toby said. "He moves fast for a dead guy. I could use him at the door on band nights. Keep the shifters from slipping in without paying the cover."

"That'll work," Beck said. "That all right with you, Tommy?"

Tommy's eyes cleared. "Yes, ma'am."

He still looked shaken, and who could blame him? Conall had scared the bejesus out of the poor guy with his testosterone explosion.

"Good. Then it's settled," Beck said with relief. She felt bad for Tommy and wanted to help him. As an added bonus, hiring him to work at the bar would bug the crap out of Captain Smug Mug. "By the way, how'd you make friends with the kitten?" she asked Tommy. "I've been trying to coax her out of hiding for days."

Tommy smiled and stroked the cat with gentle fingers. "Her name is Annie. Ain't that right, pussycat?"

"Annie." Beck rolled the name around in her mouth. "I like it. It suits her."

Tommy shuffled his bare feet on the floor. "I don't mean to be rude, but I'm hungry."

"I knew it," Toby cried. "Here we go. He's gonna eat somebody's brains."

"I done tole you I don't eat meat," Tommy said. "Wouldn't eat yo' brains no how. I wouldn't say no to some tofu, though, if y'all got any."

"Don't know," Beck said. "Tobias, stop bouncing around like a Jack Russell terrier and take Tommy in the back and ask Hank if we got any tofu. If we don't, tell him to get some, pronto. And see if you can find Tommy something dry to wear. There are extra clothes in the storeroom. Shifters are forever getting drunk and leaving their belongings lying around."

"Oh, sure," Toby said. "Send the dog off with the brain-eating zombie. Sacrifice the dog. The *dog* is expendable."

"Don't see what you got to complain about," Tommy said as he followed Toby in the direction of the kitchen. "Some crazy dude just tried to bust me open with a sword."

The lethal-looking blade in Conall's hand vanished. " 'Tis

foolish in the extreme to offer succor to such a creature," he said, frowning at Beck. "But as you refuse to listen to reason, I shall abide here until the Maker reveals his sinister purpose."

"No." Beck shook her head so hard in denial it was a wonder it didn't fall off and roll out the door and into the river. "Absolutely not."

"I detect the foul taint of the djegrali behind the zombie's arrival. 'Tis my duty to investigate."

"I don't give a rat's ass about your duty. You can't stay here."

He held up his hand. "You can thank me later. Right now, we have company."

"Thank you?" A jolt of pain shot up Beck's neck. Stress, probably. This guy was going to be the death of her. "Are you nuts? And what do you mean 'we have company'? There is no *we.*"

The front door blew open, and a troop of fairies flitted into the room on lacy wings. The tiny creatures glowed softly in pastel shades, like Christmas lights through a frosted window. The fairy in the lead was a female with skin like chocolate milk and hair of spun silver. She flew up to Conall and said something to him in a thin little voice.

"I will relay the message, little one," he said gravely. "I fear you are right and she has forgotten." He turned to Beck. "The fairies would like me to remind you that Evie and Ansgar's wedding is but an hour hence."

"Tell the fairies to kiss it," Beck said. "I'm not going. I hardly know the chick."

She stomped over to the bar and made a business of checking the stock. It had shocked the hell out of her when Evie Douglass invited her to the wedding. They barely knew each other. Sure, part of her had been secretly thrilled to be invited to *the* social event of the year. But, she'd never had any intention of *going.* Social crap gave her the hives. A few of the kith might be there, but it would be mostly norms. She'd feel awkward and out of place, and who needed that? Besides, she didn't have anything to wear.

The fairies darted after her, buzzing around her in agitated circles. They chittered nonstop, like a flock of miniature sparrows around an open bag of birdseed.

Conall followed and leaned against the bar. Beck pretended not to notice, but he was a hard guy to ignore. He was so big and so dang *male.*

"You came to Evie's defense against the djegrali," he said. "She and Ansgar are in your debt. It would please them both if you would come. The fairies also."

"Uh-uh. No can do. It's Saturday night. We got a band and the place will be packed. I can't do that to Toby."

"He has the zombie to help him now, thanks to your intercession."

She took another swipe at the bar. "Tommy's new. He hasn't been trained."

The fairy with the moonbeam hair flew up to Conall and said something in her brittle voice.

"I am afraid Silverbell insists," Conall said.

"That so? Well, you can tell Silverbell for me that I am *not* going to—"

Beck never got to finish her sentence, because that's when the treacherous little lightning bug smacked her right in the kisser with a honeysuckle-scented cloud of fairy funk.

An hour and a half later, Beck stood in the fellowship hall of the Trinity Episcopal Church along with several hundred other wedding guests—the whole freaking town was here, from the looks of it—waiting for the bride and groom to make their entrance. Correction: brides and grooms. Evie and Ansgar had gotten married in a double wedding ceremony with Addy Corwin, Evie's friend, and Brand Dalvahni, another demon hunter.

The brides had been exquisite in their frothy wedding gowns, the grooms magnificent in formal attire—tall, supernaturally handsome, and muscle bound. Normally, the cloud of euphoria and oh-my-God-I'm-so-frigging-happy-and-I-love-you-so-much-smoochie-smoochie that had permeated the sanctuary during the ceremony would've made Beck hurl. But thanks to Silverbell's burst of fairy feel-good to the face, Beck sat through the whole thing spellbound by the perfection of it all, like everybody else. Once, she'd almost *cried*.

Okay, she had cried. Twice. The first time was when Ansgar, the blond, gray-eyed demon hunter that Evie was marrying, had gotten choked up during his vows. There was something about a big alpha male revealing his inner mush that really got to Beck. She cried again when Ansgar and Evie kissed at the end of the ceremony. That kiss had been perfect, flipping fairy tale perfect. Beck could swear she heard little tinkling bells, and the air in the chapel went thick and hazy and turned all buttery and golden, like in a movie.

Conall wasn't kidding when he'd said the fairies liked Evie Douglass. The little glow worms had been everywhere, flitting around the flower arrangements, in the stained-glass windows and on the altar, sliding down the silk ribbons at the end of the freshly polished, high-backed wooden pews, and hovering around the happy couples standing at the front of the church. Judging from the comments of the people around her, most folks had no idea the fae were among them. They thought they were flower petals tossed by the attendants.

People see what they want to see. The vast majority of the people in the church probably had no idea that the guy playing the pipe organ was a ghost. Nope, not a clue, and that was a good thing. In Beck's experience, most norms wanted nothing to do with the supernatural. They'd rather put their fingers in their ears and say *la la la,* and pretend it didn't exist.

Take her dad, for instance. He sure lived in denial. Live in a town where the weird factor is off the charts? Ignore. Shapeshifter ex-partner? Ignore, ignore.

Half-demon daughter? Ignore, ignore, ignore.

Beck yanked at the hem of her dress, a slinky above-the-knee garment of midnight blue jersey with a daring scoop back. Fairy magic, she thought darkly, giving the garment another tug. The dress didn't belong to her and neither did the shoes she wore, a pair of glittery sapphire sling-backs with matching bows and four-inch heels that put her over six feet. Totally impractical and probably cost a couple hundred bucks to boot. If she was going to spend that kind of cash on footwear she'd buy something useful. Boots to muck around the bar in maybe, or a pair of sturdy hiking sandals to wear in the woods and along the river—not a pair of girly slut pumps.

She sneaked another admiring peek at her daintily shod feet. The shoes might not be sensible, but she had to admit they were the bomb diggity. Like something a fairy cobbler would come up with, shiny and sparkly. They'd been waiting on the end of her bed along with the dress. Her memory was patchy because of the fairy dust, but she remembered that much . . . as well as her squeal of delight when she'd seen them.

Princess shoes, she remembered shrieking like a five-year-old girl, followed by a lot of undignified jumping up and down on her part. Her cheeks burned at the memory. Who knew she was such a *girl?* She'd never been into froufrou shit, never had the chance. Her dad had treated her like one of the guys growing up. She'd never been to prom or a high school dance. Never been on a date . . . unless you counted a hurried, fumbling grope in the woods with a passing shape-shifter when she was nineteen. Which she so did not.

The bar was all she knew, all she'd ever known. She'd been serving drinks before she was ten, running the office and ordering supplies for her dad by the age of thirteen. She knew how to talk down a mean drunk and break up a fight. But she didn't know how to mingle with townies, and she sure as hell didn't know how to make small talk at a wedding.

She looked around. The fellowship hall of the Episcopal church was narrow and long with arched windows along both sides and gleaming wooden floors. Candles glowed softly in the windowsills amid glossy bunches of magnolia leaves and white ribbons. At the far end of the room in front of three windows, two enormous wedding cakes commanded center stage. Additional cloth-covered tables flanked the wedding cakes, groaning under the weight of silver trays laden with a mouthwatering array of hors d'oeuvres, and a champagne fountain sparkled in one corner. Beck didn't recognize half the fancy food on the platters. It was a far cry from bar food; that was for sure. Not a chili cheese dog or a chicken wang in sight.

The noise level in the crowded room was incredible. Guests swirled around the loaded tables in impatient eddies, eager for the happy couples to appear. Beck caught snatches of conversations as people brushed by. The subject of football reigned supreme, followed by talk of the wedding and the food.

Beck hung back near the door that led into the church garden, uncomfortably aware that she did not belong here.

She caught several curious stares directed her way and wondered if she was overdressed. She'd been to exactly one other wedding in her life, and that was her dad's, a simple ceremony at a country church with a preacher and a few friends. Not a formal society affair like this.

Although she'd never lived in the city limits or gone to school in Hannah, she recognized a lot of the guests from the "What's Going On In Town?" section of the local paper. Folks with money and comfortable, predictable lives; steeped in a sense of belonging and an unshakeable knowledge of who they were and their place in the scheme of things.

She, on the other hand, ran a bar on the river for demonoids. She had plenty of society, just not the elegant kind.

Beck took another quick look around. The fairies ignored her and swarmed around the wedding cakes in an ecstasy of anticipation. Fairies obviously liked sugar. Now would be a good time to try to sneak out, while the little stink bugs were distracted.

Pasting a wide smile on her face for the benefit of anyone who might be looking, Beck edged closer to the exit. The fairies were trilling a song in their thin, little voices. "A Rhapsody to Wedding Cake," most likely, Beck surmised. It was only a guess, because she didn't speak fairy. The norms, of course, were clueless.

The door was only a few feet away. She'd make a run for it, and hope like hell Silverbell didn't catch her and gobsmack her with fairy dust again. She'd sat through the ceremony. She'd be damned if she'd stick around for the rest of this nauseating crap.

She scooted around a group of guests, keeping her smile in place. Almost there.

"You look lovely," a deep voice said, stopping her in her tracks.

Beck whirled around and almost fell off her princess shoes. It was Conall, looking all bad boy and delicious in a perfectly tailored dark suit and a blazing white dress shirt, open at the neck. She'd never seen him in daylight or in a well-lit room, for that matter. Until now, that is, and it was something of a shock to her system.

Something of a shock? Try 9.0 on the Richter scale.

The Dalvahni demon hunter pain-in-her-ass was a total babe.

Chapter Five

He wasn't wearing a tie. No surprise there. Somehow, demon hunters and neckties didn't go together.

Swords, mayhem, and evisceration, yeah. Neckties . . . not so much.

His ragged dark hair gleamed in the light, and his eyes were black as midnight—blacker, like the space between the stars.

Where did he get off being so handsome? It made her mad. He made her mad. How had she missed something so obvious? The lighting in Beck's was dim, but not that dim. Conall Dalvahni was smoking hot and she'd blanked it out, had done a mental *la la la* like a stupid norm. Obviously, her daddy wasn't the only one in denial.

She glanced around. The other females in the room weren't near as slow on the uptake. Old and young alike, they watched Conall through slanted lids in a predatory, hungry way, like they wanted to gobble him up. For some reason, that annoyed her, too.

"Who cuts your hair?" she demanded irritably.

Conall's brows rose. "I do."

"Huh. What do you use, a weed whacker?"

"No, I cut it with my knife. What is a 'weed whacker'?"

"Never mind. It was a joke."

"Ah. Levity. The Dalvahni are not adept at this form of communication."

"No kidding. I never would have guessed."

Beck tapped her foot, surveying him with a scowl. An air of

solitude surrounded him like a cloak. He looked dark and dangerous and unapproachable. Beck recognized it for what it was—a shield to keep people at bay. She was pretty good at the old shield thing herself. Don't get close and you won't get hurt. You won't get left.

"Ansgar and Brand have long hair," she said at last. "How come yours is short?"

"As captain, I must distinguish myself."

"You mean you want to stand out?"

"I do not mean to imply that I consider myself superior to my fellow warriors. Far from it. It is my honor to serve them, but . . ." He hesitated. Looking down, he adjusted the sleeves of his jacket. "I am different. I am their commander."

"I get it," she said. "You're the boss and you cut your hair short to remind them of it."

"You are perceptive. It serves as a reminder to me as well." He straightened his broad shoulders. "My men rely on me, as do those they protect."

"Save the universe and the brotherhood. Wow, you're a regular boy scout, aren't you?" He looked puzzled and she waved her hand in dismissal. "Never mind. Like I said, I get it. The bad haircut sets you apart."

"My hair displeases you? It is a matter easily remedied. It grows quickly."

Beck felt her cheeks grow hot. "It's your hair. Wear it any way you like."

"But I want to please you."

He wanted to please her? The thought flustered her, and then she remembered. He wanted information.

She stiffened. "Back to that, are we? I told you I'm not interested in working with you." She glanced up as the current of people around her swelled toward the door on a ripple of oohs and ahs. The bridal parties had entered the fellowship hall, leaving her and Conall alone at the back of the room. She lowered her voice, nonetheless. "Why should I help you or your precious Dalvahni? I'm half demon. That makes us enemies. For all I know, the kith are next on your hit list."

"And if I promise you that is not the case?"

She gave him a narrow-eyed stare. "Meaning?"

He sighed. "You are a most suspicious female. Meaning that I have only just discovered the existence of your kind and I have no plans to exterminate them without further study."

"Yeah, for now, but that could change in a heartbeat."

"Mine is not a hasty nature, Rebekah. I give you my word I have no scheme at present to kill the kith, nor will I do so without good reason. You are safe."

She lifted her chin. "I'm not worried about me. I can take care—"

"—of yourself," he said. "So you keep saying. But what if you are wrong?"

"What's that supposed to mean?"

"What if you cannot take care of yourself or those you care about?" He held up his hand as she opened her mouth to retort. "Hear me out. I mean to imply no threat. There is an expression, 'the twelfth of never.' Humans use it to indicate that something is unlikely, correct?"

"Yeah."

"We have a similar saying among the Dalvahni. We say *that will happen at Han-nah-a-lah*. That is, the end of all things."

"Han-nah-a-lah?" The meaning of the strange word sank in. "Whoa, you mean Hannah, Alabama? What's that supposed to mean?"

"I do not know, but I will tell you this. For years beyond counting, the scales have been tipped in favor of the Dalvahni. Our powers are great. We are extremely resilient and almost impossible to kill. But I fear the demons may have found a weapon to use against us. Who will stand against the djegrali if the Dal are undone? What will become of this world and all the other worlds that depend on us if the demons are allowed to run unchecked?"

Latrisse's ravaged face rose before Beck. The kith were resistant to demon possession, but humans didn't stand a chance. Her dad and Brenda, and their kids . . . all the other norms in

Hannah would be taken. Hell, the entire human population would be infected by the soul-sucking bastards, and she and the rest of the kith would be left to live among the ruins.

Some of the kith would be all right with that, but not her. There were plenty of norms she liked just fine. Ed Landrum, the mechanic who worked on her truck . . . Johnny Harvey, the good-natured meat man down at the Piggly Wiggly with his broad hands and ready smile, and Myrtle Glenn down at the drug store, to name a few. They might be norms, but they were nice folks.

Her dad was a decent guy in his own way, hardworking and faithful to his wife, always cracking a joke with his customers. Good to his employees and his children, the human ones, at any rate.

To be fair, he'd never mistreated her, either. Just shrugged her off like a shirt he'd outgrown and moved on, starting another life without her. Plenty of men did that. Started new families and left the old ones. She and her dad didn't have the best relationship, but that didn't mean she wanted him dead or possessed. The same went for Brenda and the rug rats.

Besides, she reasoned, if the demons took over the kith would be in danger, too. Maybe not in danger of possession, but she knew from experience that a demon-possessed human on the rampage could tear hell off the hinges. Living on a planet infested with them would be a nightmare. They'd be killing each other and killing the kith. Civilization would come to a screeching, screaming, bloody halt, and planet Earth would become one big reeking charnel house. Talk about your horror movies.

"All right, you got my attention," Beck said. "What do you want me to do?"

"Keep your eyes and your ears open," Conall said. "Send out feelers among the kith. See if you can discover any rumblings about this so-called weapon."

"Done."

"And I want you to give me a job."

"*What*? Are you crazy? I can't hire you."

"I will gladly offer you recompense."

"What is it with you trying to pay me off? Get it through your thick skull that I'm not for sale."

"I apologize. 'Twas not mine intent to besmirch your honor. I offered to pay you because you would be granting me a boon. Working at the bar will give me the opportunity to gain people's trust and gather information, to winnow rumor from fact."

She shook her head. "It would never work. We'd be at each other's throats within five minutes."

"I would not be at your throat. You would be my employer. You would be able to tell me what to do and I would have to do it."

"Tempting, but the answer's still no."

"You hired the zombie."

"That's different. Tommy's in trouble. He doesn't have any place else to go."

"*I* am in trouble," Conall said. "The fate of my brothers and your world may well hang in the balance, and you would turn me away whilst offering aid to the undead."

Something flickered in his dark eyes. Outrage, maybe? Nah, surely not. She couldn't hurt his feelings . . . could she?

She glanced at him through her lashes. Maybe it was the bad haircut, but he seemed somehow a little less perfect and invulnerable. Or maybe she was a big old pushover.

So what if she did hurt his feelings. She didn't care.

Did she? She examined her feelings, pushing aside her natural dislike of him.

Oh, crap, she did. Damn. She did *not* need this.

"Hang around the bar," Beck suggested, desperate for an alternative. "Buy a few drinks. Mingle with folks. You'll accomplish the same thing."

"No. As a patron, I would stand out. If I work for you, I will go unnoticed."

Blend in? Beck gazed at him in exasperation. In what reality? He was big. He was brooding, and he was gorgeous. On top of that, he exuded menace. The guy walked around with a big MESS WITH ME AND I'LL KICK YOUR ASS sign blinking non-stop over his head, for God's sake.

"What sort of job did you have in mind?" she heard herself say. She rubbed her aching temples. First the zombie and now Mr. Grumpy Pants. "What can you do? I mean, besides kill things."

"I am good with horses and a fair blacksmith," he said. "And I know something of dragons."

Dragons? Was he for real? Somehow, she managed to keep a straight face.

"Don't get many of those," she said. Actually, they didn't get any. Shape-shifters, mostly—the kith were fond of shifting—and the occasional werewolf. Oh, yeah, and fairies as of today, Beck thought sourly, recalling Silverbell and her pesky little posse of gnats, but no dragons. "I was thinking of something a little bit more useful."

"Dragon lore can be extremely useful," Conall said stiffly. "As you would know, had you ever been on the wrong end of one." He frowned and added, "Though, in truth, there is no good end."

"Lucky for me, that hasn't been a problem. But, you never can tell. Good to know who to call in case of a dragonish event."

Conall moved closer, his dark gaze intense. Beck forgot about her headache. She forgot to breathe. It was like a force field, all that intensity, buffeting her in waves. Man, this guy was good and twice as dangerous when he turned on the charm. If she were smart, she'd get as far away from him as possible, for her own peace of mind, if nothing else. She certainly wouldn't *hire* him. He'd be under her feet like a 225-pound Chihuahua.

"Give me a chance," he said. "Set me a task. I am a very fast learner. You will see."

His deep husky voice made her stomach go squishy. The last of her resolve crumbled.

"Okay," she said. *So much for being smart.* "But no sticking the customers with that sword of yours. Makes 'em cranky."

"If you insist."

His lips curved, ever so slightly. Was he amused? Nah, he didn't have a sense of humor.

"And you have to get along with the other employees." She gave him a hard look. The blood was starting to pump back into her oxygen-deprived brain, and she already regretted her impulsive decision to hire him. "I've got my hands full keeping Hank happy. I don't have the time or the energy to referee the rest of you."

"I will be the most affable of fellows."

"And you have to be nice to Tommy."

Beck waited, feeling pleased with herself. The zombie would be a deal breaker.

Conall shrugged. "I will not harry the creature without reason. You have my word."

Her last hope shriveled on the vine. "Okay, you can start on Monday."

"I will start at once."

"At once?" He was overbearing, opinionated, and full of himself. He'd be ordering her around and driving her batshit in less than a week. "You don't mean like *now?*"

"Yes, tonight," he said. "As of this moment, I am in your employ. Agreed?"

"Yes." Fine; the sooner he went to work for her, the sooner he could leave.

"And I will remain in your employ until I discover more about this weapon of the djegrali's."

Warning bells jangled. Whoa, that could take months.

"I'll give you two weeks," she said.

"Six," he countered.

"A month," she said. "Not a day more."

"Done."

He held out his hand and she shook it.

Crap. Damn and double damn. How did she get herself into these messes?

"Beck! I'm so glad you came."

Evie Douglass—oops, Evie Dalvahni—rushed up to them, a

vision in a strapless ivory gown with flowing skirts. Her fiery hair was arranged in a deceptively casual up-do. A few curls dangled around her bare shoulders, and her hazel eyes were aglow with happiness and excitement.

Beck usually felt comfortable in her own skin, at least when she wasn't wearing a slinky dress and sky-high stilettos. But Evie Dalvahni, with her generous curves and tiny waist, made her feel positively boyish.

"Wouldn't have missed it," Beck said. It wasn't a total lie. The wedding had been beautiful, and Evie looked so genuinely happy to see her that Beck felt ashamed of her sullen attitude. She summoned a warm smile. "You look wonderful, Evie. Everything is perfect, the church, the flowers, you."

Evie blushed. "It was all Bitsy—that's Addy's mama. You know her?"

Evie indicated a tiny dynamo of a woman standing on the other side of the room near the luscious blonde who was Evie's best friend and fellow bride.

Beck shook her head. "I know of her, but we've never met. She runs the funeral parlor, right?"

"That's right," Evie said, beaming. "Addy's her only daughter, and Bitsy's been planning the wedding for *months*. Ansgar and I sort of tagged along at the end."

A Viking god in a tux strode up to them. "Captain," he said, nodding to Conall.

"Well met, Ansgar." Conall arched a brow at Beck. "You remember Rebekah Damian."

Beck shot Conall an annoyed look. "The name's Beck. Congratulations on your marriage, Ansgar. It's nice to see you again."

It wasn't really, but Beck's daddy had raised her to be polite. The last time she'd seen the blond demon hunter, he'd wrecked her bar. Granted, he'd had help from a passel of demons and a few others, including Conall, but the bar had been trashed all the same.

Ansgar put a possessive arm around Evie's waist and gave his new bride a look so hot she should have been melted on the spot. He was one satisfied demon hunter. What would it be like to have someone love her like that? Beck wondered. She shrugged away the thought.

"Greetings, Rebekah," Ansgar said. "Evangeline and I are overjoyed that you could be here today."

He'd followed Conall's lead on the name thing, Beck noticed with a twinge of irritation. Unlike Conall's rough growl, Ansgar had a voice as cool and smooth as silk, seductive and mesmerizing. There was magic in that voice. Beck was beginning to understand what Conall had meant when he said the Dalvahni were powerful. These guys were the whole enchilada. Good looking, deadly efficient, and gifted with a bottomless bag of tricks. No wonder the demons were looking for a weapon to use against them.

If Ansgar's gift was his mesmerizing voice, then Conall's gift must be driving people bonkers, she reflected. Why, the citizenry of entire enemy cities had probably leaped to their deaths to escape the big Dalvahni pain in the ass.

Beck realized that Evie and Ansgar were waiting for a response, and babbled something appropriate. At least, she hoped it was appropriate.

"Sweetling," Ansgar said to Evie in his sorcerer's voice, "the fairies have grown impatient waiting for us to cut the cake and have gotten into the wine. They will be pixilated in a trice and cause no end of trouble."

"Oh, my goodness. Yes, of course, you're right." Evie flashed Beck and Conall an apologetic smile. "Y'all be sure and stay. There's a ton of food and plenty of champagne, and the cake is supposed to be delicious." She wrinkled her nose. "It wouldn't dare be anything less, not with Bitsy in charge."

Taking Ansgar's offered arm, Evie turned to leave, only to whirl back around. "Thank you so much for coming," she whispered, giving Beck a tight hug. "Really."

Dumbfounded, Beck watched Evie hurry off with her new husband. A warm, comfortable feeling bloomed in her chest. She rubbed the aching place in her sternum.

"Rebekah, are you well?" Conall asked.

"Heartburn," Beck said, not meeting his gaze. "See you later. I'm out of here."

She bolted for the door.

See you later? What kind of lame-ass thing was that to say? She'd see him later, all right. She'd hired the guy to work at the bar, *because she was an idiot.*

Good God almighty.

Beck paused at the top of the steps to take a deep breath. It was a beautiful night, star studded and clear, the air slightly chilly. She'd come out of a side door that led into a small enclosed garden with neat flowerbeds and a birdbath. Now, if she could only remember where she'd parked her truck. She'd been DUI on fairy crack when she'd driven here . . .

Ah, that's right. The parking lot had been jammed with cars, so she'd parked down the street.

As she started across the garden, Conall caught up with her. "It is dark," he said, wrapping a hand around her elbow. "I will accompany you."

She jerked away from him. "I don't need an escort. Go eat cake. Drink some champagne. Talk to a pretty woman. I've got to get back to the bar."

Conall stood with his back to the church door, his face in shadow. "I have no interest in cake or champagne, and I am already talking to a remarkably pretty woman."

"Why are you being nice? Aren't you afraid you'll break something?"

"A most suspicious woman," he said, closing the space between them. "As I have already noted."

"Female," Beck said. Her breath caught in her throat. He was smiling; a real smile, not a mere curve of the lips. The effect was dazzling, like the sun coming from behind a thundercloud. "You said female, not woman. That covers a lot more territory. I've got my pride, you know."

"So I have noticed," Conall murmured.

He lowered his head. He smelled of mountain air, clean and

crisp, a green scent laced with the tang of lemons and a hint of leather. Was he going to kiss her? More importantly, would she let him?

Maybe. It was the shoes, of course. She'd never let him kiss her if she wasn't wearing the sparkly shoes. They made her feel special, like anything could happen. Like she was Cinder-freaking-ella.

Kiss him? Was she mental?

He was a demon hunter and she was part demon, for crying in the beer. Sure, they'd called a truce. Sort of. At best, that made them frenemies.

With a reluctance that surprised her, she stepped back.

"Rebekah," he said, reaching for her.

"I don't have time for this," she said. "I gotta go."

Ignoring the flash of disappointment in his eyes, she spun around and headed for the wrought-iron garden gate. She needed to get back to the bar. She was way out of her comfort zone here, in more ways than one.

"Rebekah Damian?" a man called out of the darkness.

Beck screeched to a halt. Something about that smooth, sly voice sent a chill down her spine. The night seemed to still and her senses tightened in warning.

Conall stepped in front of her, sword in hand. "Who are you? Show yourself at once."

A man slid out of the shadows and through the gate. Tall, dark haired and handsome in a lean, elegant way, he was a young, skinny Elvis with torn jeans and an attitude, and too many piercings to count. In spite of the chill in the air, he wore a sleeveless T-shirt and carried a black leather jacket slung over one shoulder. Tattoos snaked up his forearms and curled around his toned biceps. The dark ink stood out in startling contrast to his pale skin. Jeez, had the guy never been out in the sun?

His sooty hair was artfully tousled and kohl ringed his glowing purple eyes. Kith, definitely, though not from around here. They didn't get many goth types in Hannah. This guy stuck out like a dead cockroach on top of granny's Sunday buttermilk pie.

Who was he and what did he want? Beck wondered, taking in his sneering, sullen expression.

"I'm Beck Damian," she said, stepping around Conall. "What do you want?"

"A welcome home hug, for starters." The stranger threw her a crooked grin. "I'm Evan, your brother."

Chapter Six

Dimly, Beck realized that Conall was speaking to her. His deep voice was rough with concern, and he had his hand on her arm, supporting her.

"Answer me, Rebekah," he said. "Do you know this man?"

"No." She shook her head to clear her spinning thoughts. "I've never seen him before."

Evan's grin faded. "Guess a hug is out of the question. And here I was looking forward to a tender reunion." He shoved his hands in the pockets of his jeans, not an easy thing to do when they fit like a second skin. "I'm disappointed in you, Cookie. Twins don't forget one another. All that time together in the womb, I guess."

Beck felt the blood drain from her face. "W-what did you call me?"

"Cookie, like when we were kids, 'cause you were so sweet. Remember?"

Oh, yeah, she remembered. It had been their little joke, because she'd *never* been sweet. Her childhood had been one long time-out. Like the time she'd put sand in her daddy's gas tank— that one had earned her a trip to the whup shack. Or her certainty that the ants in the ant farm she and Toby had built as a science project were suffocating, so she'd freed them, trailing syrup through the bar so they could find their way out.

Cookie.

Her heart thundered in her ears and her knees had the wobbles. "But, you weren't real. I imagined you."

"It was real to me." Evan's mouth thinned. "And then you left me."

"I didn't leave you. I grew up."

"You got your period on our ninth birthday," Evan said. "You had the cramps and you were scared. You didn't have anybody to talk to. You were in pain and confused, and then you went away." He shrugged. "Puberty's a bitch, ain't it? Hits halfsies like us early and hard." He turned his cynical gaze on Conall. "Who are you?"

"I am Conall."

"You wanna put that pig sticker away? You're making me nervous."

There was an undercurrent of sly laughter in Evan's voice that Beck didn't like.

"Good," Conall said, making no move to sheath his weapon. "You should be nervous."

Evan chuckled. "You got yourself a real character there, sis. Is he always this jolly?"

"I am never jolly," Conall said. "I work for Rebekah."

"I'll just bet you do. What are you, her boy toy?" The corners of Evan's mouth lifted in a smirk. "You like 'em big and rough, sis? This one looks like he can deliver."

"Never you mind what I like," Beck snapped. "And stop calling me 'sis.'"

"Touchy. I can see I've outstayed my welcome." Evan turned away. "I wanted to introduce myself, but it's late. I got business to attend to."

"Wait." Beck wasn't done with him, not by a long shot. She had too many questions.

He looked over his shoulder at her. "Yeah?"

Beck struggled for the words. "This is crazy. How do I know you're telling the truth?"

"You know," Evan said softly, and then he was gone.

Brother, brother, brother . . .

Beck shivered and clasped her hands together in her lap. She had a brother named Evan.

No. Everything in her rebelled at the notion. She would have known. She would have felt it.

Wouldn't she?

Unbidden, the memories rushed in. Memories she'd long since relegated to a mental file marked "childhood imaginings."

Evan, the make-believe friend of her youth, her constant companion and confidant, had seemed more real to her than the adults in the bar. He'd been the product of her isolation from other children, her fright and confusion at the things she could do, her anger and resentment at being different.

At being a freak.

And then one day he was gone. Lots of kids had imaginary playmates and outgrew them. Evan had been a childish fancy she'd set aside.

Hadn't he? He couldn't be *real* . . . could he? This had to be some kind of trick.

The rumble of the wheels over the river bridge pulled Beck from her thoughts. Conall was driving her truck, a deep red, four-wheel-drive Toyota Double Cab Tundra. She had a vague memory of him walking her across the dark lot and helping her into the passenger side of the cab.

She glanced over at him. Big Red was her baby. She never let anyone else drive her truck, not even Toby. Of course, "driving" could only be used in the loosest sense of the word to describe what Conall was doing. He sat in the driver's seat, his hands resting on his powerful thighs instead of on the wheel, while the truck glided through the night like it was on rails. Except that it wasn't on rails and nobody was driving the damn thing, which made it freakazoid and downright unnerving.

Conall's chiseled features were stern in the dim glow of the dashboard. He wasn't wearing his seatbelt. In the scheme of things, it probably didn't matter much. Conall had said demon hunters were hard to kill.

"You aren't wearing your seatbelt," she said anyway. "You could get a ticket."

He didn't say anything.

"That's a bad thing." Still no response, so she tried again. "Maybe you should pull over and let me drive."

"No. You are in shock." The muscles in his back and shoulders bunched beneath his jacket as he crossed his arms, making the whole no-one-at-the-wheel experience that much harder to ignore. He reminded her of a big, muscular, well-dressed genie. She half expected him to bob his head and blink. "Would you like to talk about it?" he asked. "I know that conversing with another sometimes eases human troubles."

"I'm not human."

"You are part human. Perhaps your human part would like to talk about it."

"Very funny," she said. "I thought demon hunters didn't have a sense of humor."

"And I expected you to stink of demon. It would seem we were both mistaken."

She smoothed the front of her dress, mostly to have something to do. She'd cleaned her truck a few days earlier, and the slightly citrus scent of the vinyl cleaner still lingered, but mostly she smelled *him*. He might be annoying, but he sure smelled good.

"You're being nice to me again," she said. "Why?"

"I am trying to lure you into complacence with my charm so I can do something nefarious to you." He lowered his arms and turned his head to look at her. "Is it working?"

"Yeah, I'm eat up with complacency. Everybody says so."

He made a noise that sounded suspiciously like a snort. "This I have not noticed."

His gaze moved to her legs and locked. Beck's skin tingled and grew warm, and it was all she could do not to squirm in her seat.

"Have I told you how much I like your shirt?" he asked, lifting his gaze to her face at last.

"What?" Why was it so dang hot in the truck? Beck took a quick peek at the thermostat. Nope, set at sixty-eight degrees, like always. "It's not a shirt, it's a dress."

"There is scarcely an ell's length of cloth in the whole garment," he said. " 'Twould pass as a chemise in most realms."

He didn't like her dress. Well, hell. So much for feeling girly and pretty.

"Take it up with the fairies if you don't like it," she said. "They made it."

"I did not say I do not like it. I like it very much, as did the other males at the wedding. They were looking at you."

The only male at the wedding she'd been aware of was him. Not that she'd let him know it.

"I didn't notice."

"I did." There was a note of barely suppressed violence in Conall's harsh voice. "You have beautiful legs, long and sleek and firmly muscled." Beck blinked at him in confusion. Had she really compared his eyes to the black emptiness between the stars? Space was cold and his eyes were hot. "They were all looking at your legs," he said. "They were looking at the rest of you, too."

He liked her legs, and she *liked* that he liked her legs. This would not do. This would not do at all.

"You sound almost jealous," she said with a nervous laugh. "And we both know that's not possible."

"Of course not."

He turned his head and stared back out the windshield into the inky pool of blackness beyond the headlights like nothing had happened.

Beck drew a ragged breath. But something had happened. Something had changed between them, although she couldn't say what.

"That thing you did this afternoon . . . when you turned into water," he said after a while. " 'Twas quite an impressive trick. Are you a naiad?"

"You mean one of those chicks from Greek mythology?" There'd been a time when she'd lost herself in the old tales, searching for some clue as to what she was. "No, at least, I don't think so. My powers are stronger near water, though."

Why was she telling him this? She never talked about this stuff with anybody, not even Toby. Silence stretched between them again as the driverless truck purred down the highway and bumped onto the narrow dirt road that ran beside the river. There were no mercury lights this far outside of town. Trees hunched overhead, branches entwined, exchanging whispered secrets on the wind. Outside the truck, it was cow-belly dark.

"I was a Happy Kids dropout," she blurted. "Actually, I was expelled."

"I do not understand."

"It was a daycare, a place where people leave their children while they're at work."

"Ah," he said. "For a moment, I feared we were speaking of goats."

"No goats—just human kids, preschool, mostly. And me."

"There were no other kith at this place?"

"Not that I know of," she said. "Course, I wasn't there very long . . . maybe a week at most before they kicked me out. I was three years old. Knew nothing about demons or the kith. Didn't have a clue what I was and neither did Daddy." She looked out the window. The river was just beyond that fringe of trees. She smelled its musky sweet scent and felt the pull of water. "There was this baby in the nursery, a little girl named Jewel. Sweet little thing with big brown eyes and a head full of curly black hair. A year old, at most. She had a growth inside her. I could see it."

"Like you can see demons inside of people?" Conall asked.

"Yeah, exactly like that. I had my hand inside her chest when the teacher came in and caught me. It freaked her out pretty bad. The teacher, I mean. They had to sedate her. Mae Givens was her name. They called Daddy to come get me. I was home-schooled after that."

"Home-schooled?"

"I wasn't allowed around norm kids again. Daddy decided it was best to keep me away from humans and under the radar, so I stayed at the bar. We lived in an efficiency apartment in the back. It's gone now. Made it part of the kitchen when I re-modeled the place a few years back. He and Toby taught me—Toby, mostly. I freaked Daddy out too much."

"Your sire bears no paternal feelings for you?"

Beck made an impatient gesture with her hand. "He loves me, but I make him nervous. He knew Toby was like me and so he turned me over to him. Like to like, I guess he figured."

"I am beginning to think I was mistaken in my initial impression of your father. I do not think I like him very much, after all."

"Oh, he wasn't ever mean to me or anything like that," Beck said quickly. "It's just that he didn't know what to do with me, so he mostly ignored me. He's such a norm, you see, and I'm . . ." Her voice trailed off. "Well, I'm not."

"No, you are something quite out of the ordinary."

Was that a compliment? Beck wasn't sure, so she plunged on. "When I got older and we got a computer, I took classes online. Passed the GED when I was fifteen."

"What is this GED?"

"It's a battery of tests," she said. Conall knew less about the so-called real world than she did. Beck cast about for a way to explain the GED to a demon hunter. "If you pass, you get a piece of paper that says you graduated from high school. It's like a rite of passage."

"High school: a secondary school that usually encompasses grades nine through twelve," Conall intoned, as though reading from a book. "It is part of the human educational system?"

"Yeah. Didn't you ever go to school?"

"No. The Dalvahni train for combat, but we do not go to school in the manner of humans. It is unnecessary. We have other ways."

"You mean you learn things by magic?"

"In a manner of speaking," he said. "Our powers enable us to adapt quickly to any culture and clime, else we would be disadvantaged in hunting the djegrali."

"Sweet."

"Sweet is not a word I would use to describe the Dal—"

"You can say that again," Beck muttered.

"—but being Dalvahni has its compensations, if that is what you mean."

He fell silent again, but Beck could feel the current of his thoughts the same way she sensed the flow of the nearby river.

"You are largely self-taught and you grew up among adults in a tavern," he said at last. "Not the most wholesome environ in which to raise a child. You were lonely and isolated from others of your kind, but for the shifter Tobias."

He said it in a matter-of-fact tone that was without pity, and that made it bearable.

"That about sums it up," she said. "Except I had Evan, too. He was my imaginary friend."

"He is not imaginary, and he is not your friend. I would advise you to proceed with caution where that one is concerned. I do not trust him."

"You don't know anything about him."

"Neither do you."

"I don't know doodly squat about you, either, except you're a demon hunter," she pointed out. "That ought to send me screaming in the other direction. Instead, you're working at my bar."

He turned his head to look at her again, his eyes shining like a wild animal's. In spite of his calm exterior, there was something deeply wild and savage in him that unsettled and excited her.

"I have been honest with you," he said in a low voice. "You have my sword arm and my pledge of loyalty. Can you say the same of your brother?"

Beck opened her mouth to say something smart-aleck and shut it again. "No, I can't, doggone it."

"My instincts tell me he wants something. I would like to know what that something is. I am also curious to know how he found you after all these years."

Her thoughts, exactly. Troubled, Beck gazed out the window. "Me, too."

"And I would very much like to know why he smells of djegrali."

"What?" She snapped her head around to stare at him. "You're wrong. The kith can't be possessed."

"I did not say he was possessed. I said he smelled of demon. A human that has been taken emits a foul odor, like rancid fat mixed with something rotten. Do you know this?"

"Yes," Beck said, remembering the nauseating odor that had poured from Latrisse's poor, ruined body when they'd found her. The putrid, oily smell had permeated Beck's clothes and skin for days. "My best friend was possessed by a demon." She curled her hands into fists in her lap. "By the time Toby and I found her, it was too late. So, yeah, I know what they smell like. It's not something you forget."

"You can say that again," someone drawled from the rear of the vehicle. "My granddaddy had him a demon and hoo-doggie did he ever stink. I still remember that God-awful smell, and I been dead since Jesus was in short pants."

The truck screeched to a halt in response to Conall's unspoken command. Beck and Conall turned to look.

The ghostly figure of a man sat in the backseat of the pickup truck.

Chapter Seven

The ghost was slim and pale, with gleaming eyes the color of faded violets. A lock of blond hair fell over his white brow. He was handsome in formal attire—black jacket and slacks, white pleated shirt, and a black bow tie. Beck recognized him at once as the organist from Evie's wedding.

"It seems we have a stowaway," Conall said with a frown in his voice. "State your purpose, shade."

"I'm William Blake Peterson," the ghost said in his Bourbon and molasses accent. "But everybody calls me Junior."

Beck had seen ghosts before, though not very often and never one this solid-looking. There was Lorraine, the wife of a steamboat captain, who haunted Jezebel Oaks plantation four miles up the Devil River. Float by the crumbling, abandoned mansion at twilight, and you might catch a glimpse of her watery figure keeping watch on the sagging balcony.

And a ghost named Hazel haunted Sardine Bridge, a creaky wooden structure located not far from Hannah in Robinsonville. To summon Hazel, all you had to do was park on the bridge at midnight, call her name three times, and she'd appear. Or so the legend went.

As a teen, Beck had dismissed it as a silly story made up by silly norms to discourage their even sillier kids from hanging out at the river at night, where they might get snake-bit or drown.

Until the night she met Hazel face to face.

On a lark, Toby had driven her to Sardine Bridge late one

evening when she was fifteen. They'd eased down the old log-ging road in Toby's battered Ford Bronco. The gravel road was snaky and overgrown, seldom used anymore except by teen-agers looking for a place to make out or party, or both.

Toby had parked and the engine grumbled to a halt. It was high summer, and the tree frogs and crickets played a raspy symphony in the thick, surrounding woods. *Dee-deep, dee-deep,* they called. The trees crowded along the riverbank and pressed against a night sky bright with stars, like shining bits of broken glass.

Somewhere in the ocean of green darkness an owl hooted a mournful song. Beck's stomach jumped at the sound. There it was again, she remembered thinking, that feeling she sometimes got. Like something special, something wonderful and exciting, waited for her beyond the bar.

The humid air thickened with possibility. Seeing a ghost might not be wonderful, but at least it qualified as *something.* Sometimes, Beck got so *bored* at the bar she thought she'd lose her mind. And when she got bored, things had a way of hap-pening, things that pissed off her daddy and made the norms edgy. Daddy didn't like it when the customers got edgy.

Toby always seemed to sense when she was feeling restless and would step in with a suggested diversion, like a ghost hunt-ing trip to Sardine Bridge.

Following Toby's instructions, Beck had rolled down the passenger window and called Hazel's name.

Hazel . . .

The bugs halted their music to listen. No answer but the wa-tery chuckle of the river sliding beneath the bridge.

Ha-a-zel, Beck called again. The excited feeling in her stom-ach faded, replaced by the niggling suspicion that she'd been had. This was beyond lame. But, at least they weren't at the bar, so what the hell. She took a deep breath.

Ha-a-a-zel, she'd hollered, one last time.

Nothing.

"Toby, you are such a jerk." Flumping against the seat in a

huff, Beck had glared at the gray-haired bouncer. "This is a crock of shit. I should've known you were jerking me around."

Her heart jumped into her throat as a piercing scream shattered the night.

"Peacocks," she'd said in a shaky voice, determined not to be taken in again. "Everybody knows they sound like a woman screaming."

"That ain't no peacock." Toby pointed to a white, misty figure rising out of the river. "That's Hazel."

With a bloodcurdling screech, the ghost swooped over the bridge and through the windshield, her pale face stretched in a horrible death mask. She plunged through Beck and out the other side. It was like being doused with a bucket of water on the inside. Icy, cold water dipped from a never ending well of despair.

"No . . . cussing . . . on . . . my . . . bridge," Hazel had said, punctuating each word with an icy pass through Beck's body.

With a final shriek, Hazel flew out of the truck and dived back into the river. Beck doubled over, rubbing her aching midsection. She would have peed her pants, but her bladder was frozen.

"Oh, yeah. Probably should've warned you. Hazel can't abide foul language," Toby said in his lazy, country drawl. "She was a Sunday school teacher at the First Methodist Church until she died in a freak boating accident. I wouldn't cuss no more on her bridge, if I was you."

"Thanks," Beck had muttered. "I'll remember that."

That had been her one and only attempt at ghost hunting. Sixteen years later, the memory of Hazel still made Beck's insides quiver. Spectrophobia was an "abnormal and persistent fear of ghosts." She'd looked it up. And, while her fear of ghosts wasn't quite that manic, she had no desire for another Hazelectomy.

Bringing her thoughts back to the present, Beck eyed their ghostly hitchhiker with unease. One ice water enema in a lifetime was enough, thank you very much.

To her relief, Junior Peterson showed no inclination to swoop. "You're Rebekah Damian, the owner of Beck's Bar, right?" he said, giving her a gentle smile.

His serene, slightly wan manner reminded Beck of Leslie Howard from *Gone With the Wind,* only younger and better looking.

"Uh, yeah."

The ghost turned his eerie, shining gaze on Conall. "And you're one of those demon hunters, aren't you? I've met one of you a few weeks back. Big blond fellow."

"My brother Ansgar," Conall said with typical brevity. "What do you want?"

"A job." Junior Peterson returned his attention to Beck. "You were at the wedding tonight. Did you enjoy the music?"

"Yes, it was real nice, but I'm not sure what—"

"I've heard that Beck's is a place for our kind," the ghost rushed on. "I was hoping maybe I could play piano there sometimes. In the afternoons, during the cocktail hour, maybe. You know, before the rowdies come in wanting something a little more lively."

Beelzebubba's raucous country rock sound was certainly more "lively" than the highfalutin music Peterson had played at the church. The kith would jump in the river if he started playing that classical stuff.

Not necessarily a bad thing, depending on the kith. Beck liked most of her customers, but there were a few she could do without, like the Skinners. Look up the word "trouble" in the dictionary and you'd find a picture of the Skinners; God's truth.

"It's a bar for supernaturals," she said. "Not ghosts."

Junior sat up straight. "So what am I, dog poop?"

"He has a point," Conall said. "In my opinion, the disembodied spirit of a dead person certainly falls in the category of the supernatural."

"Nobody asked you," Beck said.

"You wouldn't have to pay me." Junior's pale eyes glowed. "I'd work for free and a place to stay."

What he meant was a place to *haunt.* Logically speaking, a

ghost at the bar shouldn't bother her, not when she had a dead guy working the door. But it did. The incident with Hazel had scarred her. *I'm prejudiced against ghosts,* she thought. *So, sue me.*

"I thought you lived at the church," she said aloud, hedging.

"Heavens, no." Junior gave his cuffs an affronted twitch. "Evie invited me to play at her wedding, but I haven't had a place to stay since my house burned."

The lightbulb went off in Beck's head. "Whoa, you're one of *those* Petersons? The ones with all the money and the—"

She broke off with a little cough of embarrassment.

"—scandal," Junior said, finishing her sentence for her. "Yes, I'm one of them."

"Your granddaddy was the timber magnate," Beck said, awed and a little star struck. The Petersons were *the* family in Hannah, the richest, most powerful, and most influential family in Behr County. Their social standing had waned a bit due to recent events, but they were still plenty loaded. "And you're saying he had a demon?"

"Oh, my, yes," Junior said. "He was in his thirties when he got possessed. I reckon that old demon was just looking for a good time, but Granddaddy had other ideas. Cole Peterson was much a man, and ambitious. He liked the power the demon gave him. He latched on to that old demon and wouldn't let go. Together, they built the Peterson fortune."

"Ansgar has told me of this," Conall said. " 'Tis most unusual. The demon and Cole Peterson merged, somehow, trapping the demon in Peterson's body. The demon could not escape and Peterson could not die, though the fiend steadily consumed his body from within. When he could no longer conceal his obvious state of deterioration, Peterson faked his death and the family hid him beneath the house in a secret chamber. He resided there until—"

He paused, as though remembering their "guest."

"Until the fire," Junior said with a nod. "My parents and my grandfather died when the house burned. Truth is, wasn't much left of Granddaddy Cole by that time. He'd had that demon so long he was a shriveled-up fig with legs."

The Peterson mansion had been reduced to ashes. Mop Webb, a shifter and a volunteer fireman who worked for the beverage company that made deliveries at the bar, had told Beck that an old furnace beneath the house exploded.

"It was a terrible fire," Beck said. "I saw the pictures in the paper."

"Uh-huh." Junior sat back and folded his hands in his lap. He had slender hands with long, artistic fingers; the hands of a concert pianist. Or, at least the kind of hands Beck imagined a concert pianist would have. Junior was her first. Like dragons, highbrow types were scarce at Beck's. "If you read the paper, then I reckon you know about Mama's letter, too," Junior said.

Of course she knew about the letter. It was all anybody in the bar had talked about for *days*. Heck, folks were still buzzing about it. There hadn't been this much excitement in Behr County since the boll weevil devastated the cotton crops back at the turn of the twentieth century.

Clarice Peterson had left a letter in her safe-deposit box confessing to the murder of Meredith Starr Peterson, her grandson's socialite wife. Beck knew Meredith only by reputation but, according to all accounts, Meredith Peterson had been a bitch on wheels. Evie Douglass had been a suspect in the murder investigation until Trey—Meredith's husband and the heir to the Peterson fortune—had made a dramatic announcement in court that *he'd* killed Meredith.

People had been buzzing about that, too. Real *Lifetime for Women* stuff. Scuttlebutt was Trey had a thing for Evie.

Must've been a big thing, if he was willing to cop to his wife's murder and go to jail for her.

The police were still holding him for questioning when they found Clarice's letter confessing to Meredith's murder.

That was juicy, but there'd been more. Clarice had aired all the Peterson dirty laundry in that letter. By her account, Blake Peterson—Junior's father and Clarice's husband—was an abusive, philandering hound dog who'd beaten and bullied her for more than forty-five years. Clarice claimed she'd killed Meredith with one of Blake's fancy collector knives to frame him for murder and even the score. Worse, to hear Clarice tell it, Blake was a sadistic son of a bitch who'd been murdering women for years to get his jollies.

Blake could hardly deny it. He'd died in the fire with Clarice. The paper said the matter was under investigation, and that's as much as anybody knew about it.

Yes sir, that letter had caused quite a stir. But, this was the first Beck had heard about Old Man Peterson still being alive the night of the fire.

"I thought Cole Peterson was dead," she said. "I thought he died years and years ago."

"There's dead and then there's dead," Junior said with a forlorn smile. "Granddaddy and that demon were well and truly caught. Like a fox in a snare, only there was no chewing off a leg to get out of the trap. See, if he died, the demon died, and the demon wasn't having any part of that. So it held on, and they had to fake Cole's death to avoid a lot of uncomfortable questions. In the end, Granddaddy was dried up and brittle as a dead cockroach." The ghost's body wavered briefly, and Beck realized he'd shuddered. "It was a mercy, if you ask me, when Mama burned the place down, even if it did leave me homeless."

"Your mother must have been desperate to do those things," Beck said, thinking of Meredith's murder and the horrible fire.

"Yes, she was." Junior's voice was sad. "Quite desperate, for a long time."

"What about you?" Beck asked without thinking. "How did you die?"

The temperature inside the cab of the truck abruptly plummeted. Oops, somebody had their ectoplasmic knickers in a twist.

"It's impolite to ask a ghost about their demise." Junior's voice was stiff with displeasure. "You wouldn't ask a demonoid about their possessed parent, would you?"

"Sorry," Beck said. "I'm not up on my spook etiquette."

"We don't like the term 'spook,' either," Junior said in the same frosty tone. "If you're really sorry, give me a job."

Beck swallowed a sigh. This day had started out like any other. Where had it gone wrong? Her gaze moved to Conall and stuck.

He raised a quizzical brow at her. "Why do you glare at me?"

"I was wondering exactly where my day went to shit," she said, "and remembering that it started to go south right after *you* showed up."

He chuckled. The sound was deep and rich, and it made her stomach do the squishy thing again. She didn't know who she was madder at, him or herself.

Him, she decided. Definitely him.

"Well?" she said. "Don't just sit there grinning like a possum. What have you got to say for yourself?"

"Nothing, boss." Conall leaned against the door and draped his left arm over the steering wheel. Confident, arrogant, and totally at ease. "Nothing at all."

"Huh," Beck said, unable to find anything objectionable in that statement and ticked off about it. "You know what you get when you spell the word 'boss' backward, don't you?"

"No."

"Double s. o. b.," Beck said. "That means I'm gonna make sure you earn your keep."

He grinned, the cheeky bastard, his teeth gleaming white in the darkness. "I look forward to it."

"So, do I get the job or not?" Junior demanded.

"Sure," Beck said, surrendering to the craziness. "Why not? The more the merrier."

Chapter Eight

Still on auto pilot, the Tundra crunched across the gravel lot at the back of the bar and eased into one of the slots marked EMPLOYEES ONLY. Judging from the number of parked vehicles, Beck's was doing a land-office business.

The entrance to the bar lay down a lighted, wooden walkway that curved around one side of the building and disappeared into the darkness. A sign in the shape of a finger pointed the way. There was one way for customers to enter Beck's, and that was through the front door, whether you came by land or water.

At Toby's suggestion, she'd hired Cassandra Ferguson, the town "witch," to place a number of deterrent spells around the property to further discourage outsiders. Cassie was a shrewd businesswoman. Her spells had an expiration date and she charged a pretty penny. But she was worth it. She'd glamoured the building to appear menacing and shabby from the river and woods to prevent unwanted guests.

Thanks to Cassie, the private road leading to Beck's was impossible to find if you were a norm. In fact, she'd done such a good job that Beck had to hire one of the kith to haul off the garbage because Waste Be Gone couldn't find the place. Cassie had even put a spell on the heavy metal door at the back of the bar to keep out the norms. That way, they didn't have to worry about some norm sneaking into the bar through the kitchen.

Beck wasn't sure which would scare a norm worse, the things he or she might see inside the bar or a run-in with their bad-tempered cook. If she had to pick, Beck's money was on Hank. He wielded a mean meat cleaver.

Norms hadn't been much of a problem so far. The kith liked having a place where they could let down their metaphysical hair, so to speak, and they'd made sure Beck's had an unsavory reputation to keep it that way. The rumors and the fact that the bar was a private club kept most of the unwanteds away. In spite of their precautions, a few norms managed to stumble across the bar from time to time, usually around the new moon when Cassandra's spells were at their weakest. These were turned away at the door by Toby.

Nobody but nobody who wasn't a supernatural got past the Great Schnozzola. Toby could smell a norm a mile away.

Beck pushed open the passenger door of the truck. Conall zipped around the vehicle and helped her down.

"Thanks," she said, balancing on her high heels.

"You are most welcome," Conall said.

His hands lingered at her waist, and she felt the heat of his skin through the thin fabric of her dress. A few inches higher, and he'd be touching the bare flesh of her back. What would it be like to have his hands on her, to be surrounded by all that warmth and strength? Her stomach fluttered at the thought.

It had been too long since she'd been with a man. That was the problem, and Conall was undeniably handsome. He exuded danger and suppressed violence, and a raw, dark energy powerful enough to light up Behr County for a year. He was a bad boy with a capital Bad.

He was the kind of guy that made a woman's hootie switch flip to high and stay there. So naturally, she was tempted. But having sex with him was out of the question. He worked for her now. Fraternizing with an employee would be unprofessional. Besides, Beck had a feeling that sex with Conall Dalvahni would be lethal, in more ways than one.

"That you, Beck?"

The worried voice from the darkness yanked Beck's wayward mind and raging libido out of dangerous territory.

Tommy hovered at the end of the walkway with Annie perched on one shoulder like a furry copper-eyed parrot. He cast a nervous look around. "You all right? How was the wedding?"

"The wedding was very . . . wedding-ish," Beck said, smiling at his politeness.

Most of the supers she knew could learn a thing or two about manners from Tommy Henderson. The nicest guy she'd met in a month of Sundays, and he was dead.

"Everything okay here?" she asked.

Tommy's anxious gaze skittered around the parking lot. "The band's warming up and Hank's cussing a blue streak 'cause some redneck dumped ketchup on his precious étouffée. Other 'n that, everything's fine."

The back passenger door of the Tundra opened with a soft, metallic creak, and Tommy jumped back twenty feet, like a cartoon character with springs for legs.

"Who's that?" Ignoring Annie's mewl of protest at his unexpected gymnastics, Tommy peered past Beck. "You got somebody with you?"

"Yes," she said. "We met someone on our way back from town."

"Who?" A suspicious expression settled across Tommy's pleasant features, and he sounded almost querulous. "Who you done met?"

Junior slid smoothly out of the truck and straightened his jacket. "The name's Junior Peterson." He arched a blond brow at the zombie. "And you would be . . . ?"

"Tommy Henderson." Without taking his gaze off the ghost, Tommy reached up and stroked the fractious kitten. "I work here."

"As it happens, Mr. Henderson, so do I. I'm the new piano player. Now, if you'll excuse me, I'd like to check out my new digs."

Nose in the air, Junior flowed past Tommy and disappeared up the walk.

"Don't mind him," Beck told Tommy. "Junior's a little touchy this evening. He'll warm up to you. Just give him time."

Tommy frowned after the ghost. "He ain't gonna warm up to nobody. He's deader than I am."

"I know," Beck said.

"And we ain't got no piano," Tommy said.

"Oh, shoot," Beck said. "I forgot."

Following in Tommy's shambling wake, Beck picked her way along the plank sidewalk to the front entrance, taking care not to catch her stiletto heels between the slats. Conall walked beside her, his stride purposeful and relaxed, a warrior aware of his surroundings and ready for anything.

Of course he was relaxed and ready for anything, Beck thought with a mild sense of annoyance. She'd be relaxed, too, if she wasn't wearing a skintight dress and hoochie heels.

No, she wouldn't, not with Captain Hah-tay at her side. Conall had shed his jacket and rolled up his shirt sleeves, and he looked absolutely yummy, damn him.

It was getting harder and harder to remember why she shouldn't jump his bones.

It was a beautiful, clear night, and the sweet, slightly musty scent of the river hung in the air. Beck breathed in the damp, earthy smell of deep woods and water, trying to cleanse her mind of her randy thoughts. She let the slow, relentless tug of the nearby river wash over her, strengthen and center her.

There, she was back in control. She glanced at Conall and fell right back into lust. His hair looked very black against the collar of the white shirt. Her fingers itched to touch the ragged, silken strands.

She sighed. So much for her Zen moment.

As they came around the side of the building, Beck saw that the pitched, tin-roofed porch was packed with customers. It was a crisp autumn evening, and the absence of bloodsucking mosquitoes and their annoying midgie cousins called no-see'ums had lured people out of doors. Beelzebubba's rockabilly sound drifted out of the bar, mingling with the chink of beer bottles and the murmur of conversation. At the end of the pier, boats rocked in the sluggish current and a dog paced up and down—Toby, standing guard.

The double doors leading into the bar were open to the night air. Things were jumping at Beck's, inside and out, and it wasn't even ten o'clock, a fact Beck noted with mingled satisfaction and unease. It was the weekend before Thanksgiving and the air tonight had an electric quality to it, the kind that heralded the change in the season. Her blood hummed in response, and the wild streak, the one she kept firmly in check, roused and strained at the leash.

She glanced up. The moon was nearly full and glowed with a dull, orangey haze. Shifter moon, Toby would call it.

A man in the crowd outside the bar laughed, and Beck's heightened senses jangled in response. There was an edgy, brittle quality to the sound that filled her with foreboding. She wasn't the only one who felt the charge in the atmosphere and the pull of the pumpkin moon.

Alabama and Auburn had both won their football games that day, which you'd think would make folks more jovial and in the mood to celebrate. Nothing doing. All that energy and excitement could turn ugly in a heartbeat, especially with the kith.

Nothing worse than a demonoid hepped up on booze and team spirit—unless it was a bar full of them.

"Who's tending bar?" Beck asked, worrying her bottom lip with her teeth.

Tommy situated himself at the foot of the steps with Annie. "Some guy named Jason," he said. "Friend of Toby's, I think. Come up in a fishing boat not long after you left. Toby acted real glad to see him."

"*What?*" Beck said.

She hiked up her skirt and charged up the steps and into the bar. She took a quick glance around. The band ended a song and drifted off the stage on break. Daddy stood behind the lighted glass block counter serving drinks to a long line of thirsty patrons. Shapes floated inside the clear bar, like blobs of colored wax inside an enormous lava lamp. The blobs were pretty, but they weren't decorative. They were demons.

She'd learned purely by accident that demons couldn't pass through certain kinds of glass in their amorphous state. It was a discovery that gave her great pleasure. Every time a possessed human came into the bar, she extracted the nasty little demon bastards and put them behind glass. It was her little way of avenging her mother and Latrisse.

Daddy was laughing and joking as he worked, his moves practiced and efficient, a seasoned bartender in his element. He had no idea, of course, that a few inches of glass was all that separated him from a swarm of pure evil.

Beck's throat tightened at the sight of him. Just like old times.

Except this wasn't old times and this wasn't the old Beck's. Jason Damian was a norm in a kith bar. He didn't belong here, anymore than she belonged in his world.

But, whereas she might feel awkward around his kind, being around *her* kind could get him killed, especially tonight.

Even if he survived the experience, Brenda would have a conniption if she found out he'd been tending bar again. She'd never stop praying over him. Alcohol was the devil's hand-maiden, and Daddy was back on the road to ruination.

Holy cats, what was he thinking?

She worked her way through the crowd and behind the bar. The murmurs of appreciation from the females in her wake told her that Conall had followed.

"Daddy, what are you doing here?" she asked.

He grinned at her, his eyes shining. "Hey, baby doll. You look pretty. Long time since I seen you in a dress."

He wore jeans, his rubber fishing boots, and a green Guy Harvey T-shirt. A faded blue ball cap covered most of his hair, but a few wavy strands had managed to escape and curled around his ears. His sandy blond hair was sprinkled with gray, Beck noticed with a pang of dismay. When had that happened?

"There you go, darling, two Bud Lites." He slid a couple of

beers across the bar to a woman with teased bleached hair, sharply penciled-in brows, and leathery tanned cleavage.

The blonde threw some bills on the bar and swished off, making way for the next patron.

"I was doing a little fishing when Toby hollered at me," Daddy continued, slinging beers and mixing drinks as he talked. "He said you'd gone to the Corwin wedding and that he could use some help. Been meaning to come see you anyway, so I thought why not? and came on in."

"Why didn't you and Brenda go to the wedding?" Beck asked.

She knew they'd been invited. Evie had thrown it out as a lure when she'd hand-delivered Beck's invitation. She'd had no idea, of course, how awkward things were between Beck and her dad.

"Brenda's feeling under the weather, so we bowed out," Daddy said. "I was glad, to tell you the truth. I hate that kind of thing. Rather take a poke in the eye with a sharp stick."

"Me, too," Beck said. They had that much in common, at least.

Topping off a draft beer, Daddy gave Conall a speculative glance as he handed the glass to a man at the bar. "What about you, Mr. Dalvahni? What brings you here?"

Conall's expression was impassive, but he was studying everything Daddy was doing, like he was memorizing it. Beck suspected that's exactly what he was doing. She had a feeling the Dalvahni were quick learners.

What would it be like to have all that attention focused on her? Hot and intense and extremely satisfying, she imagined.

Shit. There she went again, thinking with her vagina.

"I work here now," Conall said.

Daddy's eyebrows disappeared under the brim of his hat, and he gave Beck a questioning look. "That so? Doing what?"

"Oh, you know, a little of this, a little of that," she said vaguely.

She couldn't be more specific, because she didn't know the

answer herself. This morning when she'd gotten up, things had been normal. Or as normal as things could be when you ran a demonoid bar. Somehow, in the space of a few hours, she'd acquired a zombie bouncer, a ghostly piano player, and a hunky demon hunter would-be bartender who specialized in dragons. Not to mention a long-lost brother with multiple tats and piercings who smelled of eau de demon.

Wouldn't Brenda just have a big old cow if she saw Evan? The thought cheered Beck.

A scrawny, middle-aged man with bright, darting eyes and a receding chin shoved his way to the front of the line at the bar. His flushed face and listing gait signaled loud and clear that he'd already had too much to drink.

"Hey." The man slammed his hands on the bar, his wispy mustache twitching in irritation. "Who do you have to kill to get a goddamn beer around here?"

The swirling disquiet in Beck's stomach solidified into a brick of tension. The Skinners were here.

Fan-damn-tastic. It was the icing on this birthday cake of a day.

Chapter Nine

A stocky guy with drooping jowls and mournful eyes clapped his hand on No Chin's shoulder. "Hey, asshole, wait your turn," Droopy said.

With a crack of bone and sinew, Earl Skinner—Beck knew this particular lowlife from previous encounters of the icky kind—shifted into a weasel and sank his teeth into Droopy's hand.

Droopy howled in pain. *Snap, crackle, pop.* He morphed into a mastiff and attacked Earl with a deep *bah-rooh* of rage.

"Oh, crap," Beck said. "Here it comes."

Conall was at her side in a blur of motion. "Something is amiss?"

Oh, yeah, something was amiss, all right.

People in the bar started to shift like kernels of popcorn on a hot stove. *Pop,* a tiny woman with bulbous eyes and long bangs turned into a Pomeranian and chased a calico cat out the door. *Pop pop,* a redheaded man morphed into a chow and launched himself at a scruffy terrier. The two rolled across the floor in a ball of fur and teeth.

Beck gritted her teeth. Shifting was contagious, like yawning, and her body thrummed with the urge to change. The call of the wild was especially strong tonight. Her blood sang with it.

It was that crazy orange moon.

She needed to keep her wits for Daddy's sake. Anything could happen to him in a bar full of moon-drunk supernaturals.

She dug her nails into her palms. They were longer and

sharper than they'd been a moment ago, thanks to the excitement and heat in the air. The pain cleared her head and kept her focused.

"Sonofabitchholyshitfriggingdamnbastard. It's like *National Freaking Geographic* in here," Daddy said.

He kept cussing, the swear words pouring out of him in a steady stream. It was like a dam had burst inside him, and maybe it had. Daddy had given up cussing along with booze when he found Jesus. Somewhere, Jesus was shaking his head in consternation, 'cause Daddy had lapsed tonight, in a big way.

Daddy's eyes widened as a wild boar squealed and trotted across the room, its hooves skittering on the wooden floor. "Hawg," he said in a strangled voice.

Poor Daddy was on overload. Beck knew how he felt. She was on overload, too. She had the shakes and her skin felt two sizes too small.

She shoved him to the floor behind the bar. "Stay down," she said. He gaped up at her, his face slack with shock. "It's not usually like this," she heard herself say. Why was she making excuses? They'd gone their separate ways years ago. She didn't owe him an explanation. "Most of the time, it's pretty boring. It's the moon."

"Moon," Daddy said.

A deer, startled by the noise—but even more by the hungry alligator slithering toward it—jumped through a window in a shower of glass. The alligator gave a hiss of frustration, snapped its jaws at a beagle, and missed.

Beck lost sight of the gator as Earl's relatives poured out of the woodwork in a froth of slim-boned, narrow-faced fury, at least a dozen of them, male and female alike. That was the problem with Skinners. You took on one Skinner, you took on the whole sorry lot, and they were always spoiling for a fight.

There were several weasels in the pack, but Beck spotted a few possums, a couple of foxes, a raccoon, a bony yard dog, and a bobcat in the fracas, all with the Skinner crafty looks. They threw themselves into the scrap with gusto.

Animals fought in clumps or scrabbled across the slippery floor in a frenzy to escape. The noise level was incredible, a deafening cacophony of yips, squawks, barks, growls, bleats, grunts, and hisses. In a matter of moments, the place was a mess, the floor a landmine of overturned chairs, tables, and shattered bottles. Plastic glasses rolled across the floor between islands of discarded clothing and shoes. The yeasty odor of spilled beer mixed with the fumes of hard liquor and the musky scent of hot mammals.

A skunk walked by, tail held high in indignation. Beck clapped her hand over her nose and mouth at the pungent smell. Good Lord, it would take more than a mop and a bucket of Pine-Sol to get *that* out.

She glanced back at the two who'd started it all. The mastiff shook Earl, flecks of foam flying from his strong jaws. The dog flung the weasel aside. Earl hit the wall with a thump and slid to the floor. The mastiff turned his attention to the bobcat. The feline answered with a challenging yowl. *Come on, POS,* the bobcat seemed to say, *I'll eat yo' lunch.*

Behind the snarling, spitting pair, Earl shifted into an enormous boa constrictor. Beck blinked at the reptile in surprise. The snake was at least ten or twelve feet long and as big around as her thigh. Earl was either more powerful than she'd realized, or juiced up on something other than beer.

"Snake," she screeched as Earl slithered toward the oblivious dog. "Bigass snake."

The mastiff, deep in the grip of cat frenzy and oblivious to the danger, kept barking. Too late, the dog gave a startled yip as the snake wrapped him in its massive coils and squeezed.

"Lord a-mercy, he's gonna kill him," Beck said. Kicking off her girly shoes, she leaped over the bar.

"Rebekah, *no,*" Conall shouted.

She ignored him and made a beeline for the snake, or as much of a beeline as she could make in a room full of tumbling, snarling animals. The floor was a land mine of broken glass and slippery with spilled drinks. She pushed and shoved her way through the melee, thrusting her hands into clumps of snarling animals as she went. At her touch, animals shuddered and resumed their human form. They lay on the floor, panting and shivering, bleeding from various wounds, and too startled and weak from the abrupt change to move.

Her talent for undoing came in handy in a bar for supernaturals. She couldn't undo everything, of course, but she could make a shifter revert, no problem. In her experience, it was easier to deal with a naked drunk than a riled-up animal, although neither ranked high on her list of favorites.

A few of the kith, including Beck and Toby, returned to their human form fully clad when they shifted. Most, unfortunately, did not. The result of Beck's "undoing" was a bar full of naked people.

Naked, confused, *ugly* people.

Beck put her hands on a golden retriever with a graying muzzle, averting her gaze as an older woman with breasts like two deflated balloons appeared in its stead. The man lying on the floor beside her was no prize. Beck guessed him to be in his mid-forties, though he could be younger. Skinners had a reputation for hard living. He'd been a possum before she'd touched him. Patches of gray fur clung to his skin, and a skinny, hairless tail still twitched between his flabby butt cheeks. Ugh.

Something made her look back. Conall strode toward her, his face tight with anger. A cloak of shadows surrounded him, and his perpetual aura of kickass pulsed visibly hotter. Animals and people scrambled out of his way.

What was he so riled up about? It wasn't *his* bar being torn off the hinges.

No time to worry about it. She had to stop Earl from killing that dog. Kith had never killed kith in Beck's, and she meant to keep it that way.

She'd almost reached them when a long, trembling shriek stopped her in her tracks. A second horrible scream followed, shattering the night. The hair on the back of Beck's neck rose, and cold fear slithered down her spine. The sound came from somewhere outside in the darkness, the cry of a prowling panther combined with the anguished wail of a dying woman. She'd never heard anything like it.

Toby burst in off the porch and skidded to a halt, his chest heaving. His gray braid had come undone, and he sported the beginnings of a black eye.

"Wampus Kitty," he shouted, his mismatched eyes wide with fright.

There was a moment of frozen silence and then everybody moved at once. Earl released the dog with a hiss of alarm and slithered out the door. The mastiff scooted after him, tail between his legs. Animals and naked people trampled one another in their haste to reach the exit. In a matter of moments, the bar was deserted. From outside in the parking lot, Beck heard the roar of engines starting and the screech of tires on gravel as folks fled in their vehicles.

She glanced around the bar, trying to assess the damage. The lighted MILLER sign on one wall was busted, there were a few broken chairs, and one of the windows had been shattered, but otherwise the damage seemed minimal. Aside from the clinging odor of skunk, that is. She'd have to remember to ask Cassie Ferguson if she had an anti-skunky funk spell in her repertoire.

Most importantly, the glass bar was still intact, she noted with relief. If those demons had gotten out, all hell would have broken loose. Things had been quiet for so long that she'd never worried about it.

That wasn't the case anymore. Two bar fights in a matter of weeks. Tomorrow she'd ask Conall to take custody of the demons. One less thing to worry about.

Toby whimpered in disgust. "I smell skunk."

"No kidding," Beck said. "What's a Wampus Kitty?"

"It's an Ewah, an evil critter that walks on two legs in the form of a mountain lion." Toby glanced over his shoulder, like he expected something horrible to burst through the door. "My old granny was part Cherokee. She said when the Wampus Kitty screams somebody's gonna die and be buried in three days."

"It's just a story, Tobias," Beck said. "Nobody's going to die."

"You heard that scream." Toby shuddered. "You saw the way everybody hightailed it outta here. The Wampus Kitty is real, all right."

Tommy came in from the porch with Annie on one shoulder. "Is it over? Did it work?"

"Did what work?" Beck asked.

"Folks were fighting outside," Tommy said. "Then they started turning into animals. I saw Toby get punched, and people going at it in the bar. I told Annie we needed to stop it before somebody got hurt, and so she did it."

"Did what?" Beck asked.

Tommy reached up and rubbed Annie's ears. "Show 'em, Annie."

Annie's mouth dropped open, growing wider and wider, the vast cavern bristling with teeth. A familiar, terrifying scream echoed from the enormous opening.

Toby's eyes bugged. "Holy shit, Annie's the Wampus Kitty."

Annie hushed and her mouth shrank to its former dainty size. Lifting a paw, she proceeded to wash her face.

"Ain't she something?" Tommy said, looking pleased as punch. " 'Annie,' I says, 'we got to stop that fight 'fore they wreck the place.' Next thing I know, she lets out a scream. Some folks were so skeered they jumped in the river. I almost jumped in after 'em, and then I remembered the gators." He shivered. "They'd eat a ripe one like me, for sho'."

Toby snarled deep in his throat and backed away. "Get that damn cat out of here. She's bad luck."

"Toby, you don't mean that," Beck said.

"The hell I don't."

Annie jumped off Tommy's shoulder and streaked into the night.

"Annie," Tommy cried. He gave Toby a wrathful glare. "You hurt her feelings. You better hope she comes back."

"Or what?" Toby said, glaring back at him.

"Or I might decide to eat yo' brains after all," Tommy said. "That is, if you had any, you superstitious hick."

He lumbered out the door after the kitten.

"Well, she is bad luck," Toby said defiantly. "And it ain't superstitious if it's *true*. A zombie's bad enough, but we can't have no Wampus Kitty in a bar. Bad for business. She'll run the customers off."

"You're prejudiced," Beck said, wanting to shake him. "You don't like cats. That's what this is really about."

"I'm a *dog*," Toby said. "I'm supposed to hate cats. It's in the handbook. And this ain't no regular cat. This here is a feline harbinger of doom."

"She's a kitten with a big meow. You're being ridiculous, Toby."

"You'll get rid of that cat, unless you want the customers peeing themselves."

"The kith have enough problems without turning on one another," Beck said. "Annie broke up the fight. You owe her an apology."

"I ain't apologizing to no damn cat, especially that one."

"Fine, be that way," Beck said, limping for the door.

She shrieked as she was swung off her feet and pressed against a hard, warm chest.

"Let me go," she said, scowling at Conall. "I have to find Annie and Tommy."

"No, you are hurt. Do not worry about the zombie and the kitten. They are commiserating at the end of the dock."

"How do you know?"

"I am Dalvahni."

Three words, but they were spoken with casual arrogance. *I am Dalvahni*. End of subject. Of all the pompous, egotistical . . .

He was so full of hot air it was a miracle he didn't float off into space. The only thing he didn't add was *and you're not*. But he might as well have. It was sure as hell implied.

He strode toward the kitchen with her in his arms, his shoes crunching over broken glass and bits of plastic.

"I'm fine," Beck said, squelching the urge to kick her feet like some helpless movie chick. "I need to check on Hank and the band." She caught a glimpse of her dad standing behind the bar, looking dazed and lost. "And Daddy. I need to make sure he gets home all right. He's not used to this."

"He is not alone," Conall said. "You needlessly put yourself in danger."

"Things were getting out of hand. Somebody had to stop it."

"It did not have to be you. I am a warrior. You should have let me settle it. Instead, you allowed yourself to be savaged by a bunch of wild animals. 'Twill be a miracle if you do not get an infection or some dread disease."

"The kith don't get sick and we don't get diseases."

"Thank the gods," Conall said with feeling.

"Put me down," Beck said. "That's an order. You work for me now. You have to do what I say."

"Not when you are hurt. When you are hurt, you have to do what *I* say."

Beck stared at him in disbelief. She was going to have an aneurism, and it was his fault. She'd way underestimated him on the batshit crazy thing. Plain and simple, he drove her nuts. Whatever had made her think she'd last a week around him? It had only been a couple of hours and she was already out of her tree.

A week with Conall Dalvahni and she'd be certifiable.

Chapter Ten

Conall carried her into the office and plunked her down on top of the desk. Retracing his steps, he flipped on the lights and shut the door. An interior one-way window looked out onto the bar. Her dad was moving around in the other room setting tables and chairs to rights. She heard hammering: Toby, boarding up the broken window. There was still no sign of Hank or the band.

"I should fire your ass," she said, not bothering to hide her belligerence. "What do you think of that?"

Conall closed the gap between them in two strides. Jemima, he smelled good, clean and crisp, like deep woods under winter frost.

"I think you curse too much," he said, towering over her. "I also think you are trying to goad me into leaving because I make you nervous."

He was right, of course. He made her nervous as hell. Not that she'd let him know it. She adjusted the skintight dress for the umpteenth time and slid him a furtive glance, trying to gauge his mood. A dark nimbus of energy still swirled around him, but his impassive expression was firmly back in place. Same old stern, drop-dead gorgeous Conall, perfect specimen of a perfect race.

What would it be like to be so calm and assured? she wondered with a stab of envy. Never frightened or confused, never in doubt, never a flicker of self-loathing. Sure of himself and of his place and purpose in the universe.

"Huh," she blustered, her gaze on his hard jaw. He had a very nice mouth, firm lipped and sensual. "You wish. I think you're the one who's nervous. I think you've been nervous since you found out about the kith. *I* think the fact that we exist rocks your world, because it means you don't know everything, after all."

A smile tugged at the corners of his stern mouth. "You have a high opinion of me."

"You have a high opinion of yourself."

He chuckled. The sound shot straight down her spine and settled between her legs, where it did some very interesting things.

"The kith do not disturb my equanimity," he said. "You do."

Beck glanced up at him in surprise. Big mistake. He had beautiful eyes, black, glittering, and mesmerizing. She fell into them, tumbling head over heels into space.

"Oh, yeah?"

He leaned closer, his mouth mere inches from hers. The air pulsed around them and she held her breath, afraid that he would kiss her, terrified that he would not.

"Yes," he said softly. "You petrify me."

She petrified *him*? Mr. Implacable, Mr. Emotionless, Mr. I Have Some Knowledge of Dragons? Oh, please.

She drew back, breaking the tension between them. "Right, like I believe that bullshit."

"You mock me, but I speak the truth. The Dalvahni do not lie."

Reaching past her, he opened a desk drawer and removed a blue and white plastic box.

"Hey, how'd you know where I keep the first-aid kit?"

He raised an imperious brow.

"Never mind," she said, throwing up her hands. "For God's sake, don't cue the *I am Dalvahni* speech."

He set the plastic box beside her on the desk and inspected her foot. Carefully removing a sliver of glass, he turned his attention to the other foot. His hands felt hot against her bare skin. Heat spread up her legs to her thighs and belly. Good

Lord, she was panting, hot as a fox, and all the guy had done was touch her *feet*.

She forgot her annoyance. She forgot everything but the feel of his skin on hers. His head was bent, and his dark, shaggy locks brushed the back of his collar. Her dreamy gaze drifted over him, taking in his broad chest and wide shoulders.

He was a big guy and strong. He made her feel dainty, and at five-feet-nine that was hard to do. Muscles rippled beneath the fabric of his white cotton shirt as he went about the business of inspecting her scrapes. It was fascinating; better than television. It was *Hot Guy* TV, starring Conall Dalvahni.

He smelled good, too. He was freaking smell-o-vision.

She had to tuck her hands beneath her hips to keep from yanking him down on top of her and having her wicked way with him. That would shock the hell out of Captain Grimly Perfect, now wouldn't it?

Pain yanked her from her whirlpool of lust as he probed the edges of a deep cut on her heel.

"Ow, that hurts."

"Be still. I cannot fathom what possessed you to charge into the fray like that."

"I had to stop Earl before he killed that guy."

"Earl?"

"The snake."

"Ah," he said. Brushing aside her protests, Conall removed some pre-moistened cloths from the first-aid kit and set to work cleaning the dozen or so scratches on her arms and legs. He turned his attention to a particularly ugly scratch on her right calf. "And why, may I ask, did you feel it necessary to accomplish this feat unshod?"

"The floor was covered in goo. I didn't want to ruin my shoes."

"Little fool. So you would ruin your feet instead."

The words were spoken without heat. Releasing her leg, he dabbed at a welt on her wrist.

"I'm a pretty fast healer," she said, wincing, "but I've never had pretty shoes before."

He gave her a strange look. "Why not? You are hardly poor."

"I do okay. Not much need for pretty shoes in a bar."

"Were you mine, I would shower you with beautiful things."

"Why? You hardly know me."

"I know you better than you think. I know you are beautiful and that you have a kind heart." Lifting his hand, he gently smoothed the crease between her brows with the tip of one finger. "I know you are brave, sometimes to the point of imprudence. But, mostly I would give you beautiful things because I do not think I could help myself."

He thought *she* was beautiful? Oh, please. The guy was temptation on two legs and had a voice like brandy and chocolate. With very little effort, he could wrap her around his little finger.

"Oh, you're good," she said, leaning closer. "You're real good."

Don't do it, sanity urged. *You'll regret it.*

"Oh, what the hell," she said and kissed him.

She kissed him. Astonishment surged through Conall followed by a wave of lust that almost brought him to his knees. How many times had he wondered what she would taste like?

He had his answer at last, and the reality far exceeded his expectations.

She tasted sweet and ripe, like sun-warmed berries. He could not get enough. Cupping her head in his hands, he deepened the kiss, dipping his tongue into the honeyed recess of her mouth. She gave a purr of satisfaction deep in her throat and stroked his tongue with hers. Lust gripped him, hot and fierce.

His entire existence had been about duty and service. Never had he spared a thought for himself. Indeed, he had no inkling anything was lacking, until he met Rebekah. She had changed everything.

He wanted her as he had never wanted anything in his very long life. He burned for her.

Why not? his baser self whispered. *She is warm and willing. You can smell her heat. Take your pleasure with her.*

You cannot, his logical self growled in protest. *Would you suc-cumb to the same madness as your brothers?*

Yes, he wanted to shout. *A thousand times yes.*

With a daughter of the djegrali?

No. He could not.

Cursing his inner sentinel, Conall released her and stepped back, his lungs bellowing like he'd outrun a ravenous six-legged Drakthian tiger.

Rebekah's violet eyes were wide, her luscious mouth soft from his kiss. "That probably wasn't a good idea."

His gaze caressed her flushed face, lingering on her mouth. It was wide with a slight indention in the pouty lower lip. "It was a terrible idea, but I do not regret it."

"You don't?"

"No." Unable to help himself, he touched her bottom lip with the tip of his finger. "I have wanted to kiss you for a very long time. Duty brought me here, but I stayed because of you."

He frowned, cold fingers of unease gripping his belly as he realized the truth behind his words.

Like a dog starved for affection, he'd followed at her heels for weeks, nay, *months,* craving the sight of her, fascinated by the proud set of her shoulders, the elegant curve of her back, and the tempting sway of her rounded hips as she moved about the bar. The jasmine scent of her had haunted his dreams, and the husky music of her voice was balm to his weary soul.

And her smile . . . She had a lovely smile, warm and mis-chievous. She was always smiling at someone. Tobias. The cus-tomers.

Even the surly cook.

Never at him, though, her unseen shadow. He wanted her smiles, her attention . . . her touch, all of it for him and him alone.

His reaction to her baffled him. Why, 'twas almost as if he were under some kind of strange enchantment . . .

"Of course," he said slowly. "You put a spell on me, you she-devil. That is why I could not stay away, why I have lingered near you all these months."

"*What?*" She jumped off the desk and faced him, her chest heaving. "Of all the—I can't believe you think that I—Oh, never mind. I am out of here. I knew it was a mistake to kiss you. If anyone's put a spell on somebody, it's *you*. A pretty face and a pair of bedroom eyes, and I fall for it. I should have known better."

He regarded her with gathering unease. "You think I bewitched you?"

"You're damn straight. Why else would I kiss a stuck-up, disapproving *demon hunter*?"

Every line of her strong, graceful body radiated hurt and outrage. She was telling the truth. His careless words, born of pride and frustration, had caused her pain.

Conall's belly sank to his shoes. He'd killed and wounded scores in the line of duty with nary a moment's remorse; yet the knowledge that he'd hurt Beck cut him to the quick.

She took two steps away from him and whirled back around. "And what the hell do you mean 'all these months'? How long have you been spying on me?"

"For some time now. 'Twas my duty to determine if you or your kind posed a threat."

"I'm a threat all right—a threat to punch you in your sanctimonious, judgmental nose." She clenched her hands at her sides. "How long? Answer me, Mr. I Cannot Tell a Lie."

"Since the month you call July."

"*July*? But you didn't come into the bar until the end of August."

She remembered the first time she saw him? He felt a flicker of hope. A propitious sign, surely.

And she thought he was pretty. Not the proper term to describe a Dalvahni warrior, but he would not quibble with it.

"I observed you for some time without your knowledge," he admitted.

"That's not possible, unless you can make yourself invisible."

"The Dalvahni have many gifts."

"Right. Whatever."

She did not believe him. Vexed, he vanished in front of her and reappeared.

She gaped at him for a moment before her face darkened. "You are such a creeper," she said, charging out the door.

"Rebekah, wait! "

She was still barefoot and the floor had not been swept. She would hurt herself. Again.

Conall swore and went after her.

Chapter Eleven

Beck was so mad she couldn't see straight. The big jerk thought she'd put a come-hither spell on him. She was kith. So, naturally that made her a hoochie mama from hell, a demonic Delilah sent by the dark side to lure Mr. Holier Than Thou to perdition.

He was attracted to her and it was *her* fault. It couldn't be his fault. Oh, no. He was a demon hunter. He could do no wrong.

Self-righteous jackass. She hated him. She wanted to kick his ass.

She wanted to kiss him again.

How could she want a guy so bad her teeth ached and hate his guts at the same time? It was mental.

She barreled out of the office and slammed into Toby.

"Whoa, hold your horses," Toby said, catching her as she stumbled. He looked done-in. "I'm for calling it a night. The bar's a mess, the dang cook's done run off with the band, and the customers are scattered 'tween here and next Sunday, thanks to that Wampus Kitty. I say we clean up in the morning."

Beck looked around, taking in the sticky floors, broken glass, and smears of blood. The breeze through the open doors chased tufts of animal hair into corners like frightened mice. Tables and chairs were smashed, and the place reeked of eau de skunk.

She couldn't face this. Not tonight, not when she was so hurt and mad.

"Go home," she told Toby. "We'll deal with it tomorrow."

Toby jerked his thumb in the direction of the door. "You close up and I'll give Jason a ride to his truck. He's parked up by Pell Landing."

"Sure," Beck said with a twinge of shame.

She should've thought of that herself. Daddy had no business being on the river this time of night, particularly after the shock he'd had. Her nerves were worked, and she was used to the kith. Daddy must be practically comatose after seeing a room full of people—some he'd served at the Burger Doodle for years—turn into a bunch of animals.

A tingle of awareness warned her of Conall's approach. Why didn't he just go away? She should have fired him, that's what she should have done. But, she'd shaken his hand and that was as good as giving her word. She'd made her bed and now she was going to have to lie in it.

Wrong analogy; beds made her think of sex. With Conall. No point going there, because it was never going to happen. The gulf between them was too wide, their differences too great.

Squaring her shoulders, she turned to face him. In spite of her resolution, a tiny thrill of *huzza* shot through her when she saw him. He screamed medieval warrior, in spite of his modern clothes. It was his no-quarter-given attitude and the powerful way he moved. Like the trappings of civilization were nothing but a thin veneer and he could go from GQ to killer in a nanosecond.

She gave him the squinty-eyed treatment, because looking at him full on made her heart go thumpity thump and she forgot to be furious. "What do you want?"

He held out an old pair of sneakers she kept in the office. "You forgot your shoes. I found these behind the desk. Put them on."

It was an order, not a request. He worked for her, not the other way around, a fact he didn't seem to get.

She considered refusing, but that would be childish and immature. Lifting her chin, she looked down her nose at him. Hard to do, when he towered over her, but she gave it her best.

"I'll put them on," she said, taking the shoes from him. "But only because there's glass on the floor and not because you said so."

Wow, way to be mature. Whatcha gonna do for an encore, stick out your tongue and say nanny nanny poo poo?

She shoved her feet in the sneakers. Lucky for him, he kept his mouth shut. One word out of Conall, one superior twitch of a dark eyebrow, and she'd explode and there'd be ugly all over the place. She wasn't half demon for nothing.

"Came to say goodnight," Daddy said, coming up to them.

"Thanks for helping out." Beck gave her father a bright smile. No point in taking out her bad mood on him. She was saving it all up for Conall anyway. "I appreciate it."

"Any time," he said.

Daddy didn't mean it, of course. He was being polite. His expression was dazed, his eyes slightly out of focus, like a man who's seen too much. He didn't know the half of it. He had a long-lost son. She should warn him about Evan before her brother showed up at the Burger Doodle and announced the news over a cola and fries.

She could hear him now. *Hi yah, Pops. Add another imp to the Damian family tree. I'm Evan, the son you never knew you had. Pass the ketchup.*

Daddy would have a stroke.

She'd tell him some other time. They were both too tired to deal with it tonight.

"I need to get on home," Daddy said. "I'm never this late. Brenda's probably laid an egg by now."

More like a dozen.

"Tell Brenda and the twins I said hello."

"Tell 'em yourself." Daddy removed his hat and turned it over in his hands. "We'd like you to come to the house for Thanksgiving. That's the real reason I come by. The fishing thing was just an excuse. It's past time you got to know the twins better."

Beck's smile faltered. "Thanks for the invite, but I don't think that's a good idea. Things being . . . well, what they are."

"Things are what you make of them, sugar bear. I reckon I know the score. If I didn't, I do after tonight." Daddy jammed his hat back on his head. "And I still want you to come."

"What about Brenda?"

"It was her idea," he said. "Toby's already said he's coming." He hesitated. "Course, she don't know about certain *things,* if you catch my drift."

"No duh," Beck said. "Don't worry. Toby and I won't out ourselves in front of Brenda or the twins."

Daddy looked relieved. "It's for the best. Brenda's a fine woman, but she wouldn't understand. Matter of fact, not sure I do." He glanced at Conall. "You're more'n welcome, too, Mr. Dalvahni."

Beck stiffened. "I'm sure Mr. Dalvahni plans to spend the holiday with his brothers."

"As it happens, Ansgar and Brand are out of town with their wives indulging in the traditional post-nuptial celebrations," Conall said smoothly. "I would be honored to break bread with you and your family, Mr. Damian."

"Be a whole lot more 'n bread." Daddy was starting to sound more like his old self. "My wife knows how to put on a feed. There'll be plenty to eat, so save your hungries."

"The Dalvahni enjoy a good repast," Conall said. "It is kind of you and your wife to include me in the festivities."

"It ain't nothing," Daddy said.

"What about the other one?" Beck said in a belligerent tone.

Conall gave her a bland look, as if he sensed how close she was to detonating. "The other what?"

"Your other brother," Beck said through her teeth. He was being purposely obtuse. "I don't remember his name. He married the librarian. I read about it in the paper."

"Lordy, you still pouring over that rag?" Daddy chuckled. "You used to read that thang front to back when you were little." He shook his head in wonder. "She always knew more about what was going on in Hannah than folks who lived smack dab in the middle of town."

Conall raised his brows. "Is that so?"

Beck flushed. "So I read the paper. It's not a crime. What about your other brother?"

"Rafe and Bunny are spending the holiday with her family." Conall heaved a huge sigh. "Alas, I was not invited."

"Pissed them off, too, huh?" Beck said. "I'm not surprised."

"Becky," Daddy said, giving her a look of reproach. "What's gotten into you?" He clapped Conall on the arm. "It's settled then. You'll spend the day with us."

Conall bowed. "I am honored."

"Uh, sure," Daddy said, eyeing him uncertainly. Folks in Hannah didn't go around bowing. "See you Thursday, then. Feed's on at noon." He turned to Toby. "You ready to go?"

"Yep." Toby lifted a hand in farewell. "See you in the morning."

As soon as they left, Beck pounced on Conall.

"What's the big idea?" she said. "It's bad enough I have to make nice over turkey and dressing with my stepmother without having to sit across the table from *you*. Talk about indigestion."

"You do not care for your father's wife?"

"I don't care for *you*, but that part went right over your head."

"You are angry," he said with irritating calm. "Your spleen will soon pass."

"You leave my spleen out of it."

"Why do you dislike your stepmother?"

"She dislikes *me*. She thinks I'm going to hell on roller skates because I run a bar."

"She knows you are kith?"

"Oh, hell to the no. And she's not going to find out. You keep your mouth shut about it, you hear?" To her disgust, an angry tear rolled down her cheek. She brushed it away, hoping he wouldn't notice. "Daddy doesn't need the kind of grief Brenda would give him if she found out I'm part demon. You leave it alone. I mean it."

Conall stepped closer. "Rebekah, upon reflection, I fear that I may have—"

The screen door swung open and Tommy shuffled into the bar.

"Where's Annie?" Beck asked, grateful for the distraction. Another minute and she'd be bawling like a baby.

"Hunting," Tommy said.

Face scrunched in misery, he trudged past them and disappeared into the kitchen.

"The undead creature seems desolate," Conall said.

"I'd better check on him."

"Why? He is dead. He can hardly do himself more of an injury."

"Mr. Sensitive," Beck muttered, starting after Tommy.

She screeched to a halt as Junior Peterson materialized in front of her.

"Junior," she said, clutching her chest. "You scared the hell out of me. Why don't you wear a bell or something?"

"What am I, a cow? Ghosts don't wear bells." Junior looked around. "Where's the piano?"

Beck's head throbbed. Stress; it was the stress. It was too much, all of it. She needed to get away, to think, to regain her center.

"We don't have a piano."

"No piano? What kind of rinky-dink bar is this?"

"The kind without a piano," Beck said. "This ain't the Grand Hotel."

The ghost sniffed. "No kidding? How am I supposed to play my music without a piano?"

"I don't know. I'll figure something out tomorrow."

"Tomorrow? What am I supposed to do until then?"

"Sleep?"

"Hel-loo," Junior said. "Ghost Course one-oh-one. We don't sleep."

"Listen to music, then. There's a radio in my office."

Junior rolled his lavender eyes. "Please. Unless things have changed—which I doubt—there's only one radio station and it alternates country music with the farm report."

Things hadn't changed. The hills around Hannah did funny

things to the signals from the big radio stations in Pensacola and Mobile—something about the crater rock. The only reliable signal came from the local station, WBHR. They didn't call it Bear Country for nothing. Cell phone reception was spotty for the same reason.

Beck held onto her rapidly fraying patience. "Maybe one of the band members knows where I can borrow a keyboard."

"A *keyboard*?" Junior's eyes widened in horror. "You mean one of those electronic gizmos? I studied music at Vanderbilt, darlin'. These hands have never touched a keyboard, and they never will."

"Suit yourself," Beck said. "I'm going home."

"I will accompany you to your dwelling," Conall said. "We need to talk."

"*No.*" Good Lord, she was shouting. Beck took a deep breath. "I mean, that won't be necessary."

Ignoring the protesting ghost, she shut and locked the double front doors and tidied up behind the bar. It was a tiny spot of clean in all the mess, but it made her feel better.

After a few minutes of Beck giving him the silent treatment, Junior got the message and left in a huff. Good riddance, Beck thought. *Don't know where he's going. Don't care. He's too high maintenance. I'd almost rather have Hazel.*

No, she wouldn't. Hazel had turned her insides into a slushy.

She hurried into the kitchen. Conall waited near the red exit sign like some kind of supernaturally hot sentinel, one shoulder propped against the wall, his arms folded across his wide chest. He watched in silence from his self-appointed guard post while she went about the business of closing up the kitchen.

She pretended not to see him, but he was a hard guy to ignore. Make that impossible.

Hank cleaned as he cooked, so there weren't a lot of dirty dishes. The garbage with the shrimp shells had already been hauled out to the Dumpster. She set a dirty stockpot in the sink to soak and wiped down the counters.

Deep fat fryer switched off. *Check.* Oven and stove turned off. *Check.*

Satisfied, she headed for the exit, making a last-minute detour when she noticed the door to the walk-in cooler was ajar. She peeked inside.

Zombie in the cooler.

Check.

Chapter Twelve

Tommy blinked at her from the depths of the refrigerated darkness. "I had to do something," he said, sounding defensive. "I'm starting to smell."

Beck doubted Tommy could smell himself, on account of him being dead and all. But *he* thought he could, so there you go.

Tommy needed zombie Xanax. And when Hank found out there was a dead guy hanging out in his fridge, he'd need Xanax, too.

Probably Hank was right. Probably keeping a corpse in the cooler next to the hamburger patties was a health code violation. Probably, she should do something about it.

She closed the refrigerator and walked out the door, sailing past Conall with her nose in the air. She was going for dignified and aloof, but the hot pink sneakers sort of blew the whole Ice Princess Bitch on Wheels thing.

The parking lot looked like a deserted used-car lot, since most of the owners were still chasing the moon through the woods. She fished her keys out of her purse and opened her truck. She glanced back. Conall crossed the lot toward her, his powerful stride unhurried.

Good. He wasn't trying to catch her. Maybe he'd taken the hint that she didn't want his company.

She was still mad at him, wasn't she? Of course she was.

It suddenly occurred to her that she had no idea how he'd gotten here. Maybe he'd rented a car. Maybe he'd ridden up

astride a destrier like some knight from the Middle Ages.
Maybe he slid down a rainbow on a unicorn.

Didn't matter; he was a big demon hunter. He could leave
the same way he came.

She climbed into the Tundra, cranked the engine, and
wheeled out of the lot. Three miles later, she abandoned the
paved road for one of dirt, bumping through the thick, inky
woods to her place on the river.

She parked in her usual spot under the mercury light, got out
of the truck, and slogged across the yard to the back steps. The
house was nothing fancy—a small, two-bedroom, two-bath
cabin with a pitched tin roof and a screened porch that wrapped
around three sides—but it was hers. She'd bought the land
when she turned twenty-one, put a trailer on it, and moved in.
The cabin had come later, after years of scrimping and saving.

"Hey, baby, it's me," she called, letting herself in. No answer.
No large, furry lump on the wicker furniture, nothing stirring
among the mini jungle of plants on the back porch. "Mr. Cat?"

Double French doors separated the screened back porch
from the main part of the house. Kicking off her sneakers, she
stepped inside. The floor plan was simple and open, with high
ceilings and wood floors. Lots of windows to take in the view
of the river and the surrounding sea of woods, the master bedroom and bath on one side of the house, the second bed and
bath on the other; in the center, the eating, living, and dining
areas. There was a comfy couch in the den for flopping in front
of the television, and a stone fireplace for warmth on cold
nights.

Home; her island of safety.

She walked through the house calling her cat.

Meow. The cry was faint. Beck followed the sound to the
front porch that looked out on the river, and found Conall sitting in a rocking chair with her cat in his lap.

"Traitor," she said to the perfidious feline.

"Brrrp," Mr. Cat said, returning her glower with a sated,
sleepy-eyed look of satisfaction.

Conall chucked the big orange marmalade under the chin.

Mr. Cat, the shameless lap whore, flipped his purr button to high and practically drooled.

Beck switched her disapproval to the oversized warrior on her property. "It's bad enough you put the whammy on me," she said. "Now you're whammying my cat?"

"I did not 'whammy' either of you." Conall paused. "Although, in all honesty, I am not entirely sure what that means."

Poor little demon hunter, playing the "I'm-not-from-around-here card. His translator seemed to work just fine when he wanted it to. How convenient.

"What are you doing here?"

"I wanted to make sure you reached your abode in safety."

"I'm fine." A sudden thought made her stiffen. "How do you know where I live?"

"I was curious to see where you dwelled, so I followed you home one night. I felt . . . protective of you, for some reason."

"Bullshit. You were snooping."

"Dalvahni warriors do not snoop. We reconnoiter."

"You were snooping. You thought I was in cahoots with your stupid djegrali."

"They are not *my djegrali,* and it was reasonable for me to suspect you at first."

"At first? Does that mean I'm no longer Numero Uno on the kill list?"

He removed Mr. Cat from his lap and rose to his feet. "Now you are being silly. Have I not pledged my sword arm in your defense? Have I not given you my word not to harm you?"

"You think I put some kind of spell on you."

"Ah, that," he said. "Foolish words spoken in haste. I came to apologize."

Beck turned and stared blindly out at the river. The orange moon laughed down at her. She had a feeling Conall was laughing at her, too. He didn't give a hill of beans about her or her feelings.

"Stop being nice." She folded her arms tight beneath her breasts. "It confuses me. If there's one thing I can't stand, it's a bastard who won't stay in his corner."

She blinked back tears. God, she was hormonal. She took a deep breath to calm herself. It didn't help.

She was supercharged. It was the moon and the call of the river. She needed to go for a run in the woods or a swim, something to get rid of the jitters.

What are you, the poster child for the unaware? the sly voice in her mind said with a smirk. *It's not the moon or the river. It's him.*

A sudden tingle of awareness warned her of his approach. Somehow, he'd closed the space between them without making a sound. Heat poured off his powerful body, and his cool scent enveloped her.

"This bastard will not stay in his corner. This bastard regrets hurting you more than he can say."

Beck swallowed. "Don't worry about it. I couldn't care less what you think of me."

"So very tough," he murmured. His fingertips traced the opening in the back of her dress, brushing her bare skin and sending little shivers of delight coursing through her. "But not, I think, as tough as you pretend to be."

He replaced his fingers with his lips, and her knees nearly buckled as she felt the warm, wet drag of his mouth across her naked back. A playful nip on her shoulder was followed by the soothing lap of his tongue. Goosebumps of pleasure prickled Beck's skin, and her breasts felt heavy and tight.

Sweet Sister Ruth, out of all the males in creation, why did it have to be *him* that got her motor revved?

He turned her around and pulled her into his arms. Twisting his hands in her hair, he lowered his head until their mouths were but inches apart. Her pulse skittered at his nearness.

"What are you doing?" she said.

"I should think it is obvious," he replied, and kissed her.

He took his time about it, tasting her at leisure, nibbling at her bottom lip and stroking her with his tongue like she was some kind of exotic fruit and he couldn't get enough. She felt that kiss from her head to her toes and everywhere in between.

Especially *there*, between her legs.

Her blood heated and sizzled in her veins, and the wildness

crouching inside her threw back its head and howled. She was on fire and trembling, and her stomach did a quivery, flip-floppy thing, like an army of frogs was jumping around in there.

It was too much. It was too hot, too exciting. Too everything.

She tore her mouth away from his and backed away. "I thought we agreed this wasn't a good idea."

"Yes, we did." Giving her a wicked smile that made her heart go ker-thump, he stalked her across the porch and backed her against the wall. "I changed my mind."

"Wait a minute," she said, putting her hands on his chest. The heat of his skin scorched her palms through the thin fabric of his white shirt. "What about talking? You said we needed to talk."

"Talking is highly overrated." Bending his head, he blazed a trail of hot kisses down her throat. "I am more interested in doing . . . other things."

Beck's eyes drifted shut. It felt good to be in his arms. He was big and strong and he made her feel safe, which was ridiculous. She could take care of herself. She tried to think, but thinking was impossible with him so close.

The warm puff of his breath teased her skin. There was something she needed to tell him, something important.

Oh, yeah. They hated one another. That was it.

Opening her eyes, she told him as much, but he seemed undisturbed.

"I do not hate you." He drifted feathery kisses from her temple to the curve of her jaw. "If I hated you, I would not be doing my best to make amends."

"A-amends?"

"Most definitely. I have a plan. Would you like to hear it?"

"Um . . . yeah. I guess so."

"First, I would tell you again how beautiful you are."

Beck's heart rate kicked up another notch as his hand slid under her dress and up her thigh. Her head was spinning. "Flattery's usually a good start."

"I am glad you approve," he said. "And then I would tell you that your skin is glorious. Soft and luminous, like moonlight on roses. It makes me want to taste you all over."

"Moonlight on roses?" The words came out a husky growl. She cleared her throat. "Nice, but it'll take more than a few pretty words to get you out of hot water with me."

"So fierce," he said with a chuckle. He caressed her inner thigh. He was close, so damn close. Just a little farther . . . "But I am curious. If you are unaffected, why do you tremble in my arms?" His clever fingers circled higher, inching closer to the aching spot between her legs. "And what has made you so rest-less?"

"Moon," she gasped, clutching his shoulders.

"I do not think it is the moon at all." His black eyes gleamed. "I think you want me."

She glared up at him. "Not in this lifetime, mister."

"I think you are bluffing." His fingertips brushed the edge of her panties. "Shall we experiment and see?"

Cupping his palm between her legs, he stroked her clitoris with his thumb. She went off like a rocket, waves of pleasure engulfing her.

He released her, and she slid to the floor in a boneless heap, her dress bunched up around her thighs.

"Just as I expected," he said, smiling down at her. "Bluffing."

The combination of that smile and the post-orgasmic pheromones whizzing around her brain made her woozy.

So she was easy. So all he had to do was touch the outside of her panties and she had a big old orgasm. So what?

She leaned her head against the wall and scowled up at him. "My mother may have been possessed, but you're the devil."

His smile widened. "See you in the morning, boss."

He vanished.

"Conall?"

No answer.

Beck sniffed. He was gone, not a hint of warm, green-scented male anywhere. Well, that answered her question about how he got around.

He got around just fine, she thought darkly. In more ways than one.

Mr. Cat rubbed against her hip with a reproachful meow. "Talk to the paw, buddy," she said. "You're as pathetic as I am."

She sat on the porch floor until she was certain her legs would support her before retreating into the house. She fed Mr. Cat and took a long soak in the garden tub.

While she soaked, she thought about what had happened and decided not to beat herself up about it. It had been years since she'd had sex with anyone, and she was long overdue in the orgasm department. The way she figured it, she was entitled.

Orgasms were good. This orgasm, in particular, had been a pip—the best ever, in fact. She no longer felt so jittery and antsy, and her headache was gone. Yessir, that orgasm had done her a world of good.

In fact, that orgasm had probably saved her life. Hell, that orgasm had probably saved *other* people's lives, because all that bottled-up sexual tension could have exploded and hurt someone. It was what you might call your sacrificial orgasm. She'd taken one for the team, maybe even one for *humanity*.

She was a frigging saint.

Nope, all things considered, she had no regrets. She needed to stop thinking about it though. And she really needed to stop thinking about Conall. Granted, that orgasm had been pretty darn terrific—okay, it had rocked her world—but she couldn't go there again. Mr. Sexy Demon Hunter with the magic hands and mouth and seductive words that turned her insides to goo was off limits.

From now on, he was just another employee at the bar.

She would not blush when she saw him in the morning. She would greet him with cool composure. She would be professional, pleasant but aloof. She would keep her distance. She would not allow herself to be distracted by his supernatural hotness, and she most certainly would *not* succumb to his sweet-talking ways.

And on no account would she allow him anywhere near her

panty line again. Her crotch had a mind of its own and could not be trusted. Of course, that meant she was back to living in a no-gasm zone, but it was the smart thing to do.

The thought was so depressing that she almost slid under the water and let herself drown.

She sat there until her fingers wrinkled, which is God's way of saying "Hey, dumbass, out of the water already," and climbed out. She dried off with a fluffy towel, donned her robe, and padded into the kitchen for a post-orgasmic, celebratory cup of hot chocolate. Funny how everything in her world had narrowed to that mini volcanic explosion of pleasure, like a planet being sucked into a collapsing sun.

Jeez Louise, she really needed to get laid more often. If she had a normal sex life, Captain Orgasm wouldn't have this effect on her.

Yeah, right.

She added a couple of extra marshmallows to the mug and took a sip of melted, sugary fluff off the top. A series of sharp yips from the woods behind her house startled her. Hot chocolate sloshed over the edge of the cup, burning her hand.

"Dang it," she swore, sucking on her scalded fingers.

A harsh grunt outside drew her to the window. She peeked through the blinds at the yellowed rectangle of grass behind her house.

A shaggy black bear sat on his haunches, the bulky centerpiece in a circle of tawny gray coyotes. The bear flung back his head and growled a rumbling ode to the moon. Tipping their noses skyward, the coyotes joined in.

The mystery of the missing cook and the runaway musicians was solved. Hank and the band were holding a concert in her backyard, and it looked like they'd settled in for the night.

Chapter Thirteen

The alarm buzzed and Beck aimed a bleary eye at the clock. The wild kingdom jamboree behind her house had gone on until after two. Four hours of sleep and a full day of cleanup ahead, plus a to-do list that included getting the broken window replaced.

Ugh.

She groaned and pulled the covers over her head. Her rest—what little there'd been of it—had been disturbed by torrid dreams starring a certain black-eyed demon hunter. She was wide awake and horny as hell.

Her brain might accept that her steamy interlude with Conall was a one-time thing, but the rest of her body had missed the memo.

Just her luck the one guy she wanted to scratch her itch was a big fat no-no.

Something heavy hit the mattress, and she felt the tread of kitty paws across the coverlet.

"Brrrp," Mr. Cat said, batting the blanket over her face with his paw.

"Let me guess. You want breakfast."

"Meow," Mr. Cat said.

Beck stuck her head out of the covers. "I don't suppose it's occurred to you that I might be smothering."

Mr. Cat stalked across her chest.

"I can feel your concern," Beck said. "Way to show the love, pussycat."

Dragging herself out of bed and into the bathroom, she washed her face and brushed her teeth. No point in taking a shower when she'd spend the day mopping up God knows what-all. She'd clean up later, after the job was done. Going to the walk-in closet, she threw on a pair of old jeans and a long-sleeve T-shirt, and scraped her hair into a ponytail. She found her work boots on the porch and put them on, gave Mr. Cat his morning spoonful of wet food, and headed out.

It was Sunday and Beck's was closed. If she busted her hump and got things tidied up, maybe she could spend the afternoon reading on her porch. Quiet time was precious to her, and the thought cheered her.

Her little bubble of happiness burst when she pulled into the parking lot and spotted Earl Skinner waiting near the back entrance of the bar. He wore a sweatshirt and dirty jeans. Patches of hair bristled on his unshaven, receding chin, and his stringy hair was oily and matted.

The temperature was in the low forties, but in spite of the chill Earl's face was slick with sweat and his complexion held a greenish tinge. Whatever Earl had been on the night before had worn off, and he felt like hell. As for that thing he called a beard, it looked like somebody had glued pubic hair on his face.

An older man she did not recognize stood beside him. He was roughly the same height as Earl, but there the resemblance ended. Earl was a wormy thing, and the older man had obviously never missed a trip to the trough. He was jowly, and his belly jutted over the waistband of his jeans. His thick silver hair was poofed in the "higher the hair, the closer to God" hairstyle favored by Jimbo Swafford, a televangelist out of Mobile. Silver sideburns bracketed his ruddy face.

He was dressed nicer than Earl, too. For starters, he was clean and the plaid button snap shirt he wore looked new. His small feet were stuffed into a pair of bright red and yellow boots with swirling black inlay.

An old rhyme about coral snakes went through her head. *Red on yellow, kill a fellow. Red on black, friend of Jack.* Instinct told her this guy wasn't a friend.

"What now?" she muttered, sliding out of her truck.

Fancy Boots swaggered up to her. His eyes were more blue than purple and he was showing his age, which told Beck the demon in him was pretty watered down. Halfsies like her didn't age. Cassie Fergusson had once confided to Beck that she was over a hundred years old, and Cassie didn't look a day over twenty.

"Beck Damian?" Fancy Boots said.

"Yeah?"

"Name's Charlie Skinner." He pulled a small envelope out of his shirt pocket and handed it to her. "Trey Peterson asked me to give this to you."

The initials *WBP* were embossed in raised script on the front of the cream-colored stationery.

"What's this about?" Beck asked, turning the envelope over in her hand.

"There's a gathering this afternoon at Peterson's hunting cabin. All of the kith have been invited. You and Littleton ought to be there. You ain't gonna want to miss this."

"Kind of short notice, isn't it?"

"Yeah, that's why I'm hand-delivering the invite."

"I had no idea you and Peterson knew one another."

Charlie hooked his thumbs in his front pockets and leaned back on the heels of his boots. "We're closer than you might think. When he couldn't reach you by phone, he asked if I minded running an invite out here. I said, 'Sure, why not?' Anything for my good buddy Trey."

"Uh-huh." Beck eyed him warily, her Oh Crap-o-meter on full alert. Trey Peterson was heir to the richest fortune in Behr County. Since when did he get chummy with the Skinners? "I'll think about it."

She turned to go and Charlie grabbed her by the arm. "Hold on. Earl says he started a fight here last night. We've come to make amends."

"That so?" Since it was common knowledge the Skinners didn't have a pot to pee in, just how did he plan to make amends? "I appreciate it." She pulled free and stepped away. "Keep him away from here and we'll call it even."

"Got me a better idea." Charlie stepped in front of her. "I want you to put him to work. Time the boy learned responsibility."

The "boy" had to be forty years old, if he was a day, and had been raising hell in Behr County as long as Beck could remember.

"Way I figure it, you could use a man around here," Charlie said with a toothy smile.

"Men I got."

She was *drowning* in testosterone. There was Toby, of course, and Hank. And, as of yesterday, Tommy and a certain sexy beast of a demon hunter. Conall was male with a capital M. Heck, she even had a male ghost hanging around the place.

"You talking about that partner of yours? He don't count." Charlie sniffed and tugged at the waist of his jeans, revealing a large silver buckle buried beneath his belly fat. "I done some checking. Littleton pert near raised you, but you two ain't a couple." His gaze roved over Beck in a way that made her skin crawl. "Good-looking woman like you needs a man in your bed. Might as well be Earl. Like to like, I always say. Us Skinners are always on the lookout for good stock, and you look like a healthy breeder."

"Wow," Beck said. "I'm speechless."

Charlie grunted and looked around, a calculating gleam in his eyes. Sarcasm, it seemed, was wasted on Mr. Skinner.

"Nice place you got here," he said. "Be a good thing if you hooked up with my boy." He shoved Earl at her. "Don't fret about him being littler'n you. He may be a runt, but he's carrying where it counts, if you know what I mean."

Spots danced in front of Beck's eyes. She knew exactly what he meant, and it made her want to gag.

"Well, don't stand there like a knot on a log, boy." Charlie shoved Earl on the shoulder. "Talk to the gal."

"Uh," Earl said. His throat worked and he looked like he

wanted to hurl. Beck put some space between them, just in case. "Got me a new bird dog. Brittany spaniel name of Huckleberry. Good nose and the prettiest pointer you ever seen."

Charlie slapped Earl upside the head. "Idjut. She don't care about your stupid dawg. Tell her something about yourself, something that'll get her interested in you."

"I got tricks in my jeans," Earl said, reaching for his zipper. "I got a shape-shifting penis. Wanna see?"

That did it. Beck grabbed Earl by the shirt and lifted him in the air. It was easy. Earl was a string bean and her demon blood was up.

"I don't care if you got a whale penis eight feet long," she said, giving him a shake. "I don't want to hear about it. Ever. Again. Is that clear?"

"Here now, no need to get riled," Charlie said in alarm. "We come here peaceable like to make you a respectable offer. If you don't cotton to Earl, there's plenty more Skinners to choose from."

"I'm not interested," Beck said.

Conall materialized without warning. He was dressed in jeans and a T-shirt and he looked lean, mean, and dangerous. And hot, majorly hot. Lord, how had she ever missed that fact? Her eyeballs and her brain must have been on vacation.

Conall's flat, black gaze moved from Earl to Charlie. "Is there a problem?"

Beck dropped Earl to the ground. "Nothing I can't handle."

"Who are you?" Charlie demanded.

"I am Dalvahni."

Charlie sucked on his bottom lip. "Dalvahni, huh? I don't remember nobody around here with that name. You from Hannah?"

"No."

"Didn't think so." Charlie gave Conall the once-over. "You talk funny. You a Yankee?"

"No," Conall said.

Good grief, this fun little conversation could go on forever.

"He works for me," Beck said.

Charlie swelled. "You hired a foreigner, but my boy ain't good enough for you? Folks hear about this, might be bad for business."

"Is that a threat?" Beck said. " 'Cause I don't take kindly to threats."

"It's a fact." Charlie spat on the ground. "The kith are funny about strangers."

"If the kith don't like it, they can kiss my go to hell," she said. "Nobody tells me what to do in my place."

Something rustled in the underbrush and Hank stepped out of the woods. He was back in human form, and he was naked. He lumbered across the gravel lot on bare feet shaped like cinderblocks. He had toes like a mountain troll and more body hair than a gorilla on Rogaine.

"Morning," he said to Beck.

Stalking past the Skinners without a sideways glance, he trudged through the employees' entrance.

Charlie edged away from Conall. Probably had something to do with the "I will remove your entrails through your nose and strangle you with them" vibe Conall was projecting loud and clear.

"Well, I done what I come here to do, so I guess me and Earl will be moseying along," Charlie said. "Think about my offer. The Skinners are on their way up. You play your cards right, and you could move up, too."

Oh, she'd think about it, all right. The thought of "hooking" up with Earl Skinner would give her nightmares for weeks.

Toby stuck his head out the back door. "You better get in here. Hank and Tommy are going at it."

"Oh, crap."

She'd forgotten about the zombie in the fridge.

The kitchen was empty. The walk-in refrigerator stood open. Empty tofu boxes lay scattered on the floor. Somebody had been eating their curds and whey. Not that she was complaining, considering what Tommy could have been noshing on. What was she going to do about him anyway? Even if he never ate anybody's brains, sooner or later he'd start to fall apart. Zombies have a finite shelf life.

"—can't have a dead guy in with the food," Hank bellowed in the next room. "It's unsanitary and plain old gross."

"I'll tell you what's gross, Chewbacca," she heard Tommy answer in his crème brulée voice. "You walking around with your johnson hanging out, that's what. Who you think wanna see that? *I* sure as hell don't. Take a lawnmower to that ass of yours. You could stuff a mattress with that shit."

"Uh-oh," Beck said, hurrying from the kitchen.

She halted, staring about in shock. The bar was clean. It was better than clean. It was good as new. No sticky floors, broken furniture, or shattered glass. No broken, boarded-up window. No skunky odor clinging to everything. It was like the bar fight had never happened.

"What the . . . ?" She shook her head, her sleep-deprived, caffeine-deficient brain unable to take it in. Who could have done this? There was only one person left at the bar last night.

Her gaze moved to Tommy. He clutched a bottle of Fabreeze in one hand. A wad of gauzy white rectangles protruded from his shirt pocket, and a half dozen more fluttered from his belt loops. Dryer sheets, Beck realized, catching a whiff of Tropical Breeze. Tommy smelled like the laundry detergent aisle at the Piggly Wiggly.

"Did you clean up the bar?" she asked him.

Tommy shook his head.

"You know anything about this?" she said, turning to Hank.

"Nope." Hank looked around at the immaculate room and scratched his belly in thought. "Weren't me."

Conall materialized without warning, which was his MO. "Clothe thyself," he told Hank in a voice as cold as the heart of winter. "There is a lady present."

Hank stopped in mid-scratch. "Where?"

Conall's jaw tightened. "Rebekah."

"Beck don't mind," Hank said. "She's used to shifters. It ain't no big thing."

Tommy snorted. "You can say that again."

"Why you—" Hank began.

"I mind," Conall said, silencing Hank. "Cover your manhood or lose it."

Hank drew himself up. "Beck?"

Beck searched for a way to be diplomatic. "Naked happens when you run a demonoid bar, but most people look better with their clothes on."

That included Hank, although she didn't say so.

Hank turned on his heel and stomped off without a word.

"Damn," Beck said. "I think he's mad."

Conall shrugged. "His mood is oft more foul than fair."

This from Mr. Sweetness and Light? Talk about the pot calling the kettle black.

"He may be cranky, but he's a darn good cook. What am I supposed to do if he up and quits?"

"If the cook does not return, I will take his place," Conall said. "I can roast a capon or a haunch of venison as well as the next fellow."

"Yeah, but do you know how to operate a grill and a deep fat fryer?"

"No."

Beck sighed. "I didn't think so."

The screen door swung open and Ora Mae Luker trotted into the room. She wore a baggy mauve sweater, a long flowered skirt, and brown orthopedic shoes.

"A-ha," she said, leveling an accusatory finger at Tommy. Her short gray hair was frowzy from the humidity off the river. "You ate my cauliflower, you plant mo-lester. I saw you."

"Tommy, is this true?" Beck said. "Did you raid Ora Mae's garden?"

"I was hungry. "Tommy turned his hands up in a helpless gesture. "Them cauliflower looked like brains. I got cravings, you know. It was eat them cauliflower or something else. Something *worse.*"

"Brains?" Ora Mae's expression sharpened. "What's he talking about?"

"Vitamin deficiency," Beck said, improvising. She did *not* want to explain Tommy's "delicate" condition to Ora Mae. "It makes him crave meat. Very upsetting—Tommy's a vegetarian."

"That right? My cousin Mert's a vegetarian. 'Cepting she eats scrimp. Reckon she figures scrimp don't count, somehow." Ora Mae gave Tommy a stern look. "But that don't mean you get to gobble up my produce, young man. You're worse than a plague of rabbits. I'll expect you to pay for the damage."

"Can't," Tommy said with a cauliflower-scented burp. "Ain't got no money."

"I'll pay for the damage," Beck said. "Tommy works for me. I'll run you a tab."

"That right?" Ora Mae's eyes gleamed behind her glasses. "You fronting him?"

"Yes. What say, fifty dollars?"

"Fifty dollars?" Ora Mae blew out a raspberry. "That won't even pay for the fertilizer. I had three rows of cauliflower in that garden. A hundred and fifty bucks would be more like it. Or I could turn him over to the sheriff for trespassing."

"That won't be necessary," Beck said quickly. "I'll run you a tab."

"Top shelf at the bar-brand price?"

Beck winced. Crafty old lady. But she couldn't let Tommy go to jail. He might eat his cellmate.

"Done," she said.

"How nice." Ora Mae gave them a sunny smile. "Guess I'll scooterpoot back home. Y'all have a nice day."

Beck watched her bustle out of the bar. "Now I know how Georgia felt after Sherman marched through."

"I'm going to look for Annie," Tommy announced. "You got any more of that tuna? She likes tuna."

"In the store room," Beck said.

Tommy shuffled off without another word.

"The zombie is making a valiant effort to stay true to his ideals, but he suffers for it," Conall said when Tommy had left. "He hungers for flesh. You must send him away before it is too late."

"Send him away where? He'll eat somebody and I'll be responsible."

"You will not be responsible. His maker bears that burden."

"Yeah, and when I find that son of a bitch, whoever he is, I'm gonna kick his ass. In the meantime, Tommy stays here, where I can keep an eye on him."

"And when he succumbs to his terrible need for flesh, as he surely will do?"

"Then I'll take care of it," she said, though the thought made her cringe.

"No, you will not," Conall said. "When the time comes, I will do the deed."

Toby sauntered in from the kitchen dressed in his usual uniform of jeans and a T-shirt. His long, gray hair was damp and neatly braided.

"That dang zombie's crawling around in the kudzu looking for the Wampus Kitty," he said. "Hope he finds her."

Beck stared at him in surprise. "I thought you didn't like Annie."

"Don't like her," Toby said. "She scares the hell out of me. Been thinking, though. Maybe we ought to keep her around. Kinda like a secret weapon, you know?"

Beck bit her bottom lip to keep from smiling. Toby Littleton's bark was definitely worse than his bite. It was one of the things she loved best about the old coot.

"She knows how to clear a room," she said. "Thanks for cleaning up the place, Tobes. What'd you do, call in a favor?"

"Negatory. I didn't clean squat. Went home, like you said."

"Then who did?" Beck said.

Junior Peterson materialized. "Where's my piano?"

"What piano?" Toby said. "And who the hell are you?"

Junior drew himself up. "I'm Junior Peterson, of *the* Petersons. I'm the new piano player." The ghost gave Beck an accusatory glare. "Or I would be if someone had done what they said they'd do."

"I've been busy," Beck said.

"That's no excuse," Junior said. "I can't haunt the Episcopal church forever, you know. Sooner or later, Father Ben's going to figure out I'm a ghost. He pulls out the holy water and the *Book of Common Prayer,* and I'm a goner."

Chapter Fourteen

Junior was dressed in a pair of tan trousers and a navy-and-white–checked button-down shirt. He looked elegant, urbane, and totally pissed.

"So you'll cross over," Beck said. "Is that such a bad thing?"

"Maybe I'm not ready to leave," Junior said. "Maybe I still have things to do. Besides, we made a deal."

"Hold the phone." Toby looked at Beck in disbelief. "You hired a ghost and didn't tell me? And not just any ghost, one of them uppity Petersons?"

"I forgot."

"You forgot?" Toby waved his hand at her. "Remember me, your partner?"

"Things broke out in crazy and it just sort of happened."

"Huh." Toby folded his arms across his narrow chest. "How do you even know the guy can play?"

Junior stiffened. "I beg your pardon. I'm classically trained."

"Hear that?" Toby said. "He's classically *trained*. He plays Old Dead Guy music. Like anybody in a bar wants to listen to that."

"I can play anything," Junior said. "Put me in front of a piano and I'll prove it to you." He did a head smack. "Oh, wait. You haven't *got* a piano."

"Hannah's a small town and pianos are expensive," Beck protested. "Besides, I'm still trying to figure out who cleaned up the place."

Junior rolled his eyes. "Buy a clue, honey, and ask your boyfriend."

"Conall is not my boyfriend."

"Yeah, whatever."

"Is he right?" Beck demanded. "Did you do this?"

Conall returned her perusal, calm and impassive. "Yes."

"Why? *How?*"

"I wanted to be of service. I do not wish you to regret your decision to hire me."

"*What?*" Toby's eyes bulged. "You've gone and hired him, too? Have you lost your mind?"

"Yes, yes, I'm certifiable," Beck said. She waved her hand at Conall. "Explain."

He shrugged. "The djegrali seldom come peaceably. The Dalvahni must be able to set things to rights once the battle is won, or else we are in violation of the Directive Against Conspicuousness."

"The what?"

"The Directive Against Conspicuousness."

Conall enunciated each word like she was slow, or something. And maybe she was, because she was having a hard time with this. He was talking about magic. Magic she knew about; she was a demonoid. But it was one more weapon to add to his already overstocked arsenal.

"You are dissatisfied with the results?" he asked.

He was doing it again, studying her like she was some kind of science project.

On any other guy, it would have come across as anxious to please, but not on him. On him, it came across as predatory, the Big Bad Wolf sizing up Little Red Riding Hood for a snack.

"The results are Jim Dandy, but you should've damn well asked first," she said. "I don't like being beholden to you."

"Now, Becky, that's plain rude," Toby said. "I don't appreciate you hiring him without my say-so, but the guy did us a favor. I mean, jeez, look at this place."

"Favor schmavor. You don't know him. He's not the type to do something for nothing."

Conall raised his brows. "You had no such complaint last night."

Beck's cheeks grew hot. How dare he bring up last night in front of other people? She glanced at Toby and the ghost. Junior was studying the edges of his perfectly starched cuffs, and Toby was staring off into space pretending like he hadn't heard.

She knew better. Junior was being polite, and Toby's hearing was just fine.

Conall moved to her side. "I have embarrassed you. Forgive me," he said in a low voice. "You were upset last night and I wanted to give you ease."

Oh, he'd given her ease, all right. They probably heard her "ease" clean over in Baldwin County.

"So, what did Charlie Skinner want?" Toby asked. "I saw you talking to him out back."

Beck tried to collect herself. "He heard about the fight last night and wanted to square things."

Toby snorted. "Bet he didn't offer to pay Earl's tab."

"No. He wanted to leave Earl at the bar to work it off."

Toby hooted in disbelief. "Earl, *work*? He ain't never hit a lick at a snake in his life. Don't even help his daddy with the family b'ness."

"Which is?" Conall asked.

"Moonshine," Toby said. "And b'ness must be pretty good. You get a load of them boots Charlie had on, Becky?"

"Couldn't miss them. They were butt ugly."

"Ugly, hell," Toby said. "Them boots were Paul Bonds. Custom made. Pair like that'll run you fifteen hundred, easy."

Beck gave a low whistle. "That's a lot of moonshine."

Toby chuckled. "Sho' is."

"Earl said he had a new hunting dog," she said, thinking. "A Brittany spaniel."

"Pure bred?" Toby asked.

"I got that impression."

"Well, well, well." Toby's nose twitched like he was on the scent. "Looks like the Skinners are living high on the hawg."

Beck pulled the envelope out of her pocket. "Charlie delivered this invitation. Seems the kith are gathering at the Peterson hunting cabin this afternoon." She looked at Junior. "Charlie said he and Trey are tight."

"Charlie Skinner and my son don't run in the same circles."

"And since when do the kith gather?" Toby asked.

"I was wondering the same thing." Beck smoothed the wrinkled invitation against her palm. "I'm going to the meeting to find out."

"I should not be surprised if your brother is at this gathering," Conall said. "It cannot be a coincidence that this meeting and his arrival coincide."

Toby's bright gaze darted from Conall to Beck. "Brother? What brother?"

Oh, boy. This was going to be hard to explain.

"A guy came up to me as Conall and I were leaving the wedding," Beck said. "His name is Evan. He's my twin."

"Baby girl, you know that ain't possible." Toby's tone was gentle. "This feller, whoever he is, is pulling your leg."

"I don't think so," Beck said. "When I was a little girl, I had an imaginary friend named Evan. Only, turns out, he's real."

"You had an imaginary friend?" Toby's eyebrows disappeared into his hairline. "You never told me this."

"Evan said grown-ups wouldn't understand." Beck looked away. "Daddy already thought I was a freak. I was afraid he'd send me away if he found out."

Send her away from Toby; she couldn't have borne that.

Toby gave a low whistle of surprise. "My God, Becky, you're serious. You really think this guy's telling the truth."

"I know he is."

"Son of a gun. Does your daddy know?"

"No, and we're keeping it that way." She pressed her lips together. "I want to find out more about Evan and what he's been up to all these years."

And, more importantly, why he smells like demons.

"I'm going with you to this meeting," Toby said. "I want to take a gander at this Evan fellow."

Junior heaved a plaintive sigh. "I'd go, too, but Trey can't see me. He doesn't want to."

Poor Junior. Sometimes, family sucked.

"I'm sure that's not the case," Beck said. "Lots of people can't see ghosts."

Junior's face tightened. "He can see that bitchy dead wife of his just fine. He blocks me because it reminds him of—"

He stopped.

"Reminds him of what?" Beck prodded.

"My death, all right?" Junior snapped. "Trey saw me die when he was ten years old."

Beck's eyes widened. "The accident out at the mill back in the eighties—that was you. There was an article about it in the paper. They named the annual turkey shoot after you. It was a big deal."

Junior's eyes blazed. "I *loathe* hunting, and my death was no accident. My father threw me into a saw to teach Trey a lesson." Energy whirled around the ghost, lifting Beck's hair and making her skin prickle. "He said he didn't want Trey to grow up to be like me. He said I was weak because I love music and play the piano." His eyes glowed hotter. "That son of a bitch murdered me in front of my own son. That's why Trey can't see me. It hurts too much to remember."

Crack. Junior disappeared, shattering the MILLER LITE sign on the wall in his wake.

"Whew, somebody's touchy," Toby said.

Conall repaired the broken sign with a negligent lift of his hand. "I will accompany you to this gathering in the event things should go amuck."

Amuck. Not a word people used much anymore, Beck reflected. A mucking shame, too, because it was so apt. Things frequently went amuck when the kith were involved.

"Bad idea," she said. "You stay here and keep an eye on things while we're gone."

Conall frowned and Beck could have sworn the lights in the room dimmed. "No."

She propped one hand on her hip. "You said you trusted me. Time to put your money where your mouth is, Mr. Dalvahni."

"This has nothing to do with trust and everything to do with duty," Conall said, his deep voice stiff with disapproval. "One of the kith may have information about this secret weapon the djegrali have discovered. If so, it is imperative I be at this meeting."

"You're not from around here and you're not kith. You'll stick out like a turd in a bucket of buttermilk."

"I concede the rationality of your argument that my presence at this gathering might draw attention—"

"Duh, you think?" Beck said. He was big and beautiful and he radiated power and menace. Showing up with Elvis in drag might create a bigger stir, but she doubted it.

"—therefore I will make myself invisible."

"No," Beck said. "The place will be crawling with kith. Just because *I* can't see you when you're wearing your invisible Underoos doesn't mean no one else can. The kith have different abilities. Right, Toby?"

"Yup," Toby said.

"Toby and I will go to the meeting," Beck said. "Alone. We'll be your eyes and ears."

"Rebekah, I do not think—"

"I want your promise."

Conall fell silent. "Very well," he said at last. His mouth thinned. "We will do it your way this once. But not unless I get a promise of my own." He slipped a silver ring off his hand and slid it on her left index finger. It was way too big, but the band magically shrank until it fit. "At the first sign of danger, speak to the ring. Do not hesitate. This you must promise me."

Speak to the ring? What was she, Gollum? She'd feel like an idiot.

"Sure. Whatever you say."

He stepped closer, his eyes hard as agate. "I gave you my word, Rebekah. Now I want yours."

"Okay, okay, keep your panties on. I promise I'll speak to the fricking ring if there's a problem. There, satisfied?"

"No. I am not accustomed to sitting idly by whilst others ride into battle. But I am inured to this course, for the moment."

"Relax. Nothing's going to happen. It's beer and barbecue. Says so on the invitation. People will get drunk and run around naked and throw up, and somebody will get their truck stuck in a ditch. I've seen it a million times."

"Proceed with caution," Conall said. " 'Tis an age-old trick to lull one's enemies into complacence by plying them with food and drink." He made a slashing motion in the air. "Once they are sleepy and replete, you move in for the kill."

Hoo boy—Mr. Look on the Bright Side of Life.

"Thanks, I'll remember that," she said, shoving the invitation back in her pocket. "Don't overeat and don't get wasted. Piece of cake."

Later that afternoon, freshly showered, her hair washed and dried and a smattering of makeup applied, Beck stood in her walk-in closet trying to decide what to wear. After some deliberation, she opted for comfort, pulling on jeans, a moss-green cable-knit sweater, her favorite brown boots, and a leather jacket. No sense getting gussied up to go tromping around in the woods.

"Nice," Toby said, getting to his feet when she emerged from the bedroom. "We'll take my truck. Wouldn't want that fancy ride of yours to get scratched, and you can't hurt old 'Retta."

Beck smiled to herself. Loretta was Toby's name for the ancient Ford he kept as a second vehicle. Loretta was kind of like Toby, a little worse for wear on the outside, but the innards worked just fine.

They climbed in the truck and took off, following the directions in the invitation. The Peterson hunting cabin was located on a chunk of privately owned land in the northwest corner of Behr County. Privately owned by the Petersons, of course—more than ten thousand acres of thick woods stocked with game for the Petersons' pleasure.

The closest bit of civilization was Musso, a one-traffic-light hole in the road with a gas station. But Musso was three roads and ten miles back, leaving them drowning in trees. Beck was at home in the woods. But these woods made her nervous. She couldn't shake a feeling of unease. The trees seemed to press in around them, like silent, green giants. These were not friendly woods. These were scary woods straight out of *Grimm's Fairy Tales* or Middle Earth, full of dark, hungry things.

Death crouched in those trees. Beck felt it waiting.

Get a grip, she scolded herself. *This is Conall's fault. All his talk of enemies lying in wait has made you jumpy. Don't let him spook you.*

She gripped the seat with both hands to keep from bouncing onto the floorboard as Toby aimed his battered pickup down yet another dirt road. Hog trails disappeared from the road into the thick brush.

"Good thing that invitation included a map, or we never would've found the place," Toby said, taking a right at a fork in the road.

"No kidding," Beck said. "And I thought we lived in the boonies."

"We must be getting close." He eased the old truck through a line of vehicles parked along both sides of the road. "Look at all the cars."

They rounded a curve and came into a huge clearing.

Toby slammed on the brakes. "Cheezy Pete, that ain't no hunting cabin. It's a freaking hotel."

A sprawling two-story lodge built out of logs hunkered on a stone foundation. Smoke curled out of a towering chimney at one end of the building. The dirt road gave way to a white gravel drive that curved past the house and beyond to a multicar garage.

A bonfire blazed in a stone pit in front of the palatial home, and wood smoke and the scent of roasting meat wafted from an industrial-size grill on wheels. Plank tables loaded with food banked the wide porch steps, and burly servants with trays wandered among the guests offering festive drinks in plastic cocktail glasses.

Hundreds of people milled around the lawn, a lush oasis of winter rye grass in the middle of the vast hunting preserve. Beck recognized some of the faces from the bar or from around town, but there were quite a few folks she didn't know. Everybody was laughing and drinking and talking. It was a par-tay, and the kith were out in force.

The crowd hummed with restless expectancy, like a large animal stretching its muscles in anticipation. But in anticipation of what? The atmosphere was reminiscent of the primal tug of the shifter moon the night before, and yet different.

Darker and more dangerous.

Beck was gripped by a sudden, unreasoning urge to turn and run, and keep on running.

She glanced over at Toby. His expression was tense and alert, his long nose aquiver. He sensed it, too, the Big Ugly lying in wait.

He gripped the steering wheel. "I've got a bad feeling about this."

"Me, too." She swallowed the nervous lump in her throat. "I don't think this is our kind of party after all. Let's get out of here."

"Roger that."

Toby slung the truck into reverse, backed up a few feet, and stopped.

"Shit," he said. "Road's gone."

"What?" Beck wheeled around to take a look.

Behind the Ford, rye grass undulated in the breeze; beyond that, nothing but thick woods. The road was gone, swallowed up by the trees.

Chapter Fifteen

A no-neck goon yanked the passenger door open and pulled Beck out of the truck. The smell of cheap cologne climbed up her nose and coated the back of her throat, making her sneeze. Jeez, somebody needed to ease up on the aftershave.

Squatty and heavy with muscle, the goon had closely cropped muddy brown hair and small, unblinking dark eyes. His conservative dress—crisply starched khakis and a pink shirt embossed with an oversized pony on the front—was at odds with his brutish appearance. The result was jarring and just plain *wrong,* like a rhino in a tutu.

"Hey, what's the big idea?" Beck said, trying to wrest her arm from his iron grip. "Let go of me."

It was a waste of time. The guy had hands like meat hooks.

"Boss say bring you," the tank said, tugging her toward the house.

His speech was guttural and thick, like talking was a newly acquired skill. Sharp as a spoon, this one, Beck thought.

And loaded with personality; Tommy was more animated than this guy, and Tommy was dead.

"Toby," Beck yelled over her shoulder.

"Right behind you, baby girl."

Toby came around the other side of the truck accompanied by a baldheaded slab of beef in khakis and a royal blue shirt with cheery lemon yellow embroidery. The two thugs marched Beck and Toby up to the house and onto the spacious front porch.

"Stay here," Meat Hooks and Baldy growled in unison.

Lurching back down the steps, they took side-by-side posi-
tions and froze in place like a couple of grotesque Polo-clad
refugees from the Island of Naboombu.

"What the hell?" Toby said. "Something wrong with them
two. They smell funny."

"No kidding. I think the one in pink took a bath in *Axe*."

Toby grunted. "Trying to cover up something with all that
stinkum."

Beck's stomach did a queasy flip-flop. "Demons?"

"Don't think so. Demons smell rotten." Toby rubbed the end
of his long nose. "These guys smell more like dirt. Like when
you're digging in the leaves after a vole and you get to the
mulch underneath where the worms and blind things live.
Know what I mean?"

No, she didn't. But, then, she'd never been a dog. "What are
they?"

"Dunno," Toby said. "Not human. More'n that—couldn't
say."

Charlie Skinner staggered around the side of the house, an
open Mason jar in one hand. He stomped up the steps in the
red and yellow boots.

"Lookee here what the cat done drug up," he twanged. "If it
ain't Miss High and Mighty and her fav-o-rite hound. Figured
you's too good for the rest of us." He took a swig from the jar
and gave Beck a knowing leer. "Wuzza matter, you smell
money and come a-running?"

"I don't know what you mean," Beck said.

"Big changes in the wind. You throw in with the right folks,
and you could make a pile."

Charlie *was* a pile. The kind treated with Preparation H.

"Which folks?" She kept her tone pleasant. "You mean the
Petersons?"

"Hell no. Trey Peterson ain't no big thang, not compared to
them."

"Them?"

Charlie waved his arm, sloshing the contents of the jar. "The big kahunas, the guys in charge. If you's smart, you'll go along with the plan."

"Oh, yeah? What happens if we don't go along with the . . . uh . . . 'plan'?"

"You can kiss it good-bye, bay-bay, that's what. These guys don't mess around. But I ain't saying no more." He gave her a lopsided grin. "You be nice to Old Charlie and he might put in a good word for you."

"Nice, huh?" Beck's stomach lurched. "What did you have in mind?"

Like she didn't know. Yuck. *Play along,* she thought. *Be smart. You can do this.*

Charlie leaned closer. Good God, Charlie's breath would peel paint.

"For starters, you can have a drink with me." He waggled the jar at her. "And then you and me can go upstairs and play horsey. I'll be the horse and you can ride." He winked. "Earl ain't the only-est Skinner with talent down there, if you catch my drift."

Sweet baby Jesus, Charlie Skinner was talking about his parts. *Vomitous maximus.*

Toby took the jar from Charlie. "The gal ain't much of a drinker, but I'll have a swig."

Charlie grunted, watching closely as Toby took a swallow.

Toby's eyes widened. "Man, that's good."

"Smooth, ain't it?" Charlie said. "M' own special blend. I call it 'kith-a-poo joy juice.' 'Kith-a-poo,' get it?"

"I get it. For the demon in you," Toby said.

"Hey, I like that." Charlie slapped Toby on the shoulder. "That 'ud make a damn good slogan. You're all right, Littleton."

"So is this here 'shine," Toby said, taking another gulp.

"Take it easy," Beck said in alarm. "That's strong stuff."

"Quit pecking at him," Charlie said. "A man don't need no nagging woman. He can drink all he wants. Plenty more where that come from." Charlie waved his arm at the crowd.

"Trey asked Old Charlie to provide the booze for this here event. Whadda you think's in them fancy little glasses? Skinner moonshine, that's what."

"Hot damn," Toby said, draining the jar.

The front door opened, and Evan stepped out of the house. His dark hair was glossy and straight today. Swept in a dramatic fashion across his white brow and over one eye, it gave him the appearance of a brooding, bad boy. The torn jeans and white T-shirt were gone, replaced by dark blue slacks and a purple shirt topped off with a black leather jacket. He'd removed the loop from his bottom lip, but the long earring and numerous silver studs were still in place. His long nails were painted a sleek navy blue.

Trey Peterson was with him; Beck recognized him from the paper.

Through the years, Beck had followed Trey Peterson and his golden crowd in the paper with avid interest and more than a twinge of jealousy. Rich, handsome, and from a socially prominent family, Trey had always seemed to have it all. She'd often wondered what it would be like to be him. Living a privileged life, a big fish in Hannah's little pond, part of the in-crowd. Belonging, not looking in on things from the outside like her.

But that was before she'd met Junior and learned what kind of monster Blake Peterson had been. A murderer who'd killed Trey's father in front of him in the most brutal fashion *to teach him a lesson*.

She examined Peterson carefully, taking in the expensive cut of his dress slacks and his cashmere sweater. The sweater alone probably cost more than most people made in a week, but Trey wore it with the casual assurance of someone used to good things. The fancy clothes didn't disguise the fact that he looked tense and unhappy. Lines of strain were etched around his mouth and eyes.

Evan strolled up to them with Peterson at his heels.

Working at the bar, Beck had learned to read people, but she couldn't get a bead on Evan. He was a still pond, with things moving beneath the quiet surface. What kind of things, though, she could not tell.

"Hello, Cookie," Evan said. "Peterson, introduce yourself."

"How do you do, Miss Damian? I'm Trey Peterson. Evan mentioned you were coming." Trey held out a trembling hand to Toby. "And you must be her partner, Toby Littleton."

Toby swayed, staring at Trey's hand without shaking it. Toby was pounded.

"Thanks for the invite, but we can't stay," Beck said. "Toby doesn't feel well."

Evan chuckled. "You seem out of sorts. What's the matter, Cookie, that big stud not hitting it the way you want?"

"You shut your filthy mouth," Toby said. His wiry body quivered with hostility. "You don't talk to her like that."

Beck laid a quieting hand on Toby's arm and looked at Trey. "Toby and I need to get back to the bar. Tell your men to let us through."

Peterson's eyes widened. "What? Uh, I mean, I don't know if that's—"

"No one leaves until after the meeting," Evan said, cutting him off.

"Y-yes, that's what I meant to say." Trey nodded. "No one leaves until after the meeting."

O-k-a-a-y. Trey's name might be on the invitation, but he wasn't in charge.

She turned to Evan. "You can't keep us prisoners here."

"Why not?" Evan said. "We're all prisoners of something. Right, Peterson?"

Trey jumped. "What's that? I-I'm afraid I wasn't listening."

Peterson wasn't nervous. He was flat out *scared*. The queasy feeling in Beck's stomach returned. She glanced around, looking for a way out. The forest had crept farther in; the trees crouched a few feet behind Toby's truck. As she watched, the trees crept closer. No getting out that way.

If Toby were sober, they could shift and make a run for it, maybe get past Meat Hooks and Baldy and hide in the woods. Not a pleasant thought, going into those moving trees.

She took a deep breath. She was letting her imagination run away with her. It was a party. Folks were laughing and dancing, and getting sloshed on moonshine. The thing with the trees was unnerving, but weird was normal around the kith, especially when alcohol was involved. She could handle this. She'd find out what was going on and prove to Captain Joy Suck she could be trusted. That just because she was kith didn't mean she was *evil*.

Why, exactly, it was so important to prove herself to him, she did not know.

"I don't feel so good," Toby announced and promptly turned into a dog.

"Toby?" Beck reached out for him, snatching her hand back as he snapped at her. "What's gotten into you?"

Toby snarled and went after his tail, circling in a maddened frenzy.

"This is your fault," Beck said, turning on Charlie. "You got him drunk."

Charlie drew himself up. "It ain't my fault the man can't handle his liquor. He ain't the only one, neither." He spat in disgust. "Look at 'em. Bunch of pussies."

Beck took a closer look at the crowd. Toby wasn't the only one having a bad reaction to Charlie's home cooking. As she watched, several people ran screaming for the woods, only to be turned aside by the trees. One man flung himself blindly at the unyielding trees until a flailing limb struck him in the head. He fell at the edge of the clearing and lay still, blood trickling from his mouth and ears.

Still others reverted to their animal forms; foxes, dogs, cats, and sundry other animals darted between the legs of the drunken kith, adding to the confusion. A man and woman at the edge of the crowd shifted helplessly, going from human form to animal and back again, until they collapsed, naked and quivering, on the ground.

Evan gestured, and a crew of big guys carried the injured man and the unconscious couple off the field and started rounding up the crazed animals.

Beck watched them carry the bleeding man into the house. "You've poisoned your own kind," she said to Charlie. "So help me, if you've hurt Toby I'll—"

"Aw, hell, don't get your dander up. The mutt will be fine," Charlie said. "Might have a little head on him in the morning, but that's all."

Toby leaped off the porch. Dodging the lumbering guards, he streaked toward the woods, letting out a startled yelp when the trees lashed at him with their branches.

"Let him go, Skinner," Evan said.

Charlie shook his head. "They said don't let nobody through."

"They don't give a shit about a part blood mutt. Do as I say."

"All right, but I ain't taking the heat if they don't like it."

Charlie waved a fleshy hand and the trees stilled. Toby disappeared into the woods.

Charlie noticed Beck's shocked expression and chuckled. "You thought Old Charlie was no-count? You was wrong." He hitched up his belt. "Us Skinners are late bloomers. Maybe we ain't zombie makers like our boy Evan, but we got skills. How you think we've run moonshine all these years without being caught?"

"The trees," Beck said, putting two and two together. "You move the trees around to hide the stills."

"Bingo." Charlie grinned. "Them revenuers ain't caught us yet and they ain't going to."

Beck hardly heard him. Her gaze was on Evan. "You're the zombie maker?"

Evan jerked his head at Charlie and Trey. "Give us a minute. Alone."

"Fine by me," Charlie said. "Peterson, you look kind of peaked. What say we get us a little drinky poo before the meeting starts?"

"Can't," Trey said. "Got to get back inside."

"Suit yourself," Charlie said. He stomped down the stairs,

grabbed a drink from a waiter, and cozied up to a brunette half his age.

Trey gave Beck a weak smile. "If you'll excuse me, I'll—"

"William Blake Peterson the Third," a petite blonde screeched, materializing on a suffocating cloud of citrus perfume. "What do you think you're doing?"

Beck's spinning brain did a triple flying WTF. She recognized the chic blond bob, the blue eyes, pert nose, and carefully crayoned mouth from the society page. This woman was a big whoppeedoo deal in Hannah.

Or, more precisely, she *had* been. The blonde was Meredith Starr Peterson, Trey's recently departed and very dead wife.

Meredith wore jeans that hugged her size two frame, five-inch beige suede ankle boots with leather stitching and trim, and a cashmere sweater.

She pointed a perfectly manicured pink nail at Trey. "You told me you were *golfing*. I can't let you out of my sight for a minute."

"I did play golf," Trey stammered. "And now I'm at a business meeting."

"Huh." Meredith tapped an expensively shod foot and looked around. "What kind of business? I don't see anyone from the club." Her gaze narrowed on the drunken crowd. "Who *are* these people and what are they doing on our land? I don't see anyone from the club." She stiffened. "OMG, is that Earl Skinner? I've seen his picture in the paper. He steals car radios and broke into the Gas 'N Gulp. What's that he's waving around, his *penis*?" Her face melted into a ghoulish mask. *"What kind of party is this, and why are you doing business with those white trash Skinners?!"*

Trey looked embarrassed. "I'm not doing business with the Skinners, Merikins. Stop making a scene and come inside. I can explain."

"I doubt it." Meredith flounced after Trey. "Here I am, spilling my guts to a therapist, doing my best to make our marriage work, and you're hanging around in the woods with the

People of Walmart. What's next, Neck Car? I am telling you, I absolutely despair that you will ever—"

Trey bolted into the house and slammed the door.

"Oh, no, you didn't," Meredith said.

She sprang after him, a pint-size velociraptor in designer high heels, and shot through the closed door, ghost fashion, leaving Beck and Evan alone on the front porch.

Beck considered Evan, trying to reconcile his sulky bad boy demeanor with what she now knew about him. He didn't just see dead people; he played with them.

"You sent Tommy to the bar to find me?" she finally asked.

"Who's Tommy?"

"The zombie. You don't know his name?"

Evan shrugged. "Why bother? They're lumps of rotting meat."

"Tommy's different. He knows what he is and he *hates* it. He's suffering. You need to let him go."

"He's not suffering. He's *dead*."

"You're wrong. He's very much aware."

"Forget the stupid zombie," Evan said. "What matters is I found you."

"You mean Tommy found me. How do you two communicate, anyway? Zombie telepathy?"

"I get flashes of what they see and hear. That's how I knew you were going to the wedding."

"What do you want, Evan? Why are you here now, after all these years?"

"Don't you think I wanted to find you sooner?" To Beck's surprise, Evan grabbed her by the shoulders and shook her. "I couldn't. I never had a chance."

Stunned by his outburst, Beck looked down at his hands. Tattoos writhed in sinuous loops across the pale canvass of his skin.

He looked past her at something and pushed her away. "They're here. We'll talk about this later. Keep your mouth shut and do what they say, Cookie, and you'll be all right."

"Who's here?" Beck said, turning to look. Two shambling figures stepped out of the woods on the far side of the clearing. "Who are those people? Do you know them?"

Evan's mouth twisted. "Oh, yeah. I know them. They're my parents."

Chapter Sixteen

Conall paced the length of the empty bar, nervous as a hart at the scent of a pack of hounds on the wind. Something crackled beneath his foot. He bent down and picked it up. It was a discarded bag of some kind. The lettering on the torn package said *Select Brands Variety Pack* and the words *Nerds, Smarties,* and *Sweet Tarts* were emblazoned across the front in bright colors. He wadded up the package and slammed it into the trash with unnecessary force. It was this damnable waiting. He was ill equipped for it.

'Twas ironic, this sudden lack of fortitude. He'd laid siege to cities until they crumbled and stalked the djegrali for centuries with the relentless persistence of water upon stone. Yet, he had no patience for an evening's wait.

Puzzling in the extreme.

His worry was rooted in inactivity and his eagerness to uncover the djegrali's secret. Certainly his restive mood had nothing to do with Rebekah. Granted, she was beautiful in spite of her demon blood; perhaps *because* of it.

Memories of the evening before made his blood race. The taste of her had been sweet, he admitted, remembering the way she'd come apart in his arms.

He wanted her. The Dalvahni were renowned for their sexual appetites and he had denied himself physical ease for too long. Rebekah was a fire in his blood. He lusted after her, plain and simple. The fact that she was forbidden fruit only added to her appeal.

He wanted her. There; he'd acknowledged it and felt better for it. Lust he knew and understood. *If this be nothing more than desire, why the gnawing ache in your belly, like some great animal consumes you from within?* a sly voice whispered.

Perhaps he was ill. He considered the possibility and rejected it. The Dalvahni did not know sickness or disease. They were famed for their regenerative powers. Physical hurt was but a brief sensation, quickly forgotten in a moment's healing.

Not so humans. Images from a hundred battles rose unbidden in his mind, soldiers, broken and spent, their mangled dying bodies littering the blood-soaked fields. Mortal flesh was fragile, as easily crushed as the tender folds of a flower beneath a booted heel.

Rebekah is half human, the voice of worry whispered in his mind. *You sent her unprotected into the unknown.*

"The shifter is with her," he said aloud. "He will protect her."

And if Tobias is no match for the djegrali? Even now, she could be hurt or dying while you do nothing.

With a roar, Conall smashed the room to bits, breaking chairs and tables and blowing out the windows, taking care, even in his rage, not to shatter the glass counter and release the demons. Chest heaving, he surveyed the damage, his ire unsatisfied. His gaze moved to the bar and the demons floating within the confines of their translucent prison.

He could free the djegrali and engage them in battle, destroying them one by one. 'Twould be an epic battle, a song written in flame in the Great Book.

The warrior in him longed for the physical respite. He raised his hand to destroy the bar and lowered it again. Such a thing would be the act of a child indulging in a tantrum, not behavior behooving the leader of the Dalvahni.

Conall cursed, loud and long, dredging up every swear word he knew. His vocabulary was extensive and he was fluent in a multitude of languages. He had seen and heard much, and he had a very long memory.

When his anger was spent, he went about the business of setting the place to rights. He was putting the finishing touches on the job when the woman and the talking dog walked into the bar.

"*Man. See man, Cassie?*" the dog said, straining at the leash.

"I see him." The woman's hand tightened on the strap. She was beautiful, with smoky purple eyes and shining blond hair that brushed the tops of her shoulders. "Settle down."

An aura of magic hung around her, confirming Conall's suspicion that she was a demonoid. Clad in tan trousers, a white shirt with the sleeves rolled up, and sturdy, sensible shoes, the golden-haired stranger was an alluring mixture of femininity and practicality.

"Nice dog," Conall said, giving the animal a dispassionate perusal. "It talks."

" 'It' is a she, and, yes, she does. I must say, you're handling it well. Most folks would be freaked out."

Freaked out: a heightened degree of emotion, particularly fright.

Conall shrugged. "A talking dog is unusual, but not unheard of."

"Glad you're okay with it." She looked around. "Is Beck here?"

"No, she is at a meeting."

Her eyes widened in dismay. "Don't tell me she went to the gathering."

"Yes. Tobias accompanied her."

She sank into a chair, her expression distracted. "Oh, dear. I meant to call, but Dooley ran away and it took me hours to find her." She patted the dog's yellow fur. "You led me on quite a wild goose chase, didn't you, you bad dog?"

Dooley wagged her tail and gave the woman a black-lipped grin. "*Dooley not chase goose. Dooley chase squirrel.*"

"You scared me half to death," the woman scolded. "How could I face Addy if I lost you?"

Dooley's ears perked. "*Addy? Addy here . . . and Brand Man?*"

"No, Dooley. They're still gone."

"*Gone?*" The dog flumped to the wooden floor. "*Dooley hate gone. Want Addy and Brand Man home.*"

"They'll be back soon. I promise."

"Go-oon-ne," Dooley repeated with a mournful yowl, laying her head on her paws.

"She misses her owner," the woman said. "I'm Cassie, by the way. I'm dog-sitting for my friend Addy while she's on her honeymoon."

"Adara Corwin?"

She smiled at him, her eyes brightening. "Yes, although she's Addy Dalvahni now. You know her?"

"I am Conall, Brand's brother."

Her smile faded. "Oh. You're a demon hunter."

"You do not care for my brother?"

"Brand? I hardly know him." She got to her feet. "I came to see Beck. Since she's not here, I'll be on my way."

"Hold," Conall said. "You are kith. Why are you not at the meeting?"

"What's a demon hunter doing in a demonoid bar?"

"That is my affair."

"Ditto."

He processed the strange term. *Ditto, meaning the same.* He clamped down on his impatience. She knew something, something that might affect Rebekah. He felt it in his gut. Something fluttered in his chest, an odd sensation that made his heart race and his thoughts scatter.

Panic, the hateful voice whispered. *You fear for the demon wench.*

He took a deep breath and willed his galloping pulse to slow. "You came to warn Rebekah of something? If so, you must tell me."

She hesitated, her dislike and distrust of him plain on her face.

"Please," he said, pushing the word past his unwilling tongue.

She straightened her shoulders and gave him a challenging look. "I see things sometimes, okay?"

"You are a seer?"

"That's one word for it," she said. "I found the invitation this morning in a pile of junk mail. I opened it and this awful smell hit me, like rotting meat. I caught a glimpse of woods and dark shapes and then I went cold. It was like every good thing had been sucked out of the world." She shivered. "I didn't want any part of it. I came to warn Beck, but Dooley ran off. Looks like I'm too late."

Too late. Too late. The words rang in Conall's head.

His desire to smash things returned in full measure. He drew another deep breath into his lungs. There was something he should remember. Something important . . .

The ring—of course! By the sword, how could he have forgotten? The ring would lead him to her.

Opening his mind, he sought the ring and found it. It showed him a jumble of images—a thick stand of trees, a curl of smoke against the evening sky, a crowd of drunken people. A man and woman shuffled out of the woods, ghoulish and loathsome in appearance.

Demons; and he had sent her among them. Rebekah had the heart of a warrior. She would challenge the fiends and be hurt or killed.

"This meeting," he said. Calm; he must remain calm. He could not help Rebekah if he gave in to the killing rage. "Can you tell me where it is?"

"I can do better than that. Let me drop Dooley off at the house, and I'll take you there."

Dooley sat up and wagged her tail. *"Dooley ride? Dooley like ride."*

"Not this time, girl," Cassie said. "It may not be safe. You'll have to stay, I'm afraid."

Dooley flumped back to the floor. *"Dooley HATE stay. Stay make Dooley sad."*

"Be a good girl and I'll cook you a cheese omelet for supper." Dooley's ears lifted. *"Dooley like cheese."*

"I know," Cassie said. "Come on. Let's get in the truck."

Seething with impatience and a gnawing sense of urgency, Conall exited the building with them. "Your abode is not far?"

"It's a little out of the way," Cassie said. "But I'm not taking D-o-o-l-e-y. If something happened to her, Addy would never forgive me."

"Addy?" The canine launched into a panting ecstasy about her owner. *"Addy, Addy, Addy?"*

Conall clamped his jaws together to keep from roaring in frustration. Each passing moment was an agony of worry. Where was Rebekah? What was happening to her? Would he reach her in time?

Was she already dead? His mind recoiled.

"I thank you," he forced himself to say. He was Dalvahni, an unemotional creature of logic. "I am in your debt."

"Forget it. I'm not doing it for you. I'm doing it for Beck."

Conall wondered briefly who or what had made this woman so bitter, and pushed the thought aside.

It mattered not. All that mattered was Rebekah.

"Your *parents?*" Beck shook her head in confusion. "No way."

The creatures crossing the lawn were thin and wasted, with filthy bodies and clothes, matted hair, and sunken cheeks. Demon-possessed humans, gross caricatures of the people they'd once been, before the fiends twisted and consumed them.

"Not a pretty sight, are they?" Evan spoke without emotion, as though he were commenting on the weather. "They get this way at the end of a cycle. They'll shed soon, and then it's not so bad. For a few months, anyway. The morkyn go through bodies pretty quickly, because they're so powerful."

"Morkyn?"

He gave her an odd look. "You don't know much, do you? There are different castes of demons. The morkyn are at the top of the food chain."

"I know enough to stay away from them, which is more than I can say for you."

"You think I wanted this?" Evan's mouth tightened. "They found me in a flop house where our bitch of a mother dumped me. I didn't have a *daddy* like you, princess."

"Princess, my ass," Beck said. "I was raised in a bar by a man who could hardly stand to look at me."

Evan laughed. "Please. You had a home and plenty to eat. I'll bet your mean old daddy never broke your arms and legs or burned you with cigarettes until you begged him to stop. I'll bet you got to go to school and learn to read and write, instead of running from place to place to avoid the police." His eyes glittered feverishly in his white face. "I'll bet he never took you to a crack house and locked you in a room with a dead man for three days while he got high. Did he?" His voice rose. "Did he?"

"No." Beck wanted to weep for the young Evan, abandoned, unloved, and abused. "He never did anything like that."

Clasping her trembling hands together, she felt something hard rub against her finger. Conall's ring; his stern, implacable face rose before her, steadying her.

"H-how old were you?" she asked.

Evan slammed his fist into a porch column. "Six. The guy was already dead when they threw me in with him. He was my first zombie. I was so scared. I just wanted someone to talk to. Instead, he tried to eat me."

"What did you do?"

Evan laughed. "I learned how to control a zombie in one hell of a hurry, that's what. I used him to break down the door and I ran. Almost got away, but they caught me. That's when they—"

He stopped.

"When they what?"

"Nothing. It doesn't matter."

"You could have left," Beck said. "You didn't have to stay with them all these years. You had a choice."

"Did I, Cookie?" The rage seemed to leave Evan in a rush, leaving him deflated. Rubbing his bruised knuckles against his thigh, he watched the gruesome twosome approach. "Like I said, you don't know much."

Chapter Seventeen

The sun was setting behind the trees, and the temperature had dropped. In spite of the chill, the creepy couple crossing the lawn wore summer clothing. The man's stained, sleeveless shirt hung open to the waist, exposing his emaciated chest and sunken belly. Grimy cargo shorts flapped around his bony knees. The female was dressed in a faded cotton shift. Both of them were barefoot. Bruises and scabs covered their arms and legs, and their hair was greasy and matted. Patches of crusted scalp showed through the woman's thinning locks, and she dragged one blackened, swollen foot as she walked.

Just like Latrisse, Beck thought with a shudder. All used up.

The drunken kith shouted and followed the hideous creatures like a herd of eager paparazzi at a red carpet event. As if in response to some unspoken command, the crowd halted at a respectful distance as the two demons neared the house.

The couple paused at the foot of the steps and grinned up at Evan with blackened teeth. They were even more horrifying up close, with wobbly, liquid eyes like dark pitch. The odor of spoiled meat assaulted Beck's nose. Demon-possessed humans stink like a butcher shop Dempsey Dumpster in July, and these two were no exception.

The smell was so awful that Beck had to breathe through her mouth to keep from throwing up. Evan didn't seem to mind. Maybe he was used to it.

"All is prepared?" The man's raspy whisper sent a shiver up Beck's spine.

"Yes, Elgdrek," Evan said.

Elgdrek's ghoulfriend was in particularly bad shape. She was no doctor, but Beck suspected the woman's foot was gangrenous. This pathetic wreck had once been somebody, a teacher maybe; someone's wife or mother. A beloved daughter, perhaps.

How old had she been when she was taken? No telling; the body was too far gone. Young, though, Beck guessed. In her experience, demons were attracted to youth and vigor. Not much point in possessing an aging body. Why take a used clunker for a joyride when you could steal a brand-new sports car?

What if there was still a spark of human consciousness trapped inside that prison of decaying flesh? Beck didn't want to think about it.

Charlie Skinner pushed his way out of the horde and swaggered up to the female cadaver. "Hey, gorgeous." He grinned at the she-monster. "Where you been all my life?"

Gorgeous? Charlie's words were slurred and he was unsteady on his feet. Drunk or not, there wasn't enough alcohol on the planet to make this gal passable, much less gorgeous. Charlie's moonshine wasn't joy juice, it was psychotropic.

Her theory was confirmed when the female thing grabbed Charlie and gave him a lingering, open-mouthed kiss. Skinner threw himself into the caress to the accompaniment of hoots and catcalls from the onlookers.

Kissing this chick would be like licking a toilet. Charlie was drunk on Crazy Kool-Aid, no doubt about it.

Releasing Charlie, the woman smiled up at him and stroked his big belly. "I am Hagilth," she said. "Later, we will have sex."

Charlie flung his arms in the air like he'd won the lottery. "Yee-hah."

Beck didn't much like Charlie—okay, she didn't like him at *all*—but she felt bad for him. Sex with Old Haggy would be like screwing a maggoty corpse.

Hagilth's oozing gaze fastened on Beck. "This one is young and pleasing to the eye," she said with a sickly grin. "You have done well, servant."

Holy smokes, Haggy thought she was her new ride. Beck's brain went fuzzy at the thought. Thank heavens she was kith and couldn't be possessed.

Evan shook his head. "She's not for you."

"*What?*" Hagilth's face stretched and her mouth widened to the size of a washtub. "You dare refuse me, you insolent pile of rat droppings?"

Evan collapsed to the floor, his body twitching. The tattoos on his throat and hands squirmed and tightened, cutting into his skin like wire. Blood welled from the wounds.

Not tattoos, Beck thought with a ripple of shock. *Bindings. He's their prisoner.*

"Not human," he gasped, clawing at the inky garrote around his throat with a bloody hand. "Can't h-have . . . not . . . human."

Hagilth sucked on a lock of her slimy hair. "I see. She is part demon, like you?"

"Yes," Evan croaked.

"Disappointing," Hagilth said, releasing him. "I hope you have others, for your sake."

Evan rolled to his knees, coughing, and staggered to his feet. Blood dripped from his hands and throat, staining the front of his silk shirt. He reeled across the porch and rapped on the door.

"Bring them out, Peterson," he said. Reaching up, he rubbed his throat with shaking hands. "It's time."

"You okay?" Beck asked.

Evan's mouth twisted. "Feeling sorry for me, Cookie?"

"Maybe."

"Don't." He snatched a handkerchief out of his pocket and dabbed at the oozing cuts on his hands. "I can take care of myself."

He sounded just like her, a chip on his shoulder big as Montana. The realization made her squirm.

The door opened and Trey stepped onto the porch. Two young teenagers, a boy and a girl, accompanied him.

The boy was good looking in a high school heartthrob kind

of way, with shiny brown hair and long, thick bangs that swept across his brow at a precise angle. The girl was attractive, too, round-faced and smooth-skinned, the girl-next-door type. Her shoulder-length blond hair was pale gold, with the silky texture that didn't need a flat iron to achieve uniform straightness.

"Where's the music and the DJ?" The girl looked at Trey with wide, green eyes. "You said this was a rave."

Hagilth made a horrible snuffling noise. "Juicy," she said. "Bring them."

Beck's stomach clenched. Oh, God, those poor kids. She knew what was coming next.

The girl took one look at Hagilth and started screaming, and the boy bolted. Trey shoved the girl at Evan and went after him.

This was her chance, maybe her only chance, while they were distracted.

Beck leaped over the porch rail and hit the ground in a crouch. Evan shouted something, but Beck's attention was on the demons. She sprang at Hagilth. Beck was sure she could take her. The bitch couldn't weigh a hundred pounds soaking wet. She'd snap her neck like a twig.

A pair of hard hands closed around her waist and yanked her back. She caught a flash of pink; Meat Hooks. The guard tucked her under one arm like so much baggage, and resumed his frozen stance at the foot of the steps.

"Let me go," Beck said, kicking.

Meat Hooks' arm tightened and Beck cried out in pain. Much more, and the son of a bitch would crack her ribs. Demon stink coated the back of her throat, and the overpowering smell of the guard's aftershave made it hard to breathe.

Lifting her head, she saw Evan and Trey shove the teens off the porch and into the waiting arms of the demons.

"Leave them alone," she shouted. "Dammit, they're just kids."

"Don't be a pain in the ass, Cookie." Evan shoved the bloody handkerchief back in his pocket. "You can't help them. It's too late."

Smoke poured from the ghouls' gaping, broken-toothed

maws and into the mouths of the helpless boy and girl. The teens stiffened and arched their backs, their limbs twitching and convulsing. When they straightened, their eyes were puddles of goo.

The bodies the demons had abandoned collapsed to the ground in a rubbery heap, as limp and formless as a deboned chicken. Evan barked an order, and the bald guard shuffled forward, scooped up the gelatinous remains, and threw them into the bonfire. The husks went up like tissue paper. Baldy trudged back to his place at the bottom of the steps.

The boy turned on the girl with a snarl. "I wanted the girl. You always get the tender ones."

"Stop whining, Elgdrek." The girl tossed her silky hair. "The boy is stronger and will last longer." Turning, she gave Beck a gooey-eyed appraisal. "What ails this one? She seems excitable."

"She's drunk. Skinner put something in the moonshine, remember?" Evan said. "I'll deal with her."

He motioned, and the guard trudged up the steps and dumped Beck on a porch bench.

"I don't like her," Hagilth said. "If she gives you any more trouble, kill her." She gave a voluptuous stretch and crooked a finger at Charlie. "Come here, you."

Charlie's face lit up. "Hot damn."

"Not yet." Elgdrek halted Charlie in his tracks with a look. "Business first."

Hagilth pouted. "I suppose you're right. But let us hurry. I want to play." She threw back her head and laughed. "Ah, the bloom of youth is sweet."

Youth's sweet all right, you parasitic bitch. Beck sat up and pushed her long hair out of her face. *For a few weeks, a couple months, maybe, a year at most, and then you'll toss this poor girl aside like an old sock.*

Not if I can help it, Beck thought. She could see the demons pulsing inside the teenagers like malignant tumors. The right tool and the right opportunity, and she'd pull the bastards like a couple of bad teeth.

She got to her feet and looked around for something, anything, to use. There, sitting on a table next to a pitcher of fruit juice and several bottles of Skinner moonshine, a bottle of liqueur with a bartender's metal tip. Perfect.

Hagilth and Elgdrek pranced across the lawn, and Charlie and the rest of the crowd followed.

"What the hell's the matter with you?" Evan said. "You pull a stunt like that again and I won't save your ass."

"Fine by me." Beck started down the steps. "Don't do me any favors."

She paused as the guards moved to block her, staring up at her with dull, unblinking eyes. She flapped a hand in Meat Hooks' face; nobody home.

Looking over her shoulder, she found Evan watching her from the porch, one shoulder propped against a wooden post. "Where do you think you're going?" he asked.

"To get a drink, if Dumb and Dumber will let me by. I'm thirsty."

The kith cheered as the two demons climbed onto the bed of a pickup truck and started to speak.

"No more shenanigans, Cookie. I mean it," Evan said.

"Don't worry. I know when I'm licked."

"Good. I'm in no mood for heroics."

She patted her back pocket. "Yep, left my cape in my other jeans."

"I'm glad you've decided to cooperate." Evan slunk down the steps with loose-limbed grace. "Let's have a drink together, to celebrate."

Shit, shit, shit. She did *not* want to play auld lang syne with Evan, especially with that poison Skinner had concocted. Nothing to do but be cool and fake it.

"Why not?" she said, tossing him a bright smile.

She sailed past the two loutish guards and sauntered over to the drink table. Evan followed.

Elgdrek was speaking to the kith in his slithery voice.

"—no longer have to be ashamed of what you are," he said. "Join us and be rulers of this world. Oppose us and be destroyed . . ."

"Resistance is futile." Beck turned her back on the drunken revelry, sickened by how easily swayed the kith were. Crowd mentality, she thought. "Guess this is where we get assimilated into the hive. Happy day."

She grabbed two glasses, poured two fingers of moonshine into one, added ice, orange juice and peach schnapps, topped it off with an orange slice, and handed the drink to Evan.

"It won't be like that," he said, taking a sip. "The kith will be running things."

"You mean, like you're running things now?" She cocked her brows. "No thanks. I saw what they did to you."

He stared at the tattoos on his hands. "It's not so bad, so long as you keep them happy."

"And if you don't, look out," Beck said. "They can do whatever they want to with you, 'cause you're their slave."

"I'm *not* their slave." His eyes flared with heat. "I'm their partner. When things go down, I'll be at the top of the heap. Play your cards right and you could wind up at the top of the heap, too."

At the top of a heap of *bodies,* maybe. Given their way, the demons would turn Earth into their own personal theme park.

"You give Charlie this same speech?" she said. "'Cause it sounds familiar."

"Skinner's a tool. He's greedy and conniving, but not very bright. I need someone smart, like you." He frowned at her empty glass. "You're not drinking."

Damn. She'd hoped he wouldn't notice.

She splashed a little moonshine into her glass for show, but he put his hand on the bottle and tipped it. Glug glug, the liquor poured into the tumbler. Crap; so much for keeping her wits about her.

"What about Peterson?" she asked, dumping some OJ on top of the booze. "Why's he in this? It's not like he needs the money."

Evan shrugged. "He wants to get rid of his wife. She's a raving bitch. The poor bastard can't take a leak without her giving him hell."

Beck stirred her drink to buy time. "How do you get rid of a ghost?"

Evan waved his hand in the direction of the truck. The demons had finished their "we are the world" speech and were knocking back a tray of drinks while the kith danced around in celebration of the new order.

"He's made a deal with Hagilth and Elgdrek," he said. "He gives them what they want, and they take care of Meredith."

That made Beck's antennas go up. "What's Peterson got that would interest a couple of demons?"

Evan shook his head. "Not going there with you. Not yet."

"What's the matter, bro? Don't you trust me?"

"I don't trust anybody."

Beck's brain whirled. Trey wanted to get rid of Meredith badly enough to make a deal with the demons, but what did he have to offer the demons in return? Did he know something about this secret weapon the djegrali wanted? A streak of excitement shot through her. She was onto something. She could feel it.

She couldn't wait to see the look on Conall's gorgeous face when she told him.

Evan closed his eyes and took a deep breath. "God, smell that fresh air. I can breathe again."

So, he did notice the smell. She'd feel sorry for him, except for the whole pimping-humans-out-to-demons thing.

He opened his eyes and leveled a pointed look at her glass. "You still aren't drinking. I'm beginning to think you don't like me."

Busted.

Beck lifted her glass. "Here's to you and here's to me, but if we ever disagree to hell with you and here's to me."

She took a slug of the drink, shuddering as the fiery liquid scorched its way down her throat and hit her stomach. What had she eaten today? Let's see . . . nothing.

Great.

She tugged at the neck of her turtleneck and peered down her shirt.

"What are you doing?" Evan asked.

"Looking for the hair on my chest. That shit is strong."

"You get used to it." His brooding gaze moved to the cavorting demons. "You can get used to anything."

"Yeah," Beck said. "That's what I'm afraid of."

Chapter Eighteen

The alcohol rushed into Beck's bloodstream and sent her flying. Blood like pure spring water; that's what Toby always said about her. She'd never been much of a drinker. She liked to keep a clear head. Stuff happened when a demonoid lost control. Things got broken. People got hurt. Norms saw things they weren't supposed to see. Questions got asked with no easy answers.

The kith-a-poo joy juice hit her brain and the world burst with color, layer upon layer that pulsed and flowed into one another in dizzying patterns. She'd always had excellent sight, even for a demonoid, but not like this. Her vision was magnified. Tiny insects crawled along a branch on a tree more than a hundred yards away. A mockingbird perched in an oak on the far side of the clearing. She saw every detail, the intricate swirl of feathers, the dark line around the umber eyes, as clearly as if the bird sat on her finger.

"Wow." She felt her mouth stretch in a goofy grin. Charlie was a lecherous old coot, but his moonshine was kickass. "This is *soooo* cool."

"What?" Evan said.

Her grin widened—she couldn't help it, her lips moved of their own accord. Much more and the dang things would slide right off her face. "I can see everything."

Evan shot her a sullen look from beneath his dark swoop of hair. "You're looped, and on one lousy drink."

"What can I say? I'm a cheap drunk. You?"

He snorted. "I grew up in flop houses. The closest thing I ever got to a juice box was a margarita or a screwdriver."

"That sucks."

She meant it. Daddy had ignored her, but Evan's childhood had been something out of a horror novel, only the nightmare never ended, because the demons still owned him. She studied the markings on his hands. There had to be some way to help him. Thanks to Charlie's special mash, she could clearly see the spell—more of a curse, really—tiny squiggles etched into Evan's skin.

Ilgrith unduth, the curse read. It meant "bound unto death."

Holy shit, she could read the language of the demons. The knowledge shocked her. And she could see the end of the spell line. It was right there, in the web between two of Evan's fingers. If she tugged on it, would it unravel?

She reached out to touch it and jerked her hand back in surprise as the kith let out a collective roar.

"What now?" Evan muttered, turning to look.

The demons were still lording it over the kith from the back of the truck.

Charlie Skinner stood near the tailgate holding a young woman by the arm. She wasn't much to look at; too pale and thin. Her head was bowed, her gaze downcast. She wore a bandanna over her hair. The ends sticking out of the kerchief were frizzy and dry as autumn wheat. Her clothes were mismatched and ill-fitting, like she'd picked them out of a rag bag without looking. She wore cheap flip-flops, one pink and the other blue. Her slim, bony feet looked cold.

Elgdrek held up his arms and the kith fell silent. "Our friend Charlie has offered his youngest daughter as tribute to prove his loyalty to us and the Plan."

"That's right, she's all yours," Charlie said, his words mushy with drink. " 'Bout time she made herself useful. Ain't never been nothing but a dud. Not a drop of talent in 'er."

"Such a treasure," Elgdrek said dryly. "How generous of you to share it with us." He raised his voice, regarding the assembled kith from the back of the truck. "What say you, brothers and sisters? Shall we spill the blood of this wretched female to seal our covenant?"

The kith murmured in anticipation. The Big Ugly that Beck had sensed when she and Toby arrived stirred and lifted its head. Beck went cold and some of her buzz faded. Sacrifice; he was talking about making the girl a sacrifice.

"I told them no killing, but they never listen," Evan said, stepping closer to the truck. "It's always the same, and I'm the one left to clean up the mess."

He had his back to her. Reaching over, Beck hefted the peach schnapps bottle; too big and heavy. She pried the metal spout loose and looked around for a container, something smaller and less conspicuous. There, on a table near the grill, a half-empty container of *Hot Dang* habanera pepper sauce. It would be easier to handle and the pour spout should fit.

Keeping one eye on Evan, she scooted to the other table and snatched up the bottle of hot sauce. With trembling hands, she unscrewed the metal cap and stuck it in the front pocket of her jeans. She pried the stopper out and slid the metal spout into place. It fit.

The nervous fluttering in her stomach eased. She was armed, and the whole thing had taken less than thirty seconds. She slipped the bottle in her jacket pocket and eased back over to Evan. He was engrossed in the unfolding drama, and hadn't noticed she was gone.

"I was thinking we'd have us a little sport," Charlie was saying to Elgdrek. He listed on his custom-made boots, first one way and then the other, like a tree in a high wind. "Verbena can't shift, but she can run like a deer. We turn the dogs loose on her regular, so's to keep 'em exercised."

Something stirred in Beck, something hot and angry. Compared to Charlie Skinner, the devil's asshole was a bright spot in the universe. She'd never seriously considered killing anybody before, but she was thinking about it now. She was thinking about it hard.

Charlie Skinner needed killing.

"A hunt?" Hagilth clapped her hands in delight. "I adore a hunt."

"An excellent notion," Elgdrek said. He raised his voice. "And to make things more interesting, I will sweeten the pot." A small cloth sack appeared in his hand. He shook several gold coins into his palm and held them up for the kith to see. "A pouch of gold to the one who brings me the bitch's pelt. What say you?"

The kith roared in answer. Money, power and now blood: Elgdrek had them eating out of his hand.

"Remove your spell from the trees," Elgdrek told Charlie. "Our friends are eager to begin."

"Already done." Charlie swatted Verbena hard on the back of the head. "Go on, gal. Git. You's the rabbit."

Verbena gave him a startled look and darted across the field in a blur, running right out of her flip-flops. The bandanna came undone and fluttered to the ground behind her. Her quick reflexes surprised Beck. The girl ran like a greyhound, but she didn't stand a chance, not with a bunch of drugged-up supers on her trail.

Elgdrek kept the kith in check until Verbena was swallowed up by the trees. He raised his arm and brought it back down. "After her," he shouted.

The kith gave chase. Some shifted and some didn't. Charlie Skinner was knocked flat and trampled in the rush. Served him right, Beck thought with vicious satisfaction, watching him roll around on his back like an upended beetle.

Charlie's moonshine thrummed through her veins, working its magic. She felt strong and powerful. And she was feeling a little blood lust of her own. She sprang through the air and came down on the roof of the truck with a thud.

"What are you doing?" Hagilth scowled up at her. "The bitch ran that way. Go after her. Bring me her head, if you want the gold."

"No thanks." Beck pulled the bottle out of her pocket. "The bitch I'm looking for is right here."

She pounced, landing soft-footed as a cat on the bed of the truck, and rammed the tip of the pour spout into Hagilth's chest beneath the collar bone. Hagilth's licorice goo eyes widened in shock and turned green as the demon leaked out of the girl's body and into the hot sauce bottle. The girl's eyes rolled back and she slumped to the floor of the truck. The pour spout popped loose and rolled off the truck.

Beck put her thumb over the top of the bottle to keep the demon from escaping. Fumbling in her pocket, she found the bottle cap and screwed it back on.

"Release her," Elgdrek roared.

Beck whirled around. Elgdrek's teeny-bopper heartthrob face twisted and distorted. His jaw lengthened and sprouted a bristling set of teeth. Claws sprang from the ends of his gnarled fingers. Lord-a-mercy, he was ugly, a cross between Predator and the creature from the Black Lagoon with Bama Bangs.

And she'd lost the pour spout. Damn.

If Conall were here, he'd whip out his sword and beat some demon booty. But Conall wasn't here. He was miles away. She'd started this fight, and she'd have to finish it, somehow.

Elgdrek leaped at her. Beck stepped to one side, narrowly avoiding having her head ripped off. He slammed into the cab of the truck with bone-crushing force, denting the metal and shattering the back windshield. He shook himself and sprang at her again, venom dripping from his slavering jaws. Beck slipped on a puddle of spilled drink and went down on one knee. Elgdrek slashed her across the face with his claws. Pain exploded in her head. She dropped the bottle and it rolled away. She scrambled after it.

Elgdrek stomped after her and jerked her upright by the arm. His claws sliced through the sleeve of her leather jacket and punctured her skin.

"Got you," he said, his eyes red with rage.

"Got you back, asshole," Beck said, plunging her left hand into the monster's chest.

She wrapped her hand around the dark blob that pulsed near

the boy's heart. She expected heat, the kind that melted stone. But the demon was cold.

A spasm of agony shot up her hand and arm. She gasped and yanked her hand back, taking the demon with her. She tried to let go, she *wanted* to let go, but the ring had a mind of its own. A look of stunned surprise crossed Elgdrek's hideous face and his nightmarish features blurred and disappeared. Beck stumbled back. The boy swayed in front of her, his face a ghastly white. He did the eye roll thing, same as the girl, and down he went.

Beck hardly noticed. She held a twisting, coiling thing in her grasp. The wraith tried to free itself, but the ring held on, intractable and relentless. Like Conall, she thought, gritting her teeth against the pain. Her hand was frozen, chalky white as marble, and it hurt like a son of a bitch. The petrifying cold moved up her arm, turning her flesh to stone.

The ring flared and Elgdrek dissolved into dust with a shriek of anguish.

Beck spotted the hot sauce bottle lying on its side near the back of the truck. She walked over and picked it up. There were moth-eaten holes in Haggy's smoky form. Beck tilted the bottle and the demon skittered to the other side.

Pepper sauce; demons were allergic to pepper sauce. Beck threw back her head and laughed. Bet that was something else Conall didn't know. She couldn't wait to lecture Mr. Know-it-all on the djegrali. He'd probably explode.

Nearby, a man was screaming; probably one of the kith, injured in the stampede. Beck looked around and saw Evan, rolling around on the ground. His skin blistered and smoked. She blinked in confusion. What ailed him? Her gaze moved from Evan to the hot sauce bottle, and back again. Her brain made the connection, and her amusement fled. The bindings; Evan felt Hagilth's pain as his own.

Evan struggled to his knees. "Get her," he screamed at Charlie. "Bring her and the bottle to me."

Time to go. Maybe she could help the Skinner girl. Cradling

her useless left arm close to her breasts, Beck jumped off the back of the truck.

Charlie was on his feet and staggering around, looking dazed. "Wha? Whudda you want me to do?"

Beck rammed him with her good shoulder as she ran past, knocking him on his can.

It felt good—maybe not as good as beating the crap out of the lowlife, but pretty damn good.

Grinning, she raced for the woods. She reached the trees and looked back.

Her elation died. Evan was astride an enormous, thick-bodied creature with leathery, mud-colored skin. The burns on his face were already healing and his skin and clothes no longer smoked. Beck checked the bottle. The demon had wedged itself in the neck of the container like a cork to avoid the scalding pepper sauce.

"Cooo-kie," Evan said. His monstrous steed bounded across the meadow in awkward, jarring leaps. "You're not playing nice with brother."

The monster paused to sniff the air. Meat Hooks' pink shirt hung in tatters around the creature's thick neck like a frilly collar.

Beck stepped out of the trees and into view. "Sorry, bro. I never learned to play nice."

Evan urged his hideous mount forward a few lurching steps. "Give me the bottle now, and I won't let her hurt you."

Yeah, right. He'd turn Haggy loose. He wouldn't have a choice. Somehow, she didn't think Haggy was very happy with her, not after she'd killed Elgdrek and given the bitch an acid bath.

Somewhere back there, two teens were lying on the back of the truck. If she lured Evan away from the lodge, they'd have a chance to come-to and find their way home. She had to give them that chance.

"I mean it, Cookie," Evan said. "No more games."

He was closer now, maybe fifty yards away. A couple of leaps, and he'd be on her. She needed time. She needed to stall him.

She knew what she had to do, though the thought made her cringe.

"You want it?" she said. She held up the bottle for him to see. Tears trickled down her cheeks. "Come and get it."

"No, Cookie, no," Evan shouted, throwing his hands over his head.

Beck shook the bottle. Hard. Pepper sauce coated the demon wedged at the top. Haggy thrashed and flailed like a runover snake.

Beck turned and ran into the woods. She ran until she couldn't hear Evan screaming anymore.

Chapter Nineteen

Beck stopped to catch her breath and held up the bottle, taking care not to tip it. The demon clung to the glass like a sickly black spider. The sun was setting and the shadows were deep. A slight breeze rustled through the woods, scenting the chilly air with the smell of pine needles and the musty odor of dried leaves and lichen. Somewhere in the woods up ahead, she heard the frenzied cries of the kith on Verbena's trail.

Or at least she thought they were up ahead. She'd flailed through the woods in a blind panic, eager to put distance between her and Evan, and now she was completely turned around. She had no idea where she was or how to find the Skinner girl. She wished she had Toby's snoot. Tracking was not one of her gifts.

As if summoned by her thoughts, a lean, shaggy dog slunk out of the bushes with his head down.

"Don't give me that hang dog look," she said, adopting a scolding tone to hide her relief. "You should be ashamed of yourself. You tried to bite me."

Toby rolled over and showed his belly.

"Oh, stop." She set the bottle on the ground and gave the dog an affectionate rub. "You know I can't stay mad at you. Are you feeling better?"

The dog bounced back to his feet, and barked.

"I'll take that as a 'yes.' " She wasn't surprised. Most kith metabolized alcohol at a rapid rate, which was good for business at the bar. Shifting took a lot of energy and speeded up the process. "I need your help to find someone."

She held out Verbena's bandanna for Toby to inspect—she'd snagged it off the ground on impulse as she made her mad dash for the woods. Toby gave the cloth a brief, disinterested sniff, and turned his attention to her injured face and arm. He cocked his head and looked at her as if to say *What happened to you?*

"I had a run-in with a demon," she explained. She rested her good hand on his rough head. "I'll be fine. We need to find the girl who was wearing this scarf. Her name is Verbena and she's in big trouble." The mournful, yodeling howl of a coyote rose above the noise of a large pack of animals on the prowl. "Hear that?" Beck said. "That's the kith. Charlie Skinner set the pack on his own daughter. Nice, huh?"

Toby swallowed a yowl.

"Yeah, I think it's shitty, too." She picked up the bottle, taking care not to slosh the contents, and got to her feet. She couldn't care less about Hagilth, but the sound of Evan's screams would haunt her for a long time. She hoped he'd given up the chase, for both their sakes. "Do you think you can find her?"

Toby rolled his mismatched eyes as if to say *duh.*

"Good. I'm counting on you, 'cause I'm totally lost."

BOOM.

Something big crashed in the woods to the east. Beck's pulse quickened. It was a tree. A tree had fallen, that was all. Trees fall all the time. Storms, insects, and disease weaken them. They topple from age and—

BOOM. Another crash.

Two trees falling? Unlikely but not impossible, especially if they grew close together. The first one could have hit the second one going down.

Maybe it wasn't a tree at all. Maybe it was thunder. Yeah, that made sense. A storm was coming.

A mocking voice made her jerk in alarm and brought her pleasant little trip through the Land of Denial to a screeching halt.

"Cooo-kie."

Ah, hell. Not thunder and not a tree; Evan. She should have known he wouldn't quit. *Couldn't* quit, until he freed Hagilth. It was the bindings.

She held the bottle aloft with shaking hands. "Let him go, you sick piece of shit," she said to the shriveled demon. "He's suffered enough because of you."

Words formed on the surface of the glass.

He is mine and you will die.

"Predictable," Beck said. "You know, Haggy, I'm starting to dislike you."

She shoved the bottle back in her pocket.

BOOM. BOOM.

"You've been a bad girl, Cookie." Evan sounded closer now. "I'm not happy with you."

Toby gave a questioning whine.

"A lot happened after you left," Beck said. "I found out that Evan's the zombie maker."

Toby cocked his head.

"Yeah, it surprised me, too," Beck said in answer to his unspoken question. "There was a fight. I killed a demon and trapped another one. Turns out, the demons put some kind of curse on Evan." She patted her pocket. "He won't stop until he gets this one back. He can't—she controls him."

Toby growled.

"No, leave it alone." Beck grabbed him by the scruff of the neck. Toby was a big dog, but nowhere near big enough to tangle with Evan and that thing he was riding. "Let's find the girl and get out of here."

Toby whined in disgust, but put his nose to the ground. He ran this way and that, his tail waving like a flag as he sought the scent. Beck tried to keep up, but her adrenaline high from the fight was wearing off and so was the alcohol. The scratches on her cheek throbbed and her arm hurt like a son of a bitch.

"Coo-kie."

Beck swore and broke into a jog. Evan was toying with her,

trying to break her. Trying to make her feel like a hunted animal.

It was working.

"Coo-kie. ."

"Shut the hell up," she muttered.

She pressed her hand against her leather jacket. The hot sauce bottle bulged against her palm.

Shake it. That'll slow his ass down. So what if it burns him? He's nothing to you. A stranger. Think of the things he's probably done, the people he's hurt. He sure as hell won't hesitate to hurt you.

It's you or him. Do it.

She drew her hand away. No; not unless she had no other choice. She kept running.

She was gasping for breath when Toby disappeared into a stand of scrubby bushes. The shrubbery shook and something moved in the branches, something big.

Beck halted, staring at the trembling shrubbery with unease. What now? Bad enough Evan and My Little Monster Pony were behind them. God-knows-what waited in the bushes.

Beck picked up a stick and edged closer. "Toby?"

The underbrush parted and Toby trotted out. At his heels was a black bear—Hank.

Verbena Skinner rode astride Hank's broad back. Her arms and legs were covered in scratches, and her fried hair stuck out every which way.

Verbena gave Beck the once-over. Beck didn't blame her for being skittish, not after the way she'd been treated.

"Who are you?" Verbena demanded. Her large eyes were slightly bulbous, like a purple-eyed cocker spaniel, giving her a perpetually startled look.

"I'm a friend of the bear's."

Verbena poked the bear with her finger. "That so?"

Hank rumbled in response.

"That must be why he took off a-running. He smelt you." Verbena seemed to relax a little. "I tried to git him to turn, but he weren't having none of it." Her pop eyes widened at a chorus of yodeling yips in the woods nearby. "We'd best git. The bear done kilt two of them, but the rest are coming on, fast, and there's a passel of them."

BOOM.

"*Coo-kie.*" Evan's voice rang through the woods, closer still. Verbena clutched the bear's thick, black fur. "What's that?"

"My brother."

"He sounds pissed."

"He is. I'm at the top of his shit list at the moment."

"Know what that's like," Verbena said. "I got brothers."

Yes, she did, Beck thought with a shudder. Compared to Earl, Evan was a prize.

"*Coo-kie.*"

BOOM. BOOM.

Then again, maybe not.

"If you can get us to the road, Toby can hotwire a car and get us out of here," Beck said. "Right, Tobe?"

Toby barked.

"Road's this a-way," Verbena said.

She kicked her bony heels against the bear's flanks, and Hank turned and padded off. Toby ran ahead of the bear. Beck followed at a clumsy trot. She was winded, her ribs ached from Meat Hooks' embrace, and her brain felt hot and fuzzy. Her frozen arm hung useless at her side, hard and heavy as concrete. The slashes on her cheek throbbed.

If this was what "sick" felt like, then it sucked to be a norm. Sweat trickled between her breasts and down her back, and every step was an effort. Elgdrek's claws were probably poisonous, she reflected glumly. If she weren't kith, she'd already be dead.

Unbidden, Conall's face swam before her. Poison or no poison, she couldn't die. She had to tell Conall about the hot sauce. It was important, and *she'd* discovered it, not him. She was looking forward to telling him about it. It was going to be sweet.

Thinking about Conall made her feel better, stronger. Not that she gave a flying flip about him. God, no. That would be pathetic. Poor little demonoid crushing on the big bad demon hunter.

BOOM. *BOOM.*

BOOM.

Her heart rate slowed. They were losing Evan. She stumbled and almost fell. Her lungs burned and her jaw and neck felt stiff. Slowing to catch her breath, she listened. A warbling howl drifted from another section of the woods. By some miracle, they'd eluded the kith, too.

The sound of a slow-moving truck reached her ears. Relief surged through her. They were close to the road. They were going to make it.

Toby and the bear broke into a lope, and Beck struggled to keep up. She huffed up a gentle slope, her boots sinking into the thick carpet of fallen leaves. She was tired, so tired, but eager to get out of these creepy woods. Toby, Verbena, and the bear waited at the bottom of the swell.

Toby stood stiff-legged, hackles raised, his gaze fixed on a shallow ravine in front of them, one of many that creased the rolling woodland. Most were dry and filled with rotting leaves, tumbled, mossy stones, and slender saplings stretching eager limbs toward the sunlight. This one, though, held a small spring. It wasn't visible from here, but the steady trickle of water sang its presence.

Beck's weariness and pain eased. Being near water always strengthened her.

She joined them at the foot of the hill. "What is it?"

"Dunno," Verbena said. The bear grunted and swayed back and forth, his snout in the air. "They smell something."

Verbena dismounted and picked up a stout branch.

"Just in case," she said.

Beck was looking around for a stick of her own when the kith attacked.

Conall slammed his fist into the padded panel in front of him. "By the sword, this machine is infernally slow. Can you not make it go faster?"

"Take it easy," Cassie said. "You crack my dashboard and you'll pay to have it fixed."

"I will gladly buy you an entire fleet of conveyances, if you will but hurry."

"I've never been here before. It's private land and most of these dirt roads are unmarked," Cassie said. "If we don't go slow, we'll miss the turn."

Conall tamped down his rage and frustration. The ring had been activated. He'd felt it blaze to life and consume the demon. And then it went dark.

What was happening? Rebekah was somewhere near and in need. He could feel it. And because he could not see her or her surroundings, he could not hasten to her in the way of the Dalvahni, navigating through space and time in the blink of an eye.

Instead, he was trapped in this modern coach traveling at a snail's pace down yet another nameless dirt track.

It was enough to drive a warrior berserk.

He rested his fists on his thighs and willed his roiling impatience to dissipate. This insanity must cease and desist. Rebekah's well-being had become far too important to his peace of mind. He would end it now.

Today.

He would find Rebekah and ensure her safety. Then he would leave, reconnoiter, and find another base from which to uncover the djegrali's plans. He would never see her again. Things would be as they were before. He would fix his thoughts on duty and the hunt, and forget Rebekah Damian. His strange fascination with her was an aberration. It would fade in a year, a decade, a few centuries at most.

Cassie slowed the truck to a crawl. "Let me see. It may be that we should have turned back there . . ."

Conall seethed with irritation as she checked the directions on the invitation for the thousandth time.

Not strictly true. The actual number was twenty-seven. He had counted.

A warrior does not exaggerate, he reminded himself sternly.

Such uncharacteristic behavior strengthened his resolve to

leave. The Dal did not engage in hyperbole. A Dalvahni warrior was calm and rational, succinct and economical in speech and thought, his actions ruled by logic and unfettered by emotion. Embellishment, overstatement, and flights of fancy were a human indulgence outside the purview of his kind.

"Third road on the right." Cassie swung the wheeled contraption down yet another nameless rough trail. "Yep, this is it."

"Thank the gods," he muttered. "We have explored every infernal pig track in the past ten leagues and wasted the better part of a day doing it."

Cassie shot him a look. "We left Beck's less than an hour ago, and we've made one wrong turn."

"Exactly," Conall said through his teeth. He lifted his head, listening. "Stop the carriage."

"It's a truck, not a carriage."

"Stop *now.*"

"All right, all right." Cassie applied the brakes. "You don't have to bite my head off."

There was a hollow boom from the northeast.

"Hear that?"

"We're in the middle of the woods. Somebody's cutting down trees," Cassie said. "Big deal."

"At nightfall?"

"People do all kinds of stupid things, usually prefaced by, 'Hey, y'all, watch this,' followed by some bubba getting himself dead."

Deep in the woods, there was a strange, wavering cry, followed by another and another.

Conall's senses sharpened. "Wolves," he said, "coursing large game, a deer perhaps."

"We don't have wolves in Alabama. Those are coyotes."

Conall processed the strange term with his translator. *Coyote: a small wolflike carnivore with slender build, large ears, and a narrow muzzle. Similar to the jackals of Algroth, only with four legs, not six.*

The excited yips and howls of the coyotes mingled with the deep bay of a hound, the unmistakable growl of a large feline, and other animal sounds Conall did not recognize. The scene in the bar from the night before flashed through his mind, a strange menagerie of shape-shifters wreaking havoc before running off into the night.

"Do these coyotes run in packs with other wild creatures?"

"No," Cassie said, frowning. "That must be the kith. From the sound of it, their blood's up about something."

He flung open the vehicle door and climbed out.

BOOM. BOOM.

No woodcutter, that; a behemoth moving through the woods, destroying everything in its path. The djegrali had such power. He opened his mind and caught a faint trace of demon, too faint and weak to be the cause of such havoc.

BOOM. BOOM.

"Coo-kie," someone shouted.

Evan, the brother; headed in the same direction as the kith and seeking the same prey.

Rebekah.

A black rage seized Conall. He clamped down on it, calling instead upon the detachment that had served him so well for centuries. He was steel and ice, relentless and unforgiving. Cloaking himself in the merciless cold, he stalked through the woods toward the sounds of battle.

Chapter Twenty

The kith boiled out of the gulch, dozens of them in animal form. They'd divided their numbers, clever creatures. While a few sounded the chase in another part of the woods, the rest had crouched in the leaf-choked gorge, waiting to spring the trap.

Beck gave up looking for a stick and broke off a tree limb to use against them. Exhaustion and her injuries made the task more difficult than it should have been, given her kith strength, but staring a snarling posse of wild animals down the throat was sufficient motivation to get the job done.

A group of coyotes with dingy fur, black markings, and the Skinner sneaky looks led the attack. Eyes glowing red from the combined effects of blood lust, gold fever, and Charlie's magic elixir, and they charged.

Hank met them head-on. The bear swung a great paw and a coyote went flying. He swatted another one. It yelped and hit the ground in a limp heap.

Toby went after a third. He caught the smaller canine in his jaws, slung it to the ground, and went for the belly.

The rest of the kith wised up. Making a wide circle around the dog and the bear, they swarmed Verbena.

"Go 'way," she shrieked, batting at the snarling animals with her stick.

A raccoon with eyes the color of blood latched on to one of Verbena's skinny legs and dug in with teeth and claws. Verbena screamed and danced around, but the animal held on. Wading into the fray, Beck pulled the coon off Verbena's leg and flung it aside. A collie–German shepherd mix slunk forward, belly to the ground, and rushed them. Beck downed it with a kick to the head.

"Put your back to mine," Beck told Verbena. "We'll fight better that way."

Verbena complied. The next few minutes went by in a blur. *Thwack.* Beck bashed a bobcat in the head. *Thwack, double thwack.* She knocked aside an oversized ferret and two gigantic possums. On top of everything else, Charlie's moonshine had supersized some of the kith.

Creepiest of all was a jumbo bunny with burning eyes and incisors like a saber-toothed tiger. The Velveteen rabbit on Skinner crack. She punted it aside. It was soft and squishy, like kicking a teddy bear. Ugh.

Verbena was crying. Racking sobs shook her thin body, but she kept swinging her stick.

Kick, jab, bash, bonk, smack, thunk. The fight took on a rhythm of its own.

Beck ignored the pain in her head and the leaden weight of her frozen arm and concentrated on fending off the kith with her makeshift club. Her right arm ached from use, but she gritted her teeth and kept moving, always moving, back to back with Verbena.

Sweat poured down her face and stung her eyes. She was exhausted but the kith were tiring, too. Unconscious and injured animals lay in heaps on the ground. A Doberman limped off on three legs. Other animals followed.

Beck wiped her brow and looked around. Two coyotes remained. They were baiting the bear. Hank smacked one to the ground. Growling, he chased the other one into the brush. Toby went after them.

Beck dropped the tree limb and sank to the ground. Verbena collapsed beside her.

"It's over," Verbena said. Her voice sounded hoarse. "We won."

A twig snapped and Earl Skinner stepped from behind a tree. "I wouldn't be counting your chickens just yet, baby sister."

Verbena jumped up, her expression wary. *"Earl."*

There were half a dozen men and women with him, all with the sly, narrow-faced Skinner looks. Damn. The decoy group; Beck had forgotten about them in the excitement of the fight.

Earl slapped one of the men on the back. "Told ya if we bided our time she'd be ours for the taking."

Beck struggled to her feet and hefted the tree limb. "Go away. There's been enough killing for one day."

"I want that gold." Earl jerked his thumb at Verbena. "Git over here, shit for brains. Don't make me come after you."

"Leave her alone," Beck said. "You want the gold, it's yours. It's back at the house."

It was a bluff. She didn't know squat about demon gold. For all she knew, it had dissolved in a puff of ash along with El-gdrek. She hadn't stuck around long enough to find out.

Earl spat. "Them demons ain't gonna give us diddley unless we do what they say."

"The demons won't be a problem," Beck said. "I killed one of them and I got the other one in my pocket."

"Hear that?" Earl nudged his nearest kinsman. "She's got a demon in her pocket. Bet mine's bigger."

The Skinners laughed.

"Don't you ever get tired of waving your dick around, Earl?" Beck said.

Earl's amused expression vanished. "Tell you what I am tired of. I'm tired of you treating me like a dumbass. You ain't kilt no demon and you don't give a damn about my worthless sis-ter. You want that gold for yourself."

Verbena took a step back, her eyes wide. "Is it true? Are you after the gold?"

"No," Beck said. "Don't listen to him."

"You think a bunch of strangers care about you more 'n your family?" Earl said. "Now, git your skinny ass over here and make yourself useful for once."

Verbena shook her head. "I won't. I heard what they said. You're gonna hurt me."

"Aw, hell, Beenie, I'm your brother. Blood takes care of blood. We got your back. Right, y'all?"

The Skinners made noises of agreement.

Verbena hesitated, fear and uncertainty plain on her face.

"Hell with this," Earl said. "I'm done being nice."

He lifted his arm and Beck saw the gleam of metal.

"Look out," she cried. "He's got a gun."

She dropped the stick and tackled Verbena as the gun went off. The bullet thudded into the forest floor, missing them by inches.

Furious, Beck rolled to her feet. "Drop the gun."

Earl laughed. "Or what? We got you outnumbered and you ain't armed."

He whirled around at a noise. "What's that?"

A large, gray animal launched itself at Earl from the bushes.

"Toby, *no*," Beck screamed.

Earl squeezed the trigger, and the dog crumpled at his feet.

The rage simmering inside of Beck boiled over. Watery hands plunged out of the ground and grabbed the Skinners by the legs. The gun sailed out of Earl's hand and behind a tree as he was jerked off his feet and buried up to his waist in the dirt. Cursing and screaming, the rest of the Skinners were dragged down beside him, planted in the ground like a bunch of butt-ugly tulips.

Beck ran over to Toby. He shifted and sat up, holding his injured leg.

"You're bleeding like a stuck pig," Beck said, hunkering down beside him. "How bad is it?"

"Just a flesh wound."

She handed him Verbena's bandanna. "Tie this around your leg. We've got to slow the bleeding till we can get out of here."

BOOM. BOOM.

"What's that?" Earl's voice was shrill. "What's that noise?"

Evan had heard the commotion. When it rained, it poured.

"Shift back, Tobes," Beck said. "It'll be easier to walk on three legs."

"Can't. Too tired and wrung out."

BOOM. BOOM.

"Coo-kie."

Shit. She had one nerve left, and Evan was stomping all over it.

"Cookie? Who's Cookie?" Earl said.

"Let's get you on your feet," Beck said, ignoring Earl. "We need to get out of here."

"Here, let me help." Verbena looked at Beck and flushed. "I owe you."

"You git your ass over here and dig us out, Beenie." Sweating and straining, Earl tried to pull himself out of the ground. "You hear me?"

The rest of the Skinners added their two cents' worth, which mostly consisted of a lot of cussing and name calling. It would take a sensitivity coach a month of Sundays to make a dent in the Skinners' lack of couth.

"No," Verbena said, shouting them down. "I'm through with you. Dig yourselves out or stay there till spring for all I care."

Turning her back on them, she helped Beck get Toby to his feet. He draped his arms around their shoulders. Together, the three of them started for the road.

The cries of the Skinners faded behind them, and the woods became quiet but for the crunch of their feet on the leaves and the strained huff of their breath. No more taunts from Evan, no more nerve-racking booms and thumps and crashes.

Beck should have been relieved, but the unnatural silence stretched her nerves tighter and tighter. Where was Evan? He hadn't given up. She knew better than that. He was playing with them, a cat toying with three mice.

The forest held its breath, waiting.

"Something's coming," Toby muttered. He paused to catch his breath in the hollow between two tree-covered slopes. "Feel it?"

Oh, yeah, she felt it. A dark, brooding force was headed their way, something cold and deadly; something single minded and tenacious.

Beck swallowed. "It's Evan. He wants Haggy."

"It ain't Evan," Toby said. "This here's something worse."

What could be worse than Evan and the Neanderthal twins? The morkyn. Beck's heart lurched into a crooked rhythm. They'd found out about Elgdrek. They were coming to avenge his death.

OhGodohGodohGod. She tried to think, but her brain was mush.

A thought trickled through her panic. Leave, she should leave, lead the demons away from Toby and Verbena.

The sound of a gunshot made her jump. She stilled, listening. Somewhere in the forest, a large animal bawled in pain. She heard the howl of a coyote, followed by a man's startled shout.

"That sounded like Hank," Beck said. This was her excuse to get away, to separate herself from Toby and Verbena. "I'd better go see."

"Let me," Verbena said, darting away.

So much for that idea.

Beck tightened her arm around Toby. "Come on, let's keep moving."

They took a few steps and the hillside in front of them rumbled and broke away. A hulking creature rose out of the dirt and leaves. The smell of wet and rot choked the air.

"Hello, Cookie," Evan said, looking down at them from the shoulders of the mud monster.

Beck's stomach did a queasy flip. Evan's skin was red and oozing, and pockmarked with blisters. She had done this to him.

"You look terrible, bro."

Evan's swollen, peeling wreck of a mouth curved. "Gee, I wonder why."

The ground shifted again, and a second monster rose out of the ground. A tattered bit of blue cloth hung around the ugly creature's muscular neck.

It was Baldy, the other guard. Evan had called in reinforcements.

"No more games, Cookie," Evan said. "Give me the bottle or I'll turn Ragluk and Algg loose on you. Trolls are always hungry and not very picky about what they eat."

Wonderful; Meat Hooks and Baldy were flesh-eating trolls. This day just kept getting better and better.

Beck closed her hand around the bottle in her pocket. A long, gray tongue shot out of Baldy's mouth, coiled around Toby's waist, and lifted him off the ground.

Toby pounded his fists against the rubbery binding. "Let me go, you ugly sum bitch."

"Shake the bottle again, Cookie, and it's snack time for Algg," Evan warned. The troll retracted his tongue and gave Toby's wounded leg a hungry, lingering sniff. "Or you can stand there and watch your friend get eaten alive."

"Beck?" Toby's voice went up a couple of notches.

Beck opened her senses. There was an underground stream nearby, but it was buried deep beneath earth and stone, and she was tired, so very tired. She couldn't use Conall's ring. It was fused to her frozen hand. She couldn't shift and leave Toby. Algg would make a Happy Meal out of him.

"Okay, you win." Beck held up the hot sauce container. "Take the damn bottle. Just don't hurt him."

Ragluk snagged the jar from Beck with a flick of his long tongue.

"I thought you'd see it my way," Evan said, taking the container from the troll. "You're too soft, Cookie. That's your problem."

"I don't suppose you'd give me and Toby a head start before you open that bottle?" Beck asked.

"Sorry, Cookie." There was genuine regret and something like sorrow in Evan's eyes. "No can do."

He had his hand on the bottle cap, about to untwist it, when the morkyn attacked.

Chapter Twenty-one

The demon streaked out of the trees, black and formless as the darkness at the bottom of a well. Beck had never seen anything move so fast. There was no time to react, no time to move. It was simply *there*. Beck felt its pulsing rage. It wanted blood and death.

A claw flashed out of the darkness, and the troll Evan rode bellowed in pain. A red line formed across the troll's distended belly and widened, like a gaping, grotesquely lipsticked mouth. Ragluk's innards spilled out of the wound and onto the leaves with a wet, sickening plop. The troll stared at the steaming gray mass at his feet, an expression of dull incomprehension on his blunt, ugly face.

The troll toppled over and Evan jumped free. His right leg crumpled under him as he fell. Evan grunted in pain and dropped the bottle. It rolled away. Hot sauce slopped against the glass, engulfing the wraith inside. Evan screamed in pain as he and Haggy began to burn.

With a roar, Algg dropped Toby and attacked the morkyn. The troll was strong, but his movements were slow and ponderous. He swung a ham-size fist. The shadow darted out of the way. Again, the troll attacked, and the dark blur danced aside. The demon was toying with the troll, pitiless and relentless, a killing machine.

Beck looked around. Evan had vanished. The hot sauce bottle lay abandoned under a bush. Snatching it up, she shoved it back in her pocket and ran over to Toby.

"Let's get out of here," she said, tugging him to his feet.

"Becky, wait—"

"Not now, Toby."

She pulled, half carried Toby up the hill, terror giving her strength. Something, morbid curiosity, maybe, made her look back, like Lot's wife.

The little glen was coated in sheets of ice. The demon circled Algg once, twice, three times. Blood spurted. The troll bawled like a wounded calf and crashed to his misshapen knees. The claw flashed again and the troll's head hit the leaves with a muffled *thunk*.

The demon turned in their direction. Cold and hate and power poured from the black cloud in sickening waves. It had taken out the two trolls in a matter of seconds, and they were next.

Beck threw Toby over her shoulder in a fireman's carry and ran like hell. She forgot about being tired and injured. It didn't matter that her heart chugged like a diesel engine from terror and exertion, or that her legs burned from the strain of running with Toby's extra weight. She kept going.

Which way was the road? Her feet sank in the thick carpet of leaves, slowing her down. Her muscles screamed. Tomorrow, she would be sore.

If there was a tomorrow; the back of her neck prickled and her nerves shrieked in warning. The demon had followed. The temperature plummeted, and the air crackled with the energy and fury of a building ice storm. Trees groaned and shattered around them, sundered by the morkyn's arctic passage.

Don't think about it. Don't look back. Move your ass, Damian, or you and Toby are done for.

Twilight was fading. Sweat stung her eyes, making it hard to see. She tripped over a log and fell. Toby rolled free, clutching his wounded leg with a muffled curse.

A blast of cold swept over them, riming the ground with frost.

"Run, Toby," Beck said. "Get away. *Run.*"

Darkness enveloped her and Beck screamed as she was lifted in an icy, iron grasp.

"Calm yourself," a dispassionate voice said. "You are safe."

The mantle of gloom dissolved and she was in Conall's arms.

Relief surged through Beck and, on its heels, disbelief. "Conall?" She stared up at him in shock. "I thought you were a demon."

"I tried to tell you." Toby sat up with a groan. "But you wouldn't listen. I recognized his scent."

"Why didn't you *say* something?" Beck said, struggling in Conall's grasp. "You scared the hell out of me."

"I was occupied." Conall set her down and stepped back. His cold gaze moved to the scratches on her cheek. "You are hurt."

"It's nothing. Toby's been shot."

Conall picked Toby up and threw him over his shoulder. "A female demonoid named Cassandra brought me here in her truck," he said with glacial calm. "She is waiting for us some distance down the road."

"Cassie?" Beck said. "How do you know Cass—"

Conall grabbed her arm and pulled her close. The world shifted and blurred and they were standing in the road by a long-bed Chevy Silverado.

Beck stepped away from him, irritated by his caveman manner and Ice Man attitude.

"Look here, buddy," she said. "I don't know who planted the bug up your butt, but I don't appreciate being manhandled."

"Now is not the time for discourse," Conall said. His black eyes were cold and hard as flint. "We will discuss this later."

"I don't have anything to say to you."

"Perhaps not, but I have a great deal to say to you."

The driver's side door opened and Cassie Fergusson climbed out.

"I see you found her." Cassie's gaze moved to the man on Conall's shoulder. "That a sack of flour you carrying, or Toby?"

"Har de har har," Toby said as Conall shrugged him to the ground. He balanced on his good leg. "Earl Skinner shot me. Next time I see that little weasel I'm gonna tie his dick in a knot."

"That must've been some party." Cassie jerked her thumb

toward the eight-foot cargo hold. "I got four naked guys and an injured bear in the back. There's a girl with them."

Hank and Verbena. Beck hurried to the back of the truck, glad for the excuse to get away from Mr. Freeze.

Verbena sat cross-legged on the truck bed beside the wounded bear. Hank's eyes were open and he was panting. The fur on his left shoulder was bloody.

The members of Beelzebubba huddled together under two blankets, looking cold and miserable.

"What happened?" Beck asked. She climbed over the tailgate with some difficulty due to her petrified arm.

Sam, the drummer in the band, spoke up. "Two men were in the woods with guns. They shot Hank."

"Would've kilt him, too," Verbena said, " 'cepting these here coyote fellers runned 'em off."

"Kith or norms?" Beck asked.

"Kith," Sam said. He stroked the soul patch under his bottom lip. "They were hepped up on something. Kept shifting back and forth like they couldn't control it. Whatever they were on made them crazy." He shook his head. "Hank wasn't the only one they shot. Them idiots was shooting at anything that moved. I'm pretty sure they killed Lloyd Hagenbarth's boy, Phil."

Phil Hagenbarth was dead? He was twenty-two, and a nice young man. He drove a beer truck with his dad. Beck felt sick. How many kith had been hurt and killed because of Charlie's poison?

"What are you guys doing out here, anyway?" she asked. "It's a long way from the bar. You coming from the Peterson party?"

Sam shook his head. "Don't know anything about a party. Hank likes to run these woods. We were having a good time when all of a sudden he growled and took off. He came back a little while later, and that's when them idiots shot him." Sam's eyes glowed hot in the gloom. "Me and the boys went after the bastards. I hamstrung one of them." His mouth curved in a vicious smile. "He'll walk with a limp from now on."

"They got away?" Beck asked.

"Yeah," Sam said. "They jumped in a car and took off. We shifted and got Hank out of there." He gazed at the bear with a troubled expression. "What we going to do about him? We can't take him to a hospital, He's too weak to shift."

"We'll think of something," Beck said. She sat down near the tailgate to give the bear and the band members plenty of room. "Thanks for helping Hank."

"My ass is cold," Bill the sound guy complained, shifting with an audible pop.

Harry and Joe shifted too. Three tawny gray coyotes aimed identical laughing grins at Beck.

"Sorry," Sam said. Hair sprouted on his face, and his nose and jaw lengthened. "Can't help it. It's a pack thing."

Beck picked up one of the discarded blankets. She felt not the slightest urge to shift. She was too tuckered out. On the plus side, coyotes took up less room in the back of the truck.

"Coyotes." Toby shook his head in disgust. "I think I'll ride in the back with you so I can keep my leg straight."

He lowered the tailgate and eased in butt first, favoring his injured leg.

"Here." Beck tossed him the other blanket. "The temperature's dropping."

Conall appeared without warning. He held out his hand to Beck. "Come. You will sit inside with me where it is warm."

It was an order.

He could go suck an egg. She didn't sign up for his army.

"No, thanks," she said, trying without much success to match his frigid tone. "I'm staying here."

A muscle in his jaw twitched. It was the first reaction of any sort she'd seen from him since he'd shown up in his Grim Reaper guise.

"If it pleases you," he said.

Pleased her? Nothing about the past few hours had *pleased* her, especially his frostbitten attitude. It might be a cold ride in the back of the truck, but it was better than freezing her butt off around the Arctic Alpha Male.

Conall climbed in the cab of the truck and closed the door without another word. He didn't even slam it. Oh, no, not Mr. Control. You'd get more of a reaction out of a fire plug.

Fine by me, Beck thought as Cassie eased the truck onto the road. *Let him ride up front with Cassie. See if I care.*

The truck rolled through the tunnel of trees, kicking up a cloud of clay dust. The dry smell of dirt mingled with pine in the night air. The temperature had dropped with nightfall. Beck was cold and miserable, but she'd never admit it.

Images of the past few hours kept cycling through her head like scenes from a horror movie. So much bloodshed and mayhem. So much ugliness. She couldn't shake a heavy feeling of gloom.

She'd feel better once she got home and had a bath and a cup of tea, and a little kitty cat therapy. Mr. Cat was an excellent listener. She had lots to tell him.

She wiggled, trying to get comfortable. She was exhausted and sore, and the scratches on her face hurt. What if the damage to her arm was permanent? She was worried about the teenagers she'd left behind, and about Hank and Toby. She needed to figure out what to do with Verbena, and she was uneasy about Evan's sudden disappearance. Her bad mood had *nothing* to do with Conall.

Toby lifted his nose to the wind, like a dog hanging its head out a car window.

After a moment, he lowered his head and gave Beck a searching look. "Your arm hurt?"

"No, I can't feel it."

"Then why are you crying?"

Beck wiped her wet cheeks with the back of her hand. "I'm not crying. I *never* cry."

"It's for the best, Becky." His tone was gentle. "It wouldn't work. You're too different. A cat don't mate with a dog, you know."

"Don't worry about it," Beck said. "I'm not stupid enough to fall for a demon hunter. That would be crazy. I might as well take a nap on the railroad tracks, like Claude Dolan."

"Glad you're being sensible. I don't want to see you get hurt."

She'd known all along there couldn't be anything between her and Conall. That was a no-brainer.

She heard a low rumbling sound and looked back. The dirt road collapsed in on itself, and Evan rose out of the ground like an angry Poseidon bursting forth from an earthen sea, dirt flowing around him.

"Cookie," he shouted. He raised his arms; the earth crested and fell around him in giant waves. "This isn't over."

Evan brought his arms down, and a deep crack opened in the dirt road and raced toward them. A hailstorm of rocks pinged against the tailgate.

Toby pounded his fist against the side of the truck. "Put the pedal to the metal, Cassie," he shouted. "We got trouble."

Beck saw Cassie glance in the rearview mirror. The truck accelerated and they sped away.

Beck brushed the dirt off her jacket with her good hand. "That was close."

"Too close." Toby tucked the blanket around his legs. "You're going to have to do something about that brother of yours."

"What would you suggest?"

"Reckon that depends," Toby said. "He's running with them demons, ain't he?"

"Yes."

"You thinking of joining him?"

"Tobias Littleton. You know better."

"Don't get your knickers in a twist. I went MIA on you, and I needed to know." Toby tugged on his braid. "If you're going against them demons and your brother, you're gonna need help. I'll say one thing for our new bartender, he's a handy feller in a fight."

Handy was an understatement. Conall was death walking. He'd kill Evan.

"I'll handle Evan," she said. "I'll talk to him. Try and convince him to leave."

Toby snorted. "Not likely. Not as long as you got something he wants."

He was right. Evan wasn't going anywhere without Haggy.

"He's not going to change, baby girl," Toby said. "He is what he is, and there's no turning back."

"You talking about Conall or Evan?"

Toby closed his eyes. "Yep."

Chapter Twenty-two

After what seemed like a small forever, they left the woods and turned onto the paved, two-lane county road. They were a few miles outside Hannah when the blue lights came on.

Toby squinted at the Jeep Cherokee behind them. "Sheriff," he said with a grunt. "There ain't no end to this frigging day."

Beck's sentiments, exactly.

There was no emergency lane, so Cassie pulled onto the grass on the side of the road and rolled down her window. The coyotes and Toby exchanged a silent look of communication. The coyotes jumped out of the truck and vanished into the darkness, as silent as ghosts.

A tall, lean man wearing a sheriff's badge exited the Jeep and approached the driver's side window.

"Evening, ma'am," he said to Cassie. "You've got a broken tail-light."

"Really?" Cassie said. "I must have hit something on the road."

More like the road hit them, Beck thought, remembering the shower of earth and rocks from Evan's little temper tantrum.

The sheriff scribbled something down and handed Cassie a piece of paper.

"I'm issuing you a warning," he said. "But you need to get that tail-light fixed."

"Sure thing, Sheriff."

He walked back and shined his flashlight in the bed of the

truck. Toby stiffened and his nostrils flared. Something about the sheriff had sure gotten his attention.

The flashing lights on top of the patrol car cast the officer's face in relief. He was a handsome man, with a strong jaw and a firm-lipped mouth. Stubborn, more like it.

His eyes were shaded beneath the brim of his hat, but Beck got the impression he didn't miss much.

The beam of light came to rest on the bear's furry body. Hank lifted his head and growled.

"Shh," Verbena said, stroking him. "It's all right."

To Beck's amazement, Hank quieted back down. Verbena had a way with animals, or at least a way with one bear of a cook.

"It's against the law in Alabama to trap a black bear," the sheriff said.

"We didn't trap him," Beck said. "Some idiot shot him."

Beck winced as the sheriff moved the beam of light to her face. She could swear the sheriff's nose twitched.

"You a vet?" he asked.

"No, but—"

"My brother is learned in the care and healing of wild creatures," Conall said. "We are taking the animal to him."

Beck blinked in surprise. Conall had done the demon hunter thing, exiting the truck and moving to her side, swift and silent.

"That right?" the sheriff drawled. He pulled the pad back out of his pocket. "What's your name?"

Most cops would have been startled, to say the least, by Conall's *now you see me–now you don't* routine, but the sheriff didn't seem the least bit rattled.

"I am Dalvahni."

"Dalvahni?" The sheriff looked up. "Any relation to an Ansgar Dalvahni?"

Conall inclined his head. "He is my brother. You know him?"

"We've met." The notepad went back in the sheriff's pocket. "You folks been anywhere near the Peterson hunting preserve tonight?"

Cassie stuck her head out the window. "We were on Peterson land, but we had an invitation. Is there a problem?"

"One of my deputies got a call that a truck had run into a ditch near Musso," he said. "When he got there, he found two teenagers in the vehicle. They were pie faced and ranting about monsters at some fancy lodge. The description of the place sounded like the Petersons' hunting place."

Beck did a mental fist pump. The kids were safe; one less thing to worry about.

"Where are they now?" she asked.

She felt the sheriff's gaze on her and wished she'd kept her mouth shut. There was an air of intensity about this man that made her uneasy.

"On their way to the hospital in Paulsberg to be treated for alcohol poisoning," he said. "I'd sure like to know who got a couple of underage kids that liquored up. Don't suppose you know anything about it?"

"Nope," Beck lied. "Can't help you."

The sheriff's nose twitched again. "I see." He turned to go and looked back. "You can tell those coyotes to quit skulking around and get back in the truck. I'm leaving now."

He climbed back in the Jeep and drove off. Verbena got up without a word and lowered the tailgate. The coyotes slunk out of the darkness and sprang back into the truck. Verbena closed the tailgate and climbed back in.

"If you're afraid of wolves, stay out of the woods," Toby said as the truck bounced back onto the road.

"What's that supposed to mean?" Beck asked.

"It means that sheriff ain't no dummy."

No, he wasn't. He'd known about the coyotes, and she had a hunch he knew she hadn't told him the truth.

It was almost like the sheriff could smell a lie.

They made it back to the bar without further incident. The parking lot was empty except for a black and red truck with BEELZEBUBBA emblazoned down the sides, but the place was lit up like a Christmas tree.

"What's with all the lights?" Beck said. "It's Sunday. The bar's closed."

She hoisted herself to her feet. Oh, goody. She wasn't going to have to wait until tomorrow to be sore. The long ride in the cold night air had made her muscles stiff. She couldn't wait to get home and soak in the tub.

She took a deep breath, drawing the mossy scent of the river into her lungs. It was good to be out of those woods and back on her turf.

Cassie opened her door and got out. "Someone's playing a piano. Whoever they are, they're good."

Conall moved to the back of the truck in a blur of motion.

"I grew weary of the shade's incessant whining," he said. He crossed his arms and looked up at Beck, his expression as cold and hard as her marbleized arm. "So, I purchased a noisemaker. It would appear the instrument was delivered."

"Where'd you find a piano on a Sunday?" Beck said. "The nearest music store's in Mobile."

"I struck a bargain with the priest at the shade's former haunt."

"You talked Father Ben into selling you the piano at the Episcopal church?"

Conall shrugged. "I made it worth his while."

Beck felt a flutter of alarm. No telling what he paid for that piano. She'd have to reimburse him. "How much?"

"I do not recall the exact sum. Money is of no moment to the Dalvahni."

Money is of no moment to the Dalvahni. Well, it was damn sure "of moment" to most folks, including her. She and Toby had a business to run, and buying pianos for dispossessed ghosts wasn't in their budget.

Conall studied the latch on the tailgate a moment and then lowered it. The coyotes leaped out and trotted over to the black and red truck. Beck caught a flash of four naked butts as they shifted and jumped in their vehicle.

Sam rolled down the passenger window and held his thumb and little finger to his ear. "Call me and let me know how Hank's doing."

Beck waved good-bye. "Will do."

Toby scooted across the tailgate. Beck jumped off the truck and planted herself in front of him.

"Hold it right there, old man," she said. "Where do you think you're going?"

"Home."

"Think again. You've got a bullet in you. I'm taking you to Doc Dunn."

"No, you ain't. Take your own self to the doctor and see about that arm. I ain't tangled with no demon."

"What is this?" Conall said. "You fought one of the dje-grali?" Ignoring her protests, he pushed up the left sleeve of her jacket. She heard his sharp intake of breath. "Rebekah, what have you done?"

She looked down. Cassie had parked under a light pole, and visibility was good. Her arm and hand were fish-belly white and hard as concrete. The fingers of her left hand were curled into a fist. Her stomach did a slow roll. She was maimed, probably for good.

She shook off the awful thought. No, she wouldn't think about that now. She'd do a Scarlett O'Hara and worry about it later.

"I am taking you home," Conall said in a tone without compromise.

"I'm not going anywhere." Beck tugged her sleeve back in place. "Not until I make sure Toby and Hank are okay."

"Don't worry about me. I'm fine." Toby lowered his good leg to the ground and stood. "See?"

Cassie joined them at the rear of the truck. "Tell you what, Beck. I'll drop Toby off at Doc Dunn's house on my way home. I'll check on Dooley and then swing back by and pick him up. I'll call you and let you know what the doc says."

Toby waved his arms around. "Toby's right here. He ain't deaf and he ain't going to no dadflabbed doctor."

"You're going, Tobias Littleton, and that's it," Beck said. "You've got a bullet in your leg."

"It'll work its way out."

"You could get an infection."

"You go, then, if you're so all fired set on going to a doctor. You need it worse than me."

"Be sensible, Toby," Beck said. "I can't go to the doctor with a petrified arm. How will I explain it to Doc?"

"Tell the old coot to mind his own business."

"Enough." Conall picked up Toby and deposited him in the cab of the truck. "You will go to the leech and then you will let Rebekah know what he says. Understood?"

"Now see here—" Toby sputtered.

Conall put his hand on the open passenger door. A thick sheet of ice formed on the window and coated the metal frame. "Understood?"

"Yeah, yeah, I got it," Toby said. "No need to freeze my go-nads off."

"What about Hank?" Verbena asked as Conall closed the truck door and strode past her. "He's hurt real bad."

"My brother will see to the bear. He is here now." Conall turned and stared into the inky woods surrounding the bar. "Well met, Duncan."

Cassie made a choked sound. "Duncan?"

She scrambled back inside the truck and slammed the door. Beck caught a brief glimpse of Cassie's blond hair through the windshield before she ducked.

Beck was still puzzling over this odd behavior when a tall, broad-shouldered man melted out of the darkness. His shoulder-length hair was somewhere between blond and brown—hard to tell the exact shade in the dim light. In spite of his size, he moved with a stealthy grace, treading over the gravel in his booted feet without a sound. A form-fitting long-sleeve shirt clung to his taut torso and arms, and tobacco-brown breeches molded to his powerful thighs. Strapped across his wide chest was a leather and metal vest. He carried a sword on one hip.

The sheer size and masculine beauty of the stranger screamed Dalvahni. So did his solemn, unyielding expression. Jeez, was the entire Dalvahni race emotionally constipated?

"You sent for me, Captain?" he asked in a colorless voice.

Yep. Roger that. A truckload of Ex-Lax wouldn't loosen these guys up.

Conall pointed to the truck. "There is a wounded creature in yon carriage that needs your help."

In the blink of an eye, Duncan was kneeling beside the injured bear. Hank bawled and thrashed about in alarm.

Beck felt a subtle push of power, and then Duncan spoke. His deep voice was soothing, like a warm, healing balm.

"Easy, little brother," he said. "I mean you no harm."

Hank grunted and went limp.

"Wow." Verbena's thin face split in a goofy grin. Doctor Feelgood had whammied her, too. "Everything's all sparkly. Say something else."

Duncan examined the bear with gentle but practiced efficiency. "The shot went through the shoulder and entered the lung. I can save him, but he has lost much blood and the wound has festered. It will take time to heal. Have you a cage or stall to keep him in whilst he heals?"

"There's a room in the back of the bar with a bed and a small bathroom," Beck volunteered. "He can stay there until he's well."

Conall put his hand on Beck's shoulder. Cold spread from his palm and through her jacket, making her shiver. Holy smokes, he was running at subzero.

"Brother, this is Rebekah Damian," he said. "The tavern belongs to her and her partner. Yon bear is her cook."

"She has ensorcelled the creature to do her bidding like the Witch of Blandor?"

"Nay, the bear is a shifter," Conall said. "He was in his animal state when shot. No human leech would treat him. That is why I summoned you."

"Ah," Duncan said with a knowing nod. "He is kith."

"How do you know this?" Conall asked sharply. "I myself learned of the kith's existence but a few months past."

"'Tis not my first trip to this realm." Duncan got to his feet in a fluid movement, his face without expression. "I am sure I mentioned the demonoids in my report. Perhaps you overlooked it. The djegrali were causing much mischief in Tartolla at the time, as I recall. No doubt you were absorbed with weightier matters."

The words were accompanied by another subtle push of magic. Holy cow, Duncan was trying to whammy Conall.

Fat chance, Beck thought with a mental snort. "Conall" could be an acronym for *cynical overbearing naturally arrogant leery leader.*

Conall's grip tightened on her shoulder, sending another chill down her spine. Duncan Dalvahni was hiding something, and Conall knew it.

"Perhaps you are right," Conall said without inflection. He motioned and the employee door swung open. "The sleeping chamber Rebekah spoke of lies through that portal. Do you require assistance?"

"No. I will tend to the bear and report back to you."

"My thanks, brother," Conall said.

Duncan waved his hand, and the unconscious bear floated off the truck, across the parking lot, and through the open door.

Verbena shook herself out of her daze and climbed out of the cargo hold. "I'll stay with Hank." She gave Beck a shy look. "If it's all right with you, ma'am."

"Sure," Beck said. "Make yourself at home. Rustle you up something to eat in the kitchen and you'll find fresh towels in the bathroom. I keep extra clothes here. Help yourself to whatever you can find." She sized up Verbena's thin frame. "On second thought, they probably won't fit. I'll bring you something else to wear."

"Tomorrow," Conall said firmly. He draped his arm around her shoulders. "Rebekah has done enough for one day."

Verbena blushed. "Course. I owe her my life already."

Head down, she scooted through the back door of the bar.

Beck rounded on Conall. "Who died and left you in charge?"

"I do not understand the question."

"You know good and damn well *exactly* what I mean."

An engine roared to life. Cassie wheeled past them in the big Silverado, exiting the parking lot in a shower of gravel.

"That woman," Duncan said, staring after the truck. His formerly soothing voice was harsh and the patented Dalvahni wooden expression was gone. "Who was she?"

Beck eyed him curiously. "Cassie Fergusson."

"Cassandra," Duncan said, somehow making the name both a curse and a prayer.

Beck opened her mouth to ask Duncan how he knew Cassie, and the world slid out of focus and she fell.

Chapter Twenty-three

Beck spun through a whirling tunnel and stopped, landing on something solid. Home; she was home on her porch overlooking the water. She knew it before she opened her eyes. The wind rustled through the trees, scenting the night air with the smell of fern, mist, musty leaves, and damp earth. Nearby, the river sloshed against the shore in a familiar steady rhythm. On the far bank, a heron *go-go-go-go*ed, a slow croaking sound that built to a harsh *grawnk*.

Conall's arms were around her. He smelled clean and woodsy and he radiated strength and safety.

And a deep, intense cold. The guy seriously needed his thermostat adjusted.

She slipped from him arms. "What's the big idea? I was talking to Duncan."

"You are injured and exhausted. I decided it was time you came home."

"You decided?" Beck saw red. "News flash. You don't get to decide what I do. I'm not one of your men."

"I am well aware of that."

Brr, his tone was icy and aloof, almost robotic. What a difference a few hours made. This morning, Conall had been all macho concern: overprotective, testosterone ridden, gallant and solicitous. He'd threatened to remove Hank's nuts for prancing around in front of her naked, for Pete's sake.

Conall had been tender and teasing, and totally hot. And now he was a six-foot–four Popsicle. His Jekyll and Hyde transformation left Beck reeling and confused. Why the frigid attitude and the thundercloud of displeasure? She'd done what he asked, gone to the stupid party, and gotten information. For him. Not that he'd bothered to ask her about it.

Beck's chest ached and tears burned behind her eyes. Oh, no, she would not do this. She would *not* let him matter.

She lifted her chin. "I'm going inside. Good night."

"I will see to your injuries."

"No." Beck realized she had raised her voice and took a deep breath. "I mean, thank you very much, but I'll be fine."

It was a lie, of course. Her arm was totally messed up, and she had no idea what to do about it. Norm medicine couldn't fix it, but her arm could fall off before she'd ask Mr. Freeze for help.

Turning, she strode toward the porch door, back straight and head held high. Her splendid, dignified retreat lasted all of two steps before she stumbled over something large and furry.

She had time to register Mr. Cat's affronted yowl and the humiliating fact that she was about to bust her ass, and then she was in Conall's arms.

The world shifted and blurred and they were in the living room, and Conall was lowering her feet to the floor.

"Meow," Mr. Cat said, rubbing against her legs in welcome.

Conall had entered her house without using the door, but at least he'd remembered to let the cat in, too.

Mr. Cat padded off to investigate his food bowl. Mr. Cat was all about the chow.

She scowled at Conall. "Aren't there rules about this sort of thing? Don't you people have to be invited in?"

"We are not vampires. Remove your jacket so I may examine your arm."

"No. Go away. I don't want your help."

A knife appeared in Conall's hand. "I am in no mood for games. Take off the jacket or I will cut it off."

"You wouldn't dare."

Conall gave her a stony look. He didn't say a word, but the temperature in the room dropped. Ice formed on the windowpanes and swirled in lacy patterns across the wood floor. Fuming, Beck shrugged out of the leather jacket and tossed it onto the couch. What choice did she have, unless she wanted her living room turned into the Snow Queen's palace?

As soon as Captain Bossy Pants got his way, the winter wonderland routine ended. Big bully, Beck thought.

"I cannot believe you have the nerve to threaten me in my own house."

"I did not threaten you," Conall said. "I threatened your garment, a significant difference." He motioned at her sweater with the knife. "Remove your tunic."

"Go to hell."

He closed his eyes and opened them again. "I warn you, Rebekah. My patience is at an end."

"Your patience?" Beck said. She was tired and mad and hurt, not least of all by *him*. "You've got a nerve. First, you scare me half to death with your crazed Frost Giant routine, and now you expect me to perform a strip tease. I. Don't. Think. So."

She turned to stomp out of the room, but he did the demon hunter thing and got in front of her. He would *not* let her have a dramatic exit, dammit.

"I frightened *you*?" The veins stood out on his neck. Beck gaped at him, watching in shock as his frozen expression cracked and melted, revealing the volcanic fury beneath. "You have no idea what I have suffered this day because of you. I thought you were dead."

"Are you saying you've been acting like a world-class jerk because you were *worried* about me?"

"No." He reached out and yanked her close. "Worry is too pale a word to describe what I have been through. I have been out of my mind. Mad with fear. Nigh unto berserk." He gave her a little shake. "Do you know what that means to a Dalvahni warrior? No, of course you do not."

Tangling his hands in her hair, he kissed her. His lips were firm and demanding, and *warm*. So was the rest of him. The ice man was gone.

His touch unleashed something inside Beck, something she'd

always denied, the demon part of her hungry for physical pleasure, the human part of her longing for acceptance and inti-
macy. It had been years since she'd allowed herself to give in to
desire, afraid to unleash the demon in her; afraid that she would
hurt someone or turn into someone or something she did not
recognize. She moaned and kissed him back, pressing her body
against him, stroking her tongue against his. The hard length of
his erection pressed against her stomach. He wanted her. She
smiled. And she wanted him. In spite of their differences, they
had that much in common.

And judging from the size of his . . . um . . . desire, that was
no small thing.

Are you crazy, the sane part of her shouted. *Sleeping with him
is a mistake. Don't do it. Don't—*

She tore her mouth free. "I want to have sex with you."

"What?" Conall's deep voice was hoarse and his chest
heaved, which did some very interesting things to the T-shirt
hugging his muscular torso.

"I said I want to have sex with you." She swallowed and
stared at the cleft in his chin. Gathering her courage, she
blurted, "I had my tubes tied when I was sixteen. Daddy took
me to a kith doctor to have it done."

Silence stretched between them. *Way to go, Beck. Way to
make things awkward.*

She peeked up at him. His expression was distant. Was he put
off by what she'd said, or just checking his translator?

"You had a procedure to prevent conception?"

Checking his translator. Beck nodded with relief.

"Daddy and I agreed it was the right thing to do. S-so, you
don't have to worry about getting me pregnant."

"I confess, you have had me so befuddled by lust that I had
not considered the possibility."

The ball of tension in her belly dissolved. "Oh, yeah? Does
that mean you want to have sex with me?"

"I have thought of little else since first I saw you."

"Really?" Beck felt her mouth stretch into a delighted grin.
"I'm glad. Really, gla—"

"But you are injured. Did you think I would forget?"

"I don't see why not," she grumbled. "I had."

Conall kissed her injured cheek, a slow drag of his lips and tongue that made her throb with longing.

"W-what are you doing?" she gasped.

"Healing you."

The puff of his breath and the graze of his lips against her skin made her shiver. Her breasts tightened, and heat pooled in her stomach and between her legs. The warmth spread until she felt hot, inside and out, and all he'd done was kiss her on the cheek.

"Um, couldn't it wait until later?"

"No."

Damn.

He took his time, kissing the marks on her face. Then he hooked his fingers in the bottom of her sweater and pulled it over her head. Beck shivered, feeling stupid and awkward, standing in front of him half-dressed with her ugly, calcified arm hanging out.

"Ah, Rebekah," he said. "What have you done?"

"I didn't do anything. It was the ring. It grabbed the demon and wouldn't let go." Beck swallowed. Seeing her arm like this made her sick to her stomach. "Can you fix it?"

"Yes, but 'twill be uncomfortable."

"I'm a big girl. I can take it."

He gently stroked the frozen flesh of her arm, starting at the shoulder and working his way down. Light poured from his hands and heat. An electric shock startled Beck, followed by a sharp burning sensation.

"Ow, that hurts," Beck said, trying to jerk away. "Stop it."

"I told you it would be uncomfortable."

"Yeah, but I didn't think it would—Ow! Son of a bitch that hurts."

"You look a trifle pale," Conall said. "Do you need to lie down?"

"Hell no."

"Then be still," Conall said. "The nerves are regenerating. I must repair the damage." He turned his attention to her clawed hand. "Talk to me. Tell me how this happened. 'Twill take your mind off the pain."

"I doubt it," Beck muttered, but she started talking anyway.

"Two demons showed up at the party, a real couple of doozies," she said, gritting her teeth as the icy-hot sensation spread to her fingers. Little silver dots danced in front of her eyes. She would not faint. She would *not*. "Th-the bodies they occupied were all used up, so Trey and Evan brought out two more. A couple of kids." Sweat broke out on her forehead. Her arm and hand were no longer frozen; they were on fire. "I objected to that."

"Why am I not surprised?" Conall murmured.

"I used a bottle on the first one, like I did that night at the bar. Do you remember?"

Conall looked up. "Oh, yes, I remember. The memory gives me nightmares still. I take it you extracted the first demon and the second one attacked?"

She nodded with an effort. "I p-panicked and removed the other one manually."

"I beg your pardon?"

"I stuck my hand inside the boy's body and pulled the demon out." She made a face. "Can't say as I recommend it."

Conall said something underneath his breath, something rude. Beck had heard enough cussing in her lifetime to know a bunch of swear words when she heard them, even if they were in another language.

"Done," he said, releasing her.

Beck looked down at her hand. To her surprise, healthy color flooded the tissue. She moved her arm and wiggled her fingers. A little stiff and sore, but otherwise, good as new.

"Wow, thanks."

"You are most welcome."

"*Now* can we have sex?"

His eyes creased at the corners. He was laughing at her. What had made her think he didn't have a sense of humor? It was there, buried under all the layers of badassery.

"Your eagerness is most gratifying," he said.

"Take off your shirt. Now *that* would be gratifying."

To her surprise, he whipped the cotton T-shirt over his head and threw it aside.

Beck's jaw sagged and her insides went wobbly with lust. He was a freaking work of art. Wide shoulders, sculpted chest and arms, strong, powerful legs, and a ripped belly, all covered in smooth olive skin—the perfect specimen of the male animal in his prime. A man, not a boy, a warrior tried and proven in a thousand battles, the leader of a ferocious, ancient race. Everything about him screamed strength, assurance, and sexual prowess.

"Jesus, Mary, and Jerome," Beck said. "Look at you."

His beautiful mouth curved. "Am I to infer from that peculiar statement that I meet with your approval?"

"Oh, yeah," Beck said. "Infer away."

She closed the gap between them in one long stride, pulled his head down, and kissed him. He went still for a moment, as though surprised by her aggression, and then he kissed her back, his tongue tangling with hers in a nerve-sizzling dance that melted her bones.

Heat exploded between them. Beck was no stranger to passion—her demon blood made her run hot, but she'd never felt like this, jumpy and tingly, and so *alive*. She wanted to weep. She wanted to laugh. She wanted to shout for joy. She wanted to do him until one of them begged for mercy. And it for damn sure wouldn't be her.

Conall groaned her name, his voice rough with desire.

"No, don't talk," Beck panted. "Help me out of these clothes."

He grabbed the waistband of her jeans and pulled. To her astonishment, the material ripped like rotten cloth. Another tug and she was standing in her undergarments and boots. Darn demon hunter super-strength.

"Hey, those were new jeans," she protested.

"You asked for my help."

"You're right. Forget it."

Beck unfastened her bra and let it slide to the floor. Conall's jaw tightened, and she could swear little flames danced in his ebony eyes. The fire in her blood sparked hotter. It was hard to think through the haze of desire. She wanted him inside her, hard and hot and moving. Now, before she went up in flames. She'd never felt this hungry, this frantic with need.

Boots; she should take off her boots.

Bump it.

She threw herself at him and wrapped her legs around his waist. He gripped her thighs with easy strength. God, she loved that he was so big and strong. She loved—

Her mind balked. Not *loved;* she lusted. This was about sex, no complications; no strings.

Her thoughts scattered as he pressed her against the living room wall and ravaged her mouth with his lips and tongue, grinding himself against her. His hands moved over her, frantic and warm, urgent.

"Rebekah, I have wanted you for so long."

His deep, raspy voice sent a shiver of longing down her spine. Heat bloomed in her breasts and belly at his touch. The hard ridge of his erection rubbed the throbbing place between her legs. Her greedy body, so long denied, tightened in anticipation.

"Your jeans," she gasped between searing kisses. "Hurry."

She felt him fumble with the metal fastening at his waist. The hot, hard length of him pushed against the damp patch of nylon between her legs. She was wet and aching for him. With a sound of impatience, he ripped off her panties and pushed inside her, filling her, stretching her, impaling her on his cock.

Oh, God, it felt wonderful. Beck clenched around him, sobbing.

He stilled. "Am I hurting you?"

"No," she said. She grabbed his massive shoulders and held on. "Don't stop. Don't you dare stop."

He moved his hips, slowly at first, and then faster, driving his body into hers, taking her higher.

She threw her head back and let the pleasure take her, riding the wave to the crest and over the top. One, two, three more hard delicious strokes and Conall came with a ragged shout, sending little pulses of pleasure through her. The throb of his flesh inside her sent her spiraling into a second orgasm.

Now you've done it, Beck thought, floating back down from bliss. *That was perfect, and you know it. And you can't wait to do it again, can you, Little Miss Horny Pants?*

It's a good thing this is only about sex, or you'd be in big trouble.
Yeah.

Chapter Twenty-four

The strength of Conall's sexual release shook him to the core. He had hungered for Rebekah for months. Pleasure and satisfaction he'd expected from their joining, but this . . .

He waited for the familiar postcoital emptiness that inevitably followed a session in the House of Thralls, but it did not come. Instead, he was flooded with sensation, his body and mind attuned to the woman in his arms. The satin feel of Rebekah's skin beneath his palms, the graze of her soft breasts against his bare chest, the scent of heated jasmine that clung to her hair and body filled his senses. Sweetest of all, the exquisite pull of her womanly flesh around him as she climaxed again.

He opened his eyes and looked down at her. Her luscious mouth curved in a smile of satisfaction, her cheeks were flushed, her skin dewy from the heat of their sensual play. He nuzzled her neck, tasting her, delighting in her shiver of response. A hint of salt clung to her skin. Bits of leaves and straw clung to her hair from her long flight through the woods. A smudge of dirt marred one cheek. Ugly bruises dotted her arms and knees.

A sweet, sharp pain pierced the hollow of his chest, robbing him of breath. Something inside Conall cracked open—the last of the ice encasing his warrior's heart. She was disheveled and dirty and clad in naught but a pair of muddy boots, and she was the most beautiful thing he had ever seen.

You love her. You have loved her lo these many moons, though your stubborn will and warrior's pride made you deny it.

The knowledge settled in his bones. The events of the day, the terror and regret he'd felt when he'd feared Rebekah might be hurt or dying at the hands of the djegrali, had torn down the barriers his intractable, rational mind had erected.

He loved her. He could no longer deny the stunning truth of it. For centuries, his existence had been duty and the Dalvahni way. It was all he knew, all he'd thought he wanted or needed, all that existed for him.

And his reward for such devotion? The universe had set him squarely in the path of a half-demon enchantress who'd shattered his every belief and turned him inside out. The universe was a strange and unfathomable thing, marvelous and capricious in its perversity.

Rebekah wrapped her arms around his neck and smiled up at him. "Hmm, that was nice," she said, arching her hips against him to the delight of his eager cock.

"Nice?" Conall raised his brows. "More than merely nice, methinks."

"Ooh, someone has a high opinion of himself."

Her face was upturned, her lips mere inches from his. She had a beautiful mouth, wide with a slight indention in the bottom lip, that fascinating sweet spot he had longed to explore for months. Giving in to temptation, he bent his head and touched the dimple in her pouty lower lip with his tongue, enjoying her quiver of response. Her eyes drifted shut, her lashes feathery crescents against her flushed cheeks.

He wanted her again already, hungered for her.

"It can hardly be conceit when the result is so evident," he murmured against her mouth. "Behold what we have wrought."

She opened her eyes and looked around. "What the—?" she said in shock.

Blue light pulsed around them and shot in whizzing sparks around the room. But that was the least of it. The cooling mechanism humans call a refrigerator had malfunctioned, spitting out cubes of ice onto the floor, the kitchen pipe was running and so was every machine and device in the house, including the squawking box called a television.

Her startled gaze met his. "We did this?"

She jerked in surprise as the refrigerator spewed out another stream of ice. "I can't believe I didn't notice it before."

"It is understandable. We were . . . uh . . . otherwise engaged. Battle adrenaline is likely to blame."

"Good to know we won't cause a blackout every time we have sex. That is, if we have sex again."

Conall tugged her closer. "If?"

Mr. Cat streaked out of the kitchen, a small mechanized dirt-sucking device in hot pursuit.

"Mr. Cat," Rebekah cried. A jolt of pleasure-pain shot through his cock as she wiggled out of his arms. "I've got to save him. He's terrified of the vacuum cleaner."

Bemused, Conall watched her dart after the cat like a startled nymph. There was much to be said, he reflected as he went about the business of turning off the various electrical devices and shutting the water tap, for keeping one's lady love naked. Particularly when the lady in question was a lithe beauty with high, full breasts, a narrow waist and flat stomach, and long, supple legs.

Rebekah clomped back into the room in her boots, the wild-eyed feline clutched against her breasts. "Poor baby," she cooed. "He's had a bad scare."

She made a sound of dismay as the feline jumped down and stalked away, tail twitching in outrage. Conall opened the door with a wave of his hand, and the cat streaked into the darkness.

"I wish you hadn't done that," Rebekah said, her brow creasing in worry. "What if he doesn't come back?"

Conall swept her into his arms. "He will return. He loves you." Unable to resist, he stroked her bottom lip with his tongue once more. He would never tire of the taste of her. "He will not be able to stay away."

She blinked up at him. "Think so?"

He looked into her eyes, and the strange ache returned to his chest. The air grew thin and hard to breathe, and the room seemed to tilt beneath his feet.

"Yes," he croaked. By the sword, she sundered his every re-sistance. He cleared his throat and tried again. "I am certain of it."

He carried her into the bathing chamber, set her down, and pointed to the tub. "Run a bath whilst I fetch us something to eat."

He left her standing there and fled into the kitchen, as though all the fiends from the darkest recesses of The Pit were at his heels. He opened the door to the cooling device and stared blindly inside. Should he tell her that he loved her? Was it too soon? What if he was mistaken? What if his reaction to her was the result of proximity and sexual deprivation?

Best to wait. His feelings were still too raw and confused, and he too unsteadied by emotion.

He looked down at his shaking hands. Ah, gods, but he was undone.

Perhaps he should speak to someone, one of his brothers. Brand and Ansgar had passed through a similar fire. They could give him counsel.

Alas, Brand and Ansgar were away with their new wives. They would not thank him for disturbing their . . . er . . . cele-brations.

His brother Rafe perhaps? He resided in Hannah with Bunny, his pregnant wife. Bunny's pregnancy had caused Conall no small amount of concern. To his knowledge, 'twas the first time one of the Dal had produced progeny. The thralls were sterile and the Dalvahni, out of habit and custom, confined their appetites to them.

Until recently, that is, when certain of their numbers had come here in pursuit of the djegrali. The rules did not apply, it seemed, in Hannah.

The Great Book instructed the Dal to spend their lust and rid themselves of excess emotion in the House of Thralls. But, the thought of returning to the cool, draining clasp of a thrall held no thrill for Conall, not after the warmth and fire he'd found with Rebekah. He remembered the feel of her in his arms, the look on her lovely face when he brought her to pleasure, and his own shattering release within her delectable body.

She was an intriguing mixture of strength and vulnerability, his Rebekah. Her father might not have outwardly abused her, but his denial and revulsion of her demon nature had left its mark.

Conall's jaw tightened. Jason Damian was an insensitive clod. Rebekah thought she should not have children, that she was *unworthy*. At her father's behest, she had taken steps to prevent such a thing when little more than a child.

Conall would gladly thrash the man within an inch of his life but for the knowledge that he had committed the same transgression. He, too, had condemned and rejected her for her demon blood. The memory of his blind censure made him squirm.

This then, was what humans called regret. He did not care for the feeling.

She had been in harm's way this day because of him. That, also, he bitterly regretted. Using his Dalvahni powers to repair her injuries had done little to assuage his guilt. He grimaced. Guilt; another new experience. How did humans bear the dizzying onslaught of emotions?

His eyes widened at a sudden thought. What if he had repaired the damage to her reproductive organs when he'd healed her other hurts? His hand tightened on the cooler door. Nay, such a thing was not likely. He had not deliberately done so. Even if such a thing were possible, it did not mean he could sire a child with Rebekah.

He would not think on it yet. The Great Book said, "Worry not about wetting your boots ere you reach the river."

He and Rebekah had but dipped their toes in the water.

Beck saw her reflection in the bathroom mirror. Eek! Her hair was windblown and full of leaves, and she was covered in dirt and mud. She'd scare a flock of crows off a dead cow.

She examined her face. A few pale pink stripes were all that remained of the ugly claw marks on her cheek. Her bruises were already fading, and her arm was back to normal, thanks to a certain demon hunter and his magical powers.

She pulled off her boots and socks, grimacing at the orange gunk smeared on them. Good thing she had wooden floors. Alabama red clay was hell on carpets.

Selecting a bar of Evie's jasmine-scented goat's milk soap, she sank into the bath. The oversized, freestanding oval tub had been her one splurge in the bathroom. The tiny apartment she'd grown up in had boasted a cramped tub/shower combination. At five-feet-nine, she'd outgrown the small bathtub by the time she was eleven. By necessity, it had been showers from then on.

She still opted for a shower most days for speed and convenience, but she adored an occasional soak in the tub. She'd special-ordered the composite stone bath from a shop in Mobile, selecting the largest one she could find to accommodate her long legs. Toby would croak if he knew how much the thing cost, but it was worth every penny.

She washed her hair and body, using the handheld attachment on the side of the tub. The water felt wonderful, and she took her time. She was sore all over. Even *there,* she thought with a smile, remembering Conall's passionate possession.

Being with Conall had been the hottest, most explosive, most deliciously glorious sex of her life. Not that she'd had much experience. She'd spent pretty much her whole life in the bar, and there wasn't much to choose from around here, unless you counted Earl Skinner and his circus dick.

Which she most certainly did *not.*

She couldn't wait to be with Conall again. She sat up in the water. What if he didn't feel the same way? What if he was already bored with her? He'd probably been with scads of women, beautiful, *sophisticated* women. The thought shouldn't bother her. It wasn't like she and Conall were in a relationship. But it did bother her. A lot.

Conall entered the room carrying a tray with two glasses of

iced tea and a plate of fruit and cheese. He was still shirtless and his jeans rode his lean hips, exposing his broad chest, muscled arms, and washboard stomach. Lord a-mercy, he was a fine specimen. Looking at him made her brain short-circuit and sent the rest of her into full-blown lust.

Careful, girl. Enjoy the scenery, but don't get attached. This is temporary.

He set the platter down on the counter. "Why are you scowling?"

Beck sank deeper into the water. "I'm not scowling. See?" She pinned him with a bright smile. "Um, look . . . It's been nice and all, but don't feel like you've got to stay. I mean, if you've got someplace else to be."

"Where else would I be?"

Hooking the vanity stool with one foot, he dragged it over to the tub and sat down. He'd taken off his shoes and was barefoot. Even his feet were beautiful, lean and strong and bronzed, like the rest of him.

Oh, jeez, now she was fixating on the guy's *feet*. What the hell was the matter with her?

She cleared her throat. "I dunno, wherever it is you go when you're not *here*. I . . . uh . . . don't want you to think you have to hang around because we had sex." She tucked her legs close to her body and studied her kneecaps like they were the most interesting things in the world. "I mean, I'm totally cool with it if you need to leave."

Liar. You want him to stay. You want it bad. You want to have sex with him again and again and again, until you wipe all those other women out of his mind. You want . . .

What? She had no claim on him and vice versa. This was a fling. Fun and exhilarating, but it wouldn't last.

See, this is what comes of going without for too long. You should have bought that Flying Radish from Frannie Lee Buck when she had that sex toy party at the bar two Christmases ago. Everybody swears by the Flying Radish. Ora Mae says it's better than a man. She says who needs a man when you got the Flying Radish?

Thoughts of vibrators disintegrated as Conall leaned forward and rested his elbows on his thighs. Beck's mouth went dry. It was a slight, ordinary movement performed by ordinary mortals throughout the world on any given day. All the guy did was rest his elbows on his knees, for God's sake. But he raised it to an art form, a miniature ballet of muscle and sinew that was captivating. She could not look away. His lean belly rippled, creating a fascinating, deep ridge down the middle of his abs. God, he was beautiful. She wanted to lick that hard cleft. She wanted to drink champagne out of it. She wanted to—

"And if I stay?" he said, interrupting her lusty thoughts. "Is that a matter of indifference to you as well?"

"Sure." She lifted her shoulders with studied nonchalance, though it almost killed her. "Okay."

He shucked off his jeans and climbed in the tub, facing her.

"What are you doing?" Beck said as he pulled her onto his lap.

His erection nudged the aching place between her legs. Her heartbeat quickened in anticipation. She was a glutton for it, a glutton for him.

"I should think that would be obvious. But, as you appear to need clarification, I am attempting to engender a more passionate response from you."

"Huh?"

It was the closest thing to an intelligent reply she could muster lying next to all that wet, hard, delicious male flesh.

"You have a fondness for using words like *nice* and *okay,* and *cool,* words that imply a measure of indifference," he said, licking the water off the tops of her breasts. Beck shivered, though not from cold. "Such a lack of enthusiasm lessens this warrior's confidence."

Something warm bubbled up inside her, a different kind of heat than lust. She was happy. At this moment in time, she was happy. With Conall. It was such a rare and unexpected gift at the end of a truly horrendous day that she wanted to throw her head back and laugh.

She traced the outline of his beautiful, serious mouth with the tip of her damp forefinger. Wisps of steam rose from the water and curled around them.

"Bruised your ego, huh?" she murmured.

"Fractured it." Catching her finger with his teeth, he nipped the pad at the end, sending a jolt of desire zinging through her body. "I fear the damage is beyond repair."

"I doubt it. Your ego is the size of a planet."

"Harpy," he said without heat. He picked up the soap and gave it a sniff. "Jasmine, heady, elusive, and complex . . . like you." He dipped his hand in the water and trailed the wet bar of soap across her collarbone and down her shoulders. "You have no idea how your scent has haunted me all these months."

"You sat in the corner and glared at me like some dark avenger." Leaning closer, she took his face in her hands and pressed feathery, little kisses on his cheeks, his nose, and along the hard line of his jaw, memorizing the taste and feel of him, the shape of his face. *For when he's gone. So I can remember.* "I thought you hated me, but I had no idea why."

"You bewitched me." He stroked her breasts with the soap, dragging the bar across her wet skin, teasing the undersides and the sensitive tips. "For the first time in my life, I was not in control, and it made me angry."

"But, I didn't—"

He put his finger over her lips. "Perhaps not a-purpose, but the result was the same. Like your overfed feline, I kept coming back for more."

He dipped his hands in the water and poured the warm liquid over her soapy breasts. Beck held her breath as his hot gaze fastened on her puckered nipples. She wanted his hands on her, his mouth on her, *there.*

"Beautiful," he said. His deep rough voice sang along her nerves and made her body thrum. He stroked her cheek with the back of his fingers. "You take my breath away."

She closed her fingers around his wrist and brought his wet palm to her lips. "Babe, I know exactly how you feel." Rubbing his wet knuckles with her mouth, she explored the crevasses between his fingers with her tongue. "Looking at you makes me ache all over."

"This sounds serious." His slow smile made her insides flutter. "What can we do about it?"

"I don't know." She sighed. "I was hoping you could maybe give me some relief."

"I feel sure I can think of something. Show me where it hurts."

She touched her bottom lip. "Well, for starters, here."

He bent his head and licked the spot with his tongue. "Better?"

"A little, but now it hurts here."

She curved her neck, offering him her throat. His hot mouth moved along the tender flesh and nibbled at her collarbone. Warmth, languid and intoxicating, spread to her breasts and belly.

"Where else?" he asked.

She lowered her chin and met his smoldering gaze. "Here," she said, circling her breasts and aching nipples with her fingers. He watched her, his black eyes glowing hotter. "But, this . . ." She lowered her hand and touched the throbbing place between her legs. "This is where it really hurts."

He rested his hand on her inner thigh. "Here?"

"Not . . . quite," she said. Her heart pounded. "A little more to the left."

He cupped his hand over her. "Here?"

"Close."

"Here, perhaps?" he said, sliding his finger inside her. He flicked her clitoris with his thumb. "Or is this the spot?"

"Y-you're getting warmer. Definitely."

He lifted her by the waist and set her down on his straining shaft, stretching her, filling her.

"And now?" he asked. He blew on her wet nipples, licking first one and then the other.

"Red hot," she said with a gasp.

Taking her nipple in his mouth, he began to move, the hot suckling pull on the tight bud in rhythm with the stroke of his cock. The sensation was exquisite, almost more than she could bear. Beck held onto him and let the feelings take her higher and higher.

She heard Conall groan her name, and then she fractured into a million little pieces of bliss.

Chapter Twenty-five

Conall held Rebekah in his arms. She lay relaxed against him, her cheek upon his chest, eyes closed. She smelled of jasmine and soap and something else, an indefinable, subtle scent that was hers alone. The sweet exhale of her breath danced across his damp skin. He was afraid to move, to breathe, for fear of ending the moment. She reminded him of a wild animal with her sleek, supple beauty and restless, barely contained energy, a fierce falcon he had gentled for the moment, but could never fully tame.

He smiled against her hair. He liked the wildness in her. He would not have it any other way.

"Rebekah?" he murmured at last.

Her eyelashes stirred against her cheeks. "Hmm?"

"The water grows cold."

"Don't move. Not yet." She snuggled against him. "I'm comfortable."

"We cannot stay here forever." Ignoring her protests, he extricated himself from her silken limbs, and climbed from the tub. He held out a towel. "Come. I am taking you to bed."

"I don't want to go to bed. I'm not sleepy."

"Who said anything about sleep?"

She made a playful grab for the towel. "I can do it myself."

"That is not the point." He lifted her, dripping, out of the bath and set her feet on the mat. "I want to take care of you."

He rubbed her damp hair with the towel and dried her arms

and shoulders. He moved the towel over her slender back and lower, caressing the firm, round curve of her bottom. His heartbeat tripped into a gallop. It took all his strength of will not to bend her over and take her from behind, right then and there.

"Turn around."

His voice sounded cracked and husky. She faced him with a sultry smile, the vixen. She knew very well her effect on him.

"Bossy," she said.

"I prefer commanding."

Her violet eyes darkened as he moved the cloth over her breasts, her nipples puckering from the friction of the cloth. Unable to resist, Conall took one of the pink buds in his mouth. She was as changeable as quicksilver, with the hidden depths and mystery of the river outside her door. He would never tire of her. His hand moved lower, to the silky curls at the juncture of her thighs. The velvety skin there was warm. His fingers slid farther, to her womanly core.

She was slick and ready for him. The knowledge made the blood pound in his veins and groin. He had thought to tease her, to make her beg. Instead, he was the one rapidly losing control.

He carried her into the bedroom and tossed her onto the mattress. She landed on her back in a graceful sprawl and gazed up at him with a smile in her eyes. He opened his mouth to tell her that he loved her, but the words caught in his throat. Mere words were too trifling, too inadequate to convey what burned inside him.

She was so beautiful, so infinitely precious to him. All the long years of his life, the darkness and blood and struggle, disappeared and there was only Rebekah.

He stretched out beside her on the bed and kissed her, his tongue dancing with hers, delighting in her shudder of longing. He explored the rounded slopes of her breasts, the taut plane of her stomach. She squirmed restlessly beneath his sensual ministrations, but he took his time, enjoying the rapid hitch of her breath, her soft moans. He wanted to punish her a little for shredding his control, for making him love her.

A shrill ring interrupted them.

He raised his head. Rebekah's eyes held a soft, dazed expression and her mouth was swollen from his kisses.

"That's the phone." She sat up, blinking in adorable confusion. "I'd better get it. It could be Cassie with news about Toby."

"I will answer it." Conall rose from the bed and pointed his finger at her. "Do not move."

He approached the jangling machine and picked up the listening device. Conall was not entirely comfortable with the contraption, but he'd been on Earth long enough to know the basics. There was a moment of confusion when he spoke into the wrong end, but the matter was soon rectified.

"Yes?" he said, holding the thing to his ear.

He listened to the person on the other end and nodded.

"I will tell her," he said, remembering that the speaker could not see him.

He put down the telephone and strode back to the bed.

"That was Cassie," he said. "The doctor removed the projectile from Toby's leg and gave him medicine. He is at home and resting."

Rebekah flopped back onto the coverlet. "Thank goodness."

"Now, where was I?" Conall looked down at her. She was spread before him, a luscious cream and rose feast for his sampling. "Ah, yes, I remember. I was kissing you."

He grabbed her by the ankles and yanked her across the bed. Kneeling on the floor, he stroked the delicate pink flesh between her legs with his tongue.

"*Conall,*" she gasped. "You weren't kissing me there."

"Do you not like it?"

She gave him a feminine growl of enjoyment and wrapped her hands in his hair. "What do you think?"

"Good." He bent once more to the task, exploring her intimate creases with his fingers and tongue. "Let go, sweetheart. Let me give you pleasure."

He felt her body tighten with a delicious tension, sensed the thrumming heat in her blood that matched his burning desire. She arched against him and came with a little shriek.

She was still pulsing when he pushed inside her. It felt so good, so *right*.

Mine, he thought, as he started to move. *Mine. And no one, man or god, can keep me from her.*

It was his last conscious thought before the pleasure took him.

A familiar thump on the mattress woke Beck the next morning. She opened her eyes to find Mr. Cat staring at her from the adjacent pillow.

"Hello, you old poothead," Beck said, giving the cat an affectionate rub. "Glad you decided to come home."

"I told you the creature would return, did I not?"

Conall stood in the doorway, one shoulder propped against the frame. To the casual eye, he looked at ease, but she knew he could go from relaxed to lethal in a millisecond. He was fully dressed in clean jeans and a deep blue cotton tee. She liked the blue shirt. The color looked good on him, with his gleaming dark hair. Of course, he looked good in everything.

And even better naked.

Mr. Cat meowed.

"That is a blatant falsehood, you deceitful feline," Conall said. "Do not listen to him, Rebekah. He has been fed."

"Now you speak cat?"

"Yes." He shrugged. "It is no great thing. As a rule, animals are more straightforward and easier to understand than humans."

Beck drew the sheet around her, although it was a little late for modesty after the things they'd done the night before. Fevered images crowded her brain. Way, way too late, she thought, recalling an old saying about a horse and a barn door. Conall had been insatiable and so had she.

She'd have to put her hootie back in moth balls when Conall left. No one else could compare to him.

"Where'd you get the extra clothes?" she asked, to take her mind off her sudden melancholy.

"I am Dalvahni. We have our ways."

Translation: he'd used magic.

She turned her head to check the alarm clock and bolted upright in bed. "It's after eight. How could I have slept so late?"

"Not so late, when you consider how little we slept."

Conall's deep, rough voice sounded gruffer than usual. Glancing up, Beck found his gaze fastened on her naked breasts. A wave of heat washed over her, and she forgot about the time. Tossing back the covers, she knelt on top of the bed.

"Come here." She crooked her finger at him. "I forgot to do something."

He blipped across the room to stand in front of her. Pushing up his shirt, she unfastened his jeans and took him in her mouth, working the hot, hard length of him with her tongue.

"Rebekah," he said with a strangled groan of pleasure. "Wha–what is it that you forgot?"

"I forgot to say good morning. Now that wasn't very friendly of me, was it?" She looked up at him through her lashes and gave him another leisurely lick. "Good morning, Conall."

He pushed her onto her back and got on top of her. "Good morning," he said, entering her in one, swift stroke.

She clenched around him, loving the feel of him inside her. What *would* she do when he was gone?

She wouldn't think about it, not now. Not when he was doing such delicious things to her body, not when he was taking her for another glorious ride.

She wrapped her legs around his waist and held on.

An hour later, Beck was showered and dressed. When she came into the kitchen, Conall had breakfast ready.

"You cook?" she said, taking a seat at the table.

He slid an omelet onto her plate and sat down across from her. "I told you as much."

"Yeah, but I didn't believe you."

"Why not?"

She shrugged. "You don't look like the domestic type."

"Perhaps not, but I am the type who likes to eat." He took a huge bite of his food, as if to prove his point. "A warrior learns many things in ten thousand years."

"Holy shit," Beck said, dropping her fork.

Ten thousand years? The gulf between them was wa-a-a-a-y wider than she'd thought.

Conall's brow creased in concern. "Is something amiss? Are the eggs not to your liking?"

"The eggs are fine. I guess I'm a little startled to find out that you're an immortal demi-god. It puts a simple country gal at a disadvantage."

"You are kith, Rebekah. You are neither simple nor a peasant."

She picked up her fork and poked at her food. "So, what's life like on your planet?"

"The Dalvahni do not come from a planet. We reside between worlds in the Hall of Warriors."

He was talking about another dimension. For some reason, that made it worse. *Weirder.* She lived in Weird Central. But this . . .

This was more than weird.

"What about your family?" she asked. "Do they live there, too?"

"A Dalvahni warrior has no family, save his brothers."

"I get it. There's no need to play the Dalvahni fight song. I'm asking about your parents."

He chewed another bite of omelet and remained silent.

"You know . . . Mom and Dad?"

"The Dalvahni do not have parents. After Pratt tore the veil and released the djegrali to roam the worlds once again, Kehvahn made us."

"Kevin made you do what?"

"Keh-vahn," Conall repeated, putting emphasis on the second syllable. "He is the god who created us."

Beck's head pounded. "And this Pratt fellow made the djegrali? Was it some kind of competition?"

"Pratt did not make the djegrali. He is a trickster who released the djegrali out of mischief." Conall slathered a piece of bread with butter and proceeded to eat it. "It is what he does."

"He sounds like Loki."

Conall nodded. "That is one of his incarnations. He has many names."

Jeez, this was a strange conversation.

Beck took a deep breath and asked the thing she'd wondered about all her life, a question no one had been able to answer, not even Toby.

"So where do the djegrali come from?"

She held her breath, eager and terrified to hear the answer.

"I do not know," Conall said. "The djegrali simply *are*. They are older than the gods, older than the first star." He eyed her untouched plate. "You do not eat."

"I'm not hungry," she said. "What else can you tell me about them? The demons, I mean."

He pushed aside his plate and sat back. "They are powerful and capable of great magic. Being formless, they crave physical sensation and have an insatiable appetite for sex and stimulants of all kinds. They consume food and drink and drugs in prodigious quantities, thus wearing out the bodies they inhabit at an alarming rate. If the body they inhabit dies, they die also. Thus, they move from body to body, consuming them like locusts."

Beck thought of Latrisse, and her stomach did a slow roll. "Unless a demon hunter comes along and kills them, right?"

"Yes, but we give them a choice. If they quit their victim willingly, we return them to the Pit."

She glanced up at that. He was watching her in that intent way of his. "You mean, like a jail?"

He nodded.

"Why not put this veil thingy back in place? Wouldn't that be simpler than chasing them all over the place?"

"Which is the simpler task, to create a tree or hack it down? Kehvahn has tried, but he cannot repair what the Maker has wrought. For this great mischief, Pratt was banished."

"The Maker?" she asked.

"The One Who Made All Things."

He was talking about God; *the* God. The squishy feeling in her stomach spread to her brain. It was too much to think about.

She jumped to her feet. "Thanks for breakfast. I gotta get to work."

She snatched her jacket off the couch and ran out the back door.

Chapter Twenty-six

Beck dashed across the lawn and opened the door of the Tundra. Conall was waiting inside. The Flash had nothing on this guy. She climbed in without a word and cranked the truck.

Conall did not speak until they were on the road. "What has distressed you?" he asked.

She tightened her grip on the steering wheel. "Oh, I don't know, maybe the fact that I just found out you're ten thousand years old? I don't expect this thing between us to go anywhere but, I gotta admit, that intimidates the hell out of me."

"Why?" he asked.

"Why? I'm thirty-one years old and I run a bar outside a hick town. You're prehistoric and can talk to *cats,* for God's sake."

"And you are a shape-shifter and can suck demons out of humans with a metal spout. Such things are incidental. Why do you think what we have is temporary?"

"Because. How can it be anything else? We're enemies and—"

"You are not my enemy. I do not have sexual congress with my enemies."

"Sexual congress?" Beck snorted. "That sounds ever so much nicer than *I screwed the demon girl.*"

The truck screeched to a halt without warning. "Hey." Beck pressed the gas pedal, but nothing happened. "What's the big idea?"

"I do not like this word 'screwed.' " Conall's face was tight with anger. "It is a cheap and common term for what we shared. You will not use it again in reference to us."

The demon hunter was a prude. It should have annoyed her. But, for some reason, it cheered her up.

She shrugged. "Call it whatever you want. Bottom line, I'm sure there are rules against the two of us having sex."

That shut him up. He released whatever spell he'd put on the truck, and the Tundra rolled down the road. So, there *were* rules against them being together. The cheerful feeling evaporated.

Beck seethed in silence for maybe a mile and a half. "So," she said, unable to hold her tongue, "who *are* you allowed to canoodle?"

"I do not understand."

"Run it through your processor and get back to me when you figure it out."

"Now you are being a shrew."

"That's a fancy word for bitch," Beck said. "And don't think I'm too stupid to know it."

"I do not think you are stupid," Conall said. "I think you are confused and upset by your feelings for me. It is perfectly understandable. I have had some months to grow accustomed to my . . . attraction for you. You have not had that luxury."

Oh, yay. He was *attracted* to her. What did she expect, undying love? This was about scratching an itch, for both of them. Why, then, did it feel like her belly was in her shoes?

She lifted her chin. "This thing between us has taken me by surprise. I may work in a bar, but I don't sleep around."

"That is a good thing. I do not share what is mine."

"I never said I was yours."

"Perhaps not in so many words, Rebekah. But you said it last night and this morning with your body in a thousand delightful ways."

Her cheeks burned and so did the rest of her. Wow, he was some kind of smooth talker. He melted her insides like butter. Not that she'd let him know it. A demon girl had her pride.

"Nice line, Romeo," she said. "I bet you say that to all the women."

"There are no other women."

She snorted again. She was starting to sound like a horse with a head cold. "Yeah, right. Next, you'll be telling me you're a virgin."

"I am not a virgin," he said. "I have slaked my lust in the House of Perpetual Bliss, as required by the Great Directive."

"The what?"

"It is the creed the Dalvahni live by. According to the Directive, a Dalvahni warrior should avail himself of a thrall at regular intervals to rid himself of unnecessary emotion."

He spoke in a monotone and used a bunch of highfalutin terms, but he was talking about sex, sex with someone else; some kind of paid companion. Little red dots danced in front of her eyes.

"Duty sex," she drawled, holding onto her temper. "Man, sucks to be you. Most guys would kill for a gig like that."

"Killing figures largely into our . . . uh . . . gig, as you call it."

"So, what's a thrall?"

"A species that services the Dal," he said. "You encountered one the night the demons attacked and you intervened on Evie's behalf. Her name is Lenora. Do you recall her?"

Beck stopped the truck. At this rate, it would take them a week to get to the bar, but she didn't care. Remember Lenora? Was he kidding? Lenora Thralvahni was the most sexual creature Beck had ever encountered. She *oozed* sex. Lenora had jumped up on the bar and danced the hoochie-coochie in nothing but a few ribbons, sending every male in the bar—and a few females, too—into a frenzy of lust.

"I remember her," Beck said tightly. She stared at her hands on the wheel. "Black hair, blowjob mouth, and a body that won't quit. She's married to Shep Corwin. Does he know you slept with his wife?"

"Lenora was not his wife until recently, and I did not sleep with her. I favored a thrall named Lhanna, a blonde with large—"

"Stop," Beck said. She flung up her hand, palm out. "I don't want to hear it."

"—eyes and an interest in dragons," Conall finished. " 'Tis a subject we spoke of often."

"Goody gumdrops for you and Lhanna. Let me guess. You loved her for her mind."

Beck took her foot off the brake and pressed the accelerator. The truck tires scratched in the dirt, kicking up a satisfying cloud of red dust. Redneck therapy: way cheaper than paying for a counseling session.

"A warrior does not love a thrall," Conall said. "Ours is a practical relationship. Thralls provide sexual release for the Dal. They, in turn, subsist on our emotions."

It sounded very clinical the way he described it, but he was still talking about sex with another woman, a blond bimbo with a thing for dragons; Conall's confidante. Beck concentrated on keeping the truck on the road. Not that easy when the red spots had spread and her vision was a bloody haze.

You're jealous, which makes you the world's biggest idiot. You think you can be cool about this, but look at you. You're emotionally involved. Do not make the mistake of falling for this guy. He will break your heart to smithereens.

Time to change the subject before she burst into tears and shocked the shit out of both of them.

"So, yesterday at the party, I think I may have found out what the demons are up to," she said, keeping her gaze on the road.

It was safer that way. Looking at Conall was habit forming. She didn't want to run her truck into the ditch.

"Yes? What did you learn?"

His tone was bland, but she sensed his sudden alertness.

"It was a rally, a call to arms. Join the demons and take over the world."

Conall grunted. "Divide and conquer. 'Tis an age-old tactic.

The djegrali use the promise of power and wealth to sway the weak and desperate to their cause. They employed such a strategy in the realm of Gorth and would have conquered all, but for the Dal's intervention."

"This is different," Beck said. "This time, they're trying to enlist the kith. Think about it. We're talking about an army of supernaturals."

That must have given him something to chew on, because he got quiet.

"I didn't find out any specifics about this so-called super weapon the demons are supposed to have," she said after a moment of silence. "But I think Trey Peterson may be involved."

"Why?"

"He's being haunted by his dead wife." She guided the truck around a curve in the road. "Her name is Meredith and she's a raving bitch."

"Ansgar mentioned it," Conall said. "A most unpleasant shade, by all accounts."

"Unpleasant doesn't begin to describe it. She makes old Hazel look like a walk in the park."

"Who is Hazel?"

"The ghost of Sardine Bridge. Park on the bridge at midnight and call her name three times, and she'll appear. But don't cuss." Beck shuddered. "Hazel hates cussing."

"I take it you speak from experience." There was a ripple of amusement in his rough, sexy voice. "How did you meet Meredith?"

"She showed up at the party and gave Trey all kinds of hell. Evan says Trey's desperate to get rid of her." Beck glanced sideways at Conall. "So desperate, he's made some kind of deal with the demons."

"A deal your brother has brokered, no doubt. It is as I suspected from the first. He has joined the djegrali."

"Evan can't help it," Beck said. "The demons have had him since he was born."

"Then he is lost. He is drenched in evil and has done evil's bidding."

"That's not fair. Evan never had a choice."

"There is always a choice."

"Not for Evan," Beck argued. "The demons put a curse on him, some kind of magical binding that makes him do whatever they say."

"The *morkthyngeld*," Conall said with casual assurance. "The djegrali often employ such a curse with humans, but I am surprised to learn it works on the kith. I should think your demon blood would make you resistant."

"He was a little boy when they bound him, maybe that's the difference. They've done terrible things to him, Conall. He's been starved and tortured, and that's the least of it. He raised his first zombie when he was six years old, because he was lonely and frightened. Can you imagine?"

"Your brother is the zombie maker?" Beck felt Conall's dark gaze upon her. "How came you to know this?"

"I found out yesterday at the party," Beck said. "Evan sent Tommy to find me. I know it sounds crazy, but I think Evan cares about me, in his own way."

"He has a most peculiar manner of showing it. He invited you into danger and very nearly got you killed." Conall's voice was hard as granite. "He consorts with demons and trolls, and he attacked you and Tobias. Had he not gone to ground, I would have killed him."

Conall saw things in black and white in a world that was mostly gray. Maybe it was stupid to feel loyalty to a brother she'd never known, a brother who'd threatened to feed Toby to his pet troll for dinner. But she couldn't help it. She felt bad for Evan, and she felt guilty. She remembered all the times she'd bitched and whined about her shitty relationship with Jason, and felt ashamed. But for the grace of God, she would be the one bound to Hagilth.

Hagilth.

"Haggy," she cried. "Holy freaking crap, I forgot about Haggy."

"Who in the name of the gods is Haggy?" Conall asked.

"The demon I captured yesterday." She swung the truck off the road and took the bottle out of her pocket. The wraith clung to the glass. Her smoky form was thin and watery and peppered with holes. "Her name is Hagilth. She's been in my jacket all this time. I can't believe I forgot about her."

Yes, you can. Your brain's been on lockdown since last night and your vagina has been in charge. Sex with Conall wiped out your memory bank.

Conall took the bottle from her and turned it this way and that. Hagilth skittered around inside the bottle. "What ails the fiend?" he asked.

"Hot sauce," Beck said. "Demons are allergic to it."

Conall looked suitably impressed. "By the sword," he said, holding the bottle to the light. "What dark magic created this fell elixir?"

"It's not magic at all—just habanera chili peppers. They're super hot. Hot enough to burn a demon's butt." Beck grinned. "Looks like the Dalvahni have a secret weapon of their own."

"You have done well, Rebekah. This is a remarkable discovery."

Her grin widened. "You really didn't know?"

"I really did not know."

He set the hot sauce on the dashboard and snapped his fingers. An ornate bottle of blue glass appeared in his hand.

"What's that?" Beck asked.

"A djevel flaskke." He plucked the stopper out of the blue bottle and set it aside. "The Dal use them to transport the djegrali."

"Careful," Beck warned as he loosened the top on the hot sauce bottle. "She's a nasty one."

Conall gave her a look that clearly said *This ain't my first demon rodeo* and removed the metal screw cap. Haggy leaked out of the hot sauce bottle in a thin, ragged stream and was instantly drawn into the djevel flaskke. Conall popped the stopper back in place and the flask disappeared.

"Nice trick," Beck said. She guided the pickup back onto the road. "Hope you've got a buttload of those little bottles, 'cause you're gonna need them. Hannah's crawling with demons."

"So I noticed," Conall said with his customary calm. "Do not concern yourself. I know how to handle demons."

Chapter Twenty-seven

I know how to handle demons . . .

Beck smiled to herself as she turned off the road and onto the narrow drive that wound through the trees to Beck's. Conall might know how to handle demons, but he didn't know everything. He didn't know demons are allergic to hot sauce. She'd been the one to discover that juicy little tidbit, and it tickled her pink.

Her burst of feel-good lasted until she pulled into the parking lot and saw Charlie Skinner nailed to a tree. She slammed on the brakes and threw the Tundra in park.

"Holy shit," she said. "It's Charlie Skinner."

Charlie's head was bowed and his silver hair was plastered to his skull. The red and yellow boots were gone. He seemed diminished, somehow, shrunken without his fancy footwear.

Beck jumped out of the truck and raced across the empty lot. Conall blurred past her, reaching Charlie first.

"Stay back," he said, barring her way. "It could be a trap. It would not be the first time the djegrali used a corpse for mischief."

"Corpse?" Beck swallowed, thankful that she hadn't eaten her breakfast. "You mean, he's dead?"

She couldn't stop staring at Charlie's feet. They were shrunken knobs at the end of his legs. They looked *wrong,* like they belonged on a child's body and not an adult's.

"Yes." Conall's nostrils flared. "I detect a strong odor of spirits. I think it is fair to assume that Skinner was intoxicated when he died."

It was a fair assumption, all right. Charlie stunk of booze.

"He was pretty drunk at the gathering," she said. "I'll use the land line in the bar to call the sheriff. Cell reception is spotty out here. And I need to check on Hank and Verbena." She turned toward the employee entrance and stopped. "Verbena! We can't let her see her daddy like this."

"I will make sure she stays inside until the sheriff arrives." Conall pulled her into his arms and held her close. "You are shaking."

Beck leaned against him, letting his heat and strength steady her. "Hell of a way to start the morning."

"Death sours the stomach," Conall agreed. "Wait here while I make sure all is safe within."

"No way. I'm coming with you."

He released her and disappeared. He didn't even use the door. One second he was there, and the next he wasn't.

"Dammit, Conall," Beck said, striding after him.

She opened the door and stepped inside, giving a startled yelp as Conall materialized in front of her.

"I hate when you do that," Beck said, scowling at him.

"I searched the bed chamber, but no one is there," Conall said. "Something is amiss. I sense the taint of the djegrali, but not their presence." His dark eyes glowed. He shook his head. "I do not like it."

"Evan." Beck slammed her fist into the wall. "This is my fault. He's taken them prisoner because I've got Haggy. I should never have left them alone."

"They were not alone. Duncan was supposed to be with them." His jaw tightened. "In any event, you do not have the fiend. I do."

"Yeah, but Evan doesn't know that."

Conall took her by the hand and pressed a kiss on her palm. "Do not be dismayed. Your brother did not take them. He cannot enter the bar or your dwelling, nor can the djegrali. I placed protective spells around both days ago."

"You did what?"

"I do not trust him," he said. "I did what was necessary to ensure your safety."

"Without asking me."

"Yes."

It had been a long time since she'd had anybody take care of her, other than Toby, and it felt great . . . and a little scary. Conall could be a scary guy.

"Next time, ask before you—" She paused, listening. "Did you hear that? I think it's coming from the kitchen."

She pushed past him. Somebody was pounding on the door of the walk-in cooler, from the *inside*. The fridge was equipped with a safety latch to keep anyone from getting trapped in there, but someone had pushed a loaded pallet against the door. Beck rolled the heavy cart out of the way and yanked on the handle. Verbena stumbled out wearing a pair of Beck's old flannel pajamas—they were too big and didn't fit, just as Beck had figured—and a pair of saggy cotton socks. She was shivering, in spite of the blanket around her shoulders.

Hank, still in bear form, was stretched out on a bed of flour sacks with a blanket over him. Stacks of beer and soda surrounded him. Raising his head inside the miniature igloo, he bawled at them.

"I will see to the bear," Conall said. "Take care of the girl."

He lifted the bear with ease—no small thing; Hank was no featherweight, as a man or a bear—and strode past them. Beck helped Verbena over to a bench and made her sit down.

A moment later, Conall came back into the room. "The bear is resting. He seems to be none the worse for wear. Where is Duncan?"

"Dunno," Verbena said. She huddled closer under the blanket. "He was gone when I woke up."

"What happened?" Beck asked.

"Hank and I was sleeping and this black guy come busting in," Verbena said. "He kept babbling about demons a-coming and told us to hide. Hank was too weak to move, so we loaded him on the pallet and rolled him into the cooler."

"Had to have been Tommy," Beck told her.

Verbena shook her head. "Don't know. He didn't give us no name. He was riled up about something, so I done what he said. He seemed like a nice feller—treated me and Hank real gentle—even told me to bring along a couple of blankets." Her face darkened. "Next thing you know, he's done shut us in the cooler and blocked the door."

"I think he was trying to protect you," Beck said.

"Yeah? Then why didn't he get in the cooler with us? Why'd he lock us in there and leave?"

"I'm sure he had a reason," Beck said. Yeah, like he was already *dead*. Or maybe he was hungry and afraid he'd eat them. "How long were you in there?"

Verbena shrugged. "Hours. I thought me and Hank were goners, for sure. I was scared nobody would find us. Then the ruckus started and I was scared somebody would."

"Ruckus?" Beck asked. She had a bad feeling about this. "What kind of ruckus?"

"I heard something crash and then this awful howling." Verbena shuddered. "Like folks was being skint alive. There was a lot more noise a-and a really bad smell, like a dead animal. Me and Hank caught a whiff of it from inside the cooler." Verbena rocked back and forth. "Then it got real quiet. Not the good kind of quiet, either, like when you're down by the river in the evening and it's just you and the crickets and the birds are calling, and you hear the fish a-floppin'. This here was the bad kind of still, the kind that makes your insides go soft and shaky." She closed her eyes. "Something was in here with us, something bad. I heard it snuffling and scraping on the kitchen floor. Hank and me, we didn't move." She opened her eyes again. "And then it was gone. Knew it was gone, 'cause we could breathe again."

"Verbena, why don't you go lie down?" Beck suggested. The poor girl looked done in. She'd find out about Charlie soon enough.

"I am tuckered," Verbena said. Clutching the blanket around her shoulders, she stood. "You sure you don't need me?"

"Later." Beck shooed her in the direction of the little bed-

room. "Get some sleep. I'll wake you in a little while. I promise."

As soon as Verbena was out of sight, Beck rushed into the
bar. Or what was left of it. For the second time in less than three
days, the place was a shambles, only this time it was worse. The
windows were shattered, the porch doors torn off the hinges,
and the furniture had been reduced to rubble. Broken liquor
bottles were scattered about. The smells of alcohol and something rotten, like stewed garbage, were overpowering. Junior's
piano had survived the destruction, mostly. One of the legs was
broken, and the instrument listed to one side.

Worst of all, someone had taken a sledge hammer to the glass
bar.

"The demons," Beck cried, staring in horror at the shattered
glass. "Somebody let them out."

"Perhaps the Skinner human released them," Conall said.
"And, to show their gratitude, the demons killed him and
nailed him to the tree. Such treachery is typical of the djegrali."

She frowned, thinking. "And Tommy came in and saw
Charlie ransacking the place, and put Hank and Verbena in the
cooler?"

"Perhaps," Conall said.

"*No,*" a muffled voice said from behind them. "The zombie
did it."

Conall swore and drew his sword. Beck whirled around. Junior Peterson leaked out of the piano in a smoky stream and solidified. He looked terrible, wan and pale and watery, not his
normal solid self. His clothes, usually so neat and precise, were
rumpled and his hair stood on end.

Conall lowered his weapon. "Oh, it is you."

"Tommy did this?" Beck said. "I don't believe it."

"Believe it. He smashed the bar. I saw him," Junior said. His
thin form trembled. "Those *things* did the rest. There were so
many of them. I hid inside the piano. I was afraid to come out."

"Evan," Beck said, feeling angry and sick. "He put Tommy
up to this. He was looking for Haggy."

"I agree," Conall said. "When Evan discovered he could not

enter because of the shield spell, he ordered the zombie to do it."

"Poor Tommy," Beck said. "I need to find him. He'll be upset." A sudden thought made her gasp. "The storeroom. I keep demons there, too."

She ran back through the kitchen and wrenched open the storeroom door. Several dozen Mason jars had been pulled off the shelves and lay broken on the floor.

"They're gone." Beck stared in shock at the mess. "They're all gone."

Conall picked up a candy wrapper off the floor. There were a dozen more like it scattered about the storeroom. "Someone has a penchant for sweets. Verbena, perhaps?"

"I don't know and I don't care," Beck said. "The demons are gone, all of them. This is a disaster."

"How many did you have?"

"Thirty or forty, at least." Beck raised a shaking hand to her brow. "To tell you the truth, I've lost count. This is terrible. They could take over the town. We need to warn people. Not that anyone will believe us."

She shut the door and retraced her steps.

"Do not worry. The demons will not tarry here," Conall said, striding with her into the bar. "They will flee to lick their wounds. Nevertheless, I will send for reinforcements. If they do linger here, the Dal will be ready."

"I'll get word out to the kith."

"Can you trust them? Some of them will have joined the djegrali."

"Some of them, yeah. But, surely they didn't all buy that load of crap Elgdrek was peddling." Beck's shoulders sagged. Suddenly, she was weary. "It was stupid of me to keep them here in the first place, but I didn't know what else to do. A demon would come in wearing a human suit and I'd extract it. I couldn't let them walk out of here, not *knowing* it was a death sentence for the poor norm. That would be like murder."

"Do not chastise yourself. This debacle is on my head. I knew you kept demons at the bar. As leader of the Dalvahni,

I should have removed them long ago, with or without your permission." He gazed down at her in that intense way of his, like he saw right through her and into her soul. "Instead, I did nothing because it gave me an excuse to be near you."

"Really?" She returned his gaze, her heart doing a strange little skip.

"Most definitely."

Conall's expression was odd, almost tender. He reached for her. "Rebekah, I—"

Duncan appeared without warning. Beck had seen enough of him the night before to know that he was big and handsome. Seeing him in the light of day confirmed that in spades. He had eyes the color of good scotch, a sensual mouth, and light brown hair shot through with golden highlights from the sun.

He looked around at the wreckage. "What has transpired here?"

Conall dropped his hands and stepped back, his stoic mask once more in place. "You tell me, brother. I left you in charge and return to this."

Duncan held up a cloth bag. "I went in search of herbs to treat the bear's ills, devil's claw to fight inflammation and angelica root to build the blood. I had, of necessity, to travel afar."

The metal door in the back clanged shut.

"Becky," Toby hollered.

"In here, Tobe."

Toby limped in and looked around. "What in tarnation's going on? Who busted up the place and why is Charlie Skinner hanging in a tree like a gol-danged scarecrow?"

"Oh, my God," Beck said. "I forgot to call the sheriff." Hurrying toward the office, she spoke to Toby over her shoulder. "He won't be able to find us because of Cassie's spells. You'll have to meet him at the main road and show him the way."

Toby hobbled after her. "Don't worry about that sheriff," he said from the door to the office. "He won't have no problem finding us. He's kith."

"What?" Beck paused with the phone in her hand. "Are you sure?"

"Course I'm sure. Knew it soon as he come up to us last night. M' nose, you know."

The sheriff was kith. Beck's hands shook as she dialed 911. So much had happened, she was on overload. She heard someone speaking and put the receiver to her ear.

"Yes, operator, this is Beck Damian. My partner and I run a bar on the river a few miles south of Pell Landing. The address is One hundred Catman Road. The sheriff needs to send someone out here. We got a dead guy on our property."

Chapter Twenty-eight

Toby was right about the sheriff. Not only did Whitsun find the bar without a guide, he brought two deputies and the paramedics with him. He spoke briefly to Beck and Conall and then got right down to business. It took a stepladder and two men to get Charlie out of the tree. The scene was roped off and photographed. Charlie was examined and pronounced dead at the scene. No surprise there.

"Looks like they used a nail gun to hammer him to the oak," Beck overheard Whitsun say. "The body shows signs of a struggle and there's froth around the mouth. The paramedics think he may have drowned, although we'll have to do an autopsy to be sure. My. guess is, Skinner was drowned in his own moonshine."

The sheriff strode up to Beck and Conall. One of the deputies, an older man with graying hair and a slight paunch, came with him.

"You heard?" Whitsun asked Beck without preamble.

The sheriff was a straightforward kind of guy.

"Yes," Beck said. "You think Charlie was murdered. You know the Skinners run moonshine?"

Whitsun nodded. "Sonny Bowers, my predecessor, filled me in on a lot of things before he left office. He knew the Skinners were making hooch, but he never could catch them at it. Frustrated him no end. Do you know anybody who'd want to kill Charlie, a family member looking to take over the business or somebody with a grudge?"

Was he kidding? After the gathering, any number of people

probably had a grudge against Old Charlie. People got hurt and sick because of him and his kith-a-poo joy juice. She glanced at the deputy. She could give the sheriff an earful, but she wasn't about to talk kith business in front of an outsider.

"Sheriff, if I could have a word with you?" she said. "Alone."

"Give us a minute, Cecil," Whitsun said.

The deputy strolled away to talk to one of the EMTs.

Whitsun cocked a brow at Conall. "You said alone."

Conall crossed his arms on his chest. "She did not mean me. I stay."

Yeah, just what she needed: two alpha males and a double order of testosterone.

"He's okay," Beck said. "I didn't want to talk about this in front of a norm."

The sheriff stiffened. "Norm? I don't follow you."

Maybe the sheriff wasn't so straightforward, after all. Maybe he couldn't afford to be, not and do his job. Whatever; Beck was too impatient to play games.

"Don't play dumb, Sheriff. I know what you are."

Whitsun's gray eyes narrowed. Either he wore contacts to disguise his purple eyes or he was a chameleon.

"How?" he asked.

"That's my business." She wasn't about to out Toby or his nose to the sheriff. "Let's just say I know you're kith and leave it at that."

Whitsun's jaw tightened. "I trust we can keep this matter between ourselves, Ms. Damian?"

"Your secret's safe with me, Sheriff."

"Good, because I'd be unhappy with anyone or anything that interfered with my job."

Whew, somebody was touchy.

The sheriff's steady gaze shifted to Conall. "That includes you and your brothers, Mr. Dalvahni. I know what you are and what you do. I don't have a problem with it as long as you stay out of my way. This is my county."

Conall returned his regard without expression. "The Dal are not bound by human rules or boundaries."

"So I've noticed." Whitsun looked at Beck. "Any idea who did this or why they dumped Charlie's body at your place?"

"No," she said. "I can't point the finger at anybody in particular, but—"

She hesitated. It went against the grain to talk about the kith, especially to a cop. But this particular lawman was one of them.

"But?" the sheriff prodded.

"You know about the shindig at the Peterson lodge yesterday?"

"Yes. I wasn't invited, but I hear things."

Interesting; Beck wondered if the sheriff had an informant among the kith.

"Charlie was there and provided the liquor," she said. "Only this wasn't ordinary moonshine. He made it special for the kith.It . . . did things to them. Some got sick and others . . ." She shrugged. "Let's just say, it didn't bring out the best in folks."

"Was anybody hurt?"

"Yeah." She nodded toward the bar. "Somebody shot Hank, my cook, and rumor has it Lloyd Hagenbarth's son was killed. There may have been more."

Whitsun rubbed his jaw. "I'll check on the Hagenbarth boy, but first I'll need to talk to your cook."

"You'll have to wait. Right now, he's a bear."

"I don't give a damn what kind of mood he's in. If he's well enough to talk, I need to get his statement."

"You are not listening," Conall said. "She said *he is a bear.*"

"Oh," the sheriff said. "How long do you think it will be before he's . . . uh . . . more himself?"

"We do not know," Conall said. "My brother, Duncan, is a healer. He is tending the creature."

"Was your brother here last night?"

"Yes," Conall said, "although he left in search of medicinal herbs."

"I'll need to talk to him, too." The sheriff pulled out a pad and made some notes. "Anybody else here last night?"

"Yes," Beck said. "Verbena Skinner."

The sheriff looked up. "Any relation to the victim?"

"His daughter," Beck said. "She's staying here for the time being."

Whitsun wrote that down. "Any reason she'd want to kill her father?"

"Only like a million," Beck said. "Charlie Skinner was a sorry, lowdown son of a bitch, and those were his good points, but Verbena didn't kill him. She didn't leave the bar last night."

"Duncan and the bear will vouch for her," Conall said.

"When the bear can talk," Whitsun muttered.

"Besides, she couldn't have done it," Beck said. "She spent most of the night in the walk-in cooler."

"The zombie locked her in to protect her from the demons," Conall said.

"Demons?" Whitsun frowned. "What demons?"

"The ones Rebekah captured and had imprisoned until—"

"—the zombie let them out," Whitsun finished. "If this is your idea of a joke, I am not amused."

"It's not a joke," Beck said. "The zombie's name is Tommy. He set the demons free, but it wasn't his fault. The zombie maker made him do it."

"Uh-huh," Whitsun said. "So, how do you two know this if you weren't here?"

"The ghost told us," Conall said. "You will undoubtedly wish to speak to the shade as well."

"A ghost. You expect me to interview a ghost." The sheriff shoved the notepad back in his pocket. "Which ghost? No, wait. Let me guess. Hazel?"

"No," Conall said. "The shade's name is Junior Peterson."

"Peterson?" Whitsun repeated. "As in *the* Petersons?"

Beck shrugged. "His house burned down and he got tired of haunting the Episcopal church."

The sheriff's mouth thinned. He thought they were punking him. She didn't blame him. It sounded crazy.

The employee door swung open and Toby limped out.

"Becky, you won't believe it," he said, coming up to them.

"Ora Mae called and said Clyde Wheeler died of a heart attack."

"Clyde's dead?" Beck said. Clyde had been a regular at Beck's for years. "I don't believe it. We just saw him . . . when?"

"Saturday night," Toby said. "He lit out of here like everybody else when Annie screamed. His heart gave out on him in the middle of the woods. The funeral's tomorrow at two o'clock—closed casket on account of him being a pig. His brother had to tote his body home in a wheelbarrow. "

"That's awful," Beck said with a shudder.

That's the way it was with some of the kith; if they died in their animal form, they didn't always shift back. Poor Clyde. She wondered where his family got a casket for a pig. Not from any norm funeral parlor, that was for sure.

"Don't you get it, Becky?" Toby's face was flushed with excitement. "He's getting buried *tomorrow*. Three days after Annie yowled. The legend's true."

"What's he talking about?" Whitsun asked. "Who's Annie?"

"The Wampus Kitty," Toby said. "She sort of hangs around the bar, although she's skittish with everybody, 'cept the zombie. The Wampus Kitty screamed Saturday night and now Clyde Wheeler's dead."

Whitsun gave Beck a hard look. "What the hell kind of place are you running here, Ms. Damian?"

"Sheriff, I have no idea."

He shook his head. "I'd like to see the bear and speak to Miss Skinner now, if you don't mind."

"They're inside," Beck said. "I'll show you the way. Go easy on Verbena. She's had a rough night, and she doesn't know about her daddy."

"I'll tell her," Whitsun said. "Part of the job."

Not a part of the job he liked, judging from his grim expression.

"One more thing, Sheriff," Beck said. "Yesterday, Charlie was wearing a pair of red and yellow boots."

"Paul Bonds," Toby said. "Custom made."

The notepad came back out of the sheriff's pocket. "The victim was barefoot when you found him this morning?"

She nodded. "Yes. Find those boots and you might find your killer. That is, if Charlie was murdered."

"Skinner could have fallen in a vat of moonshine and drowned by accident," the sheriff said. "But he didn't climb up a tree and hang himself out to dry. Looks like somebody wanted to make an example of him."

"Yeah, but who?" Beck asked.

Toby snorted. "Take your pick. Charlie Skinner was a pain in the ass."

Beck refused to let Conall magically repair the damage to the bar.

"Why?" he asked, knitting his brows together.

"Because I don't want to get spoiled," she said. "It's not like you're going to be around forever."

She held her breath, waiting for his answer. This was his chance to contradict her.

Instead, he said only, "At least allow me to repair the windows and doors to keep out the weather and the vermin."

That was an answer, just not the one she wanted.

Serves you right, Beck thought, angry with herself. *What did you expect, a declaration of eternal devotion?*

She turned away. "Okay, I'll get the mop and broom."

She and Toby cleaned up the mess and hauled the broken furniture outside to the burn pile. Conall fixed the broken bar without asking. Beck fussed about it, but was secretly relieved. They fetched more chairs and tables out of the back storeroom and replenished the liquor supply. By noon, things were back in order, though a residual smell of demon lingered.

"Vinegar," Conall pronounced. "It kills the stench. Unless you have any Alundrean thistle seed?"

"Fresh out," Beck said.

She filled a spray bottle with vinegar and squirted it around the bar. It helped, although Toby said the place smelled like a big pickle fart.

There was still no sign of Tommy or Annie, and Beck was worried. She stood on the end of the pier calling them, but got no answer. She left some canned food on the porch for Tommy and tuna for the kitten.

"The dang possums will probably eat Annie's food," she told Conall, who'd joined her outside. "But I have to try." She widened her eyes at him. "You're a hunter. You could go look for them."

"No." He tugged her close, and kissed her on the lips. "Do not frown. I know you are worried, but I will not leave you."

Ooh, that sounded promising. Ridiculous how much lighter that simple statement made her feel.

"Why not?" Beck asked, leaning against him.

He ran his hands down her back and cupped her bottom. "Because you may be in danger. Should any of the djegrali linger here, they will bear you enmity for imprisoning them."

"Oh, I hadn't thought of that."

"I did. It is my job to keep you safe." He gave her a slow kiss that got her heart a-pumping and the blood sizzling in her veins. "A vessel approaches. We should go inside, before we shock your customers."

The guy couldn't keep his hands off her, Beck thought, smiling as she walked back up the pier. Her earlier gloom lifted. Every cloud had a silver lining. If the demons' escape meant Conall would hang around Hannah a little longer, then she was glad of it.

The news of Charlie's death spread fast, and folks drifted into the bar to talk about it. By three o'clock, the place was packed. Toby and Conall manned the bar and Beck reluctantly took over KP, limiting the menu to burgers, chicken fingers, and French fries. Verbena had fallen into an exhausted sleep after the sheriff left. She came out of the back around five o'clock, and insisted on helping out.

"Are you sure you feel up to it?" Beck asked worriedly. "I mean, because of your daddy and all."

"He weren't my daddy," Verbena said. "My mama was sneaking around on the old man. She told me before she died.

She made me promise not to tell. Said Charlie would kill me for sure." She lifted her thin shoulders. "Sorta wish I'd told him now just to get his goat. He tried to kill me anyway."

Beck gave Verbena a closer look. Her face was thin, but she didn't have the Skinners' ferrety looks. She wore a pair of Beck's old running shorts, a Beelzebubba T-shirt one of the guys in the band had given her, and plaid canvas loafers some drunk shifter had left at the bar. Her hair was a multicolored nightmare of frizz and her legs and arms were stick thin. But there was something about Verbena, something that shone through her awkward exterior.

"You don't look like a Skinner," Beck said. "Who was your daddy?"

"Traveling man," Verbena said. "Blowed through Hannah and back out again with one of them little fairs." Her expression grew wistful. "Mama said he had more talent in his little finger than all the Skinners put together. I didn't get none of it, though. I'm a dud. Earl says. They all say."

"Forget them. You are not a dud." Beck wanted to kick some Skinner ass from here to Monroe County for what they'd done to this girl. Personally. "What are you going to do? Are you going back home?"

Verbena shook her head. "No, I can't go back there." She looked down at her feet. "I was hoping you'd let me stay here. I ain't had no schooling—Charlie made me stay home and mind the stills and the dawgs. But I ain't afraid of hard work. I'll do anything. Sweep up, mop. Whatever."

"I'll talk it over with Toby," Beck said. "I'm sure we can find something for you to do."

"Really?" Verbena looked up, her eyes wide. "You mean it?"

Beck smiled. "Sure. How do you feel about waiting tables?"

A woman stuck her head in the food pickup window that connected the kitchen to the bar, a woman with creamy brown skin, exotic features, and thick, wavy black hair.

"Aw, hell," the woman said, a familiar twinkle of mischief in her tilted brown eyes. "And here I was hoping to get my old job back."

The room spun and the floor pitched under Beck's feet. "Latrisse," she gasped.

"Hello, Becky," the woman said. "Long time no see."

Beck screamed.

Chapter Twenty-nine

"But you're dead." Beck stared in disbelief at the woman kicked back in her recliner. "I was with you when you died."

They were in her living room, and Beck was sitting on the couch in Conall's lap. Beck had taken one look at Latrisse and her head had gone all swimmy. For the first time in her life she'd fainted, passed out cold from the shock of seeing Latrisse alive and well.

Conall had been there to catch her before she hit the floor. When she'd opened her eyes she was home, in his arms. She was safe and warm, and totally confused.

"Easy, my sweet," Conall murmured in her ear. He held the brandy glass to her lips. "Take another sip."

He sounded worried, and she liked that. She *really* liked that he called her his "sweet." But she hated the brandy. It was too strong and it reminded her of Charlie's moonshine.

She turned her head. "No, I don't like it."

"Nevertheless, you will drink it." He lowered his voice to that dark, sexy rumble that did things to her insides and melted her resistance. "For me."

Beck growled in frustration and took another sip. It burned her throat. "There. Happy?"

"Yes," Conall said. "For the moment."

Latrisse grinned and crossed her legs. She wore a cropped red leather jacket over a lemon yellow knit top, jeans, and purple suede half boots with five-inch heels and bright red soles. Latrisse had always liked bright colors.

"I like this one, Becky," she said. "He's bossy. You need bossy."

"Yes, she does," Conall agreed.

Conall had whisked Beck away from the bar via the demon hunter express, and a few minutes later Latrisse and Toby had toodled up the driveway in Toby's truck.

"Closed the bar," Toby announced as they'd come through the French doors. "Nobody left anyway. Whole place cleared out when you hollered. Thought you was the Wampus Kitty." He held up two six-packs of beer and a bottle of brandy. "Figured you might need a little something to calm your nerves. It ain't every day your best friend comes back from the dead."

And here they were, sitting around talking like it was no big deal. But it was a big deal. Latrisse had been dead with a capital D. And now she wasn't. Beck had seen a lot of strange things, but she couldn't wrap her mind around this one.

"I don't understand," Beck said. "Toby and I carried your body back to your mama. She had you cremated. There was a memorial service and everything. She kept your ashes on the mantel until—" She stopped, remembering. "Your mama's house got broken into a few months ago."

Song Chung Jackson, Latrisse's mother, was a widow. Her husband, Vince, an African American airplane mechanic, had brought his wife and baby daughter back to his hometown of Hannah when he'd retired from the Air Force. He'd died two years after Latrisse. From a broken heart, Beck had always believed. Another sin she laid at the demons' door.

"Song's house got burglarized?" Toby said. He took a swig of beer. "I didn't know that."

"Yeah, I think it was in May or June," Beck said. "You should read the paper."

Toby chuckled. "Why, when you're gonna tell me what's in it anyway?"

"I didn't tell you about Song."

"Yeah," Toby said. "What's up with that?"

Beck rolled her eyes. "I called your mama and asked her what happened," she told Latrisse. "She said she got home from bingo one night and found the front door wide open. Something must've startled the thieves because they took off in a hurry. Nothing was missing, but the urn that contained your ashes was lying on the floor, broken. Your ashes were gone, nothing left but a little powder. She was pretty shaken up."

Latrisse looked at her and continued to drink her beer.

"Well?" Beck said.

Latrisse sighed and sat up straight in the recliner. "Family legend has it we're descended from a vermillion bird on my mother's side."

"A what?" Beck asked.

"A phoenix," Conall said. "A beautiful, mythical bird with magnificent plumage that rises from its own ashes."

"I know what a phoenix is," Beck said, giving him a repressive glare. "I just never heard it called that before. So why now? If you're a phoenix, why didn't you rise up as soon as you were cremated?"

Latrisse took another pull of her beer. "Beats me, Beck. I was nowhere and then I was standing in a house buck naked and these two dudes were looking at me like I was Freddy Krueger. They ran out the door and I lit out after them. I was majorly freaked out. I didn't know where I was or *who* I was. I stole some clothes and wandered around for months, working odd jobs, before my memory came back."

"How long did you have amnesia?" Beck asked.

"I started getting flashes almost immediately," Latrisse said. "But nothing that made any sense." She shrugged. "One night there was a bad storm. I woke up and it was all there."

"When was that?"

Latrisse picked at the label on her beer. "Late August."

"August?" Beck said. "That was months ago. Where have you been?"

"Trying to figure things out. I had my memory back, but I

wasn't sure." Latrisse pulled another strip of paper off the bottle. "I mean, what if they weren't my memories? What if I was bat shit crazy? I did some poking around on the Internet, found you and my mama. Decided to come back and check it out." She set the empty bottle on the table by the chair. "And here I am."

"Have you seen Song?" Beck asked.

"Of course."

"How'd she take it?"

"Better 'n you," Latrisse said. "She didn't bust my eardrums."

"You startled me."

"Remind me never to startle you in the future. You caused a stampede." Latrisse rose to her feet. "You look tired. I'll talk to you tomorrow."

"What are you going to tell people?" Beck asked.

"That Mama and I had a fight and I left."

"But, you *died*. Your obituary was in the paper."

Latrisse waggled her brows. "I got better."

"Be serious," Beck said. "Song kept your ashes in a jar."

"It was symbolic. I was dead to my mother until I made amends. It's a cultural thing."

"Oh, for Pete's sake," Beck said. "Like anybody's going to believe that shit."

"Who's to say any different?" Latrisse said. "I'm the only Blasian in town."

"The sepulchral urn in which your ashes were interred," Conall said. "Where did your mother obtain it?"

"No idea," Latrisse said. "I was sort of dead at the time."

"I went with Song to pick it out," Beck said. "It was made in Hannah by a local artist."

"From Hannah river clay?" Conall asked.

"Yes," Beck said, eyeing him. "Why?"

He shrugged. "Just curious."

Toby and Latrisse left, and Conall and Beck were alone. Mr. Cat came to the window and meowed, and Beck let him in and fed him. The cat strolled over and rubbed against Conall's legs.

Something passed between warrior and feline. Mr. Cat went to the door and asked to go out.

"What was that all about?" Beck asked, shutting the door behind the cat.

"I promised him tomorrow I would give him an entire can of the smelly wet stuff he so greatly enjoys *if* he afforded us some privacy tonight."

"You bribed my cat."

"I was desperate."

"Desperate for what?"

"For you," Conall said. He lifted her in his arms and sniffed her hair. "Also, I have an inexplicable craving for the fried edible tubers you serve at the restaurant."

"You're saying I smell like a French fry. How romantic. For future reference, that is not the way to get into a girl's pants."

"I assume that expression is another euphemism for sexual intercourse, such as *getting laid* or *having a roll in the hay.*"

His black eyes were warm. Beck wrapped her arms around his neck and grinned up at him. "Very good. Somebody's been doing their homework."

He took her into the bathroom and put her down. A wave of his hand and the shower came on.

"I have given the subject a great deal of thought," he said.

"What subject is that?"

"Coupling with you. And for future reference, *this* is how I get into your pants."

He waved his hand again and Beck's clothes slid from her body and fell in a heap on the floor. Conall's clothes went the same route. Beck's heart did a funny little *tha-thump* at the sight of him. The guy should never wear clothes, he was too plain gorgeous. That would be fine by her.

But that would mean other women would get to see him naked, and she was *not* okay with that. She was in major lust for the captain of the Dalvahni, and she wanted him all to herself for however long they had together.

"You *have* been studying," she said with approval.

"Yes, but I need more hands-on experience."

He picked her up and carried her into the shower, where he washed her hair and body with great care. The slope of her shoulders, the curve of her rump, her breasts and nipples, the sensitive skin of her belly, the aching place between her legs—all were given the same careful attention. He took his time, enjoying her soft sighs and shivers of longing, his hands hot and lingering as he carefully rinsed the soap from her skin.

"My turn," she said.

She soaped her hands and washed and rinsed him, enjoying the play of her hands over his smooth, olive skin and rippling muscles. She caressed his wide chest and bulging pecs, and traced the fascinating ridges of his taut, lean belly. Her hands moved farther down to his hard, jutting erection. He was beautiful there, too. She wrapped her fingers around him and stroked.

"Hey, I wasn't finished," she protested as he lifted her by the waist and pushed her against the wall.

"Neither am I," he said.

He stepped between her thighs and thrust inside her.

Conall Dalvahni was a very good student, Beck mused as he proceeded to show her some of what he'd learned; a very good student indeed.

Tommy waited until the moon was up before he crept out of the underbrush. The bar appeared empty; no customers and no lights. The parking lot was deserted. He slogged up the embankment to the porch. His legs didn't work so good anymore and he had trouble getting up the steps.

He found two cases of red beans on the porch beside some cans of tuna. There was a piece of paper taped to the top of the cans. The eye rot had set in for real and the vision in his left eye was gone. He unfolded the note with difficulty and read the message slowly, struggling to make out the words:

Dear Tommy,
The beans are for you. They're high in protein and won't spoil like tofu. Don't feel bad about the demons. I know Evan made you

do it. I know he's the zombie maker. Come back to the bar. We'll figure something out.

Beck

P. S. Take care of Annie.

The note made Tommy want to bawl, but he couldn't. His tear ducts were gone. He sat down on the steps instead and opened a can of beans. They were the easy-open kind and Beck had left him a spoon, bless her. His fingers were swollen and spongy, so he used the handle of the spoon to pry off the lid. He shoveled the beans in his mouth and opened another can.

The beans didn't satisfy his terrible craving for flesh, but he didn't know what else to do. He was so screwed. The burning hunger worsened by the hour, and the Maker was no longer in his head.

That should have been a good thing, but it scared Tommy. The geis was still upon him, but the Maker had left him to rot. Probably, he should throw himself in the river and let the varmints eat him.

But, what if that didn't free him? What if his spirit stayed stuck to his skeleton at the bottom of the river, trapped in the darkness and the muddy silt forever, and slimy things made a nest of his bones?

The thought made Tommy shudder, but he didn't want to hurt anyone, either. He wished he was dead, *really* dead. How many times in his life had he said that when he was having a bad day? You could take every shitty day he'd had while alive and roll them into one, and it wouldn't hold a candle to this.

There were worse things than being dead, and he was one of them.

Junior Peterson materialized at the foot of the steps. "You let those *things* loose. I spent the night inside the piano, thanks to you."

"I didn't have a choice," Tommy said, indignant. "The Maker made me do it."

"Where's the cat?"

"I run her off." Tommy flipped the top on a third can of beans. "She was getting on my nerves."

"Right." Junior paused. "Scared you'd eat her?"

"Yeah." Tommy jabbed the spoon into the slimy beans. "I almost ate a squirrel this morning. All I can think about is brains, brains, brains. I don't know how much longer I can stand it before I eat somebody."

"So what's stopping you?" Junior asked. "From eating brains, I mean." He held up his hand. "Not that I'm condoning it, mind you, but I am curious. Zombies eat brains, don't they?"

"I'm a vegetarian."

The ghost looked dumbstruck for a moment, and then he began to laugh.

"Oh, my," Junior said with a gasp. Tears ran down his face in a silver stream. "A vegetarian zombie? I declare, that is the funniest thing I've heard in years."

"Glad you think so," Tommy said. "The preservation spell is wearing off, and I'm starting to decay. Bad enough I had to die, but this? I never did nothing to deserve this."

Junior's amused expression faded. "No, you didn't, but it is what it is."

"It blows."

"Yes, it does." Junior's voice held sympathy. "So, what are you going to do about it?"

"What can I do? Nothing, I reckon but sit around and fall to pieces." He held up his left thumb. The nail had split and the bone poked through the skin. "It's already started."

"You could ask that demon hunter to cut off your head with his sword. Problem solved."

"And give my poor mama a heart attack? What you think she going do when I show up in New Orleans without a head?"

"She wouldn't have to see you. You could be buried right here, or be cremated and have your ashes sprinkled on the river."

Tommy thumped the can down on the step. "Sprinkle me? What am I, fish food? Now, you listen here. I am *not* spending eternity in this backwater shithole. I'm a city boy. I want to go home to New Orleans and be buried in the Greenwood Cemetery with the rest of the Hendersons."

"You could kill the Maker. That's bound to break the curse."

"Can't get near him," Tommy said glumly. "On account of the spell."

"Who is this guy?"

Tommy opened his mouth, but nothing came out. Great; just freaking great. The Maker had abandoned him like so much garbage, but he still couldn't say his name. Silently, he held out Beck's note for the ghost to read.

Junior's pale eyes widened. "Evan? Beck's brother is the zombie maker?"

"You know him?"

"I overheard him talking to Beck outside the church Saturday night."

"He's a bad one," Tommy said. "I make one wrong move and he'll stake me out in the sun for the buzzards to eat without a second thought."

"What you need is an intermediary, a neutral third party—someone to act on your behalf."

"Right," Tommy said. "I'll just trot my ass on down to the intermediary store and get me one of them. If that don't work, I guess I could put an ad in the paper." He waved a decomposing hand in the air. *"Zombie seeks murder for hire. Pays an arm and a leg."*

"I'll be your agent."

"I appreciate the offer, but I don't see what you can do."

"I'll haunt him, that's what," Junior said. He straightened his slim frame. "I'll make him sorry he was ever born. If there's one thing I cannot abide, it's a bully."

Chapter Thirty

Tuesday morning, Beck and Verbena rode into town in the Tundra. Beck's Dalvahni watchdog went with them.

"You should stay here. We're going shopping," Beck told Conall as she and Verbena started to leave the bar.

"I go with you," he said in his unyielding I-am-captain-of-the-Dalvahni voice.

"Okay, but you'll be bored."

"I survived the siege of Ilthanric, which lasted fourteen years. I think I can withstand a morning's excursion to the market."

"I'll ride in the back, seeing as how you're so tall," Verbena said, scampering ahead of him across the parking lot.

Giving him a nervous glance over her shoulder, Verbena climbed in the Tundra. She wore a pair of old sweatpants, the plaid loafers she'd had on the day before, and a long-sleeve Budweiser T-shirt. A ball cap covered her mangled hair. Beck understood the girl's alarm. Conall was in warrior mode this morning; everything about him, from the hard, challenging look in his eyes to the implacable set of his jaw, screamed menace.

Once, he would have made Beck nervous, too. But now she just wanted to jump his bones and kiss his stern mouth until she melted his cold, dangerous mood.

Lord, she was hopeless.

They left the bar and putted down the road in silence.

"River's down," Verbena commented as they crossed the Trammel Bridge.

Spring through late summer, Devil River Outfitters did a

brisk business renting out kayaks, canoes, and inner tubes to those seeking recreation and an escape from the heat. There was no one on the rapids today. It had been a dry autumn, and the river was baring its rocky teeth.

They drove slowly into town. Hannah was snuggled between the river and a clump of low, rolling hills created millions of years earlier when a meteor had crashed into the South Alabama tabletop. A tree-lined swath of asphalt named Main Street ran from the bridge at the north end of town, past a small business district and the Methodist and Baptist churches, and huffed its way up a hill and down the other side into North Florida. The brick shops along Main Street were neat and well-maintained, the sidewalks free of litter.

It was ten o'clock. The kids were out for Thanksgiving break and the streets were bustling for a weekday. Beck turned off Main Street onto Third Avenue and parallel-parked in front of a shop. The words JEANNINE'S KUT 'N KURL were painted on the storefront window in loopy turquoise and bright pink letters that floated between the blades of a giant pair of scissors.

"First stop," Beck said, turning off the truck.

"It's a beauty parlor." There was apprehension in Verbena's voice. "What are we doing here?"

Beck glanced in the rearview mirror. Verbena's shoulders were hunched and her mouth was pinched tight. The poor girl looked terrified.

"I thought we'd get your hair done to celebrate your new job as a waitress," Beck said. "My treat."

"Don't want to. I hate getting my hair did."

"Oh." Beck wasn't sure what to say to that. Verbena's hair was a pile of over-processed crap, at least eight different colors with the remnants of a perm gone tragically wrong. She cleared her throat. "Been to a lot of salons, have you?"

"Never been to no beauty parlor in my life."

No shit.

"So, you do your own hair?"

"Naw, it's m' cousins," Verbena said. "They're always dragging something or another home from the Dollar General and trying it out on me."

"And you're okay with that?"

Verbena tugged her hat down. "Never had no say-so in the matter. Charlie said."

Charlie said. Charlie had been a colossal dick. That explained the rainbow hair dye. They'd used the poor girl like a mannequin.

"This won't be like that," Beck said. "Jeannine knows what she's doing."

"Cousin Leaberta said she knowed what she was doing, and she burnt my hair slap up with perm solution."

"Don't worry," Beck said. "Jeannine can fix that with a good haircut."

"Oh, that was a long time ago," Verbena said. "My hair was a mess back then."

Good Lord.

"This will be completely different," Beck said. "I promise."

Verbena looked doubtful, but allowed Conall to help her out of the backseat of the truck.

Later, Beck would regret not videoing their entrance into the Kut 'N Kurl with her cell phone. The sign on the front said WALK-INS WELCOME, but it was two days before Thanksgiving and the shop was crowded. Jeannine and the other stylists were hard at work at their stations. The dryer bank along one wall was filled with customers, some in rollers; others with highlights wrapped in layers of foil. The two manicurists were chatting to their clients as they did their nails, and the shampoo girl was rinsing a matron's hair in one of the sinks. A woman waited with two restless children in chairs near the reception desk.

The salon was filled with a pleasant hum of conversation and the scents of assorted hair products, nail polish, and remover. The room fell silent when they walked in. Everybody gawked, and Verbena hadn't even taken off her hat. Not that anyone was looking at Beck or Verbena. They might as well have been invisible. Everyone was staring at Conall, the Dalvahni god of

Yowza, in slack-jawed surprise. Even the children stopped
whining and pulling on their poor mother to gape at him.

And no wonder. It wasn't every day walking sex strode into
the Kut 'N Kurl. Conall looked big and bad and sinfully delicious; a dark knight in a black shirt and blue jeans.

Jeannine Mitchell, the owner, left her client sitting open
mouthed in the chair and hurried up to him.

"I'm Jeannine," she said, breathless as a four-hundred-pound
man in a relay race. "Can I help you?"

Jeannine was on the shady side of fifty with wispy, shoulder-
length brunette hair she religiously colored to squelch any hint
of gray, a pleasant round face, and hazel eyes. Her husband Ted
worked at the paper mill in Cantonment thirty miles away.

They had two grown sons and three grandchildren, but
Jeannine was looking at Conall with the flushed, jittery excitement of a ninth grader chatting up the high school quarterback
in the hallway between classes. The pulse fluttered in her throat.
Goodness, Conall had sent the poor woman into atrial fib.

"Yes, thank you," Conall said in his whiskey and sex voice.
"Our friend requires your services."

"Oh." Jeannine's girlish glow faded. "You sure you don't
need a haircut? I'd be glad to work you in."

I'll just bet you would, Beck thought, amused and irritated.
Conall Dalvahni was a big juicy steak in a room full of hungry
lionesses.

"Perhaps some other time," Conall said. He motioned to
Verbena. "My friend needs your services. If you could help her,
I would be in your debt."

"Gee, I don't know," Jeannine said, still gazing at Conall in
shock and awe. "We're sort of busy."

"What happened to working him in?" Beck demanded.

"Easy, my sweet." Conall gave his dark head a rueful shake.
" 'Tis just as well. I fear this task is beyond her skills."

"Beyond my skills?" Jeannine bristled. "I'll have you know I
took third place in the Gulf Coast hair show two years *in a row*.
Take your hat off, girl."

Verbena removed the ball cap and a collective gasp of horror rippled through the room. The shampoo girl dropped the bottle of conditioner in her hand and screamed.

"Mommy, what's wrong with that lady's hair?" one of the children asked. "It looks like dog throw-up."

"Hush, Stevie," the boy's mother said.

An old woman in curlers pushed up the hood of her dryer. "God a' mighty, Jeannine. You can't do nothing with that."

Jeannine pulled herself up to her full height of five feet, two inches. "Maybe not, but I've got to try. I took an oath when I graduated cosmetology school." She turned to the woman sitting at her station. "Outta the way, Shirley. This here's an emergency."

"What about me? My hair's still damp. It'll frizz."

"One of the other girls can finish you up," Jeannine said. She flapped her hands impatiently at the woman. "Get on. It's my Christian duty to help this poor child."

Shirley grumbled and moved to another station.

Jeannine dragged a reluctant Verbena across the room and pushed her into the stylist's chair.

"That lady looks mad," Verbena said, clutching the padded armrests. "I don't want to be no trouble."

"She can just get glad in the same pants she got mad in," Jeannine said. "It's no skin off my teeth."

"What if she don't come back?" Verbena said. "I don't want you losing b'ness on account of me."

Jeannine snorted. "She's my sister-in-law. I cut her hair for free. Couldn't chase her away with a stick." She examined a tuft of Verbena's Brillo pad hair. "The ends are fried. You need a haircut. You okay with that?"

"Do what you have to do, Jeannine," Beck said.

"No, ma'am, that's not the way it works at the Kut 'N Kurl. Her head—her decision." Jeannine met Verbena's gaze in the mirror. "You trust me, gal?"

Verbena nodded.

"Good." Jeannine squared her jaw. "Let's get to it then. First thing, we shampoo and condition your hair. I've got this great new product called Fiona Fix-It. It's made right here in Hannah. Do you know Evie Douglass? She's Evie Dalvahni now. No? Well, Fiona Fix-It is her creation. I think you'll be surprised what it can do. And then . . ."

An hour and a half later, Beck waited for Verbena on a chaise lounge outside a dressing room at the Greater Fair, Hannah's only clothing store for women. Conall stood across the room near the side exit, glowering. There were a few other customers in the store, but they weren't shopping. They were soaking up Conall's yumitude.

"Stop scowling," Beck told him. "What, are you afraid you'll get girl cooties?"

His gaze passed over the racks of clothes and undergarments, the display case of jewelry and scents, and the stacks of high heels.

"No," he said. "But, I did not expect the process to take so long. First the barber and now this."

"Shows how much you know about women." Beck swung her legs off the chair and sat up. "You all right in there?" she called to Verbena, who was trying on clothes.

Verbena mumbled something from behind the curtain.

Dancy Smith bustled up to them wearing a pumpkin-colored orange tweed sheath dress and cropped jacket. Her hair was a perfectly coiffed gray helmet, and her wrinkled cheeks were powdered and rouged. As the proprietress of the Greater Fair, Dancy took her job as the town's premier fashion consultant deadly serious.

"How are we doing?" Dancy asked, giving Beck her best plastic, professional smile. "Shall I bring her something else to try?"

"No idea," Beck said. "She won't come out."

"Do they fit, dear?" Dancy hovered outside the dressing room. "Can we see?"

"No." There was a note of panic in Verbena's voice. "I can't. I feel naked."

"Perhaps if your gentleman friend left?" Dancy arched a thin, penciled brow in Conall's direction. "Young ladies are sometimes shy with handsome men around." She looked Conall up and down and simpered—*simpered*. "And he is so dark and dangerous, and *manly*."

Dancy Smith was having a hot flash, and it wasn't from menopause. So were the other women in the store. One woman with a beehive hairdo and a bosom like a ship's prow kept peeking at him from behind a stand of belts, as though he couldn't see her. Hah! It was like trying to hide a five hundred pound moose behind a flagpole.

Beck got to her feet. "I'll see what I can do."

"That would be nice, dear." Dancy eyeballed Conall like he was a Dalvahni snack machine. "Now, if you'll excuse me, I need to check on something in the stockroom. I'll be right back."

Beck strolled over to Conall. "Dancy says you should leave. Dancy says you're making Verbena nervous with all your hotitude."

"What?"

"Verbena's shy. She won't come out of the dressing room if you're here. Why don't you go for a little walk, check out the hardware store or the Country Behr?"

"If I wished to look at a bear, I could have stayed at the bar."

Oh, brother; Mr. Literal. "It's not that kind of bear. This is an outdoor store. There are knives and guns, and implements of destruction. You'll love it."

"Knives, you say?" There was a definite gleam of interest in Conall's eyes. "Intriguing, but some other time, perhaps. It is not safe to leave you alone. The djegrali—"

"Ah, brother, there you are," Duncan said, appearing without warning. "The bear is much improved. I am ready to accompany you on the errand you mentioned, if it suits you."

He was still wearing his medieval garb. Halloween was over; this ought to be fun to explain. She glanced around to see if anyone else had noticed. Oh, yeah, but they didn't seem to mind. Females stood in tittering clumps, gaping at the two warriors. Another minute, and there'd be a vagina stampede.

"Skedaddle, both of you." Beck pushed Conall toward the side exit. He was about as moveable as a small mountain. "Verbena and I will meet you in an hour in front of the Sweet Shop. Will that give you enough time to finish your business?"

"Of a certainty," Conall said, "but I will not leave you unarmed."

"Not to worry," Beck said. "I got this." She produced a bottle of Hot Dangpepper sauce from her pocket that had been fitted with a metal pour spout. "And I still have your ring."

"You gave her your ring?" Duncan looked shocked. "Surely, it is unwise to entrust such a thing of power to—"

He glanced at Beck and did not finish.

"—someone like me," Beck said, stung. "Can't trust the demon girl, right?" She tugged at the silver band, but it would not budge. "Don't let it pucker your ass. He can have his stupid ring back."

Conall closed his hand around hers. "The ring is mine to do with as I will, and I want you to have it."

"But, what if—"

"The ring is yours." Conall said. He tilted her chin with gentle fingers and gazed into her eyes. "Always. Do you understand?"

"Sure," she said. The look in his eyes made her heart thump like a rabbit's. "But I don't want to get you in trouble with Kevin." She flashed Duncan a look of resentment. "Or cause trouble between you and your men."

Duncan gave her a deep bow. "I beg your pardon, milady. I did not understand the situation. My brother has been a wise and steadfast leader for many years. I should have trusted his judgment, in all things, including matters of the heart." He gave Beck a crooked smile. "Please accept my apologies."

"No problem," Beck said, mollified. Jeez, these Dalvahni guys could charm the shell off a turtle. She gave him a smile of her own to show that she meant it. "You two run along and do guy stuff. I'll stay with Verbena. This could take a while."

Conall frowned. "My business can wait until you are safely back at the bar where there are protective spells in place."

"So, put a spell on the store to keep out the creepers," Beck suggested.

"I suppose I could do that," Conall said, with obvious reluctance. "But you must give me your word to remain here where it is safe until we return."

"Sure thing," Beck said. "Cross my heart and hope to die."

Conall put the anti-demon thinga-muh-jigger in place and he and Duncan left on a jet stream of yummy.

Beck clapped her hands at the gaggle of women. "Beat it. Floorshow's over."

The women trailed out of the store looking disgruntled and deflated. Coming down too suddenly from a Dalvahni high would do that to you. Jeez, what a bunch of cougars.

Beck wandered around for a while, perusing this item and that. Where was Dancy? she wondered.

She soon grew bored and drifted back to the dressing rooms, where she found a slim young woman standing before the three-way mirror, gazing shyly at her reflection.

It was a moment before Beck recognized Verbena. The change in the girl was nothing short of remarkable. The parched, cotton candy hair and baggy, mismatched clothes were gone. In their place was a fresh-faced gamin with a shining cap of strawberry-blond hair. The short haircut framed Verbena's thin face and emphasized her large eyes.

If only Jeannine could see Verbena now. The stylist had been so excited by Verbena's transformation that she'd thrown in a makeover for free, dusting the girl's fair, freckled skin with powder and blush, darkening her pale brows and lashes, and dabbing a bit of pink gloss on her lips. Everyone in the salon had jumped to their feet and cheered at the results, even Shirley and the skeptical old lady under the bonnet dryer. Verbena had marched out of the Kut 'N Kurl with her head high, a bag of makeup in one hand, and a bottle of Fiona Fix-It in the other.

The new clothes completed the picture. Verbena wore jeans and a peachy pink open-stitch cotton sweater over a blush camisole. She looked youthful and very attractive, if a bit coltish with her long, slender legs and thin frame.

She stared doubtfully at herself in the mirror. "You can see all my bits in this here outfit. You sure I don't look like a skank-ho?"

"All your bits are covered," Beck assured her. "You're used to clothes that don't fit."

That was an understatement. Verbena had commented when they entered the store that she'd never had clothes of her own, only castoffs. From the calluses on the girl's feet, Beck suspected Verbena had gone most of her life without shoes, too. If Charlie Skinner weren't already dead, Beck would beat him to death with his ugly boots.

Verbena's expression was wistful as she gazed into the mirror. "They sure are purty duds, but it don't feel right taking charity."

"It's not charity, it's a loan," Beck said. "You can pay me back out of your paycheck."

"I'll work real hard," Verbena said. "You ain't gonna be sorry you give me this chance, I swear. I—"

Verbena halted, her eyes growing round in the mirror. Beck whirled around. Dancy Smith stood at the end of the lingerie aisle, holding a large hatbox in her hands.

"Hello, ladies," she said in a slithery, un–Dancy like voice. Her eyes were watery pools of tar above the grinning line of her mouth. "Look what came in on the delivery truck."

She took the top off the box and a swarm of demons flew out.

Chapter Thirty-one

Conall and Duncan strode into the Country Behr. The small shop bristled with weaponry, including an array of guns, knives, and hunting bows. Racks of clothes in a mottled pattern lined both walls, and there were shelves of boots and hats, camping gear, and bins of fishing equipment. A short balding man in a red shirt and dark trousers greeted them as they entered the store. He reminded Conall of a stubby overweight robin, with his bright eyes and beak of a nose.

"Morning," the man said, eyeing Duncan's warrior garb. "What are you, some kind of reenactor?"

Conall made a mental note to remind Duncan to obtain more suitable clothing.

"We seek information about a knife," Conall said.

"Knives, I got." The man waved his hand at the weapons on the wall and lined up inside the glass case. "I got Bowies, fixed blades, multi-blades, and survival knives, to name a few. Whatcha looking for?"

"Your wares are impressive, but we are looking for something more unusual," Conall said. "We were told that a man named Blake Peterson was a collector of weaponry. Do you know him?"

"Sure I know him. Petersons own half the town. Blake's dead though—died in a fire along with his wife." The man smoothed the front of his shirt with his plump hands, like a bird grooming its feathers. "The missus left some kind of letter behind claiming Old Blake was a wacko who liked to hurt women. You never can tell about people, can you?"

"The knife we are interested in belonged to him."

"Blake bought a thing or two from me over the years, but not much," the proprietor said with a shake of his head. "He collected specialty knives, custom made and high end. Some of those knives were worth twenty grand, maybe more. I don't carry that kind of inventory. Paper said he had something like a million dollars tied up in knives. They were all destroyed in the fire."

"A shame," Conall said. "So, Peterson did not frequent your shop?"

"Didn't say that. Said he didn't buy much. He'd stop in every now and then to show off his latest find. Called 'em his teeth. *Look at my new tooth,* he'd say, and show me a new knife." The man shook his head. "Real creepy, now I think about what he was doing with 'em. Have to give the man credit, though. He had some gorgeous blades. 'Cept for that last one he brought in here. Ugliest knife I ever saw."

Conall felt a flare of excitement. He leaned closer to the man. "Tell me about this ugly knife."

"Not much to tell. Stone blade, deer antler handle. Peterson seemed all het up about it. Said it was something special." The proprietor shrugged. "Frankly, made me wonder if he was a few slices short of a full loaf. I mean, the man has knives from all over the world and he's all blowed up about a piece of flint."

Conall and Duncan exchanged glances.

"Did he happen to mention where he got this knife?" Duncan asked.

"Right here in Hannah," the man said. "Had it made out of crater rock."

The pieces of the puzzle slid together. "The crater," Conall said. "Of course. It is as I suspected." The man behind the counter gave him a curious look and Conall reined in his spinning thoughts. "I thank you, my good man," he said. Opening his money pouch, Conall peeled off a roll of bills and handed them to the shop keep. "Take this for your trouble, along with my thanks."

"You're welcome, any time." The man stared at the wad of money Conall had given him. "And I do mean anytime."

Conall strode across the shop. "One thing more," he said, pausing at the door. "Did Peterson happen to mention who crafted this stone blade? A local knife maker, perhaps?"

"More of a jack of all trades," the man said. "His name is Claude Dolan. We call him the Key Man around here because he's our local locksmith. Runs a small repair shop, but Claude can do all kinds of things. Real clever with his hands."

"Again, you have my thanks," Conall said, turning away.

"You interested in Trey Peterson?" the man called after them. "He was in here yesterday."

Conall strode back to the counter. "Very interested. What did he want?"

The shop keep gave him a pointed look, and Conall handed him some more bills.

The money disappeared into the man's pocket. "He was asking questions about that stone knife. I told him about the Key Man, and he was out of here like a shot."

"What is the location of this Key Man's establishment?" Conall asked.

"Four blocks north and hang a Ronnie on McRae Street. The sign says KEY MAN REPAIRS. You can't miss it."

"Why are we hanging this Ronnie?" Duncan asked as he and Conall strode south on Main Street. "Is he a brigand of some sort?"

"I, too, was nonplussed at first by the human's strange instructions," Conall said. "But, upon reflection, I believe he means for us to turn right on McRae Street."

Duncan was silent for a moment. "I have checked the translator and 'Ronnie' is a name, not a direction."

"I have found our translator is, more oft than not, useless in this place," Conall said. "Humans are seldom exact in their speech."

"I have noticed this also."

"Upon which occasion?" Conall halted on the sidewalk and

gave Duncan a cold look. People flowed around them, some pausing to gape at them outright. "I checked my reports, brother. You have made numerous trips to Hannah in the past seventy years, but you make no mention of the kith in your accounts."

Duncan returned his regard with a level stare. "I have never shirked my duty."

"'Twas your duty to inform me of the kith."

"My duty is to seek the djegrali and return them to their proper sphere. This I have done without fail for ten millennia. Neither the Great Book nor our creed contain any mention of the kith."

"That argument is specious, brother, and you know it," Conall said. "You should have told me at once. I cannot lead the Dal if I am blind."

"Had I told you of the kith when first I learned of their existence, you would have wiped them out."

"You do not know that."

"I could not chance it."

"Because of the kith woman Cassandra?"

"Yes," Duncan said without hesitation. "You should thank me, brother. If I had made a timely report, you would have acted upon that knowledge with your typical ruthless assiduousness. The woman you love might never have reached adulthood."

"How noble and prescient of you," Conall said. "As it happens, the woman you love was also spared."

Duncan did not bother to deny it. He had the right of it, though, Conall admitted. The old Conall would have eliminated the kith without a second thought, including Rebekah. The thought was a blade to the heart. He would never have known the sweetness of lying with her, of loving her. Less pleasant emotions he would have been spared as well, he reflected wryly, such as jealousy, worry, and terror on her behalf.

And light and laughter, tenderness and joy; these things he would have missed also. Rebekah inspired a welter of feelings within him, some good, some decidedly uncomfortable, but he would not trade a moment of it for a return to his former existence.

"There is something in what you say." Conall resumed his former ground-eating stride. "Hate destroys reason. I would have considered it my duty to eliminate the kith." He grimaced. "Though, truth be told, the task would be nigh unto impossible. Demon-possessed humans are hard enough to track, much less those with whom they lie and produce children."

"Exactly," Duncan said, keeping apace. "That is why I did not inform you of the kith in my report. After giving the matter much thought, I have determined a simpler solution. We must find and destroy the portal through which the djegrali enter Hannah."

"Simpler?" Conall snorted. "There are no doubt dozens of portals on this plane."

"But not in Hannah. Tell me, brother. Know you of any other clime, on earth or any other dimension, where the djegrali have planted seed that begat offspring?"

Conall thought about this. "No, not in all my years of service."

"Neither have I. Were you to take a poll among the Dal, I believe the answer would be the same. Hannah is unique, a nexus of magic that draws the supernatural to it, including the djegrali." Duncan paused, adding, "And the Dalvahni as well."

Another piece of the puzzle slid into place. A star had fallen here in the distant past, folding the earth into low hills and valleys. This Conall had learned during his sojourn here. That star, Conall believed, was the source of Hannah's magic and the secret behind the knife that had wounded Ansgar. He felt it in his gut.

"If Hannah is the trouble then Hannah is also the solution," Conall said, thinking aloud. "Destroy it and it ceases to be a problem."

"Such a thing is forbidden. It is stated in the Great Book."

"Yes," Conall agreed. "Thank the gods." He was weary of battle, death, and destruction. "But there is another reason we should not destroy Hannah."

"I am eager to hear it."

"After my initial visit here, I consulted with Kehvahn," Conall said. "There are but a handful of magical nexuses in all the worlds, and they are connected. Destroy one and you run the risk of destroying them all."

"A compelling reason for Hannah's continued existence."

"Indeed," Conall said. "If magic ceases to exist, where does that leave the Dalvahni?"

"A salient point and one I do not like to contemplate. What do we do then?"

"What we have ever done, brother," Conall said. "Defend the weak against the djegrali and keep the demons in check. No easy task in a place such as Hannah."

"Yes," Duncan said. "We have much work ahead of us."

"Are you volunteering for permanent assignment here?"

"Yes, 'twill be good hunting." Duncan sounded cheered by the prospect. "Why, we might tarry here an eternity and not put an end to the djegrali or their mischief."

An eternity with Rebekah would not be enough, Conall thought with satisfaction. But it would be a start.

Assorted junk, clocks, and electrical appliances cluttered the front room of Claude Dolan's shop. Humans, in Conall's experience, possessed great fondness for their machines, even those that served no practical purpose. His gaze lingered on a large domed black and steel gadget. Who, in the name of the gods, needed an electric egg poacher?

A stand of shiny keys hung from a display on one counter. The shop walls were covered with colorful pictures of muscle-bound humans in bright, tightly fitting costumes with flowing capes, and black and white images of sultry-eyed women with pouty lips and tousled hair.

The door behind the counter swung open and a man seated on a wheeled, wooden plank rolled out. He had curly blond hair, blue eyes, and a merry face. His lower legs were gone. Thick, black straps were wrapped around his knuckles. He lowered his hands, straps down, and propelled himself across the floor on the wheeled board. He was amazingly deft at it, and his arms and shoulders were very developed in contrast to his withered thighs.

"Thought I heard somebody come in," the man said, looking up at them. "What can I do you for?"

"You are the Key Man?" Conall asked.

"Yup, that's what they call me. Name's Dolan."

"We are looking for information about a knife you made for Blake Peterson."

"Not much to tell you," Dolan said with a shrug of his heavy shoulders. He rolled over and hefted himself into a chair behind the counter. "Peterson came in with a chunk of crater rock and asked if I could make him a knife out of it. He gave me a rough sketch of what he wanted and a piece of deer antler, and I did the rest."

"Did Peterson seem pleased with the result?"

"Oh, yeah," Dolan said. "Happier than a kid in a candy store. Paid me five hundred bucks. I felt bad taking his money, to tell you the truth. It wasn't my best work. Told him I could do better, but he wouldn't hear of it. Said if it did what he wanted, he'd be back with a bigger order, and I'd be rolling in the dough. And then he went and died on me." Dolan grinned. "So much for getting rich. Ain't that the pits? And here I thought my luck was turning."

"Did you lose your legs in a war?" Duncan asked with sympathy.

"Naw," Dolan said. "I got hammered and passed out on the railroad tracks." He gave Duncan the once-over. "What about you? Take a wrong turn on the way back from DragonCon?"

Conall processed the strange term. *DragonCon: a popular gathering of humans where some participants don costumes in celebration of various characters from fiction and other forms of media, including fantasy figures like elves and warriors.*

"He is new in town," Conall explained. "He has not had time to purchase appropriate raiment." He scowled at Duncan. "But he will do so, forthwith."

Dolan chuckled. "Spoken like a man used to handing out orders."

"You have no notion," Duncan said.

"Has anyone else inquired about the knife?" Conall asked.

"Yeah," Dolan said. "Trey Peterson was in here yesterday morning nosing around."

This came as no surprise. "Did he requisition another knife from you?" Conall asked.

"Naw. He brought in some ammo and asked me to pack it with crater dust. Said it was a rush job and he'd pay extra. Came by and picked up the bullets later that day."

Conall took out his money pouch and laid several bills on the counter. Not too many; he sensed that this man had pride.

"You have been most helpful, Mr. Dolan," he said. "Allow me to recompense you for your time."

Dolan pushed the money away. "Keep your dough. I didn't do nothing but jaw at you."

"Very well, I will purchase something," Conall said. He liked this man. "Have you any items for sale?"

"Look around." Dolan motioned at the crowded window display. "Everything in the room's for sale. People bring stuff in to be fixed and never come back for it. After six months, if the owner hasn't come back for it, I put a price tag on it and sell it. What are you interested in?"

Conall surveyed the stacks of junk. "As it happens, Mr. Dolan," he said, "I have ever had a burning desire to own an electric egg poacher."

Chapter Thirty-two

Conall handed Duncan the egg poacher as they exited the shop. "Here," he said. "It is my gift to you."

Duncan regarded the unwieldy device with a sour expression. "You are too generous, my captain. However shall I repay you?"

"I feel certain you will think of something."

"You can be sure of it." The egg poacher winked from view. "This Blake Peterson was kith?"

"Yes," Conall said. "A most evil and ambitious creature, from what I gather. I believe he somehow stumbled upon the magical properties of the crater and struck a deal with the djegrali. He died before the bargain could be sealed, and the knife he stabbed Ansgar with was destroyed along with him in the fire."

"How fortuitous. And now this Trey would step into his grandfather's shoes?"

"So it would seem."

A moment later, they materialized in front of a handsome brick building on the north side of the river bridge.

"Trey Peterson's office, or one of them," Conall said. "As heir to the Peterson fortune he is well-heeled. I have been watching him for some time. To mine eye, he seemed spoiled and indulged, an ineffectual sort who posed no threat."

"What has changed your estimation of him?"

"Two days ago, Rebekah attended a party for the kith. The djegrali were there, trying to commission a new army."

Duncan grunted. " 'Tis an old trick of theirs, is it not?"

"Yes. Peterson was in attendance. He is anxious, it seems, to relieve himself of his wife and has struck a deal to that end with the devils."

"If, as you suspect, he has discovered a weapon the djegrali can use against us, he can name his own price," Duncan said. "Why not kill the wench himself? Reprehensible, perhaps, but the more logical course."

"She is already dead and, by all accounts, a most vicious scold. Peterson is desperate to be rid of her."

They entered the building. A stout matron with stiff carefully curled sooty hair sat behind a desk in the front room. She looked up, her face going slack with surprise when she saw Conall. Her gaze moved to Duncan and stuck.

"Brother, you are in violation of the Directive," Conall told him in a low voice. "You call attention to yourself."

"I will rectify the matter anon."

"Can I help you?" the woman asked, her gaze darting from Conall to Duncan.

"I would speak with Trey Peterson," Conall said.

She jerked her gaze to the calendar on her desk. "Do you have an appointment, Mister . . ."

"Dalvahni," Conall said. "No, I do not have an appointment. But Mr. Peterson will see me." He gave her a wolfish smile. "I feel certain of it."

The woman looked doubtful but pushed a button on the telephone machine. "Mr. Peterson, there are two gentlemen here to see you."

She dropped the telephones as a piercing shriek shattered the air.

"Merciful heavens," she said, staggering to her feet. "What was that?" She waddled after Conall as he strode down the hall. "Wait, you can't go in there."

Conall turned and fixed her with his icy stare. "Cease your nattering, woman, and leave us."

The matron gasped and scurried back to her desk. Rebekah would not have fled, Conall reflected. She would have stood her ground and taken him to task for his tone. But, then, his Rebekah was quite out of the ordinary.

He waved his hand, and the doors in the hall burst open. Through the portal at the far end, he spied an elegantly clad man posed with one leg dangling out an open window.

"Hold," Conall said, entering the room.

Trey looked back at him, his face stark with terror. "Leave me alone. I don't have it. It's gone."

"What is gone?"

"Th-the ammo. Somebody broke in to the office last night and stole the bullets out of my safe." Trey clutched the windowsill. "B-but, I can get more. I promise. Tell Beck I just need a little more time."

"You lie," Conall said. A furious rage iced his veins. "Rebekah would never make a deal with the demons."

"Who said anything about her? I'm talking about Evan Beck. You know him? You work for the demons, too?"

So, Rebekah's accursed brother had adopted Beck as his surname. How interesting.

"No, Peterson," Conall said. Sheets of ice covered the floor, desk, and chair, and crept up the walls, surrounding the window Trey sat in. "I am not in league with the demons."

"Who are you with then?" Sweat beaded Peterson's brow and upper lip in spite of the chill. "Maybe we can work something out. The bullets are gone, but I can get more. I swear. Bullets, knives, swords—I can get you whatever you want."

"A man most eager to bargain," Duncan murmured.

"And with whoever is most expedient," Conall said. "These stolen bullets were requisitioned by Evan Beck?"

"Not exactly." Trey fretted with the length of cloth around his neck that humans called a "tie." "He approached me about a stone knife my grandfather had. It was destroyed in a fire, but I found some notes in a safe-deposit box. The notes were sketchy, but the old man kept babbling on about crater rock, and I put two and two together."

"Your grandfather had plans to supply arms to the demons, and you mean to take over the operation."

"No! I mean, sure, I thought about it. Evan made it sound so easy. But that was before I saw *them.*" Trey shuddered. "They're worse than the old man. I want out. Maybe you and I can do business."

Conall gave him a cold smile. "I do not think so. The demon hunter your grandfather stabbed is my brother Ansgar."

"Your brother?" Trey gave him a sickly smile. "No hard feelings, huh?"

A blond apparition materialized on a nauseating wave of perfume. Hands on hips, she glared at Conall and Duncan.

"Who are you and what do you want with my husband?" She snapped her head around as Peterson made a strangled noise. "Trey, what are you doing in the window? Don't you even *think* about leaving. It's time for our marriage counseling. You've missed the last two sessions. I'm starting to think you're not committed to our relationship. Are you listening to me? Trey? *Trey?*"

Peterson shifted into a large, black and white spotted dog and jumped out the open window, abandoning his fine clothes on the floor.

"Trey Peterson, you get back here this instant!" The blonde rushed to the window, watching as the dog ran away. She turned in a huff. "Ooh, I hate when he pulls that Dalmatian shit."

"Follow him," Conall told Duncan quietly. "Bring him back."

Duncan vanished.

The ghost turned on Conall. "This is your fault. You said something to upset him." Her nose twitched and she sneezed, hard. "There's a cat in this room. Where is it?" She looked around, her eyes narrowed. "Come out, you flea bag. I know you're in here."

"Meow," Annie said, slinking out from under Trey's desk.

The cat darted past the angry ghost and ran behind Conall.

"Meredith Peterson, I assume?" Conall asked the shade.

"My, aren't you the genius?" Meredith sneezed again. "Get that damn thing out of here. I'm allergic."

"You are dead. Your reaction to the creature is imagined."

Her narrow chest swelled. "*That* kind of insensitive remark is exactly why I'm in therapy, asshole."

She disappeared with a furious pop and another heavy gust of perfume. Conall walked over to examine the open safe. Empty; as he suspected. Whoever had stolen the bullets had taken Blake Peterson's notes as well—if Peterson was telling the truth and his grandfather had documented his findings.

They would know soon enough. Duncan was an excellent tracker. Peterson would not long elude one of Conall's finest warriors.

A small sound drew his attention. Turning, he saw the cat and crouched on his heels.

"Come here, little one," he said. "I will not hurt you."

Doubt shadowed the cat's brilliant copper eyes.

"You have my word," Conall said. "It is past time you dropped this foolish guise. I know what you are."

The cat's form shimmered like a desert mirage and vanished. A dirty little girl with tangled brown hair scowled at him. She wore a large cotton shirt like a shift, and her small feet were bare.

"How?" she asked.

"Your brain patterns are different from a cat's," he said. "And I noticed the empty candy wrappers scattered about the bar. As a rule, felines do not enjoy sweets."

She looked belligerent. "You don't know it was me. It could've been Tommy."

"But it was not him. It was you."

"I don't wanna talk about the stupid old zombie. I hate him."

"You do not hate him. You are very fond of him. What happened, did he send you away?"

Her chin quivered and she looked away, scowling. "He yelled at me and threw rocks. I don't care. I don't need him. I don't need nobody."

"The zombie suffers," Conall said. "He sent you away to protect you."

"Yeah? Well, that's stupid. Friends don't do that. I'm a kid and I know that."

"You are a fierce little thing," Conall said. "You remind me of Rebekah."

"Do not. She's beautiful."

"Yes, she is. I imagine she was very much like you as a little girl."

"I saw you kissing her out on the dock. You love her, dontcha?"

"Yes, I do. Very much."

"Then why are you here? She's in trouble."

Fear sliced through Conall. "What?"

Her scowl deepened. "The demons are gonna get her. I been trying to warn you."

Duncan reappeared. He was alone.

"Peterson is dead," he said. "In his haste to escape, he ran beneath the wheels of a motorized carriage and was crushed." He looked at Annie. "Who is this dirty little imp?"

Annie kicked him. "Don't call me names."

Duncan rubbed his bruised shin. "A ferocious little thing, is she not?"

"Her name is Annie," Conall said. "Stay with her. Rebekah is in danger."

The demons buzzed out of the hat, ragged black shadows with claws and howling mouths, and flew at Beck. The ring on her finger hummed to life, like Bilbo's *Sting* when goblins were near. There were nine wraiths in all; too many. Beck yanked the metal pour spout out of the bottle and tossed the pepper sauce at them. It splattered three of the demons and they recoiled, writhing in the air, and fluttered like shreds of tissue paper to the floor.

Dancy the demon woman hopped up and down in fury, her painted orange lips stretched in an ugly snarl.

"Get her," she screamed. "Kill the demon hunter's bitch."

The remaining wraiths dive-bombed Beck. She yelped and ducked behind a rack of bras.

"Run," she shouted at Verbena. Picking up the metal rack,

she swung it at a swooping demon, knocking it aside. "Get out of the store."

The girl ran over to her. "No, I ain't leaving you."

Back to back, they watched the circling wraiths. They were truly horrible to look at, with bony, scabrous hands and fanged, hungry mouths, and they radiated hate and soul-sapping fear.

Shaking off her terror, Beck broke off part of the chrome rack. The ring flared, and the piece of metal in her hand became a shining blade of blue fire. This wasn't Sting; this was Glamdring, the mighty weapon wielded by Gandalf against the Balrog, forged by the Elves in the First Age.

The blazing sword filled her with courage. She was a hero of old. She was totally kickass. She would take Evil to the whup shack and save the Shire—uh, Hannah—from the Orcs.

A wraith attacked with a chilling cry. Beck plunged her shining blade into the heart of the thing, and it shattered with a horrible cry. Black dust rained down upon them; it smelled like charred road kill. Ugh.

"My hair," Verbena shrieked, clapping an enormous turquoise bra over her head.

Beck hoisted her makeshift Foe Hammer in the air in a gesture of triumph. "Yeah," she shouted. "That's what I'm talking about. Four of you buzzards down, five to go. Come on, dickwads. Come to Mama."

Not poetry, perhaps, or a stirring battle cry like William Wallace's in *Braveheart,* but the demons got the gist of it. They regrouped and dive-bombed her like a murder of crows. Beck caught another one on the end of her sword. A beam of light shot out and the wraith disintegrated. A second demon darted past, leaving a long, burning scratch on Beck's neck. A third jumped at her. Sharp claws ripped Beck's shoulder. She screamed in pain and whacked blindly at the demon with her sword. The demon tumbled to the floor and Beck stabbed it. The demon exploded in a puff of odiferous ash.

She turned in a circle, flailing her weapon to ward off the next attack. None came.

"Look," Verbena said, pointing. She was still wearing the bra. One cup covered her head; the other cup, large enough to hold a small watermelon, dangled next to her cheek.

Conall stalked through the store, his obsidian eyes shining with battle lust, his sword drawn. Beck blinked down at the weapon in her hand. She held the twisted remnants of a lingerie rack, not a gleaming Elven sword. Conall was death walking, and she was a chick holding a glorified coat hanger. He swung his blade and sliced a demon in half. It died with a bloodcurdling shriek. The two remaining wraiths blasted through the front display window like a couple of miniature jets, shattering the glass.

Only one demon left—Demon Dancy. Where did she go?

"There," Verbena cried, pointing again.

A huge, hairy orange spider clung to the ceiling above Conall's head.

"Conall," Beck shrieked as the spider pounced.

He leaped aside, and the spider's fangs struck the spot where he'd been standing an instant before. Shouting something in a strange tongue, Conall rushed the monster with his sword. The spider sprang away and Conall gave chase.

They ricocheted around the room, this way and that. The spider was fast, but Conall was faster; Nemesis on steroids.

The spider was no match for him. He'd kill it as easily as he'd slain the trolls. Problem was, Dancy Smith was in there, somewhere. She'd die along with the demon. Beck had to do something, and fast, or the female denizens of Hannah would be rudderless in the sea of fashion.

She scrambled around, looking for the metal pour spout. There—half buried beneath a pile of nylon panties. She snatched it up and jammed it back into the neck of the pepper sauce bottle. Conall and the demon were still going at it. The spider hissed and sputtered, bouncing around the room like a rubber ball as it tried to avoid Conall's sword. Ropes of gauze shot out of the bug's spinnerets and floated about, hanging lazily in the air and clinging in sticky strands to the merchandise in the store.

Watching the spider's frantic gyrations made Beck dizzy. The spider sprang across the room and back again, landing with her big old spider butt in Beck's face. Beck seized her chance and sprang onto the bug's back. The orange hair covering the spider's bloated body was stiff as wire and razor sharp.

She plunged the metal spout into the narrow waist connecting the spider's abdomen to the head, wincing as the sharp bristles sliced her hand and wrist.

The demon leaked out of the spider and into the bottle. With a thin, whistling shriek, the monster collapsed beneath Beck like a punctured balloon. She put her thumb over the spout to keep the demon inside.

"Umph," Dancy mumbled, her face mashed against the floor.

Beck was sitting on top of the old lady, riding her like a mechanical bull. Awkward.

With a hoarse cry, Conall yanked Beck off Dancy and into his arms. "Rebekah, are you hurt?"

"Just a few scratches."

"Little fool." His face was taut with anger. "What were you thinking?"

"I was thinking you were about to kill Dancy." She handed him the hot sauce bottle with the demon inside. "You'd better do something with this. Keep your thumb over the opening or it'll get out."

Conall snarled and crumpled the metal spout like it was tinfoil.

"Or you could do that," Beck said. The big show-off.

"What happened?" Dancy Smith sat up and spat out a glob of orange hair. "Was there a tornado?"

Poor Dancy and her store were a wreck. Both shoes were gone, Dancy's hair resembled Verbena's before the Jeannine makeover, and her stockings and clothes were in shreds.

Verbena helped the elderly lady to her feet and over to a chair.

"You don't look so good, Miss Dancy," Verbena said. "You'd best sit for a spell." She took the bra off her head and clapped it over Dancy's ruined coiffure. "There, so you don't go into shock."

Duncan appeared, a grubby child in a ragged T-shirt at his side. The little girl's dark hair was a rat's nest of filthy tangles.

"Where'd you get the kid?" Beck asked.

"I'm not a kid," the little girl said, a trifle indignantly. "I'm Annie."

"Annie?" Beck took a cautious step closer and then another, afraid she might startle the child. She blinked down into a pair of purple irises ringed in bright copper. *"Annie?"*

"Yes. Can we go now? I'm hungry."

Beck held out her hand. After a moment's hesitation, Annie took it.

"What would you like to eat?" Beck asked.

"Anything but tuna," Annie said.

Conall handed Duncan the hot sauce bottle. "Rebekah captured a demon. Transfer it to a djevel flaskke and clean up this mess." Sirens sounded in the distance. "Preferably before the authorities arrive."

He bowed to Dancy. "Madam, my brother will settle our bill. We have shopped enough for one day."

Chapter Thirty-three

The next morning, Conall got up before daybreak and went fishing. He returned from the river carrying a string of trout, three big catfish, and a five-pound spotted bass, cleaned and ready to cook. Beck's father liked to fish, but he didn't catch much. Conall, on the other hand, was the freaking fish whisperer.

While Conall pan-seared the trout, Beck fried hash browns and cut up some fruit. She liked working in the kitchen with him. Conall went about the business of cooking with the same confidence, quiet efficiency, and attention to detail that he did everything, including sex.

Especially sex, Beck thought, her stomach fluttering at the memory of the things they'd done the night before. He'd been very efficient about that, too, though not nearly as quiet. She hadn't been quiet, either. She'd sung several rounds of the Orgasm Song. Good thing he'd used his Dalvahni magic to sound proof their room, or Annie might have been scarred for life.

Beck took a seat at the table across from Conall, and glanced at the child to her left. Annie swung her legs back and forth under her chair. She'd turned her nose up at the fish and was finishing off a bowl of cereal.

We're just like a real family, Beck thought with a wistful pang. *If only . . .*

She unfolded the special edition of the *Hannah Herald* that had been delivered that morning. Trey Peterson's death was big news.

"According to the *Herald,* the driver swears he ran over a spotted dog," she told Conall, reading from a front page article. The heading read: TIMBER TYCOON KILLED IN THE BUFF." He got out of his car to check, and found Trey Peterson lying in the road, naked as a baby."

Conall took a big bite of fish and chewed thoughtfully. " 'Twould seem he shifted ere he died."

"Thank goodness," Beck said. "Otherwise, some city worker would've dumped him in a hole with the rest of the road kill." She shuddered. "And nobody would ever know what happened to Trey Peterson. At least this way, his family gets closure and he gets a decent burial."

Annie put her spoon down. "I'm done."

"Okay, go brush your teeth," Beck said. "I need to get to work."

"I'm going with you, right? Tommy might come back."

Beck felt a wave of sadness. Tommy was out there, somewhere, struggling against his zombie nature.

"Yes, but first you have to brush your teeth," Beck said.

"I brushed them last night. Jeez."

"Nonetheless, you will brush them again," Conall said calmly. "Now."

Grumbling, Annie trudged out of the kitchen.

Beck shook her head in amazement. A bath and some new clothes, and Annie looked like any other eight-year-old girl, with her dark brown hair pulled back in a ponytail and tied with a ribbon. The bath had been something of a challenge. From what they'd been able to learn, Annie's mother had died when Annie was a toddler, and the orphaned child had become a ward of the state. Annie had bounced around a lot, never staying long with any family. Reading between the lines and remembering her own childhood mishaps, Beck suspected Annie's kith abilities had freaked out her norm foster parents.

In fairness to the norms, Annie's banshee routine scared the crap out of most supers, too.

Annie had run away from her last placement, and she'd been on her own for more than two years, surviving in cat form by living off the land. Annie Glenn was one tough little cookie. Annie the cat, however, did not like water, which made bath time interesting.

The child had been filthy—it had taken two tubs of water to get her clean. She'd reminded Beck of the character Newt from the movie *Alien,* with her matted hair and sometimes feral behavior. Beck had feared she might have to shave the child's head. She'd put in a distress call to Verbena, who'd shown up with Toby and a bottle of Fiona Fix-It. Beck had no idea what Evie Douglass Dalvahni put in the miracle product she'd concocted, but Beck wanted to buy stock in it. It had cleaned and tamed Annie's grubby, snarled locks in one application.

Contrary to Conall's declaration that he'd had enough shopping for one day, he'd bravely gone back to town Tuesday afternoon armed with Annie's measurements, a tracing of her feet, and a list. Beck had asked him to get the child a few things, just enough to tide them over. Conall Claus had returned laden with packages. Dottie Wise, the owner of Toodles, Hannah's only clothing store for kids, was doing a happy dance somewhere, celebrating her biggest sale ever.

There were shoes—Sunday shoes, sneakers, clearance sandals left over from the summer, flip-flops, boots, Mary Janes, and four pairs of fuzzy house slippers in assorted colors. There were dresses, casual and flouncy; more than twenty in all. There were jeans and stretch pants, tops, blouses, sweaters, and three coats—a wool one for Sunday and two jackets. A huge shopping bag contained tights, socks, under things, and pj's; another bag was stuffed with girly doodads, including bows, hair ribbons, barrettes, headbands, and scrunchies.

A smaller sack overflowed with assorted costume rings, bracelets, and necklaces. There was a jewelry box to hold all the bling, and even a tiara. Conall also produced a teddy bear; a stuffed unicorn; a Madame Alexander doll; a hand-painted rocking horse; an easel, paints, and brushes; puzzles; a tea set; and three bags of books.

"Holy shit," Beck said when she'd seen the haul. "I asked you to get a couple of things, not buy the frigging store."

"I did not buy the store." Conall crossed his arms on his wide chest and looked superior. "I purchased enough that we do not have to go back."

"She's a *kid*," Beck had said. "They grow."

A frown line appeared between Conall's black brows. "I confess, I did not think of that." He shrugged. "Then we will purchase more."

We. Beck sighed. She liked the sound of that, way too much, but she mustn't get sucked into that kind of thinking. Conall would leave. It was inevitable. Today, tomorrow, or next month, but he would leave. The thought made her insides shrivel, so she pushed it away. He wasn't gone yet.

"Why do you sigh?" Conall asked, recalling Beck to the present.

Beck folded up the paper and set it down. "Just thinking about Annie. I don't want her raised in a bar like me."

"Come here," he said softly.

Beck got up and went around the table and sat in his lap.

"Annie will be fine," he said, nuzzling her throat with his lips. "Already, you are a wonderful mother to her. You cannot help it. It is in your nature."

Beck put her arms around his neck and kissed him. "Thanks," she murmured against his sensuous, serious mouth. "I needed that. I have no idea what I'm doing. I never thought I'd get the chance to find out."

Conall wrapped his hands around her wrists and looked her in the eye, his expression solemn.

Here it comes, Beck thought, bracing herself. *Here's where he says sayonara.*

"That is something I have been meaning to talk to you about," he said. "Are you certain this contraceptive procedure you had worked?"

"Sure," Beck said. "Why wouldn't it?"

"The kith regenerate, do they not? The situation might have reversed itself."

Beck gaped at him in shock. "I never thought of that."

She should have. Once the bullet was removed, Toby's leg had healed in a matter of hours. She felt like an idiot.

Conall cleared his throat. "Even if your reproductive organs did not regenerate on their own, it is . . . possible I unknowingly rectified the matter."

"Say what?"

"The other night after the gathering, I healed your wounds. Remember?"

She recalled his gentle touch and the light and heat that had flooded from his hands to her body—her entire body. Conall Dalvahni was nothing if not thorough.

Her heart hammered. "And we've been going at it like rabbits. You're trying to tell me I might be pregnant."

Nah, what were the odds? Some people tried for years to get pregnant, like Jason and Brenda.

And other people got pregnant at the drop of a hat.

"I thought you should know," Conall said.

A baby. With Conall. It was hard to process. It was a disaster, right? Then why did she feel like grinning?

"What about you?" she blurted. "Won't you get in trouble for fraternizing with the enemy? You could get drummed out of the Dalvahni. This must be your worst nightmare."

"My worst nightmare is something happening to you." He slipped his arms around her and held her close. "Yesterday, when you threw yourself on top of that monster, my heart stopped and my bones turned to water."

Beck held her breath. "What are you saying?"

"I am saying that I—"

Junior Peterson materialized. "You better get to the bar and quick. Earl Skinner just pulled up. Hank's at his house and Toby's in the woods looking for Tommy. Verbena's there by herself."

Beck squealed into her parking place at the bar and slammed the truck into park. "Stay with Annie," she told Conall. "I'll deal with pretzel dick."

"No," Conall said.

"Yes." Beck jumped out of the truck. "Let me handle this."

If Earl looked at her cross-eyed, Conall would take his head off. Then she'd have another dead Skinner on her hands and there'd be questions, and the sheriff, and no end of hassle.

She slammed the truck door and ran for the employee entrance. There were raised voices coming from the kitchen when she stepped inside. She hurried down the hall.

"—ain't going anywhere with you, Earl," she heard Verbena say.

"You'll do what you're told, Beenie," Earl said. Beck recognized his nasal voice. "Things are in the crapper since Daddy died. Quit screwing around and get your ass home."

"I done told you, I ain't going."

Beck heard the meaty smack of a fist hitting flesh, and a cry of pain. The sorry sack had hit Verbena.

Beck charged into the kitchen, ready to take on Earl Skinner and his whole weasel army. A cold shadow swept by her; Conall. So much for staying in the truck and letting her handle it. He was a pip at giving orders and lousy at taking them.

He lifted Earl by the scruff of the neck like a recalcitrant dachshund. Earl kicked his feet in the air and tried to shift, but something was wrong. The best Earl could manage was a ferrety button nose, some whiskers, and a few patches of fur on his hands. If he'd sprouted fur in other places, Beck couldn't see. Thank God.

"Lemme go," Earl said.

Cold rage poured off Conall, icing the kitchen floors and counters. "I should kill you for striking your sister and for shooting Tobias."

Good thing Conall had no idea Earl had taken a potshot at her and Verbena. He'd kill him.

Beck laid her hand on Conall's arm. "Don't. He's not worth it."

Conall's black eyes were flat. "It would be worth it to me."

"Please," Beck said.

"Very well." Conall shook Earl. "But only because she asked.

Hear me, varlet and listen well. Leave this place and do not return, if you value your worthless hide."

He drop-kicked Earl out the back door. Earl rolled across the gravel and got to his feet, red-faced with fury.

"You'll be sorry," he raged at Conall. "You done messed with the wrong guy, you son of a bitch."

He whirled at a low, angry growl. A dog charged out of the bushes and sprang at Earl, teeth bared. Earl yelped and ran for his truck, a blue and green low-rider with black flames painted on the front hood, but the dog was faster. He caught Earl as he was trying to open the driver's side door, and bit Earl in the butt.

Earl yelled and swatted at the dog, but the dog held on. Earl's jeans ripped, exposing his red and blue Superman undies. The dog lost his grip and Earl dived inside the truck. Cranking the engine, he spun out of the parking lot, his truck tires spewing gravel and kicking up dust.

Toby shifted to human form. He was wearing his favorite CCR T-shirt. Twigs nested in his long braid and there was dirt on the bottom of his jeans. Raising his fist, he shook it at the vanishing truck.

"I can't believe that sawed-off little rabbit turd had the nerve to show up here," he fumed. "Not after he shot me *and* tried to shoot Becky."

"What?" Conall roared, startling Beck. "The blackguard accosted you? Why did you not tell me?"

"He missed," Beck said. "And I took care of it."

"I should have killed him," Conall said. "I *will* kill him."

"Not if I get to him first," Toby said. "What'd he want, anyways?"

"Me." Verbena stepped outside. "He come to fetch me, but I wouldn't go. He said the 'shine's gone bad and the dawgs run off, like it's my fault."

"Things ain't going well for the Skinners?" Toby's eyes shone with amusement. "Can't say I'm surprised. Much as I hate to admit it, Earl's probably right. It is your fault."

Verbena blinked at him. "What?"

"You're an enhancer, gal. Knew it the first time I got a whiff of you."

"A what?" Beck and Conall asked at once.

"An enhancer," Toby repeated. "Like a walking power plant. She juices everybody up. They get stronger and better when they're around her, at whatever they do."

Verbena flushed. "No disrespect, Mr. Toby, but that can't be right. I'm a dud. Ever'body says so. I can't even shift."

"So what?" Toby said. "Any old part blood can shift, but an enhancer comes along once in a blue moon. You're something special, girl." He chuckled. "Kinda funny, when you think about it. Verbena's the only thing them Skinners ever had worth a damn, and they done throwed her away."

Chapter Thirty-four

Verbena was an enhancer. Beck thought back to Charlie's comment at the gathering. *The Skinners are late bloomers.* No duh.

Beck would be willing to bet the Skinners' rise in the moonshine trade coincided with Verbena's birth. Then there was the kith attack in the woods. The four of them—Beck, Verbena, Toby, and Hank—had taken on dozens of shifters and won, and handily at that. After the fight was over, Beck had planted Earl and his buddies up to their elbows in dirt, easy as pie, in spite of being exhausted and hurt. At the time, she'd attributed it to adrenaline and the proximity of the underground spring.

Maybe it had been Verbena, instead.

Verbena had been with her yesterday during the demon attack in the store. Beck remembered her glowing makeshift sword and her confidence and feeling of invincibility. Maybe that had been Verbena, too.

The more she thought about it, the more it made sense. Verbena was a walking talking generator the Skinners had been running off for years. A few days away from Verbena and the best Earl could manage was a half-ass shift. The Skinners had lost their one and only good luck charm. The Skinner goose was cooked, although they didn't know it. Heck, even their *dogs* didn't want anything to do with them.

Served them right as far as Beck was concerned.

She examined the bruise on Verbena's cheek. "Your face is starting to swell," she said. "You'd better put some ice on it."

"Banana peel," Toby said. "Pulp side down. Good for cuts, too."

"You heard the man." Beck pushed Verbena in the direction of the door. "Go stick a banana on your face."

"Any sign of the zombie?" Conall asked Toby after Verbena had gone inside.

"Oh, yeah." Toby rubbed the end of his long nose. "Signs all over the place, but that zombie don't want to be found. He walks in circles and he never stops moving. My nose is sore and I'm plumb dizzy from trailing him."

Beck walked over to the Tundra and opened the door. "You can come out now," she told Annie. "There's someone I'd like you to meet."

"I don't want to meet him. He's mean." Annie folded her arms and stared straight ahead. "He doesn't like me."

Beck held out her hand. "Toby doesn't know you, not really. I want you to give him another chance."

"He's a *dog,*" Annie said with an unmistakable air of feline superiority. "He hates cats. I heard him say."

"He doesn't mean it. That's just his way. Do you know what my go-to animal form is?"

"No."

"A panther," Beck said. "A black panther."

Annie gave her a look of disbelief. "Really?"

Beck nodded. "And Toby's still my friend, my oldest friend. He's more than a friend. He's family. You're my family, too—if you want to be. So, you two need to get along. You *do* want to stay with me, don't you?"

Beck held her breath while Annie digested this.

"Okay, I'll be nice to him," Annie said with a scowl. The knot of tension in Beck's belly eased. "But only if he's nice back."

Beck smiled. "Nice is a relative term. Toby puts on a good snarl, but he's all bark and no bite."

"He bit Pretzel Dick in the butt," Annie pointed out. "It hurt. Pretzel Dick screamed. What if Toby bites me?"

Pretzel Dick? Beck winced. She'd better clean up her act with the kid around.

"The man's name is Earl, and Toby bit him because he hurt Toby and tried to hurt me," Beck said. "Toby is very protective. He takes care of family, and you're family now."

Annie gave her a look that said *if you say so* and climbed out of the truck.

Beck led the child over to Toby. "Toby, this is Annie."

"Annie who?"

"*The* Annie," Beck said. "You know, meow?"

His eyes widened. "You don't mean to say that she's—"

Beck nodded. "Yep."

"Great jumping Jehoshaphat," Toby said, looking floored.

Verbena stuck her head out the back door. She had a banana peel pressed against her bruised cheek, sticky side down, like some kind of hungry alien life form. "Telephone for you, Beck."

Beck took the call in the kitchen. "Beck Damian," she said into the phone.

"Hello, Cookie."

Her hand tightened around the receiver. "Evan."

Conall was at her side in a heartbeat, his eyes like chips of black ice. "Let me speak to him."

Beck shook her head. "What do you want, Evan?"

"We need to talk."

"I don't think so, bro. I stopped listening to you after you fed those two kids to the demons." *And tried to feed Toby to a troll.*

"Where's Hagilth?"

"Where she can't hurt anyone."

He was silent for a moment. "You're not being very friendly, Cookie. I tried to come see you, but I couldn't get in."

"I know. You sent Tommy to do your dirty work. He did what you asked. Now let him go."

Evan sighed. "Still yammering about the zombie? You're good, real good—even now, I almost could believe you care. What's your angle?"

"I don't have one."

"Everybody has an angle. I just haven't figured out yours."

"Knock yourself out," Beck said. "Hope you give yourself an aneurism."

"Same old sweet Cookie. Want to know what I've been wondering?"

"Not really."

"I've been wondering if you broke into Peterson's safe."

"I don't know what you're talking about."

"Too bad. I was hoping we could work together."

"I don't think so. I don't like the way you do business, and I sure as hell don't like your friends."

"I'm not crazy about your friends, either. Why didn't you tell me your boyfriend is a demon hunter?"

"Oh, let's see," Beck said. "Maybe because it's none of your damn business."

"It occurs to me that you may be smarter than I thought." There was an edge to Evan's silky voice. "How much are they paying you to be the demon hunter's whore? Are you supposed to screw him stupid, like Delilah did Samson, so the demons can kill him?"

"What do you know about the Bible?"

"Plenty. My 'parents' possessed an evangelist and his wife when I was fifteen. Had their own cult for a while—fun times." He paused. "Or do the demons want you to do the job yourself?"

Beck hung up the phone. She looked down at her hands. They were shaking.

"Rebekah?" There was concern in Conall's rough voice. "What did he say to upset you?"

"Forget it. He's just trying to get under my skin. What's this about somebody breaking into Peterson's safe?"

"It seems Trey Peterson found some papers his grandfather left behind. Based on the information in those papers, he had the Key Man make a number of special bullets packed with crater dust. Bullets, I believe, he hoped to sell to the djegrali. Before he could accomplish his goal, however, someone broke into his office and stole the papers and the ammunition."

"I don't understand," Beck said. "What's the crater got to do with it?"

"Everything," Conall said. "I believe the crater is the source of magic in Hannah and the very reason the djegrali and other supernatural beings are drawn to this place. They find it . . . irresistible. I have thought on the matter, and I also believe the crater's unusual properties explain Latrisse's sudden and unexpected reappearance after so many years."

Beck's eyes widened. "The urn Song kept her ashes in was made from Hannah clay. Something about it kept Latrisse from regenerating."

Conall nodded. "Exactly. Until the thieves burglarized Song's house and the vase got broken. The knife that almost killed Ansgar was fashioned from crater rock. The crater has some quality, some deep magic, that renders the Dal vulnerable to harm—perhaps even death, should the wound be severe enough."

"Holy cats, the crater's like Kryptonite," Beck said. "You've got to find that thief before the demons do."

"I concur. I have assigned Duncan the task."

The back door slammed, and a clean-shaven bear of a man in olive fatigue shorts and a crisply laundered crewneck T-shirt lumbered into the kitchen. Beck stared at him in surprise. It was Hank, without the scruffy beard. His bushy black hair had been cut short, and curled at the ends. With his hair trimmed and the facial hair gone, he looked years younger.

He eyed Annie. "Who's the whippersnapper?"

"I'm Annie. You got anything to eat?"

"You just had breakfast," Beck said. "You can't possibly be hungry."

Annie shrugged.

"How about a peanut butter and jelly sandwich?" Hank asked.

Annie wiggled on the bar stool. "Peanut butter, banana, and sweet pickles?"

"You're weird, kid," Hank said. "I like you." As he went about making Annie's sandwich he talked to Beck about the menu. "I was planning to make red beans and rice tonight, but there ain't a can of beans in the place."

That's because the beans had gone to feed a certain zombie.

"You sure you feel up to cooking?" Beck asked. "It's only been a few days since you were injured. I don't want you to relapse."

"Duncan said I'm fine," Hank growled, sounding more like his old self. "Never better."

Beck looked at him closely. His color was good. For somebody at death's door a few days ago, he looked remarkably fit. Duncan had the healer's touch. She glanced at Verbena. And Duncan had help from the Enhancer.

"Sorry about the beans," Beck said. "We'll make do with burgers and dogs. Tomorrow's Thanksgiving and we'll be closed."

She braced herself. Hank *hated* cooking what he called "that trash food." To her surprise, he didn't explode.

"Don't worry about it," he said. "We'll come up with something, ain't that right, Verbena?" He noticed the banana against her cheek and frowned. "Why you got a banana on your face?"

Verbena lowered the spotted yellow peel, revealing the discolored swelling underneath.

"Who did that?" Hank said with a low rumble of fury. "Somebody hurt you?"

"That piece of crap brother of hers showed up this morning while nobody was here and smacked her around," Toby said.

"Earl and me ain't kin." Verbena tossed the banana in the trash. "Charlie weren't my daddy and Earl's mama was the old man's first wife."

"Good," Hank said. "Then you won't mind if I kill him."

"Take a number," Toby said. "Folks are lining up to kill that douche bag." He winced as the sound of piano music drifted from the bar into the kitchen. Throwing his head back, he gave a low, moaning howl. He lowered his head again, looking embarrassed. "Sorry. Sometimes, that pi-anny hurts m' ears. Reckon that Dalmatian must be hard of hearing."

"Dalmatian?" Beck blinked in surprise. "What Dalmatian?"

"Junior didn't tell you?" Toby said. "He's got him a dog. Figured you were okay with it."

Beck left Annie in the kitchen eating her sandwich and hurried into the bar. Junior Peterson was seated at the piano. His long fingers flew across the black and white keys to the notes of a fancy tune Beck didn't recognize. A large black-and-white-spotted dog sat beside him, his head resting on Junior's knee.

"Where'd you get the dog?" Beck asked Junior.

He gave her a beatific smile. "This is Trey. Son, say hello to Beck. She's our host."

The dog lifted his head and barked.

"By the sword," Conall said, joining them in the bar. "Is that the shade of Trey Peterson?"

"Yes." Beck shook her head in confusion. "The paper said he shifted before he died. Why's he a dog in the afterlife?"

Meredith appeared on a burst of perfume. *"William Blake Peterson!* What do you think you're doing?"

Junior's song ended with a discordant bang. "There's your answer," he said, giving Meredith a fulminating look. "Can you blame him?"

"Well?" Meredith tapped an elegantly shod foot. "Answer me."

Trey barked.

Meredith's face stretched into a hideous mask. "I cannot believe this. I missed my door to the other side to be with you, and this is the thanks I get, eternity with a stupid mutt?" Her voice rose to a piercing shriek. "I. Don't. Think. Sooooo."

Junior waited until Meredith's siren wound down. "Go haunt a toilet somewhere and leave us alone," he said. "I hear there's a dandy one with your name on it at the high school."

"The Peterson Memorial Powder Room," Beck said. "I read about it in the paper."

"Shut it, you backwoods skank," Meredith snarled. "Nobody asked you."

"Mind your manners, shade, or I will lock you in the Pit with the djegrali," Conall said. He paused. "Almost, I pity the demons at the thought."

"Try it, buster, and see what you get," Meredith said, swelling. "I've learned a thing or two since I bit the big one. I'll ectoplasm your ass."

"Whoo, somebody's got sand in their twat." Beck looked at the Dalmatian. "Is she always this unpleasant?"

Trey yipped.

Junior interpreted for the dog. "Trey says yes. Trey says Meredith could skin the hide off a rhino with her bitching."

"You know, it's a shame to let all that hostility go to waste," Beck said, considering Meredith. "There must be something productive she could do with it."

Meredith snapped her fingers. "Hey, shitheads, I'm right here."

"There is one thing . . ." Junior hesitated and shook his head. "Nah, she'd never go for it."

"Go for what?" Meredith demanded. "*What?* Talk to me, for God's sake, you pitiful, piddling excuse of a piano player."

"I've agreed to a haunting." Junior's expression was deceptively bland. "But I'm not having much luck scaring the target."

"Oh, please," Meredith said. "You couldn't haunt your way out of a grammar school funhouse. Who's the client?"

"His name is Tommy," Junior said. "He's a zombie. He wants to go to ground, but his maker won't release him."

"Show me this maker." Meredith's blue eyes glowed with irritation and righteous, unspent fury. "He'll cooperate. I'll make him so miserable he'll throw himself on a buzz saw." She widened her eyes at Junior in fake consternation. "Oh, wait. Somebody already did that to you, didn't they?"

"You are such a bitch," Junior said. "A total, pluperfect, stone-cold raving bitch. You're perfect for the job."

Chapter Thirty-five

Thanksgiving morning, Beck drove the Tundra into town. Conall and Annie rode with her, and Toby followed in his truck. To no one's surprise but Verbena's, Hank invited Verbena to his little cabin on the river for the day, promising her a meal of Cajun-fried turkey, onion and mushroom dressing, spicy greens, and sweet tater biscuits.

"That is, if you don't have other plans," Hank had said, turning a dull red.

Verbena blushed, too. "I'd like that."

Hank grinned, displaying a mouth full of large, white teeth. The effect was startling against his dark complexion. "It's a date then. I'll pick you up at eleven."

Hank stomped out, whistling and looking happier than Beck had ever seen him.

"He likes you," she'd told Verbena.

"I like him, too. What should I wear?" Verbena's expression grew anxious. "I ain't never had a date."

"It won't matter," Beck advised. "Wear whatever makes you feel pretty."

Verbena's hand crept to her cap of strawberry-blond hair. "That 'ud be everything. I ain't never had so many nice things, thanks to you and Mr. D."

Verbena refused to call Conall by his first name.

"Well, then, you can't go wrong," Beck said.

Verbena had nodded and hurried toward the little back room

where she was living for the time being, presumably to go through her clothes.

Toby watched the girl leave with a shake of his gray head. "This ain't good," he'd said. "Reckon it's too late to get one of them 'no fraternization' policies?"

"What's wrong with Hank inviting Verbena to his place?" Beck asked. "I think it's sweet. I didn't even know Hank had teeth until just now."

"First time they get to squabbling, you'll see," Toby said darkly. "Never pee in your own well."

"Meaning what, Confucius?" Beck asked in exasperation.

"Unhappy cooks make for bad digestion. It's all buttercups and roses now, but what happens when they fall out? We ain't got a cook, that's what."

Having deposited that little dollop of sunshine, Toby had strolled away.

Beck slowed the truck to a stop in front of a house. "This is it," she said.

Brenda and Jason lived in a ranch-style house in Meadow-brook, a neighborhood of uniform dwellings built in the sixties and seventies. Homes in Meadowbrook were small and squeezed close together. Brenda and Jason's place was red brick with blue shutters. Rings of monkey grass imprisoned two towering pines in the front yard, and a line of sickly gray-green hedges marched across the front. A few blocks over in the historic district, lawns were deep and narrow, shaded by towering oaks and maples, waxy-leafed magnolias, and frilly dogwoods, red-buds, and crepe myrtles. The houses in the older part of town were steeped in character, ranging in style from homey Crafts-man bungalows to steep-roofed Victorians and staid brick Tu-dors. In Meadowbrook, the houses all looked like they needed Prozac.

Fall in Alabama was menopausal: hot one moment and cold the next. This morning, the sky was clear and the temperature was already in the mid-sixties by eleven o'clock. With the in-constancy of Mother Nature in mind, Beck had donned a blue ruched-sleeve sweater over a white camisole, jeans, and half boots. For a millisecond, she'd considered wearing a dress to please Brenda and decided against it. Brenda would just have to deal.

She glanced at Annie. The kid looked like a catalog model in some of her new duds, a neon pink cotton cardigan over a navy cupcake skirt and matching tee, pink and blue leggings, and navy Mary Janes. Her dark hair was brushed to a soft shine and held back by a bejeweled headband.

"Remember what we talked about," Beck said. "No monkey business around the norms. It makes them nervous."

"I know." Annie clutched the teddy bear Conall had given her. "Why couldn't I stay at the house with Mr. Cat?"

"Because it's Thanksgiving and I want you with me," Beck said. "The twins are excited you're coming. It'll be fun for Jay and Darlene to have someone to play with."

"They're norms," Annie said. Her expression was pinched. "Norms don't like me."

"We'll play a game and pretend we're norms, too," Beck said. "It'll be fun."

"Did *you* play with norms when you were little?"

"No, my daddy wouldn't let me."

"Then how do you know it will be fun?"

Beck sighed. "Just try and get along with them and no funny stuff."

Brenda had insisted they didn't need to bring anything, but pride wouldn't allow Beck to show up at her stepmother's house empty-handed, so she'd brought a gallon of Hank's seafood gumbo. She'd also made Jason one of his favorite desserts: Boiled Can, a recipe from the Great Depression that consisted of caramelized condensed milk, chilled, and served over a Graham cracker and topped with whipped cream.

They got out of the truck and Beck handed Conall the heavy Crock-Pot. He wore dark wool trousers and a blue broadcloth shirt unbuttoned at the neck. His shaggy black hair gleamed in the sunlight, and he looked so freaking handsome Beck wanted to offer up her hoo-hah on the altar of his magical hotness right then and there.

She wouldn't, of course. Not on Daddy and Brenda's front lawn and not in front of the kid. But, wouldn't that just send Brenda into a paroxysm of prayer?

The thought made her giggle. It came out more of a nervous snort.

"Rebekah, are you well?" the Divine Dalvahni asked.

"Fine," Beck lied.

Annie hugged her teddy bear. "My stomach hurts. I want to go home."

"My stomach hurts, too," Beck said. "But we're here and we're going inside."

Annie looked up at Beck, her face scrunched in concern. "Do you think you're going to barf?"

"I sincerely hope not," Beck said, ringing the doorbell.

A dog barked inside the house, growing louder as the animal rushed for the door.

"They have a dog." Annie gave Beck a look of reproach. "You didn't tell me they have a dog."

"It's just Boo, their miniature dachshund," Beck said. "She's harmless."

The door opened and Beck almost dropped the dessert plate. "Latrisse! "

Latrisse wore a clingy black dress that hit her right above the knees. The dress was simply cut, conservative even, but Latrisse's shoes more than made up for it: shimmering snakeskin double-platform pumps with five-inch heels, mottled purple uppers, bright turquoise heels, and cheetah print soles. A black and tan miniature dachshund danced around Latrisse's feet, barking nonstop.

Conall looked at the dog, and Boo shut up.

"Latrisse, this is a wonderful surprise," Beck said. "I didn't know you were going to be here."

Latrisse waved them into the foyer. Boo circled them, sniffing at their ankles, before trotting off to the kitchen. The rich scents of baked ham and roast turkey, cornbread dressing with onions and celery, squash casserole topped with butter-soaked crackers, baked sweet potatoes, and warm bread wafted through the house. Brenda Smith Damian might be a Bible-thumping, holier-than-thou pain-in-the but-tocks, but she sure could cook.

"I saw your daddy at the Burger Doodle yesterday," Latrisse said. "After he finished having a heart attack because it turns out I'm not dead, he invited me and Mama to the big feed." She gestured with her hands. Her long nails had been painted purple and turquoise to match her shoes. "And here we are."

"I'm so glad," Beck said, and meant it.

Being with her norm family was awkward under the best of circumstances. Jason meant well but was always on edge with her, especially around Brenda and the kids. Oh, he tried to act like everything was okay, but it was always there, that watchful, wary look she'd gotten from him all her life, the look that said he was terrified she might do something strange. The twins were cute kids, but she'd never gotten to know them, not really. Brenda had suffered two miscarriages before she'd had Jay and Darlene and she was over protective as a hen with one biddy. She'd never let Beck babysit or, heaven forbid, let the twins spend the night at her place, because Beck lived on the river and Brenda was convinced they'd fall in and drown. Understandable—and then there was the whole you-work-in-a-bar-so-you're-going-straight-to-the-hot-place thing.

Beck looked around. Brenda had added the twins' latest school pictures to the already groaning shrine on the foyer wall, but nothing else had changed. To the right was a combination formal living room and dining room. Through the open door that connected the dining room to the kitchen, Beck glimpsed Brenda taking something out of the oven.

The foyer spilled into a paneled den with a fireplace. Down a narrow hall were three bedrooms and two small baths.

Toby loped through the door behind them. "I brought ice and a gallon of sweet tea," he announced in the triumphant tone of a conquering hero returning with the spoils of war.

"Awesome," Latrisse said. "Brenda forgot to buy ice and everything's closed." She smiled down at Annie. "You must be Annie. The twins can't wait to meet you."

"I like your shoes," Annie said, zeroing in on Latrisse's feet. "They're pretty."

"Aren't they?" Latrisse pointed one foot, tilting it this way and that. "Would you like to try them on?"

"Yes, ma'am," Annie said.

"Me, too." A blond-haired girl popped up from behind the living room couch like a prairie dog coming out of its hole. "Can I wear them, too. Please?"

Jason stuck his head out of the kitchen. "Happy Turkey Day, y'all. Don't just stand there. Make yourself to home." He hurried to take the Crock-Pot from Conall, giving it an appreciative sniff. "Mmm, smells good. Gumbo?"

"Yep. Hank made it." Beck held up the dessert plate. "I brought Boiled Can."

Jason's eyes lit up. "Hot diggity dog, you know I love it. Just set it on the sideboard with the rest of the sweet stuff."

Beck put her hand on Annie's shoulder. "Daddy, this is Annie. I told you about her."

"Nice to meet you, shug." Daddy gave Annie a distracted smile. "Toby, stick that tea in the fridge and put the ice in the cooler." Brenda called his name from the kitchen. "I'm coming, woman," he said. "Keep your apron on."

Conall followed him into the living room. "I would greet your lady wife, if it pleases you."

"Sure, sure," Daddy said. He paused to frown at Darlene standing behind the couch. "You and Jay quit horsing around and say hello to our guests."

The twins bolted into the den after Annie, who'd followed Latrisse of the Splendiferous Footwear.

Stepping around the card table and folding chairs Brenda had set up for the kids, Beck set her plate on the sideboard between an enormous bowl of banana pudding and two pumpkin pies. Brenda's oak dining table gleamed with her prized Fiestaware. In the center of the table, a covered-glass cake plate filled with fall fruits and vegetables added a decorative touch.

Having made her offering to the dessert gods, Beck went into the kitchen. Steam wafted from the pots on top of the stove, and the double ovens and microwave were going full blast. Jason stood at the breakfast table carving a turkey as big as a Volkswagen, and Toby was slicing the ham. The dachshund sat at their feet, her back legs flattened behind her like bat wings, patiently waiting for some tasty ort to hit the floor.

Over by the stove, Brenda buzzed back and forth, tending to her cooking. Brenda was eight years younger than Jason, but she looked every one of her forty-nine years, and then some. She'd never lost the baby weight she'd gained with the twins. A few inches over five feet tall, Brenda was bosomy and as soft and doughy as her homemade rolls. She wore an animal print polyester dress with a vee neck and a chunky red and black necklace. Her frosted brown hair was curled, teased, and sprayed to a fare-thee-well.

"Put me to work," Beck said. "What can I do to help?"

Brenda gave her a polite little smile, the same smile she'd been giving Beck for years, one that implied tolerance without affection. "Your gentleman friend brought flowers. You could put them in a vase for me and set them on the sideboard with the desserts, if you would."

Her "gentleman friend" hadn't had flowers when they arrived, which meant Conall had used hoodoo. Brenda would have a fit if she knew.

Beck picked up the bouquet of flowers lying on the butcher block—plump white and orange roses, a dozen each, mixed with delicate, drooping Chinese lanterns—and put them in a vase with water.

"Done," she said when she'd completed the task. "What else?"

"Nothing," Brenda said, without turning from her task. "Go visit with Song and Latrisse in the den. Too many cooks spoil the broth."

Dismissed and feeling about as useless as an ashtray on a motorcycle, Beck walked into the den. Annie and Darlene sat on the floor gazing worshipfully at Latrisse's feet. Jay leaned over the arm of Conall's plaid recliner, showing him an oversized plastic gun.

"It's an Armadillo Vengeance Blaster," Jay was saying to

Conall. "You load the plastic discs in here." He poked his finger in the chamber and wiggled it around. "And you pull this trigger to shoot."

Brenda stuck her head out of the kitchen, spoon in hand, and gave Jay a death-ray glare. "Bubba, don't you dare shoot that thing in the house."

"Aw, Mom." Jay slumped, boneless as a jelly fish, over the arm of Conall's chair.

"I mean it," Brenda said, employing the universal mom tone. "Don't make me come in there."

"Perhaps later, you can demonstrate this remarkable weapon to me outside," Conall said in his solemn way.

Jay snapped to his feet in a miracle of bone regeneration. "Promise?"

"You have my word."

Jay grinned at Conall. "Cool."

Something funny unfolded inside Beck, a warm, scary feeling that made her feel weak and floaty and altogether strange. Stress; it had to be stress. It's a well-known fact family makes you crazy.

Two worn but comfortable brown couches formed a crooked L in front of the fireplace. Beck chose a seat near Latrisse's mother, a tiny bird of a woman with black hair, almond-shaped eyes, and the wrinkled mouth of a smoker.

"Well, Song," Beck said with a smile. "Our girl gave us quite a surprise, didn't she?"

Song bobbed her head up and down. "A blessing, to be sure."

Latrisse slipped off her pumps for the girls to admire and Darlene snatched them up.

"Me first," she informed Annie, clutching her prize to her chest, "because *I'm* nine and you're only eight."

A storm gathered in Annie's purple eyes. "But I saw them first and Latrisse said—"

"It's my house and you're my guest," Darlene said in a lofty tone. "You have to do what I say."

"But—" Annie protested.

"Annie," Beck said.

Annie looked at Beck and sighed. "Okay."

The doorbell rang.

"I'll get it," Beck said, jumping up from the couch. God, this was going to be a long-ass, eternal, never-ending day.

She strode into the foyer and threw open the front door. Evan lounged on the concrete stoop, tattooed and studded, and wearing his patented pout.

"What are you doing here?" Beck said, frowning at him. "If you've come to make trouble, forget it. I'll kick you into next week."

Evan arched a pierced brow. "Cool your jets, sis. I was invited, same as you." He opened his arms wide. "I'm here to spend Thanksgiving in the loving bosom of my fam."

"Oh, shit," Beck said.

Chapter Thirty-six

Beck picked at the food on her plate. Brenda had outdone herself. There was enough food to feed half of Behr County, and everything was delicious. The turkey and ham were moist and flavorful. The sweet potato casserole was a diabetic's nightmare of brown sugar and pecans, and the green bean casserole was a creamy delight crusted with artery clogging, crunchy fried onions. But, Beck wasn't hungry. Evan had taken care of that.

Not that she'd had much appetite to begin with. She forced herself to take a bite of giblet gravy and rice. Brenda made her gravy from scratch—starting with a caramel brown roux of flour and oil, and adding rich hen's broth, sliced boiled eggs, and slivers of dark meat chicken and turkey—but it tasted like sawdust to Beck. *I'll be thankful when this rat killing is over.*

She'd taken Daddy out on the back patio before dinner to grill him about Evan. "Where'd you meet the prodigal son?" she'd demanded.

"He came in the restaurant a few days ago and introduced himself," Daddy said. "Told me he'd hired someone to find you, and that you two have gotten close. Came as quite a shock, finding out I have a grown son." He grinned. "Reckon I throw twins."

"And just like that, you invite him to the house for Thanksgiving?"

Daddy lifted his shoulders. "He's kin. He looks just like you

and he's got the Damian birthmark. He's in town alone and he
didn't have plans for the holiday. What else could I do?"

"And Brenda's okay with this?"

"Didn't say that." Turning his head, Daddy gazed through
the storm door and into the kitchen, where Brenda bustled
about. "She'll come around. Give her time. I know you and
your step-mama haven't always gotten along, but Brenda's a
good woman."

Daddy seemed to be ignoring the white elephant in the
room, so Beck decided to point it out. "Evan is kith," she said.
"Like me."

"Don't know anything about that," Daddy'd said, not meeting her gaze. "Don't want to. I expect you both to behave
while you're in my home, and not do anything to upset Brenda
or the twins."

Daddy had gone back inside and that had been the end of it.
Deny, deny, deny; that was the norm way, but Beck felt like she
was sitting on a powder keg.

Beck glanced at Conall, sitting at the table beside her. Mon-
sieur Demon Hunter seemed unfazed by the undercurrents of
tension eddying about the room. Conall was calm as a Hindu
cow, and on his third plate of food. The kids ate a little, maybe
enough to keep a flea alive, and squirmed restlessly in their
chairs. Jason and Toby were talking football with the determined zeal of two adult males doing their best to ignore a
strained social situation, and Latrisse and Song were attempting
to make conversation with Brenda. They weren't having much
luck. Brenda might be here in the physical sense, but mentally
she was out to lunch. She was pale and green around the gills,
and she couldn't stop staring at Evan. If a caravan of carnies had
trooped into Brenda's dining room and copped a squat at her
table, she couldn't have looked more shocked and appalled. Her
lips moved constantly, but she wasn't talking or eating.

Beck suspected she was reciting the Twenty-third Psalm.
Nonstop.

On the bright side, compared to Evan, Beck was Jesus' little lamb. It should have made her feel better, but it didn't. She kept waiting for the shit to hit the fan.

Evan wasn't eating much, either—whether out of habit or because he was uncomfortable, Beck couldn't say. His burns had healed, but there were dark circles under his eyes, like he hadn't slept, and he seemed tense and jumpy. He wore black jeans, black pointy-toe boots, and a black zipper shirt with draw-strings and eyelets and long, dangling fringe. With Elgdrek dead, half of Evan's tattoos had disappeared. But Haggy was still alive and kicking, though imprisoned in a djevel flaskke, which meant Evan still looked like the Illustrated Man. His black hair was mussed and spiked, sticking up every which a-way in a feathery crown, and his purple eyes were rimmed with kohl.

"What happened to you?" Toby had asked when Beck walked into the kitchen with Evan. "Yo' mama hump a rooster?"

Things went downhill from there.

Annie stood up from her folding chair. "I need to go to the bathroom," she declared in the dulcet tones of a rodeo an-nouncer.

"You may be excused," Beck said.

Annie disappeared down the hall. Embarrassed, Beck glanced at Brenda, but her stepmother wasn't paying any attention.

"W-what did you say you do for a living?" Brenda asked Evan. Her food sat untouched on her plate, and she clutched the plastic beads around her neck like a rosary. Beck didn't have the heart to remind her that she and Jason weren't Catholic.

"I helped run the family business," Evan said just as smooth as you please.

Brenda stared at the long earring dangling from Evan's ear and the stud in his lip. "What sort of business did you say your parents were in?"

"Acquisitions."

"Oh, please," Beck said under her breath. "Don't make me throw up in my mouth."

"A-acquisitions?" Brenda repeated, looking slightly molli-fied. "That sounds respectable."

Oh, yeah? Beck wanted to say. *Only if you consider death, depravity, and degradation respectable.*

"It wasn't a walk in the park," Evan said. "To be frank, I'm sort of at loose ends, with my dad dead and my mother gone." He gave Beck a hard look. "I can't really make any kind of decision until I know whether Mommy dearest is going to return."

"Where did you say she went again?" Brenda asked, eyeing his ink. In Brenda's world, tattoos were the mark of the devil and Evan was clearly possessed. If she only knew . . .

"I'm not sure," Evan said. "She flits here and there."

Beck choked on a swallow of tea.

"Rebekah?" Conall asked. His voice was full of concern. "Are you well?"

"I'm fine. I just—"

"Look, Mama, a kitty," Darlene cried, pointing to the living room window.

A black cat sat on the windowsill. The cat arched its back and yowled. The sound rattled the glass. The dog yelped and squeezed under the sideboard. Jason and Toby stopped talking football. Darlene and Jay dove under the card table, and Brenda turned white as her napkin.

Conall kept eating.

"What the hell was that, a mountain lion?" Evan asked.

"Ak ma," Song clutched Latrisse in fright. *"Ak ma."*

A toilet flushed somewhere in the back of the house. Annie walked into the dining room and resumed her place at the kids' table, innocent as you please. Beck gave her an "I will deal with you later" look and turned her attention back to her stepmother. She was worried about Brenda. She wasn't acting herself. Hazel the ghost of Sardine Bridge and Brenda Damian had one thing in common: both could be counted on to lambast anyone who cussed around them. Evan had said *hell,* and Brenda hadn't uttered a peep of protest.

Granted, the sudden and unexpected appearance of the Wampus Kitty was enough to startle anybody, but now that things had calmed down, Beck expected Brenda to whip out a Bible verse or three and use them on Evan, something from Colossians or Ephesians denouncing obscene talk and corruptive words. But, Brenda just sat there.

Beck gave her a worried frown. "Brenda, are you okay?"

Her stepmother pushed her shoulder blades against the back of her chair. "My back hurts, probably from standing on my feet too long."

Meredith Peterson appeared on a gust of icy, perfumed air, a vision of petite chic in an orange poplin shirt with cuffed, three-quarter sleeves, a flowered pencil skirt, and hot pink stilettos.

"Your back hurts because you're *fat,* you cow," she said to Brenda. "Take the feedbag off once in a while. It'll do you good." Her furious gaze turned to Evan. "As for *you,* I'm not finished with you."

"Oh, no, not again," Evan groaned as Meredith launched into a vicious tirade.

"What's the matter?" Brenda asked. Her anxious gaze moved around the table. "Is the turkey dry?"

"The turkey's just fine, Mama," Daddy said.

Brenda jumped as the dachshund exploded in a frenzy of barking under the sideboard.

"Gracious, Boo, what's gotten into you?" Brenda turned her head. "I feel a draft. The kids must have left the back door open." She pushed to her feet and dragged the yapping dog out of its hiding place. "I declare, Boo Lily, you don't have a brain in your head. You are going outside right this minute."

Clucking at the snarling pooch, Brenda walked through Meredith and into the kitchen.

If Brenda noticed the chill or Meredith's citrusy scent, she didn't show it. As for Meredith, she was in full harangue. She stood over Evan pouring out a steady stream of abuse. Evan, for his part, looked miserable.

Beck cleared her throat. "Um, Daddy?"

"Yes, sugar bear?"

"We have a situation."

"What kind of situation? Are we out of ham? You need more ice?"

She glanced at the twins and lowered her voice. "We have a ghost. Why don't you take the kids and go outside? Brenda, too. We'll handle this."

"A ghost?" Daddy jumped to his feet. "In the yard, kids. Now."

"But, Beck, I wanna—" Annie said.

"Now, Annie," Beck said, doing her best to imitate Brenda's Mom glare.

"Oh, man," Annie said as Jason herded her and the twins out of the room.

Toby pushed back his chair. "I'm gone. I can't take this caterwauling."

"Candyass," Meredith sneered as he left, taking Song and Latrisse with him.

"This is not a good time, Meredith," Beck said, once they were alone. "It's Thanksgiving."

"Like I give a flying camel fart about your stupid holiday," Meredith said. "I'm on a job."

"She keeps saying that, but what does she *want*?" Evan dropped his head in his hands. "I can't sleep. I can't eat. I can't think for the noise."

Meredith let out another deafening shriek.

Conall set down his fork. "I grow weary of your antics, shade. You are disturbing my enjoyment of this most excellent repast. State your business and be gone."

Meredith made a face at him. "Joysuck." She turned to Evan. "Very well, if you must know, I'm here on behalf of my client, Thomas Crispus Henderson."

Evan lifted his head from his hands. "Who?"

"The zombie," Beck said. "She wants you to let Tommy go."

"Well, why didn't she say so?" Evan said. "I could have gotten some sleep."

"I'm a professional. I wanted to make an impression." Meredith smirked. "And, besides, it's fun."

Conall picked up his fork again. "He will release your client. You may go."

"I will?" Evan's eyes narrowed. "What's in it for me?"

"Comply with the virago's demands or continue to suffer her ministrations." Conall shrugged. "The choice is yours."

"Okay, okay," Evan said. "I'll let the damn zombie go. Jeez."

"Hold on," Beck said. "If you take the spell off him now, can you find him again?"

"No."

"Then you need to do it later," Beck said. "Tommy wants to go home. We can't send him back to New Orleans if we don't know where he is."

"I'll tell him to come to me," Evan said. "There, happy?"

"I should wait, were I you," Conall said, spearing another piece of ham off the platter. "Unless you wish to explain the undead to the humans over dessert?"

"Oh," Evan said. "I didn't think of that."

Meredith flounced into the living room and plopped on the sofa. "I'm not leaving until my client gets satisfaction." Conall gave her a cold stare, and she added, "But I'll quit howling. For now."

The back door crashed against the wall and Daddy rushed inside. "Becky," he shouted. "I need you to stay with the kids. I'm taking Brenda to the hospital. She's having a heart attack."

Beck stood at the living room window and watched her father bundle Brenda into his truck and screech out of the driveway. The nearest hospital was thirty miles away in Paulsberg, the county seat. In the other room, she heard Conall talking to the twins. He'd been wonderful with them, calm and soothing. The guy could sell swampland. You'd think a big, stern-looking guy like him would intimidate children, but he had the opposite effect. He exuded authority and confidence, and he was gentle and patient with them.

He'd make a wonderful father.

Whoa, where had that thought come from?

She wandered into the den and settled Annie and the twins down to watch a movie with Conall while she cleaned up. He offered to help, but she declined.

"There are five of us to handle the kitchen," she told him. "I need you to stay with the kids. They like you."

"Yes, please." Darlene hung on Conall's arm. "We want you to watch *Barbie and the Diamond Castle* with us."

"No, we don't," Jay said with brotherly disgust. "That's a stupid old girl movie."

"I'm talking about me and Annie," Darlene said. "We want him to watch it with us, right Annie?"

Annie shrugged, her face closed. "I don't know. I've never seen it."

Beck's heart squeezed. Of course Annie had never seen it. She'd been too busy trying to stay alive.

"Oh, then we *have* to watch it." Darlene looked up at Conall with pleading eyes. "Please?" She shot her brother a look. "Jay watches it with me all the time. He's just being a *boy*. It's got a dragon in it, like Killer."

"Killer?" Conall asked.

Jay pointed to the glass aquarium on one wall. "My Bearded Dragon. He's not a real dragon. He's a lizard."

"You say this tale has a dragon in it?" Conall rubbed his jaw. "Methinks this sounds interesting. What say you, Sir Jay? Shall we prove our gallantry and cede to the ladies?"

"Huh?" Jay said.

"It means we get to watch the *Barbie* movie, stupid," Darlene said, jumping up and down. "Yay."

Beck left them arguing about who would sit next to Conall and went into the kitchen. She almost kept going when she saw the mess.

"Don't panic and carry a towel," Latrisse said, waving one of Brenda's kitchen cloths at her. "We'll have this place cleaned up in no time."

Toby and Song pitched in and, to Beck's surprise, so did Evan. The five of them had the food put away and the kitchen clean and tidy in a little more than an hour. Song and Latrisse said their good-byes and left, and Evan flopped on the living room sofa like he owned the place.

"Don't you have someplace else to be?" she asked, looking down at him with her hands on her hips. "Any place else?"

Evan settled against the cushions and crossed his feet at the ankles. "Nope. Jason and Brenda invited me to stay the night. Wasn't that nice of them?"

"Jim Dandy," Beck said, going to check on the kids. She found Conall sitting on the big couch between the two little girls. He seemed engrossed in the movie. Jay was sprawled on the floor on his stomach, heels up, chin resting on his hands. To Beck's surprise, Meredith was curled up in an armchair watching the movie with them.

Boo Lily the dachshund was curled in a sleek knot on Conall's lap, one eye slightly cracked and aimed at the ghost. The crotch of safety, Beck thought in amusement, looking at the contented hound. Even the dog liked Conall.

"By the sword, that Lydia was a wicked sorceress," Conall said when the movie ended. "The damsels Alexa and Liana were stalwart friends to overcome such evil."

"It's okay." Jay rolled onto his back and pointed his Armadillo Vengeance Blaster at the ceiling. "The dragon is the coolest part."

"A most fearsome beast," Conall agreed. "I am glad the witch and the worm were turned to stone."

He was discussing a Barbie movie with the same seriousness and gravity, Beck suspected, that he employed during a council of war with the Dal. She loved that about him.

Love, love, love. The word spun around in her brain, leaving her reeling and unsteady as a drunken clown teetering on a high wire.

The Big Truth, the one that she'd been trying to ignore for days, smacked her in the face like a banana cream pie. She was in love with Conall. Captain Grim, demon hunter. Mr. I-Know-Something-of-Dragons—

She loved him. She gripped the dish towel in her hands. Don't panic, she thought. *Don't panic.*

She stumbled back into the kitchen. Who was she kidding? She was scared to death.

Chapter Thirty-seven

The telephone by the breakfast table was ringing. *Jason's cell,* it blinked.

Beck snatched up the phone. "Hey, Daddy. What did the doctor say about Brenda?"

"Gall bladder." He sounded tired, but relieved. "I hate to ask this, sugar bear, but can you stay with the kids tonight? Brenda's never been in the hospital and she's scared to death."

"What about the twins?"

"Nurse practitioner," Daddy said. "They were born at home."

"Oh. Sure, I'll stay with them."

"Thanks, chickpea. I owe you one."

Click; he was gone.

This really was the day that would never end. She wanted to go home and soak in the tub, and think about what she was going to do. She was terrified to tell Conall she loved him. She was terrified not to.

Meredith materialized in front of the fridge. "That movie sucked," she said. "What kind of saccharine crappy-ass ending was that?"

"It's a Barbie movie," Beck said. "What did you expect, death and dismemberment?"

"I expected something besides puppies and sparkles and BFF shit," Meredith said. "I'm out of here."

"What happened to not leaving until your client gets satisfaction?"

"Screw that," Meredith said. "But tell Emo Evan I'll be watching him."

She disappeared in a burst of perfume.

"That was your daddy on the phone," Beck told the twins when she returned to the den. "Your mama's okay."

Jay sat up, his hands gripping the plastic gun. "D-did she have a heart attack?"

"Nope," Beck said. "Her heart's fine and she's going to be all right, I promise. Daddy's staying with her tonight, but he'll be home in the morning."

"But, who'll stay with us?" Darlene's mouth trembled.

"Me and Annie," Beck said.

"Yay, a sleepover," Darlene squealed, her fright forgotten at the thrill of spend-the-night company.

"Conall, too?" Jay asked.

Conall bowed. "I should be honored."

"Yay," the twins said, bouncing around like a couple of ping pong balls.

The back door slammed and Toby ambled in. "Garbage is taken out," he said. "I'll be moseying along."

Beck felt a sudden, claustrophobic urge to get out of the house. "Wait and we'll walk out with you. I thought I might take the kids to the park for a little fresh air." She looked at Annie and the twins. "Would you like that?"

"Can we go to the one by the river?" Jay begged. "It's way better than the old one." He pointed his gun. *"Pekew, pekew,"* he said. "I wanna show Conall my AV Blaster."

Beck hesitated. "I don't know. Your mama won't like it."

"We've had swimming lessons," Darlene insisted. "She takes us there all the time now. Besides, there's a fence, so people won't fall in."

Beck looked at her watch. Jiminy Cricket; it was after two o'clock. It would be dark in a couple of hours.

"Okay, but only for a little while," she said. "Grab your jackets. It'll be cold down by the water."

Five minutes later, they walked out of the house. With Evan.

"What are you, a tick?" Beck asked him.

Evan grinned. "Just enjoying a warm fuzzy with my beloved relatives." His smile vanished. "You and I need to talk."

"Does it have to be *today*?" Beck said.

"Yes, Cookie. Today."

Toby paused on the sidewalk, his nose twitching. "I smell something."

Conall halted beside him, his expression watchful and alert. "Is it the djegrali?"

Toby sniffed. "Nah, but it ain't—you know—*normal*. Smells like Fritos." He gave Beck a significant look. "Reckon you know what that means."

"Reckon I don't."

Toby shook his head at such ignorance. "Well, they're gone now. See ya."

"What's a juhgrahbi?" Jay asked as Toby climbed in Loretta and drove off.

"A Japanese motorcycle," Beck lied, pushing him down the sidewalk. "Get in the truck."

Evan followed them in his rental car. When they got to the park on the river, they found it empty except for an old man walking his dog along the paved path at the edge of the water. It was Thanksgiving and people were out of town visiting relatives or sitting at home in front of the television watching football.

They crossed the park to the lookout that jutted like a ship's prow over the river. To the right, the Trammell Bridge spanned the Devil. Farther upriver was Beck's and home. The kids leaned over the railing, oohing and ahhing at the thirty-foot drop to the water.

"Not so far," Beck said, grabbing Jay by the jacket. "You'll fall down and go boom."

Annie and Darlene soon grew bored and raced for the swing set.

Jay stuck his hip out and brandished his plastic gun. "Now I can show you how it works," he said, giving Conall a hopeful grin.

"In a minute," Evan said. "I need grownup time with Beck and Conall."

"Aw, shoot," Jay said. He scuffed his athletic shoe against the cement. "You promised, Conall."

Conall laid his hand on the boy's shoulder. "And I will keep that promise. Give us but a moment."

A large lizard poked his head out of Jay's jacket pocket and bulged its eyes at them.

"Good grief, Jay, you brought Killer?" Beck said. "Your mama will have a cow."

"No, she won't. Mom hates lizards." Jay poked Killer back in his pocket. "I won't lose him. I promise."

Promises; everything with kids was about promises.

"Lord a-mercy," Beck muttered as Jay ran over and joined the girls. "Now, I'm responsible for a lizard."

As soon as Jay was out of earshot, Evan pounced. "Where's Hagilth?"

Conall regarded him with a stony expression. "The demon is no longer your affair."

"The hell she ain't," Evan said. "Tell me where she is."

"You are in no position to make demands," Conall said. "But for my regard for your sister I would have killed you already."

Beck stepped between the two bristling males. "Elgdrek is dead and Haggy is out of the picture," she said to Evan. "You're *free*. You should be thanking Conall."

Evan laughed. "I'll never be free until Hagilth is dead. Where is she?"

He was like a dog with a bone. Beck couldn't blame him. She'd be the same way, in his shoes.

"Show him, Conall," she said. "Please. For me."

"Very well." Conall held out his hand, palm up, and the djevel flaskke appeared. "Hagilth is in my keeping, and will remain so until I transport her to the Pit."

"A *bottle*?" Evan shook his head. "Not good enough. What if she gets out? I want her dead. Maybe we can make a deal."

"Deals, deals," Beck said. "Why is it always deals with you? Not everyone can be bought."

"Don't be such a baby, Cookie. Everyone has a price. You

just have to figure out what it is." Evan looked at Conall, his jaw clenched. "Your boy Duncan's been snooping around asking questions about a certain doorway. I know where it is."

Conall's hard expression did not change, but Beck detected a flicker of interest in his dark eyes.

"You know the location of the portal into Hannah?" Conall said. "You will tell me."

The siren at the fire department went off, interrupting them.

"Something's burning." Beck looked toward town, but didn't see any smoke. Leaning over the railing, she looked upriver. "I see it," she said, pointing to a dark plume in the sky. "Looks like it's close to Ora Mae's place."

Jay ran up to them, his face red and streaked with tears.

Conall slipped the flask in his trouser pocket. "Later, we will talk more about the portal," he said to Evan. "I do not wish to discuss it in front of the boy."

Beck knelt in front of Jay. "What's the matter?"

"I was feeding Killer a bug and he bit me. I dropped him and now I can't find him."

"Dadflab it," Beck said, borrowing one of Toby's favorite words when she really wanted to say something worse. "I knew this would happen."

She followed Jay across the park to help him look for the missing lizard. Not far away, Annie and Darlene were swinging, kicking their legs back and forth to see who could go higher.

Beck dropped to her hands and knees. She was rooting around in the bushes when Earl Skinner stepped from behind a tree. He wore a flannel shirt under a baggy army jacket, and jeans. The ferret nose and whiskers were still in place, his hair was greasy, and he smelled like wet hay.

Or Fritos, Beck thought, remembering Toby's earlier remark. She got to her feet and shoved Jay behind her.

"Hello, bitch, looking for this?" Earl said, holding up Killer.

"That's my lizard," Jay said, peering around Beck. "Give him back."

"Finders keepers, losers weepers," Earl said. "He's mine now." He stuffed the lizard in his pocket and produced a nine-millimeter handgun. "Where's your demon hunter boyfriend?" He laughed at Beck. "Don't look so surprised. I figured that one out from Old Man Peterson's papers."

Conall shot across the park in a blur of motion and stepped in front of her.

"Here I am, Skinner," he said. "You were skulking around Jason's house earlier. Toby smelled your stench. What do you want?"

"This," Earl said, firing the gun.

Beck screamed as Conall jerked, once, twice, and fell to his knees, toppling to the ground with a wrenching groan. Blood seeped from two bullet wounds in his chest, and spread.

"Conall." Beck went to her knees beside him.

"Move out of the way." Earl pulled a cell phone out of his pocket and pointed it at the dying warrior. "I'm gonna make me a little snuff film and show it to them demons. This here demon hunter's gonna make me rich."

"Run, Rebekah." Conall's voice was hoarse with pain. "Take the children and go."

"Run, Rebekah, run." Earl mocked him in his nasal voice. He kicked Beck out of the way and stood over Conall. "Not so tough now, are you?"

"Take it easy, Skinner." Evan came up to them slowly, his hands in front of him so Earl could see that he was unarmed. He glanced at the frightened boy. "Jay, get the girls and get out of the park."

Jay looked at Beck.

"Do it," she said. "Go."

Earl laughed as Jay took off. "That's right. Run you little shit," he yelled after the boy. "I know where you live."

"Put the gun down, Skinner," Evan said. "You don't want to do this."

"Screw you. You knew about the weapons. You were gonna keep it to yourself, cut the Skinners out." He bent down and picked up the flask lying on the ground next to Conall. "Reckon I'll keep this as a souvenir."

"That's mine," Evan said, lunging at Skinner. "Give it to me."

Skinner leveled the gun at Evan. Evan froze. "Not so fast, pretty boy," Earl said. "I'd as soon kill you as look at you. Just you try me."

"I want that bottle," Evan said through his teeth. "I'll pay you for it."

"Pay me for it, huh?" Earl grinned and stuck the djeval flaskke in his shirt pocket. "Must be worth something if'n you want it so bad." He aimed the gun at Conall's head and held up his phone. "Say good-bye, asshole."

"No." Beck threw herself on top of Conall.

She flinched as the gun went off, waiting for the bullet to rip through her flesh. Nothing happened. She heard Earl swear and then the sharp crack of the gun being fired again and again

She lifted her head. Tommy stalked Earl around the park. The preservation spell had worn off and Tommy looked bad, real bad. His nose was gone and part of his jawbone peeked through his left cheek. He'd hung a string of air fresheners around his neck, but nothing could disguise the sickly sweet smell of decaying flesh.

Earl backed away from the zombie, firing the gun, but Tommy kept coming.

"Son of a bitch, why don't you die?" Earl screamed.

"'Cause I'm already dead, moron," Tommy said. He jerked the gun out of Earl's hand and threw it. The gun sailed over the fence and plopped into the river.

Tommy sat down on the ground. "Aw, hell," he said, looking at the bullet holes that riddled his body. "Now look what you done."

Evan charged Skinner. "Give me that bottle, you little weasel."

Earl Skinner turned and ran with Evan hot on his heels.

Beck crawled over to Conall and slapped him on the cheek. "Open your eyes, Conall. You even *think* about dying, I'll kick your ass."

His beautiful mouth curved in a weak smile. "Hellcat. Would that I had told you."

Beck ripped open his shirt. "Told me what?"

"That I love you."

"Yeah, but do you trust me?"

"Completely."

"Good." Tears ran down her cheeks. " 'Cause this is going to hurt like hell."

Ignoring Conall's roar of pain and surprise, she stuck her hands in his chest and pulled out the bullets. Tears blurred her vision, but she couldn't quit now. She had to get the poison out. Gritting her teeth, she held her bloody hands over the bullet wounds and concentrated. Conall arched his back and cried out again as blood and tissue contaminated with crater dust rose from the holes and dissipated. The wounds healed and closed before her eyes. Conall slumped to the ground and lay still.

Was he dead? Oh, dear God, had she killed him?

"Conall?" Beck grabbed the edges of his torn shirt and shook him. *"Conall?"*

He opened his eyes and looked at her. "You were right. That hurt."

Beck collapsed on his chest, sobbing. "Oh, thank God. I thought I'd killed you."

He put his arms around her and held her close. "No, my one and only love," he said. "You saved me."

An agonized scream pierced the air. Evan burst out of the woods. The insolent pout was gone and he looked terrified.

"Run," he shouted, dashing full tilt boogie for the park exit. "That idiot Earl opened the bottle. Hagilth's loose."

Chapter Thirty-eight

The dragon shrieked out of the sky and slammed into the park like a downed fighter jet, gouging the earth and shattering park equipment and trees. The monster was huge, the size of an eighteen-wheeler, with ragged golden wings and liquid eyes the size of manhole covers. She stank like a herd of dead cows bloating in the sun.

And she was pissed.

Hagilth bathed the park in flames, scorching the grass, melting the chain link fence, and setting the woods on fire. The acrid scents of smoke, sulfur, and ash choked the air, and embers of burning wood and sparks of hot metal flitted in the air like drunken fireflies.

"It's a dragon," Beck said stupidly. "Where did Haggy get a dragon?"

Conall got to his feet. "If you are correct and the kith cannot be possessed, then the demon must have entered the closest living creature, which, I surmise, happened to be Jay's lizard."

"That's *Killer*?"

"So it would seem."

"Holy shit. What happened to Earl?"

"I presume the dragon ate him."

"Oh, my God."

Conall drew his sword. "Make for the river. I will hold the fiend's attention."

"Are you crazy? You can't fight that thing. You've been shot."

"I am healed, thanks to you."

"You almost *died*," Beck said. "You lost a lot of blood and—"

He pulled her close and gave her a hard kiss. "I trusted you. Now you must trust me. I know what I am about."

I know something of dragons. The words echoed in her head. Had it only been five days ago he'd said them? So much had happened since then. So much had changed. *She* had changed. She loved him. The thought of losing him was unbearable.

"I do trust you," she said. "But you don't have a shield and I can—"

He ran out into the open. "To me, demon," he shouted. "Come. Let us grapple on the field of death."

Of all the idiotic, melodramatic—

Haggy turned on Conall and spat out a sheet of flame. The dragon's roar swallowed Beck's scream of terror. The fiery blast baked the spot where Conall stood, melting a bronze statue of Jeb Hannah, the town father.

No, please no, he couldn't be dead. Not now, not when she'd found him. Not when she knew what it was to *love* him. Life without him yawned before her, a big, empty nothing. What would she do if he—

The smoke parted and she saw Conall. He was safe; he'd done the demon hunter thing and blipped out of the way.

Beck's knees buckled and she sagged against a tree for support, lightheaded with relief. You just wait, Conall Dalvahni, she thought. *When this was over, I'm going to put a bug in your ear you'll never forget. Meredith's bitchfests will seem like a heavenly choir of angels in comparison.*

"Here I am, worm," Conall said. "Come and get me, if you can."

It was the Dalvahni version of shooting the dragon a bird, and it got the desired reaction. Haggy snarled and swung her barbed tail. The bony spike slammed into an oak, showering the park with deadly sharp pieces of wood. Conall plucked a long shard of oak from his shoulder and tossed it aside. The wound healed before the piece of wood hit the ground.

He sprang lightly aside as the furious dragon struck at him like a snake. Haggy's jaws snapped on thin air. She hissed and lashed out with teeth, claws, and barbed tail, but Conall seemed to anticipate her every move, appearing and disappearing, and driving the beast mad with fury.

As she watched the battle, the frightened tattoo of Beck's heart steadied to a slow, angry thump. Why, he's enjoying himself, the big alpha jerk, she thought, furious with him. *I'm having a heart attack, and he's having FUN.*

She could stay meekly behind a tree while he battled Hagilth the Horrible, or she could help. Maybe Conall knew something about dragons, but she had a few tricks of her own.

Keeping one eye on the battle, Beck crept closer to the river. She opened her senses and let the power of the river fill her, saturate her, build within her, steady and relentless, until she was near to bursting with it.

A flicker of movement drew her attention to the lookout. Tommy; he lumbered to his feet, his movements sluggish, as if the bullet holes in his worn body and the fight with Earl had sapped the last of his strength. Head down, he staggered toward the battle.

He was going to try to help Conall. Haggy would burn him to a crisp.

"No, Tommy, stay back," she cried. "You're too slow."

The dragon heard Beck's cry and turned, her horned head swinging like a lantern at the end of her long neck.

"Mine," she said in a raspy voice like stone on stone. "I have you now, bitch."

Beck met the dragon's oozing gaze and time seemed to slow. She was falling, falling, into those dark wells of emptiness and hate. She watched, bemused, as Haggy thundered toward her like a golden Godzilla, knocking Tommy aside with a swipe of her tail. He flew through the air and landed several hundred feet away in a jumbled heap.

"Rebekah. *Rebekah.*"

Conall's agonized shout penetrated the dragon's spell, rousing Beck from her stupor. Haggy was almost on top of her. The dragon opened her jaws and vomited out a ball of flame.

Beck shifted into water and flowed out of the way. The heat from the dragon fire was withering, baking the concrete under Beck until she felt like an egg sizzling on a hot griddle. She cried out in pain and the river answered. A wall of water surged over the railing and washed over Beck, forming a watery shield between her and the dragon. She floated, safe, in the cool arms of the river.

Haggy roared in frustration and spewed flames at the liquid wall. Steam rose in billowing clouds. Through the hot haze, Beck saw Conall leap on the monster's back and raise his sword. The sword flashed and Beck heard the solid swish of metal on meat. The dragon's head hit the ground with a wet plop.

"Conall?" Resuming human shape, Beck looked around. Conall rode the dragon's headless body. Haggy collapsed beneath him and disintegrated into dust.

Conall strode over and caught Beck in a crushing embrace. "You are soaked," he said roughly. "The dragon's breath— Are you hurt?"

"Just singed a little around the edges." She buried her face against his wide chest, heedless of the drying blood. "Your shoulder—I saw you get holed by a piece of wood."

"Oh, that. 'Twas nothing."

"Good." She put her hands on his chest and shoved him. "What the hell were you thinking, taking on a dragon? Are you insane?"

"I?" Conall shouted back at her. His dark eyes blazed with anger. "When I said make for the river, I meant for you to take shelter there, not throw yourself in front of the beast." He grabbed her by the shoulders and shook her. "By the gods, Rebekah, I thought you were dead."

"Welcome to my world. I thought you were toast."

"I was in no danger. This was not my first dragon fight."

"Yeah? Well, it was for damn sure *my* first. You scared me out of my wits."

He snatched her back in his arms and ran his hands over her, as though to assure himself she was alive. "Impetuous little fool. Will you never learn to obey?"

"Doesn't seem likely." The shock was wearing off and Beck had the shakes. She wrapped her arms around his waist and held on. He was safe. He was alive, and so was she. "Will you?"

"I give commands. I do not take them."

"No, really? I hadn't noticed. Guess it's safe to say neither one of us will be making any promises to obey when we take the vows."

Conall's hands stilled. "What vows?"

"The wedding vows. You *are* going to marry me, aren't you?"

"Is this what humans call a proposal?"

"Yep. So, what's it going to be, yes or no?"

"That depends." Conall gave her a smile that made her heart go flippity flop. "Do you love me?"

"What do you think?"

"I do not know what to think." Cupping her bottom in his hands, he tugged her close. "As I lay dying, I swore you my eternal devotion. In response to my passionate avowal, you stuck your hands in my chest."

"To save your life. From now on, when you leave the house, you're wearing full body armor."

"I thank you for saving my life, milady." Conall tilted her chin and looked into her eyes, his gaze hungry. "Still, I would have the words." Bending his head, he brushed his lips against hers. "Say the words, my love. I need to hear them."

Beck had meant to make him suffer just a little bit longer, to even the score for giving her the scare of her life—twice in one day. But, when it got right down to it, the guy was hard to re-sist. Make that impossible. Not only was he gorgeous and badass, he was looking at her like she was the most beautiful, precious thing on earth.

And to top it off, he had the remarkable good sense to fall in love with her. Who could say no to a guy like that?

"I love you," Beck said, relenting.

"Again," Conall murmured. Lowering his head, he brushed his mouth against hers. "Say it again."

"I love you, Conall Dalvahni, with my all heart. And I don't care what anybody has to say about it. Kith or kin, or the gods themselves—I'll fight the whole stinking Dalvahni army, if I have to, to be with you. Satisfied?"

"Yes," Conall said, and gave her a scorching kiss that melted her insides and made her brain go loopy.

"I am sure this is all very gratifying, Captain," a deep voice said, "but the human authorities will be here anon. Of a certainty, they will have questions."

Conall lifted his head, ending the kiss. Duncan stood a few feet from them, surveying the ruined park.

"I trust you to rectify matters," Conall said, keeping Beck safely tucked against his side.

"As you command," Duncan said. He pointed to a crumpled heap on the ground. "What about him? 'Twould appear he is beyond help."

Beck saw Tommy and ran over to him. Conall grabbed her by the arm and pulled her back.

"Not too close, Rebekah," he said. "He is in extremis. He might not recognize you."

Tommy looked even worse up close, bloated and brownish green. Getting knocked around by a dragon hadn't helped matters. From the odd angle of his limbs, Beck was pretty sure both of his arms and legs were broken.

"Don't come no closer." Tommy's voice was slurred. "I'm a hot scrambled mess."

"Oh, Tommy," Beck said, aching for him.

Conall put his arm around Beck's shoulders. "You saved our lives," he said. "Rebekah and I are in your debt."

"Then find me that zombie maker." Tommy closed his eyes and let his chin drop to his chest. "I'm done with this shit."

"I'll find him." Beck swallowed. "You have my word."

"Be at ease, my love," Conall said in a low voice. "He is here."

Evan moved across the park like a sleepwalker.

"You killed her?" he asked hoarsely. "Hagilth is dead?"

"Yes," Conall said.

"I'm free." Evan stared at his hands. The tattoos were gone. "After all this time, I'm finally free. I don't believe it."

Tommy lifted his head, his gaze unseeing. "That him, Beck? That the Maker?"

"It's him, Tommy."

"He going to let me go?"

"Oh, yeah," Beck said, giving Evan a challenging look. "He'll let you go. Or else."

Tommy sighed. "That's good. Make sure they send me home. Promise me, Beck."

"I promise."

"Tell Annie—" Tommy's rich drawl faltered. "Tell her I'm sorry. Tell her I chased her away because—" He shook his head. "Because—"

"I know," Beck said, fighting back tears. "I'll tell her. I'll make sure she understands."

Tommy nodded. "Good. I'm ready now."

Evan raised his hand.

"Good-bye, Tommy," Beck said. "We won't forget you."

But Tommy was already gone.

Beck wiped the tears from her cheeks with the back of her hand. There was nothing more she could do for Tommy, except make sure he got home.

"Take Tommy to the bar," she said to Evan.

"No way. He smells."

Beck slapped him, hard. "He *smells* because you did this to him, asshole. We are *not* leaving him here. It could take the police months to identify him."

Evan rubbed his red cheek. "That's no way to treat family, Cookie."

"You're kith and you may be kin," Beck said, "but you're not family."

Something like hurt flickered across Evan's face and vanished. "Message received, loud and clear."

"Good," Beck said.

She meant it, didn't she? Evan wasn't her family, not really. She didn't trust him and she didn't owe him anything.

Then why did she feel so low and mean?

"I will take care of Tommy," Conall said. "Go and find the children."

She shot him an annoyed look. "Is that an order or a request?"

"A request, naturally," Conall said. He fixed Evan with a cold stare. "Your brother and I have things to discuss."

Evan's expression grew wary. "What kind of things?"

"The location of the portal in Hannah, for one," Conall said. The ground froze and cracked, and frost crept up Evan's boots. "Where is it?"

Evan swore and jumped back. "Okay, okay. You know that pasture on the edge of town, the one with the big oak covered in Spanish moss?"

"No," Conall said. "You will show it to me."

Beck left them discussing it and went to look for Annie and the twins. She found them huddled behind her truck.

"It's all right, the bad man is gone." She knelt and took the cowering children in her arms. "And he's not coming back."

"H-he's dead?" Jay asked. "Did the dragon get him?"

Darlene wiped her nose and scowled at him. "There's no such thing as dragons, Bubba. Mama's gonna whup your behind for telling fibs."

"You tell on Jay, and I'll tell your mama you said a bad word," Annie said.

Darlene's face reddened. "I never did. You made that up."

"Prove it," Annie said.

"No one's going to tell on anyone," Beck said firmly. "Everybody in the truck. We're going home."

"What about Killer?" Jay's mouth trembled. "We can't leave him here."

Crap, she'd forgotten about the lizard.

Jay read the answer in her expression. His mouth trembled. "He's dead, isn't he, Becky?"

"I'm afraid so, Jay. I'm sorry."

"It's your fault, Bubba," Darlene said. "You shouldn't have brought your dumb old lizard to the park."

Annie jumped to Jay's defense, and she and Darlene started arguing again. Beck was in the process of wrangling the squabbling kids into the truck, when the old Ford screeched up.

Toby jumped out, looking half-wild. "It's gone, Becky. The son of a bitch burned it down."

"What are you talking about?"

"The *bar*," Toby said. "Grease fire. Earl Skinner broke in through a window, turned the deep fat fryer on high, and left it. Junior saw the whole thing. It's gone. All of it."

Beck blinked at him in shock. The column of dark smoke and the agitated wail of the fire trucks had been the *bar*?

"I don't believe it." She sagged against the side of the truck. "What about the alarm system and Conall's protective spells?"

"Earl got around them somehow," Toby said. "He's good at breaking into things. That's his talent."

Correction: *was* his talent. Earl had broken into Trey's safe and into the bar, and he'd opened the djeval flaskke and released Haggy. Bet that was one jar Pandora Earl wished he'd never opened.

"You wait until I get my hands on him," Toby fumed. "I'll make him wish he was never born."

"Earl's dead," Beck said.

"What?" Toby said. "How?"

Jay stuck his head out the truck door. "I think the dragon ate him."

"*Bub-bah*," Darlene wailed. "There's no such thing as dragons. I'm telling Mom."

The bickering erupted once more. Good grief, it was *The Song That Never Ends*.

Beck shut the truck door, muting the noise. "Stop back by Brenda and Jason's and we'll talk about things over supper. There's a ton of food left."

Toby looked slightly cheered at the prospect of leftovers. "You talking turkey and dressing?"

"Yep."

"Giblet gravy and rice?"

"Yep," Beck said. "Plenty of that, too."

"Don't mind if I do." Toby turned his head as a car sped past. "There goes that brother of yours. Reckon what he's up to?"

"No telling."

What *would* Evan do now that he was free? Where would he go? Would she ever see him again? Probably not; not after the way she'd left things. Did she even want to?

Too many questions with no answers; she'd think about it later.

"Does Verbena know about the bar?" she asked Toby.

"Yeah, she and Hank drove up right after I got there. She was hopping mad at Earl, 'cause her new clothes got burned up."

"Tell her not to worry," Beck said. "We'll get her some more clothes. Tell Verbena she can stay at my house tonight. Ask her to feed Mr. Cat for me."

"Sure," Toby said. "I'll take her there myself. I've got a key."

Conall and Duncan were putting the finishing touches on the cleanup when the police arrived. Officer Dan Curtis got out of his patrol car and strolled up to them. Beck recognized him from the paper.

"Old Man Willis called the station with some crazy story about a dragon in the park." The officer shook his head. "That old geezer must be smoking wacky weed in his pipe." He gave Beck a squinty eyed look. "I smell smoke. You folks been grilling? That's a fire hazard. There's a drought, you know."

"We haven't been grilling," Beck said. "We brought the kids to play in the park."

"Huh," Officer Curtis said, looking around.

A few moments ago, the park had been a smoking ruin. There was a circle of dead grass where Haggy had died. Beck would be surprised if anything ever grew there again. One of the swing sets was upside down, a slide was wilted and crooked from Haggy's furnace breath, and the monkey bars looked *wrong*. Apparently, the Dalvahni info bank was a bit sketchy when it came to playground equipment.

"You probably smell the smoke from the fire," Beck said. "I heard the sirens earlier."

"Yeah, could be," Officer Curtis said. "Dispatch said somebody torched that bar on the river. Beck's, I think was the name." He adjusted his hat. "Never been there m'self. Heard tell it was rough—a real dive. You know the place?"

"Yeah, I know it."

That "dive" had been her childhood home and her livelihood. Later, she would grieve about it and worry what to do next. But, right now, she was too numb.

"That right?" Officer Curtis said, with a touch of censure. "Well, you won't be going there no more. The fire trucks got lost trying to find the place. By the time they got there, the building was gone." He turned back for his car. "Park closes in half an hour. Don't hang around too long. The boogedy woogedies come out after dark."

Chapter Thirty-nine

The next morning, the back door slammed and someone tramped into Brenda and Jason's kitchen.

"Becky? Kids?" Jason hollered. "I'm home."

"In here, Daddy," Beck said.

She rolled off the pallet and crawled out of the makeshift tent she and the girls had made using Brenda's dining chairs, a bedspread, two quilts, and a butt load of safety pins.

Her father walked into the den. "Rise and shine, sleepyheads."

"What time is it?" Beck got to her feet, sandy eyed from lack of sleep. Conall had built a fire in Jason's metal fire pit and they'd stayed up late roasting marshmallows and hot dogs, and telling stories.

"Almost seven."

"How's Brenda doing?"

"Fretting and complaining, which means she's on the mend," Daddy said. "I saw Toby's truck on the street."

"Yeah, he came back for leftovers and ended up spending the night. We built a fire and Toby told the kids the story about the Howling Hag of Catman Road. You remember that one?"

Daddy chuckled. "Sure do. Toby used to scare you silly with it. What about Evan? Did he stay too?"

"Evan took off yesterday afternoon. I think he left town."

"So soon? We were just getting to know him."

No you weren't, Beck thought with a twinge of sadness. *He doesn't even know himself.*

"I think he had some things to work out."

"But, he's coming back, right?"

"I don't know. He didn't say."

"You okay with that, chickpea?" Daddy asked. "You look upset."

Of course, she was upset. She and Evan had parted on bad terms. Part of her grieved to think she might never see him again, but Evan had more issues than *National Geographic,* and she had Annie to think of now. Bottom line, Beck didn't trust Evan. But it wasn't something she wanted to talk about with Jason. It was too complicated. Daddy was doing his best to be open minded, but he had his limits. How did you explain to your oh-so-normal father that his long lost son ran around with demons and played with dead things? You didn't.

Conall would understand. Okay, maybe he wouldn't understand. He'd never had a twin, he was overprotective as hell, and he didn't like Evan worth a damn, but she could talk to him about it and he would listen.

And he wouldn't think she was off her rocker or go all bug-eyed at the mention of magic, because *he* was magic.

In more ways than one, she thought, shivering with delight at the memory of the hot and heady good-night kiss he'd given her a few hours earlier.

"Becky?" her father said, frowning in concern.

"Sorry," Beck said. "I'm not awake yet and I'm a little stiff from sleeping on the floor. The girls and I decided to let the guys rough it in the backyard."

"You call that roughing it? Fanciest tent I ever saw."

"What?"

Beck looked out the French doors and into the backyard. A black and red striped pavilion sat on the yellowing autumn grass. Flags fluttered from the peaked top. It was something straight out of King Arthur, large enough to sleep several armored knights. The bright cloth parted and Conall strode out, looking every inch the hard muscled warrior, albeit a modern one in jeans and a short sleeve tee shirt. His arms and feet were bare in spite of the chill—the outdoor thermometer hanging next to the birdfeeder read 40 degrees.

Beck caught a glimpse inside the tent before the flaps closed, and it was *plush,* with a table and chairs, a glowing brazier, several cots, and soft bedding. Oh, yeah, the men folk had really suffered.

Conall turned his head and looked straight at her, as if sensing her regard. The expression on his lean face was positively wolfish, and just like that, she was hot and bothered.

Jeez, she really needed to get a grip. She was in a hormonal haze, and her daddy was standing two feet away.

She took a calming breath and willed her raging libido to cut it out *now.* She and her inner slut were still having a come to Jesus, when Conall materialized in the den and yanked her into his arms. He smelled of wood smoke and some kind of spicy scent, and he radiated heat like a furnace.

"I missed you," he said, nuzzling her neck.

"I missed you, too." Putting the palms of her hands flat against his chest, she smiled up at him. "Daddy's here."

Conall turned to face him, keeping one arm draped possessively around her. "Well met, Jason. How fares your lady wife?"

"Better, thank you," Daddy said, making a visible effort to control his shock at Conall's sudden appearance. Beck made a mental note to remind Conall that people didn't teleport in Hannah. "Came home to pick up a few things and check on the kids. I sure appreciate y'all looking after things for me."

"Nonsense," Conall said. "Rebekah and I have enjoyed ourselves immensely. We built a fire and toasted marshmallows. You are familiar with this confection?"

"Uh, sure," Daddy said. "I'm more of a circus peanut man, myself."

"Circus peanuts?" Conall looked intrigued. "Do you skewer and roast them, as well?"

"Nah, you just open the bag and eat 'em."

"It is different with marshmallows," Conall confided. "There is more challenge to the thing. The trick is to caramelize the outer skin whilst retaining the molten sweetness at the center. I sacrificed six to the flames ere I mastered the art of it."

"You don't say?" Daddy said.

Toby came inside. "Morning, Jase. Did Becky tell you about the fire?"

"What fire?"

"That turkey buzzard Earl Skinner burned down the bar."

Daddy's face went slack with shock. "What?"

"Yep, nothing left," Toby said. "Total loss."

Beck left Toby to explain things and slipped into the bathroom to wash her face and brush her teeth. She scraped her hair into a pony tail and went into the kitchen to start the coffee. When she reentered the den a few minutes later with a tray and cups, Toby was finishing his tale of woe.

"—and then the little sneak went and got himself killed," Toby was saying. "I don't even get the satisfaction of ripping him a new one."

Daddy accepted a cup of coffee from Beck. "That's terrible news about the fire. Y'all going to rebuild?"

"Yes." Beck studied the steaming contents of her mug. "But not right away, and maybe not another bar."

"Say what?" Toby yelped in surprise.

"I was thinking maybe we'd open a restaurant," Beck said. The words tumbled out, surprising her. But as soon as she said them, they felt *right*. The idea had been there for a while, she realized, percolating in the back of her mind. She was tired of wrassling drunks and cleaning up vomit and soured beer. "If Hank agrees to stay, that is, and I think he will. He seems smitten with Verbena. What do you think, Tobes?"

He rubbed his jaw, looking thoughtful. "I don't right know. What if we can't prove Earl started the fire? If we can't collect on the insurance, we're screwed."

"That will not be a problem," Conall said. "I will be your backer."

"No, you won't," Beck said. "How many times do I have to tell you I don't want your money?"

"As often as you like," Conall said calmly. "Nevertheless, you shall have it."

"Sounds like a man who knows his own mind." Her father set his cup on the tray. "Guess I'd better grab a shower and head back to the hospital. Brenda's sister's staying with the kids today. Doc says Brenda can come home tomorrow."

Annie and Darlene crawled out of the makeshift tent.

"I don't want Aunt Terri." Darlene's face puckered. "I want Annie and Beck and Conall to stay with us."

"They need to get home, shug," Daddy said. "Mr. Dalvahni and your big sister have things to do."

Big sister; Beck decided she liked the sound of that. All this time, she'd been avoiding her norm family because she was afraid they wouldn't accept her, that she wouldn't fit in. Maybe it was time she gave them a chance.

Beck smiled at her little sister. "He's right. We have to go. But, we'll see you again, real soon. I promise."

"Tomorrow?"

"We'll see."

Darlene groaned. "That means no."

Beck laughed. "Okay, tomorrow. I promise."

Conall cleared his throat. "I would like to make an announcement. Rebekah and I are to be wed."

"Well, I'll be doggoned," Daddy said. "Hear that, Toby? Becky's getting married."

"Huh." Toby crossed his arms on his chest. "I don't recollect nobody asking my permission. What about you, Jase?"

"No, now that you mention it, I don't."

A warm feeling bloomed inside of Beck. "I didn't know I needed permission."

"Course you do," Toby said. "You may be grown, but you'll always be my baby girl." He gave Conall a measuring look. "So, when did you propose?"

"It wounds my masculine pride to admit it, but I did not do the asking."

"Popped the question herself, did she?" Toby grinned. "Can't say as I'm surprised. Becky's always had a mind of her own."

"Indubitably," Conall said. "Although I believe the correct term in this realm is 'bossy.' I dared not refuse her."

"Me?" Beck gasped in outrage. "You've got a nerve."

Conall pulled her into his arms. "You know I love you madly."

"Huh," Beck said. "Don't think that's going to get you off the hook."

He smiled down at her. "Termagant."

"Termagant, is it?" She thumped him on his chest. "You're gonna pay for that one too. Big time."

"Promise?" Conall said, and kissed her.

"Ew," Darlene said. "They're smooching."

"They do it all the time," Annie said. "Grownups are weird."

Chapter Forty

Five months later

It was springtime in Alabama and everything was in bloom, including Beck. She rested her hand on the slight swell of her belly, still marveling at the life inside her. Conall had healed her—in so many ways, though he argued the matter differently. He claimed she'd saved *him,* but she knew better. She'd used the bar as her safe house, walling herself away from her family and the world out of habit and fear of being rejected. Until her shadow warrior had come along and broken through her defenses.

Smashed them down, more like, she thought with a smile.

The day after Thanksgiving, Conall had swept her away to the Hall of Warriors. She caught a fleeting glimpse of a cavernous space with columns marching into blackness and a starry canopy above, and then they were in a library filled with scrolls and books. A frozen waterfall on one wall displayed an ever changing slideshow of strange and wonderful images. When Beck tried to take a closer look, the whirling pictures made her dizzy.

A slim, bespectacled fellow with thinning brown hair and the distracted, studious air of a scholar rose to greet them. To Beck's surprise, Conall introduced the man in the wrinkled brown robe as Kehvahn, the creator of the Dalvahni. He looked more geek than god.

"You're not what I expected," she'd said, without thinking.

Kehvahn turned to regard her. His gaze was penetrating, fathomless. Beck squirmed, feeling stripped bare, like Kehvahn saw her, *really* saw her, all the way through, the good and the bad.

"Neither are you," he said at last with a nod. "I had my reservations, but I believe that you will do. Yes, I believe you will do quite well."

His form shifted and swirled like smoke, and he disappeared.

"Where'd he go?" Beck asked, looking around. "I thought we came here to get his permission."

"We have it," Conall said. "He approves of you. How could he not?"

Taking her by the hand, he led her over to an enormous leather bound tome and handed her a bronze quill. She looked around for an ink well, but didn't see one. She pressed the nib of the quill tentatively against the page, jerking her hand back as sparks flew from the end of the pen.

"What the hell?" she said.

"Try again," Conall said. "You have the right of it."

Beck shrugged and scratched her name on the parchment with the quill. The letters burst into flame and burned away, leaving her signature shining on the page. Conall took the pen from her and signed his name with a flourish. A bell gonged somewhere in the distance, deep and sonorous. The room dissolved around them and the next thing Beck knew, they were home.

"That's it?" she had demanded. "I expected a test or a trial by fire. An *argument* at least. Something besides scribbling our names in a stupid guest book."

"It is not a stupid guest book," Conall said. "It is our most sacred text. The history of our race lies within those pages, along with the signature of every Dalvahni warrior sworn to service. By signing our names in the Great Book, we are bound together as one."

"You mean we're *married*?"

Conall's lips twitched. "That is the human term for it."

"I don't feel married," Beck said.

"You do not?"

She shook her head. "No, I don't. I want a wedding. It doesn't have to be anything fancy, but I want a wedding."

"Then you shall have it." Conall took her in his arms and kissed her. "It will be the grandest wedding Hannah has ever seen. You will be reading about yourself in the paper, for once." Satisfaction and challenge gleamed in his dark eyes. "But make no mistake about it, Rebekah. Wedding or no wedding, you are mine."

Beck had protested but, secretly, the thought of her picture in the *Hannah Herald* alongside the society muckety mucks tickled her to pieces. And she was determined to make everything perfect.

The wedding plans kept her busy for the next few months. There was so much to do; a date to be decided on, as well as a thousand other details, including the selection of her wedding dress, the bridesmaid dresses, flowers and music—the list went on and on.

Hank had suggested a caterer out of Mobile. Food was *very* important. The captain of the Dalvahni was getting married, and in Dalvahni Land, that was a Really Big Deal. The Dal would be there in numbers, and they were all about the chow.

"But, no chocolate," Evie had cautioned Beck. "I know it's traditional for the groom's cake to be chocolate, but take my advice and choose something else, unless you want a bunch of schnockered super beings at your wedding. The Dalvahni can drink an ocean of beer without getting a buzz, but a handful of M&Ms or a few Raisinettes and the big guys are wasted."

In addition to planning the wedding, Beck and Conall had set the paperwork in motion to adopt Annie.

"Don't get your hopes up," the harried social worker at DHR had told them at her office. "It's a slow process, and the court system is backlogged."

Beck wasn't worried. She and Annie had a very determined demon hunter on their side.

Toby had been right about Beck's. There was nothing left but a few charred beams and a half melted *Budweiser* sign, but the insurance company had coughed up the money. The day of the fire, Bill, the sound guy from *Beelzebubba,* had stopped by Beck's to check on some equipment, and he'd seen Earl sneaking out a back window. A phone call that his wife was in labor sent Bill scurrying to the hospital in Paulsberg, but he'd told the police about the break-in. Earl, of course, was never found for questioning.

Construction was scheduled to begin on the restaurant the week after the wedding. To Beck's delight, Hank had agreed to be their chef. He suggested they call the new place Fleuve Magie, but Toby had set up a howl.

"Floove may-gee?" Toby said. "What kind of fancy ass lah-dee-dah name is that?"

Hank scowled. "It's French. It means river magic."

"Huh," Toby said. "If you're so all-fired set on naming the place after the river, why not call it Devil's Food, and be done with it?"

That nearly sent Hank packing, and it had taken both Beck and Verbena to soothe the bear's ruffled fur. After much discussion, they'd settled on Chez Beck's, a name elegant enough for Hank and Junior and not too difficult for Toby to pronounce— in theory, at least. He managed to mangle the name on a regular basis, mostly to annoy Hank, Beck suspected.

Junior had moved back to the Episcopal church for the time being, taking a certain Dalmatian with him, but not without leaving detailed instructions about the kind of piano he wanted for the bar at Chez Beck's. As for Meredith, she appeared to have shuffled off this mortal coil.

"I hope she found her door to the Beyond, and took it," Evie confided to Beck one day with a shudder. "I know it's mean of me, but she's *so* unpleasant."

Unpleasant? Meredith was a world class pain. Beck doubted she was gone for good. Meredith was somewhere in an ecto-plasmic snit, biding her time. She'd show up when least expected, and spew ugly all over the place.

But not today, Beck thought, checking her reflection in the

oval, full length mirror. Nothing and no one would spoil her wedding day.

She was waiting inside a specially built gazebo for the ceremony to start. In the distance, she heard the low murmur of the wedding guests. Trees surrounded the little building on three sides, offering Beck and her attendants, Evie, Latrisse, and Verbena, privacy and seclusion. A gentle breeze stirred the bright green leaves outside the pavilion and the sultry perfume of the river mingled with the scent of the climbing roses outside their shelter.

It was late afternoon, Beck's favorite time of day, that magical time known as the gloaming, when the veils between the worlds thin and anything seems possible.

Even true love, Beck thought with a surge of happiness. The stern, unforgiving captain of the Dalvahni had fallen in love with a tough, prickly demonoid be-yotch, and she loved him right back, something fierce.

The world was a strange and wonderful place.

Latrisse placed a flower in Beck's hair, a pale peach rose to match her sherbet tulle ball bridal gown. The bodice of the dress was pleated silk satin organza with a sweetheart neckline, secured at the waist with a floral jewel encrusted band. A chapel train embellished the full skirt. It was an over-the-top romantic, girly-girl gown, and Beck loved it. It more than made up for a childhood and adolescence of missed parties, spend-the-nights, playing dress-up, dances, and proms.

She glanced in the mirror at Latrisse, who was standing behind her. Latrisse was stunning in a pear green silk taffeta bridesmaid gown with an asymmetrically pleated sweetheart bodice and a banded, jeweled waist.

Latrisse gave the rose a final twitch and stepped back. "There," she said. "You're perfect."

Verbena hugged herself. "Oh, Becky, you look purtier 'n any princess."

Happiness and Hank's cooking had filled out Verbena's too skinny frame. She was still slender but much healthier looking.

"Don't forget Tommy," Annie said, hovering anxiously at the edge of Beck's circular skirt.

Beck held up her arm to show Annie the rhinestone bracelet on her wrist. "I wouldn't dream of it. He's my something borrowed and my something blue."

Thanks to Conall's woo woo and Sheriff Whitsun's connections in law enforcement, Tommy's body had been identified and safely returned to New Orleans for burial. Beck had waited a few weeks before sending Tommy's mother a condolence card, concocting a story about meeting Tommy in a cooking class in the city. She'd expressed her fondness for Tommy and her deep sadness at learning of his death, and left it at that. To her surprise and delight, Tommy's mother had written back, and they'd struck up a regular correspondence. When Mrs. Henderson learned of Beck's wedding plans, she'd sent the bracelet along with a note:

Tommy gave me this on Mother's Day, the year he turned twelve. He earned the money raking yards. I know he'd want you to wear it on your special day.

Tommy would be with her on her special day, but not Evan. She hadn't seen or heard from her brother since that day in the park. It seemed he really had left town. Wherever he was, she hoped he was happy and doing well. She'd gotten her new beginning. Evan should get one, too.

Evie entered the gazebo with Darlene, distracting Beck from her thoughts of Evan. "The music's started," Evie said, her eyes alight. "It's showtime."

"It's time to go, it's time to go," Darlene sang, dancing around the gazebo in excitement.

Beck kissed Annie on the cheek and gave her a gentle shove toward the door. "See you in a minute, love."

Evie and Latrisse hugged Beck and left with the little girls.

Verbena hung back. "Oh, Beck," she said, throwing her arms around her. "I'm so happy for you I could bust wide open."

Blushing, she scurried out the door, leaving Beck alone in

the pavilion. But not for long; a moment later, her daddy appeared at the entrance, looking uncomfortable in his formal wedding duds.

He held out his arm. "Ready, Becky?"

"Yes, Daddy."

She walked down the steps and into the lush garden where Beck's had once stood. This had been Ora Mae's wedding gift to her, this magnificent floral wonderland, raised from the ashes of her former life. Ora Mae could grow anything, anywhere, and grow it bigger and better; that was her talent. The overgrown patch where the bar had once stood had been cleared, and now burst with roses, spring flowers and shrubs, all abloom. A wide carpet of grass sparkled like a brilliant green jewel in the late afternoon sun. On one side of the lawn, huge tents and cloth covered tables had been set up for the reception. The wedding guests, norms and supers alike, sat in covered chairs lined up in neat rows. The norms were clueless, unaware that the neighbor, friend, or relative sitting next to them might be something other than they appeared. For once, the norms were in the minority, with the inclusion of the kith and Conall's men. The Dalvahni were here to see their captain married; some two hundred strong.

Beck paused at the top of a gentle slope, her hand on Jason's arm. A white fabric ribbon strewn with rose petals wound between the seated guests to the river where Conall waited on a floating dock, resplendent in a black tuxedo, white shirt and black tie. Jay stood beside him, a proud groomsman in a miniature black tux. They were surrounded by a sea of Conall's brothers in formal attire. The Dal turned to face her as one, in a show of respect. Their hair and skin color varied, but there wasn't an ugly one in the bunch. Beck hardly saw them. Her attention was riveted on Conall, her dark haired, dangerous love.

A wiry, gray-haired man stepped forward to meet Jason and Beck. It was Toby, looking dapper and ten years younger in his black tux.

"You look beautiful, Becky," he said. He cleared his throat. "Course, you've always been beautiful to me."

"You look beautiful too, Tobes."

"Horse feathers," Toby said with a growl.

Everyone was looking at them, warriors and guests, as they stood there at the top of the hill. Beck felt Conall's gaze upon her, too, hot and possessive and full of love. She shivered in anticipation.

"They're waiting," Daddy said. Stepping aside, he shook Toby's hand. "Your turn, you old dog, and rightly so. You raised her right."

Beck gave Jason a quick hug. "Thank you, Daddy."

She turned to Toby and took his hands in hers, blinking back happy tears. "This is it, Tobias. Take me the rest of the way?"

His odd colored eyes were bright. "I'd like to see somebody try and stop me."

He walked her down the aisle, stiff and proud, to the platform on the river where Conall stood.

"Thank goodness you are here," Conall said. "I thought you would never come."

Beck smiled up at him. "Did I keep you waiting long?"

"Only forever, my love." Conall raised her hand to his lips. "But you were worth it."

Evening wrapped the river in dusky arms, and the crickets and tree frogs joined in their nightly serenade. On the opposite bank, twinkle lights and lanterns glowed, turning the clearing where Beck's had once stood into a fairyland. The band began a slow, lilting melody and couples drifted out of the crowd and onto the gleaming dance floor. They twirled to the music, tossing bits of laughter and conversation into the breeze. Evan stood in the dark, his brooding gaze on the festivities. A few feet away, the river flowed past stone steps and set a small boat nodding at the end of a dock. Weeping willows at the water's edge dipped their frothy branches into the current.

"It was a beautiful wedding," Ora Mae said at his side. "You should have gone."

"She thinks I left Hannah." Evan shoved his hands in his pockets. "It's better this way."

"Family can be tough," Ora Mae said. He heard sympathy in her voice. "Come up to my place and I'll fix you a nice cup of tea. I made a fresh batch of scones this morning. Blueberry, from my own garden. Blueberries are a super food. Did you know that?"

"No," Evan said, not bothering to conceal his impatience. Christ, why was he here with this lame old lady?

He followed Ora Mae up the path to her house. She was short and pudgy, but spry for an old broad, with thick calves ropey with muscle. Evan had trouble keeping up. The flowered dress she wore hit her just above the ankle, a belted, long sleeve affair with a lace collar. Her small, square feet were encased in sensible walking shoes.

"You said on the phone you wanted to talk," Evan said, huffing a little. "What's this about?"

"Patience, all in good time," Ora Mae said. "You'll feel better when you've had a little something to eat. Your blood sugar's low. I can hear it in your voice. That's why you're so cross. It's very important to keep your blood sugar level, you know. Those dips can make you cranky."

Cross? He was mad as hell, and it didn't have a damn thing to do with his blood sugar. When he'd first realized he was free, he'd been stoked out of his mind. Then reality had set in. He'd spent the last five months in purgatory, drifting and unmoored. What the hell was he supposed to do now? He'd never been on his own. Hagilth and Elgdrek had always called the shots, telling him what to do, but they were dead.

Freedom, he'd discovered, was scary as hell.

He left Hannah for a while, but he'd soon come slinking back. He didn't fit in anywhere. He had no skills, no education, and no training, unless you counted the criminal kind. Hell, he could barely *read*. And he was wanted by the police in half a dozen states, thanks to his loving "parents."

"How'd you find me, anyway?" Evan asked. He'd rented a rundown trailer in Froggy Bottom, a seedy, dilapidated area of Hannah, and had taken pains to stay under the radar. He didn't want Beck or Conall to know he was around. He wasn't family, huh? Well, screw her and the big demon hunter she'd rode in on.

I'm lying low, he told himself. *Taking some time to figure things out, and then I'll blow this one horse shithole of a town for good. Later, losers. I'm gone.*

"Oh, a little birdy told me," Ora Mae said. "It's hard to keep secrets in a small town."

Reaching the top of the slope, she opened a twig gate fashioned in the shape of a cobweb. A lamppost with a wrought iron lantern illuminated her round, pleasant face and her eyes glinted behind her spectacles.

She motioned him through the gate. "Up the path and through the garden. My goodness, I'm tickled you're here. I haven't had company in a coon's age."

"Whatever the hell that means," Evan muttered to himself. Her stupid Aunt Bea from Mayberry routine was getting on his nerves.

He stepped under a greenery arch heavy with hydrangea blooms. The garden on the other side of the gate was a riot of assorted flowers and blooming shrubs. The redbuds and dogwoods were blossoming, and the sweet scent of roses and honeysuckle mingled with the sharp, green tang of herbs. A hedge bunny stood frozen beside the path, a hedge hound in close pursuit. The lighted, pebbled walkway curved toward the house, a stucco cottage with ivy covered walls, and a metal bound door. Smoke curled out of the chimney and light spilled out of the snug leaded windows.

"Come in, come in," Ora Mae said with a smile in her voice. Opening the door, she shooed him inside. "The bathroom's that way, if you want to freshen up. I'll put the kettle on."

The bathroom was charming, with a claw foot tub, a toilet with a pull handle, and a pedestal sink. Evan washed his hands and wandered back out, poking around a bit while Ora Mae made tea and warmed the scones. The bottom floor of the cottage consisted of a cozy sitting room with a fireplace and a low, beamed ceiling, a small kitchen, and the bath. A narrow stair led to the second floor.

Having seen all there was to see, Evan slumped into a chair at the table and listened to the old lady's chatter with half an ear. Like the fixtures in the bathroom, the kitchen appliances were nostalgic. The stove was shiny white porcelain with oversize knobs, four black burners, an oven and a bottom broiler. A red and silver emblem on the front of the appliance bore the name *Wedgewood*. The squat, old-timey, white fridge had a v-shaped handle, and an audible hum.

"There." Ora Mae plunked a platter of scones on the table beside a steaming blue teapot. Seating herself across from him with her back to the door, she handed Evan a plate with two scones and poured him a cup of tea. The tea was fragrant, the scones warm and redolent of butter, sugar, and ripe berries. "I'm anxious for you to try these. It's an old family recipe."

Evan sweetened his tea and took a bite of scone to be polite. He'd never been a big eater, probably because Elgdrek and Hagilth had forgotten to feed him half the time, but he was suddenly ravenous.

The pastry melted on his tongue and his eyes nearly rolled back in his head, it tasted that damn good. He'd been living on Ramen noodles, and the pastry was flaky and delicious. Better than delicious; it satisfied some deep, unfilled *need* in him, a need he hadn't even known existed. He ate the scones on his plate, and helped himself to two more.

"I do like to see a man eat," Ora Mae said when the platter was empty. "Now we can talk."

Evan sat back in his chair and tried to focus on his hostess. He'd eaten too much and it had made him sleepy. His lids drooped and he jerked himself awake.

"This is about Beck, isn't it?" His speech sounded thick. "I know you two are friends. You found out I was still in town, and you're trying to patch things up between us."

"Cut the crap," Ora Mae said. "I didn't call you here to talk about your sister. She's a nice kid and I'm fond of her, but I have a problem with you. You told that overgrown bag of steroids she married where the portal was, and he destroyed it. You've screwed up my plans."

Evan wanted nothing more than to put his head down on the table and go to sleep. Just for a minute or two. *The scones.* The thought drifted through his groggy mind. *She put something in the scones.*

Ora Mae folded her hands in her lap and waited. He frowned and tried to think. What did she say?

"Plans?" he mumbled. His lips felt numb.

Ora Mae leaned closer. "Where do you think Charlie Skinner got the secret ingredient for his special 'shine?"

Evan blinked at her dully. Behind her, a splash of color drew his befuddled gaze. Boots; sitting by the door next to the umbrella stand. Red and yellow boots with intricate black scrolling. Charlie's boots.

A trickle of dread crept down his spine. He couldn't move.

He dragged his gaze back to Ora Mae with an effort. "You killed Charlie."

Ora Mae slammed her hands on the table, rattling the Little Dutch Boy and Girl salt and pepper shakers.

"Charlie was a no-talent slug who couldn't find his ass with both hands and a road map." Her eyes burned red in her motherly face. "He spied on me and he snuck into my garden and cut down one of my mimosas. Trees I grew from seedlings. Trees I watered and fertilized and fretted over like babies. Trees I spent *years* cultivating. Charlie took one of them. He came on my property and stole from me. And the idiot didn't even know what he had. He chopped up that mimosa, put it in that paint thinner he called liquor, and fed it to the kith. Do you have any idea what that tree was worth? No, of course you don't."

"Drugs," Evan said, forcing the word past his lips. "You sell drugs."

"Any two bit hood can sell drugs. I sell nirvana, quality plants unmatched by any grower in the world. Ever hear of Purple Haze?" Ora Mae tilted her head. "No? It's a strain of marijuana, and I grow it right here in Hannah. People come from all over to get my product. It's a good business, but those trees were something special. They contain a powerful hallucinogen—the most powerful hallucinogen the world has ever known." She gave Evan a look that made his blood run cold. "Your parents and I were working out a deal until Skinner interfered. Now your parents are dead and the portal's closed. Thanks to you, I'll have to find new associates."

Evan watched, helpless, as the old lady rose from her chair and stomped around the table.

"You've caused me no end of trouble," she said. "I've got plans for you."

She lifted him from the chair and slung him over her shoulder like a sack of flour. Carrying him into the garden, she threw him inside a musty shed.

"Go to sleep, pretty boy, and dream," Ora Mae said. She slammed the door and threw the bolt. "Dream about cakes and pies, and slabs of roasted meat. I'm going to fatten you up."

Did you miss the other books in Lexi's hilarious series?

DEMON HUNTING IN DIXIE
A warrior, a demon, and the girl next door . . .

Looking for Trouble

Addy Corwin is a florist with an attitude. A bad attitude, or so her mama says, 'cause she's not looking for a man. Mama's wrong. Addy *has* looked. There's just not much to choose from in Hannah, her small Alabama hometown. Until Brand Dalvahni shows up, a supernaturally sexy, breathtakingly well built hunk of a warrior from—well, not from around here, that's for sure. Mama thinks he might be European or maybe even a Yankee. Brand says he's from another dimension.

Addy couldn't care less where he's from. He's gorgeous. Serious muscles. Disturbing green eyes. Brand really gets her going. Too bad he's a whack job. Says he's come to rescue her from a demon. Puh-lease. But right after Brand shows up, strange things start to happen. Dogs talk and reanimated corpses stalk the quiet streets of Hannah. Her mortal enemy, Meredith, otherwise known as the Death Starr, breaks out in a severe and inexplicable case of butt boils. Addy might not know what's going on, but she definitely wants a certain sexy demon hunter by her side when it all goes down. . . .

DEMON HUNTING IN THE DEEP SOUTH
Demon-slayers, evil forces, and an über-bitchy ghost . . .

Hotter Than a Demon in Panties

Evie Douglass doesn't know what's worse—the demons secretly infesting her small Alabama hometown or . . . human belle-from-hell Meredith Starr Peterson, who's made her life miserable since high school. But when the "Death Starr" is brutally murdered and Evie is the number-one suspect, she's suddenly besieged by the evil-not-dead-enough and Meredith's furious specter. The only way she can clear her name is to get out from under demon hunter Ansgar's grim protection. He's blond, breathtaking, and the most lethal of all his kin, but—after years of teasing—Evie is wary of anyone who swears her plus-size self is beautiful. However, having Ansgar all over her is sparking outrageous powers Evie didn't know she had. And she'll face any ultimate evil to keep this sexy slayer in this dimension and in her bed for all eternity. . . .